Bones Don't Lie

A Nathan Wolf Adventure

Books by James Duermeyer

Nathan Wolf *series*
Trail of the Outlaw
Singing Creek
Counterfeit Rodeos
Bones Don't Lie

Novels
Flint Bluff
Market Time Conspiracy

Nonfiction Books
Heroes in Obscurity
The Capture of the USS Pueblo; the Incident, the Aftermath, and the Motives of North Korea

Bones Don't Lie

A Nathan Wolf Adventure

James Duermeyer

SPEAKING VOLUMES, LLC
NAPLES, FLORIDA
2023

Bones Don't Lie

Copyright © 2023 by James Duermeyer

All rights reserved. No part of this book may be reproduced or transmitted in any form or by any means without written permission.

The views expressed are solely those of the author.

ISBN 979-8-89022-016-5

Dedicated to all law enforcement officers in gratitude
for their exceptional service and commitment, as they
confront uncertain and dangerous situations daily without hesitation.

Chapter One

Late Spring, 1820
The Southern Plains of the Fledgling United States

A talented pastoral poet would have cause to apply his/her skill of verbosity to such a day and such a landscape. The azure blue sky was unspoiled, save for a few wispy white cloud traces moved by gentle breezes. The seemingly endless sea of gently moving green prairie grass and vegetation stretched as far as the eye could see, broken only by an occasional grove of oaks, cottonwoods, or mesquite trees, and periodically slashed by a crossing creek or arroyo. Red, yellow, blue, and orange wildflower and weed blooms appeared to be the colorful ribbon ties of a giant green patchwork quilt. The air carried no sound other than the active calling of the native birds. Red-winged blackbirds perched on a slant at the tops of the taller and stiffer weed stalks, their calls intended to attract mates and ward off interloper males. Those calls were joined by meadowlarks, shyly remaining hidden as they constructed their nests in the dense grass. From the groves of trees, quail whistled their distinctive calls in attempts to lure partners to their covey. Occasional red-tailed hawks floated effortlessly on the slight breezes above, watching with keen, hooded eyes for movement in the prairie grass below. And there was a multitude of wildlife within and near the prairie grass. Prong-horn antelope and deer foraged in the grass and within the oak groves. Rabbits, voles, mice, snakes, and other small prey animals fed the hawks, foxes, bobcats, and coyotes, balancing the robust food chain of the prairie, a world that was ageless and servile to the passing of yearly seasons and weather events, and generally quiet in nature.

But that tranquility and quiet could occasionally be broken. As if anticipating an unseen yet faintly heard noise, the songbirds of the prairie became quiet, their heads moving to pick up the sound, a sound that at that instant would have been inaudible to a human. Unheard, that is, until the phenomenon moved closer. But before that, at well over a mile in the distance, a dark tan smudge faintly appeared on the horizon. The apparition remained low on the sight line and seemed to shimmer and dance in the sunlight. But it did not remain in the same place. Instead, it seemed to move across the distant prairie at a slow pace, as if blown by the breeze. The brown shape continued to move and began to grow slightly taller. It was still over a mile away when the first sounds could be heard. It was the sound of low and distant thunder, much like that of an approaching powerful storm. But unlike a thunderstorm, the sound continued without pause between thunderclaps and grew in intensity. The brown shape also grew and perhaps could be speculated to be a windblown dust storm. But then another aspect of the apparition became apparent. A very faint vibration in the ground could now be felt by those ground-dwelling small animals in the deep grass, and it too, grew in intensity. In a short time, the noise slowly became louder in volume as the dust cloud moved ever closer. Songbirds, so prevalent only moments before, began taking flight, coursing to the nearby oak groves.

Then, it appeared as if the lower portion of the dust cloud parted, and at the base of the now rapidly approaching dust storm and roaring pandemonium, they could be seen. A great multitudinous army of dark brown shapes undulated beneath the huge dust storm. Hundreds of dark, round-backed creatures approached the idyllic prairie setting, all seemingly in unison, running toward some location or running away from an unseen danger. Bison, the largest land animal on the North American continent, in a herd of over two hundred with each animal weighing from one to two thousand pounds, now created a roar of hooves over which nothing else could be heard, and a vibration that shook the ground beneath the prairie grass. This herd was small, a mere pittance of the estimated fifty to sixty million bison that roamed the midsection of the United States in ancient history and until the early 1800s. Only a fire caused by nature, indiscriminate buffalo hunters, or Native American hunters would cause such a flight by the bison. In this instance, the herd was being chased by the Lords of the Prairie, Native American Comanche hunters, who were driving the small herd of bison to an arroyo with a high and steep drop off where many of the bison would be killed in the fall and would subsequently feed the *Kotsoteka* (buffalo eaters) band of Comanches for many weeks. As they ran toward their demise, the herd lost its leaders to the fall into the arroyo. The remaining herd split, ran to the ends of the arroyo, crossed the dry creek bed and merged together again on the other side, where they continued their flight from the Comanche hunters who now remained at the arroyo to begin dressing out their kill. A messenger from the hunting group was sent back to the Comanche encampment so that the women of the camp could come to the kill and assume the bulk of the work in dressing out the slain bison and their hides.

In 1534, when the expedition of Luis de Moscoso Alverado left the first horses behind after exploring what would become Texas, little did Moscoso know that he had installed the catalyst that would drastically change the Comanche culture. Moving southeast from their original northern hunting lands of the Great Basin, the Comanches moved to where they had access to wild mustangs and bison, and with the help of those wild mustangs, the Comanches evolved into equine masters and horseback hunters. In addition, with their mastery of the wild mustangs, the Comanches became mounted warriors, a powerful people capable of dominating other tribes in battle, and able to forage for their primary source of food, shelter, and clothing, their lifeblood, the bison of the Southern Plains. The Comanches had no equals on horseback and swept rival tribes, including the Apaches, from the Southern Plains. They would remain the Lords of the Prairie until the onslaught by the U.S. Army and white settlers greatly reduced the American bison herds, thereby nearly starving the Comanches, at least those who had not been killed by the introduction of European diseases. These factors ultimately forced the Comanches to move to federally controlled reservations. Many years later, Marshal Nathan Wolf would investigate a case that touched the Comanche Nation at their reservation near Lawton, Oklahoma.

Chapter Two

May 11, 1825
Cork Harbor, Cork Ireland
On the Quay by the British Sailing Ship *Brunswick*

Morris Conley was the oldest child in his Irish Catholic family living in the crushing grip of poverty. His family was no different from thousands of other families attempting to stay alive in a country suffering the scourge of poverty and limited food to keep its citizens from starving to death in 1824 and 1825. There had been six children born to the Conley family, but the two youngest children had died shortly after birth from a mother who could barely keep herself from starvation. Their deaths were grieved at the time, but it was certainly understood that Mrs. Conley would not have been able to feed either one of them in her emaciated condition.

Since the age of nine, Morris had worked at any job that a child could do. The money he earned was contributed to the family's subsistence, but not all of it. Morris furtively kept a portion of his earnings for his own use. Today, he would use the money he had saved over several years for a down payment on his future.

Ireland, at the time, was in dire straits as a British colony, but England had problems feeding its own people, let alone those subjects living in its outlying colonies. As a result, the British crown looked for methods to rid itself of a portion of its desperate population in order to lessen their severe impact on the British. Ireland, being geographically close to England, was a likely and easily managed target to which the poor were sent. Yet, Ireland was not large enough, nor self-sufficient enough, to take in all of Britain's needy. The British solution, then, was to ship a considerable portion of the Irish population to Quebec province in Canada, a more substantial and stable British colony that could more easily absorb the poor and starving British subjects. Mr. Peter Robinson was appointed by the British to oversee the emigration project of resettling over 2,500 Irish citizens in Canada, where they would establish their own communities. Almost all of the Irish evacuees came from the Blackwater River region in County Cork. Eleven different ships were used to transport the Irish emigrants, and they all departed on various shipping dates from the Cork Harbor. On this day, it was the sailing ship *Brunswick* awaiting the loading of its passengers destined for Canada.

Twenty-year-old Morris Conley stood apart from the crowd waiting on the quay. He intended to leave Ireland with the gathering emigrants, but he knew it might be difficult. To his credit, he had worked for and saved a fair amount of cash that safely rested in his pockets, but in addition to a small boarding fee, the authorities were only allowing families to board the ship. As Morris was alone, he did not meet that criterion. But that was of little concern for Morris, as he had no intention of boarding the ship destined for Canada. He reasoned that because he had witnessed the morale-breaking rules and taxes imposed by the British, he was of no mind to go to Canada, another British protectorate.

As he had learned earlier and was now observing, there was another sailing ship moored astern of the *Brunswick*. It, too, had a group of Irish citizens waiting to board. It was the British ship *Weatherall*. In a previous conversation with sailors on that ship, Morris had learned that other emigrants would be boarding that ship, chartered by the crown to leave Cork and sail to the Virginia colony in the United States. Morris intended to be on that ship, and he had a plan, an audacious plan that required willing partners, and one that would, unbeknownst to him, shape his destiny. His plan was so bold, he was unsure that he could carry it out successfully. Thus, he was agonizingly and intently studying the crowd. After a moment, he saw the situation that he would attempt to use to his advantage. Just like everyone else waiting to board the *Weatherall,* the Charles Blackston family had the look of impoverishment and consisted of parents with too many children to look after. Of the six Blackston offspring, one of their children was an attractive young lady named Patricia, who appeared to be nearly the same age as Morris. Her well-worn clothing and lace up, hard, brown leather shoes spoke of her life status. From his study of the crowd, Morris selected her and her family to help complete his plan. Gathering up his courage, Morris strolled up to the waiting family.

He tipped his scully cap to Mr. and Mrs. Blackston and introduced himself. Charles Blackston, the husband and father of the family, responded warily and looked Morris Conley up and down, wondering what this young man wanted. He soon discovered Conley's purpose.

"You see," said Morris, "I have no family, and therefore, cannot board the ship. Could I offer you a half crown to allow me to claim your daughter as my wife when boarding so that the ship's purser will allow me on board?"

A half crown was only the equivalent of two shillings, and Mr. Blackston very nearly said "no" in immediate response. But Blackston was a desperate man, and money spoke plainly to him. Of great worry to him was that he had a family to feed, and his meager funds may not last for the crossing. He had heard that unscrupulous ships' captains, while they were paid by the British to transport the emigrants, sometimes charged their passengers for food. He was unsure how much it would cost to feed his family for the lengthy sea journey. Blackston was no fool and was also astute enough to recognize an opportunity, even if it meant a slight compromise to his daughter, albeit harmless enough.

"You say you have no family," said Blackston.

"Aye," replied Morris.

Blackston stroked his chin and again physically appraised Morris before speaking. "Her name is Patricia. We call her Tricia."

Morris again tipped his cap, this time to Clarkston's attractive daughter. She merely stared coldly in return.

Blackston paused again as he methodically worked out details in his head. He then said, "A half crown is of no interest to me, boy. But I will make you a fair proposition. For two crowns you may borrow her for your deception." Two crowns were nearly a pound in value, and the equivalent of several meals that could feed his family during the ocean crossing. At his side, Patricia Blackston listened to the conversation. Her eyes were open wide, and her mouth was agape as her father consented to "rent" her out to enable this brash young man to board the ship bound for the United States. She was not at all pleased, but she saw no immediate harm in the plot and remained quiet. In addition, she was somewhat intrigued by the handsome young man.

Morris had thought that more money may have been needed, so, inwardly he was relieved. He said, "Mr. Blackston, you drive a hard bargain, but I will agree to two crowns. And I thank you, sir."

"Just a moment, young man," said Blackston. "I'm not through." Blackston had seen a long-term opportunity that would benefit him and his family. His desperate plight of poverty and trying to feed eight mouths left him with little choice. He knew that he might face the wrath of his wife and daughter, but his mind was made up.

Blackston cleared his throat and continued. "In addition to allowing you to board the ship with my daughter posing as your wife, you will marry Tricia while we are enroute to America. I'm sure that the ship's captain will consent to marry you and Tricia once we are well underway. You will, indeed, make her your legitimate wife."

Morris was shocked at this turn of events and was struggling to grasp Blackston's idea. Marriage was the farthest thought from his plan. But again, Blackston was not finished. "You will be responsible for Tricia's safety and well-being and ensure that she is properly fed during the voyage. And one more thing, if there is a fee charged by the captain for your wedding, you will pay that yourself. Those are my terms."

Morris Conley stared open mouthed at Charles Blackston. Morris's plan had seemed to be working until Blackston interjected additional terms. Marriage! He was dumbfounded. He happened to glance at Patricia and saw the same look of disbelief on her face, a face that he now saw for its beauty, but also its bewilderment. Beauty or not, the thought of marriage had never entered Morris's thinking. Morris very nearly spun on his heel to flee from the proposition, but he knew from rumor that the British plan to transport Irish citizens to Canada and the United States was nearly complete and another opportunity might not come again in the near future. Some members of the crowd waiting to board the *Weatherall* had begun moving toward the gangplank. Boarding was soon to begin. He looked again at Patricia and could see that she was just as confused as he was. Nevertheless, he slowly walked to Patricia Blackston's side, where Charles Blackston held out his hand. Morris Conley placed the two coins in the man's hand.

It was at this point that Patricia Blackston finally spoke as she looked at the two men. "You can't do this to me, Father. I don't know this man. I'm not a child; I'm eighteen years old, and you can't just fling me away. I want no part of your disgusting plan. Do you hear me? I won't do it!"

Blackston replied. "Settle yourself, lass. I am doing this for your own good and for the good of our family."

Patricia was furious. "I will not do this." She spun on her heel and took the first step to walk away. Her mind was spinning, and she was trying to think of how she could make her way without the shelter of her family, but she was determined to leave.

As Patricia took her first step to flee, Charles Blackston's beefy hand reached out, grasped her arm, and spun her back around. "Now you listen to me, Tricia. I will not have any of your shenanigans. For the good of this family, you will come with us, and you will marry this young man. You are of the age to marry at any rate. My decision is final, and I believe that a young man with the spunk that Mister Conley has shown will move on to success. You could do much worse. Now, let's get on that ship."

Blackston did not let go of his daughter's arm and forced her to walk by his side as they climbed the gangplank. Patricia's face was bright red as her father explained to the purser that she was his daughter, and that Morris Conley was his son-in-law. The purser nodded and moved his attention to the next group of boarders. The Blackstons and Morris Conley settled themselves into the open sleeping area below decks to await the ship's sailing.

Crossing the Atlantic in 1825 took from six weeks to three months depending upon the weather. The emigrants had little to do but conserve their energy and look after one another. After three weeks at sea, Morris and Patricia had established a somewhat tenuous relationship, and to the surprise of each of them, the relationship slowly grew from platonic to a genuine romantic interest. Morris was not sure how he would support himself in America, let alone placing a wife into the situation, but he had, by now, determined that Patricia should become part of his life. After six weeks at sea, the captain of the *Weatherall* did, indeed, perform a civil ceremony to complete the marriage of Morris Conley to Patricia Blackston, a ceremony witnessed by the other passengers, followed by a rousing cheer from all. The cheer was even louder as the young couple kissed one another for the first time as husband and wife. The simple wedding of the two young adventurers lifted the morale of the other passengers who, by this time, were fatigued and bored from their long voyage.

After two months, the *Weatherall* reached the port of Norfolk, an American port that had been active since the middle of the eighteenth century. The Blackston family and the Conleys took separate rooms at a cheap boarding house. Both Charles Blackston and Morris Conley soon found back-breaking work on the waterfront as stevedores. It was difficult, heavy work, but it was steady and paid a fair day's wages. The reason they were able to find work was that a great portion of immigrants left Virginia to head west for adventure and opportunity. Thus, Norfolk had many transient workers, and, many times, not enough workers to handle the near-constant shipping trade.

* * *

A year went by, and while the couple knew reasonably well how to read and write English from their British teachers in Ireland, they honed their skills during that year. Also, of great importance, as was his habit, Morris was managing to save a portion of his pay. This was helped by Patricia, as she assisted in the kitchen of the boarding house. She received no pay. Instead, the rent for the Conley's room was reduced, thereby enabling them to save a bit more money. Morris knew that he did not want to spend the rest of his life as a dockhand. As time passed, he began developing another plan. He had watched as emigrants landed at the port, purchased hard goods and sundry items as they readied themselves to travel to the West. The stout-hearted of them walked, and others, who had the necessary funds, purchased wagons and any spare horse or mule that could be found.

Morris was determined to follow other immigrants and travel to the interior of the United States. He had feared that Patricia would not want to go with him, but he needed not to worry. When he shared his thoughts with Patricia, while reluctant to leave her family, she was in agreement. She told him that she was in love with him and would follow wherever he led. Within herself, she was frightened, but she would never tell Morris of her trepidation. In truth, Patricia was stronger of spirit than she believed of herself. She had the will and determination to be a cherished asset to their adventurous goal.

The final impetus for implementing the plan came on the day that Morris happened to purchase a newspaper. A headline on a front-page article had caught his eye. After paying a half-penny for the paper, he stood on the sidewalk near the newsstand and reread the article over and over. A smile crossed his face. He refolded the paper and walked briskly home.

Within a few moments, Patricia was reading the same newspaper article. Morris watched her as she read. He smiled at her when she looked up from her reading, a questioning look on her face.

"Tricia, what do you think?" Morris asked.

She looked back to the paper, looked up again, and answered with a question, "Does this mean we're going to this Mexico place?"

"Indeed, it does, dearie. When the last of winter has gone, we will leave," said Morris.

The newspaper article that had mesmerized Morris was a narrative of a recent colonization law that had been enacted by the Mexican Government. That 1826 law stated that Mexico would begin giving grants of land to those Americans living in the territory known as Mexican Texas, (the territory that would later become Texas). Each family requesting it would be granted one *sitio,* 4,428 acres to be used for grazing, and one *labor*, 177 acres to be used as cropland. The only stipulation to the grant was that the grantees, no matter what their nationality, upon being assigned their individual grants, would automatically become Mexican citizens. The intent of the Mexican government was to ensure that Mexican Texas remained a Mexican possession, bolstered by the fact that all the citizens living in Mexican Texas were now Mexican citizens. It stood to reason, then, that those Mexican citizens would fight on the Mexican side if Mexico ever had to defend its territory. At least that was the intent, not knowing that later unrest by Texans would precipitate a revolution to free Texas from Mexico.

Morris Conley, and his wife, Tricia, intended to take advantage of the land grants from Mexico in order to begin their married life as ranchers in Mexican Texas. True to his word, when winter had released its cold grip from the east coast of the United States, Morris Conley and his wife, Tricia, set out on their journey to Mexican Texas. Carrying their meager possessions in a two-wheeled pushcart, they walked from Virginia to make their way west. In their journey, they were seldom alone. Other travelers used the same network of trails in their own westward treks. At times, Morris and Tricia were able to secure rides on traveling wagons. Driving the slow freight wagons westward was a long and lonely task, and at times, the freighters welcomed them, happy to have a bit of companionship and conversation.

Their journey ended in May of 1827. They had arrived in Mexican Texas and forthwith staked a claim for their ranch in what later would become northern Texas. Their never-ending work to build a cattle ranch from scratch could now begin.

The couple would certainly need shelter from the elements, so the first thing that Morris did was to build a lean-to from dead-fall trees and limbs. As crude as it was, the couple would live in that shelter for nearly a year while Morris planted a garden and began work on another project before he could begin building their house. That other project was the digging of an underground room and tunnel. It would eventually become the root cellar and escape room. Morris wanted a place that he and Patricia could hide if they were attacked by hostile Indians. As he dug underground, he was able to bring the dirt up from the tunnel and spread it around the homesite. He would not have been able to do this if he had built the house first. With the help of Patricia, the underground work was completed, and Morris and Patricia began building their house. By their own sweat and perseverance, the Bar Lazy C Ranch began to grow.

* * *

The house would need to be large enough to accommodate what they hoped would be a growing family. Yet even while the construction was being carried out, the couple lost their first newborn to natural causes. Morris interrupted work on the house in order to clear off a small portion of land at the top of one of the hills near the ranch house. This would be the family burial plot, and the baby that the couple had lost was the first of the Conleys to be buried there.

With the complications of that earlier pregnancy, Morris and Patricia Conley wondered if they would be able to have other children. But nature has a way of making believers out of non-believers. Thinking that she may not have the opportunity to raise a child, Patricia surprisingly became pregnant again, and in late 1828, she gave birth to a son whom the couple named Michael. They would have no other children. The construction of their ranch house continued in earnest.

The northernmost edge of Morris and Patricia's ranch land butted up against the Red River near the small settlement of Spanish Fort. For the rest of his life, from the sweat of his brow and with the help of his wife, Tricia, and their son, Michael, Morris Conley built the Bar Lazy C Ranch from the ground up, making it one of the premier ranches in North Texas. Even the name of the ranch reflected the handiwork of Morris as he had no alternative but to learn every task of ranching through trial-and-error experience. For example, when he first began forging and repairing metal implements for ranch use, he constructed the first branding iron to be used on the ranch. As he forged the metal to make a Bar C brand, he made an error while shaping the metal, which left the C appearing to slant to the side as if leaning on the bar. From then on, the ranch with its iconic brand was officially named the Bar Lazy C and was known locally as the Lazy C Ranch, a thriving cattle ranch operation.

When he was old enough, Michael Conley became a driving force for his father and assumed any task required to manage a cattle ranch, tasks that over the years, his father had lovingly taught him. As Morris Conley became less able to carry out the hard physical labor of running the thriving ranch, Michael took over the day-to-day management of the business. At his skilled hands, the ranch continued to grow and prosper. And in 1850, when Michael felt that he was prepared as he ever would be, he asked Miss Sylvia Jennings, the daughter of a farmer near the village of Spanish Fort, to marry him. They married, and in the following years, after the natural and quiet passing of Morris Conley and Patricia Conley, who were buried in the Conley family plot on the ranch they loved, Sylvia became the matriarch of the Lazy C Ranch. The life of a rancher or farmer is one of unending days of hard work from sunrise to sunset, but Michael and Sylvia thrived. They loved the land, and they loved their lives at the Lazy C.

* * *

Chapter Three

1898

Decades passed and with the hard work of Michael Conley, his wife Sylvia, and the cowhands who worked for them, the Lazy C Ranch flourished. It grew into more than five thousand acres of grazing land as Conley bought up nearby property when it became available. A modest well-appointed adobe ranch house with its attendant out-buildings served as testament that smart, frugal, hard work reaped rewards. Michael and Sylvia were blessed with good rain and good cattle, as well as two children of their own, Sean and Jane. Sean was for all practical purposes, stepping into the shoes of his father. He loved the ranch and the unassuming life of a cattle rancher, spending many hours accompanying his father in his daily activities. Jane, the daughter of Michael and Sylvia, could not have been more different.

Michael and Sylvia's daughter Jane's early life was pathetically sad. Disillusioned by the never-ending work associated with running a cattle ranch, at the age of seventeen, she left home to seek her fortune. But it was not necessarily a fortune that she encountered in her search. It was not long before she met a glib-talking opportunist by the name of John Malone who lived in Dallas, and who had organized and was running a wildcat bank in that city. What soon followed was Malone and Jane producing a squalling son. Yet, Malone had absolutely no intention of marrying Jane Conley. Malone's shady business practices were soon discovered by bank examiners and investors who took the law into their own hands and ran Malone and his family out of town. In short order, Malone abandoned Jane and the child, whom they had named Ivan. Even though he had sired a child with Jane, Malone wanted no part of either of them. He drove to Fort Worth and literally threw them out of his carriage and onto the streets of Fort Worth. John Malone never made any further attempt to see either Jane or Ivan. Thenceforth, Jane lived the life of a domestic servant, securing cleaning and laundry jobs wherever she could to make ends meet to buy food and keep a roof over her and her son's head. Being a somewhat comely woman who appealed to men's baser instincts, Jane was also not above earning a bit of money in the world's oldest profession. As the years went by, her son, Ivan Malone, grew to be a huge brute of a man. Without a father to challenge and channel his development, Ivan discovered that it was easier and more profitable to walk down a crooked path in life. Ivan had been given the surname of Jane's short-term paramour, a name that Jane Conley grew to hate. In addition to making his mother's life miserable, Ivan Malone would soon play an integral, yet infamous, role in the life of the Lazy C Ranch.

The son of Michael and Sylvia, Sean Conley, was the obverse of his sister. Sean Conley learned and absorbed the lessons given to him by his loving parents, took them to heart, was a hard worker, and had a deep love for ranch life. There was little doubt that he would be able to skillfully take the reins of the ranch when his father was ready to slow down. But neither Michael nor Sylvia had anticipated that the time for Sean to take over the ranch would come sooner than expected. Life is funny, yet sometimes sad and cruel about such matters.

Over the years, Sylvia Conley had attempted to remain in contact with her daughter, Jane, sending a letter to her at every opportunity when her daughter's whereabouts were rumored by cattlemen friends who sold their livestock at the Fort Worth stockyards and who had become acquainted with the police officers who patrolled the hard-fisted, hard-drinking stockyard neighborhood of bars and bordellos. With those rancher friends passing information regarding Jane's whereabouts along to the Conleys, some of those letters reached Jane, and she kept the small stack of letters from her mother. Yet no matter how her mother pleaded with her to return home, Jane had reached a level in her squalid life whereby she was certain that she would never be welcome at the Lazy C, and her somewhat compromised health caused by her hard scrabble life was becoming a never-ending situation of aches and pains, along with the inner depression of knowing that she had thrown away her life. She felt that she would be far too embarrassed to ever return to the Lazy C. But the letters, kept by Jane, so carefully and lovingly sent by Sylvia Conley to her wayward daughter, were not just read by Jane. On occasion, the letters were also perused by Jane's son, Ivan.

It was through the same rumors from cattlemen friends in Fort Worth that Sylvia knew that Jane had a son named Ivan who lived somewhere near Jane, thus making Sylvia aware that she had a grandson. What Sylvia Conley did not know, was that Ivan Malone was a shiftless, no-account as he grew to manhood. He was a grifter, a man without scruples with a soul devoid of compassion. His trail of criminal acts grew ever wider through his young life and included murder in the course of robbery. Yet, he had not been caught for any of his crimes, as he was careful to leave no witnesses. After all, dead witnesses cannot talk. The lives of other people held no value to Ivan Malone.

Ivan did not live with his mother. He preferred the company of other ruffians who made their way on the dark streets of Fort Worth. On occasion when he needed money for liquor or other vices, Ivan would pay a visit to his mother. Jane had little money, and certainly none to spare. Her current job as charwoman at a nearby Fort Worth stockyards brothel furnished her with money enough to barely eke out a living.

Primarily because of the way Ivan had always treated his mother, Jane and her son had developed a mutually strong dislike for one another. Even in Ivan's teenage years, Jane saw Ivan as a malicious and evil money grubber who came to her to extract a few coins by threatening or causing physical harm to her. Ivan saw his mother as a detestable, broken-down harlot from whom he could extort money. If Jane protested, Ivan slapped or beat her into submission. Jane bore the bruises to her body for several days following each visit by Ivan. It was during these periodic visits to Jane's hovel that Ivan read the letters sent to his mother by his grandmother, and from the letters, he became familiar with the Lazy C Ranch in North Texas, deducing that the ranch operation was an opportunity to somehow extract his pot of gold.

Ivan's plan to reach that goal would soon begin its bloody unfolding, pushed forward by another visit to his mother. But this visit was different from the earlier occasions. His mother, Jane, sat at a table in her low-rent room, drinking a mug of tea made from the last of the scraps of tea leaves in the tin box tea container as Ivan stepped through the door. Jane's eyes reflected fear as she slowly rose from her chair. She could smell the liquor on him and knew she was in for another bad time.

"Where is it, woman?" The quiet whisper came from the lips of Ivan.

"I don't have any money, Ivan. I had to pay the rent on this 'palace' this morning," Jane replied, gesturing at the pathetic surroundings where she lived.

"A likely story, Mother, just another of your lies to keep me from enjoying myself," said Ivan. He reached out and grabbed the arm of his mother. "Tell me where it is, or I'll hurt you."

Jane knew then that she was going to be hurt, and she tried desperately to wrench her arm free. Her strength was no match for her son who stood a foot taller and weighed well over a hundred pounds more than she did. The first blow was a solid slap to the side of her face that jerked her head to the side. She suffered this blow in silence. Ivan's grip on her upper arm tightened even more to the point that it was painful. The second blow was a backhand slap to the other side of her face.

"You better speak up, old woman. Now where's your money?" growled Ivan.

"I told you I don't have any money. I had to pay bills," Jane stoically replied. She looked distraughtly at her son. It was at this moment that she feared for her life. The man she was looking at was now demonstrating that within his soul, he would feel no remorse for killing her in his rage. She felt hopeless and resigned to the thought of dying at the hands of her son, the very man she had nurtured as well as she could as he had grown to manhood.

This time he shouted, "You are lying to me," said Ivan. With his free hand he grabbed his mother around the throat. "Tell me where it is."

Jane was silent. There was nothing she could say. She simply had no money to give him. She knew how the situation would play out, as her son had abused her on numerous previous instances. She knew she would be hurt at the hands of her son. Her resolve meant that she would need to remain silent. There was simply nothing she could say that would stop the heartless physical violence rendered by her son, a man who Jane was convinced was insane. But her silence further enraged Ivan. With his hand still around his mother's throat, he forcefully shoved his mother toward her bed, sending her tripping backwards, sprawling across the bed, and falling off the opposite side of the bed, wedging her next to the wall. Jane was stunned and a bit dizzy. She struggled to take a breath while willing herself to be silent. She decided that it would be better if she stayed on the floor wedged between her bed and the wall where Ivan could not reach her. She lay listening as Ivan began to physically tear apart her room, but she remained motionless. Jane was still alive, and as she struggled to draw air into her lungs, she was certain that her injuries would soon close her life. Her sad passing thought was that she would soon die, accelerated by the actions of her own child. A quiet gasp passed her lips. Yet, even in her bruised and damaged condition, another thought formed in her mind as she drew a quiet raspy breath. Her thoughts began to clear and her resolve to live steeled to the point that she formed the idea that if she ever recovered from her injuries, she would find her son, and when she found him, she would kill him. A wisp of a thought passed her mind that it was unthinkable for a mother to want to kill her own child, but the thought passed as quickly as it had occurred. Her course of action became crystal clear to her.

Not a shred of remorse rose within Ivan. Without a further glance to the inert body of his mother, he rapidly ransacked the room, still looking for money or anything that he could sell for cash. His search was futile. A broken-down two drawer wooden cabinet yielded only a few articles of clothing, a half bottle of cheap perfume, and the stack of letters that Jane had saved from her mother, Sylvia Conley. Enraged, Ivan threw the letters across the room, watching them disperse across the floor. But then he glanced back into the drawer and saw it. It was a small cloth pouch with a drawstring at the top. He lifted it and opened the pouch. Turning the pouch upside down, a gold necklace with a small pendant figure of a horse slipped into his fingers. He turned the horse in his hand and that's when he saw the engraved writing on the reverse side. The engraving read, *To Janie from Mom.* Ivan's initial reaction was that he would be able to fence the necklace for a small bottle of whisky, but then he sat motionless on the edge of the bed. An idea began to form in his head. A self-satisfying smile crossed his face, as he put the necklace back in its pouch and shoved it into his pocket. He walked over to the door, quickly looked up and down the alleyway, and walked out. It was time to travel.

Chapter Four

Wise County, Texas

U.S. Marshal Nathan Wolf, his wife Claire May, and little Bobby had been living in their cabin for nearly two months. Their move from the Summer Prairie Ranch in Kansas to Wise County, Texas, had been a traumatic event for the couple, especially for Claire May, as she had left her mother, Virginia, and brother, Will, and the ranch where she was born and raised. Each step taken in preparation for the move had been worrisome to her. She remembered the moment she had broken the news to her mother and brother that she and Nathan would be moving to the Texas ranch bequeathed to her by her deceased uncle, John Summers. She recalled the time spent with Virginia as the two women walked through the Summer Prairie ranch house deciding which furniture and furnishings could be given to Claire May and Nathan for their new home in Texas. But at the completion of that task, she remembered that both women had sat on Claire May's bed and cried while hugging one another.

Claire May had said to her mother, "I don't feel right taking things that had belonged to you and Dad." Robert Summers, Virginia's husband and Claire May's father, had died several years prior.

"Claire May, we've been over this many times. You and Nathan deserve anything I can do to help," said Virginia. "This bed of yours and the other furniture and household items will remind you of Summer Prairie, and that your mother and brother love you and want to help you." Virginia paused as Claire May looked at her while wiping away tears with the palm of her hand.

Virginia continued, "I remember when your father and I first came to this ranch to start out. I remember like it was yesterday, but I can tell you, it scared me to death. We had nearly nothing when we started out, and it was a hard life building this ranch. We could have used some help."

Claire May squeezed her mother's hand. She had always been in awe of her mother, a very attractive, yet strong and forceful woman in her own right. The graying process of Virginia's hair only added to her mother's regal appearance. Claire May admired her mother's strength, a liberal dose of which had been passed down to her.

Virginia gazed out of the window in Claire May's bedroom. It was painful yet satisfying to think of her daughter leaving her. But she had known from the first time that she had read the telegram describing the death of John Summers, the brother of her late husband, Robert, that Claire May would be foolish not to move to Texas and take over John's ranch. It was a wonderful opportunity for Nathan and her. They would be able to start their married lives managing a working ranch, albeit hundreds of miles away. After receiving and reading the telegram, and knowing Claire May's adventurous spirit, Virginia had known that her daughter and son-in-law would eventually leave for Texas.

Virginia turned to face her daughter and continued their discussion, "Sweetheart, you remind me so much of me when I was younger. You are strong and you have a good heart. And I see how happy you make Nathan. He's a good man. As for me, I think you know that it is about time that I turn over the whole operation of Summer Prairie to your brother," said Virginia. "Will has a good head on his shoulders and has taken over where your dad left off. He can handle the ranch by himself. And he won't be alone very long, since he and Alice Morgan will soon set their wedding date. Even so, I intend to stay on here at Summer Prairie, but I also intend to spend a lot of time with my grandchild. So, I will be traveling at various times between Kansas and Texas, and when I visit you in Texas, I like the idea of seeing some of the items that have been here at Summer Prairie. Dry your tears. In a day or two, we will have the ranch hands load up all these things and put them on a train car headed to Texas. We will wire your man, Mr. Carillo, to get your things at the other end of the train line. It will all work out, you'll see."

Just as her mother had predicted, when Claire May, Nathan, and little Bobby had arrived at their new home, the furniture and other goods had already been placed inside the cabin and were waiting for Claire May to tell Nathan and Pablo Carillo where to place each item. The projects to paint the interior of the house, hang cupboards, and install countertops were ongoing when the Wolfs arrived. In Claire May's opinion, the most astonishing additions to the house were the additional bedroom and a commode room that had been added to the cabin. For the first time in her life, Claire May would have an indoor toilet and the luxury of a bathtub.

The construction and completion of the addition onto the cabin had been started by instructions and funds wired to Pablo by Nathan so that materials could be purchased by their hired man. Claire May had not been told the details of the construction in order for it to be a wonderful surprise to her. Per Nathan's instructions, Pablo had hired some helpers, and along with the addition, other repairs and modifications had been made to the cabin. A major undertaking in the construction and remodeling had been the installation of a clay tile sewer line that led to an underground concrete septic tank to which leech lines had been attached. Completing the project had been the installation of a manual water pump that let water flow into the toilet tank. While the system was a bit cumbersome, it meant that the family would not need to walk to an outhouse in inclement weather.

Claire May had made use of the time that she needed to be outdoors while the men finished the final details inside the house. With lumber and other materials brought to the house by the workmen, Claire May had wielded her own hammer and saw. It was not long before she had built a coyote-proof chicken coop. She had been determined that the family would have fresh eggs. She also was able to plant a small garden, no small feat as she had to work around Bobby's insistence that she not stray too far from him. The addition and other remodeling projects were now nearly complete, but Pablo and his helpers continued their hammering, as the last of the wood shingles were attached to the roof to make it impervious to rainy days.

In addition to being completely surprised when they arrived at their new home, Claire May had laughed when she saw the new additional bedroom. She remembered the words of her mother, who said, "You're going to need to put an addition on your house for when I come to visit you." Aside from that, Claire May was very grateful that they would have a bit more room in the cabin. She had her own suspicions about why they might later need more room in the house.

Bobby's arms and legs flailed as he became restless in his basket that was on the floor of the cabin's porch. He did not like that the sun had moved in the last thirty minutes to the point where a partial ray of sunlight now crossed his tiny face and hit him in the eye. He vocalized his displeasure, which in turn, alerted his mother, Claire May Wolf, to his situation. Claire May, her tawny blonde hair askew and a paint brush in her hand, was on the grass next to the porch, putting a fresh coat of paint on pieces of the tired-looking cabin furniture. She put down her paint brush, pushed her hair to the side, stepped up onto the porch, and bent down to pick up the baby.

"What's the matter, little man? Did the nasty sunbeam get in your eye?" she cooed while holding him and moving the basket with her foot to a shady spot on the porch. Her blue eyes met the blue-eyed stare of her now-smiling son, Bobby Wolf.

But that was not Bobby's only irritant. He reached his small hands out to grasp his mother's shirt. "Hmm," murmured Claire May. "I guess I know what you want." She sat down on the edge of the porch with her legs dangling over the side and unfastened the top buttons of her chambray work shirt. Bobby's small face was soon hidden as he nursed from his mother. After a short time, the infant had had his fill and slowly began to drift off to sleep. Claire May gently placed the baby back in his basket and rebuttoned her shirt. While Bobby slept, she returned to the grass and continued her painting chore.

Chapter Five

Lazy C Ranch
Near Spanish Fort, Texas

This was not the first time that Michael Conley was extremely riled up. Yet, he was also ashamed, ashamed because his anger was directed toward his wife, Sylvia, whom he worshipped. But for the life of him, he could not understand what had gone through his wife's head to allow that no-account tramp to stay on the property. He was standing in the doorway of the barn watching as his cowhands slowly rode away to begin their day's work. The group accompanied a horse drawn wagon that contained their tools, and they were headed out to round up strays and take care of some periodic calf branding. But due to his size, one of the cow hands stood out from the others as they rode slowly away. That man wore a dull yellow shirt in an attempt to set himself apart from the other hands, but he needn't have bothered. He stood apart by his sheer size and by the way he sat a horse. Even at a walk, he bumped in the saddle, jostling his head and arms. Ivan Malone was not a cow man and never would be. As Michael Conley said many times, "He barely knows the crappin' end from the eatin' end of the horse and is downright worthless."

Malone had no work ethic, and the other hands complained to the foreman, Lee Stark, who in turn, complained to Michael about the man's disregard for helping his fellow cowhands get their work done. When confronted by the foreman, or by Michael, Malone always seemed to have a lame excuse for not keeping up with work he had been assigned. Michael had given so many tongue lashings to Ivan Malone that he was tired of trying to make a ranch hand out of him and would just as soon see the back side of Ivan Malone ride off into the sunset. Michael and Malone had had another of those shouting sessions this morning before the ranch hands had ridden away. Malone could not get his horse to stand still to throw a blanket and saddle on it and had taken a whip to the horse before Michael was able to stop him.

Michael vividly remembered his words to Malone. "If I ever see you whip another of my horses, I will personally take a whip to you and kick you off my property. Is that understood?"

Malone had simply glared back at Michael, but slowly nodded his head in agreement. But the look on Malone's face when Michael had chewed on him caused a shock in Michael's chest. Directed toward Michael, it was the look of pure, cold evil, the eyes of a killer without conscience. Even so, Malone was at least smart enough to know that for the time being he had to get along with his grandfather and Sean Conley until such time as he could carry out his long-term goal.

As the men rode away, Michael's mind wandered as he recalled the day last July when Ivan Malone had ridden onto the ranch sitting astride one of the sorriest looking horses that Michael had ever seen. The animal had been ridden nearly to death and was clearly malnourished. Rib bones were evident through the dull sides of the animal, living proof that the horse had not had proper feed in quite some time. The horse walked with a limp and was near the point of being unable to walk any farther. Michael's immediate thought when he had seen the stranger was that a man was measured by the condition of the horse for which he was responsible, and it was plain to see that the stranger was a man who cared nothing for his horse. Michael knew that such a man was as low as vermin. What possible reason could such a man have for coming onto the Lazy C? Michael had soon found out and remembered the conversation.

The man had dismounted his horse, leaving the animal hanging its head nearly to the ground. It was clear that only with immediate care would the horse last through the night. The stranger was a big man with wide shoulders, and it was evident that he would have been a heavy load for the played-out horse. The man had several days' growth of whiskers, and he appeared dirty and unkempt.

"You're on private property, mister," growled Michael. "Now who are you, and what do you want?"

One of the ranch hands who was lunging a green horse in the nearby round pen had seen the conversation between the stranger and his boss, Mr. Conley. He stopped his work and climbed up on the corral fence. He could tell from the appearance of the stranger that he had no business on the ranch. He slipped down from the fence and furtively drew his sidearm, as he could see that Mr. Conley was not armed. With the handgun held behind his hip, he slowly walked to where he was only a few paces from his boss. Ivan Malone only glanced at the ranch hand.

"Now, now, mister, I don't mean any harm," said Ivan. "Are you Mr. Michael Conley?"

Michael answered. "I might be. Who wants to know?"

"Well, my name's Malone, sir, and I'm just lookin' for a job," said Ivan.

"Ain't got no jobs, mister, and I can sure as hell see you ain't no cowhand. So, I'm of the opinion that you should just turn around and start walking," said Michael. "Oh, and when you start walking, your horse, if he is your horse, is staying here. Making that horse walk again would probably kill it. I don't tolerate any man abusing a horse. Now, git!"

Michael turned to the ranch hand and told him to holster his pistol and take the horse that Malone had been riding into the barn. "Make sure it gets plenty of water and feed."

"Hey, mister, you can't just take my horse like that. It's my horse, and you're stealing it," said Malone.

Michael answered, "Well, if I'm any judge of men, I'd bet that you stole that poor animal yourself. You can tell me if I'm wrong."

Malone had not answered Michael's accusation. In truth, he had stolen the horse and a saddle from an unattended stock barn in Fort Worth, but he puffed up at Conley's accusation just the same. Then he said, "Well, I'm not walkin' just yet, Mr. Conley. I've got a story you might like to hear."

Michael Conley was losing his patience. But he decided to hear the stranger out. "Story, huh. So, spill it."

"Well, Mr. Conley, I reckon that before you kick me off your place, you probably ought to know that I'm your grandson."

"I ain't got no grandson," replied Michael, yet his face had a slight questioning look, as he remembered a conversation he had had some time back with Sylvia.

"I beg to differ with you, sir. You see, your daughter, Jane, was my mother." Malone used the word 'was' because he was sure that Jane had been killed during their last meeting. After all, she had not moved or made a sound while she lay on the floor next to her bed where he had thrown her.

Malone's mention of Jane brought a flood of sorrowful memories to the mind of Michael Conley. His daughter had rebelled against all attempts by Michael and Sylvia to mold her into a woman capable of running the Lazy C along with her brother Sean. Instead, she had run away from the ranch well over twenty years ago. The rumor was that she was living hand to mouth in Fort Worth. Michael remembered his reaction to Malone's words. "You makin' some kind of joke, mister?"

"No joke, Mr. Conley, and I can prove it," said Malone.

Their conversation was interrupted as they turned their heads to observe Sylvia Conley approaching them. Sylvia's hair had turned a lovely salt and pepper shade over the years, and she still walked ramrod straight, with determination that showed in her mannerisms. She wore the clothes of a rancher, a man's shirt and pants for working around the ranch house. She had seen her husband and the stranger talking in the yard and joined them to learn the cause of their discussion. "Mind if I listen in?" she said.

Ivan Malone smiled inwardly. Now he knew that he would not have to get past Michael to see Sylvia. She had come out to meet him. *Just what I hoped*, he thought to himself.

"Howdy ma'am," said Malone as he doffed his well-worn hat.

"Howdy yourself," answered Sylvia.

Michael turned to Sylvia. "Now, Sylvia, you don't need to be concerning yourself to come out here. This gent was just leaving. Ain't that right?" he said as he looked sternly at Malone, inwardly hoping that Malone would get the hint and leave.

Cool as a cucumber, Malone ignored Michael and turned to Sylvia. "I'm Ivan Malone, Jane's boy," he said. "I reckon you must be my grandma."

Malone's statement did not have the same effect on Sylvia as it had had on Michael. She was certainly shocked, but she had known that her daughter had at least one son, a bit of news that she had learned from her friends in Fort Worth and shared with Michael years ago, even though he had chosen to dismiss the rumor. However, she knew no other details as her daughter had never answered any of the many letters that Sylvia had sent to her. She studied the face of the stranger. It was then that she could see a slight trace of her daughter's face in that of the man in front of her. Her heart skipped a beat. *Could it be?* She asked herself.

Michael was now angry. "Mister, you got no right to come here and make some outlandish claim. You're upsetting my wife, and I'm about a half minute from going to get my shotgun."

"Now, now," said Malone. "Maybe this will put your mind at ease."

Malone had reached in his pocket and retrieved the necklace he had taken from Jane. He walked toward Sylvia and held out his hand. Malone was certain that his last beating had probably killed his mother, but he said, "My mother gave me this necklace the last time we were together. I think you might recognize it."

Sylvia took the necklace from his hand and looked closely at the horse pendant, reading the engraved letters on the back. She stood motionless for a moment. Then a tear rolled from her eye. "You say Jane gave you this?"

Malone quickly let a lie cross his lips. He did not truly know whether his mother was dead or alive. But he replied, "Yes, ma'am. You see, she was quite poorly and wasn't sure whether she had much longer to live. She was alive the last time that I saw her, but later, I believe someone said she might have died of consumption."

"And you're her son?" replied Sylvia.

"Yes, ma'am," said Malone. "And the last time we were together, she gave me this here necklace and told me that I should come to see you and maybe you might have some work for me. She said you'd know that the necklace was from her."

Of course, Jane had never said or done any such thing, but by now, Malone knew that his grandmother was the person to make or break his scheme. "She had mighty kind words to say about you, ma'am."

Sylvia still held the necklace in her hand and glanced at it again before studying the face of her grandson. Michael knew what she was going to say even before she spoke. Sylvia turned to Michael. "I reckon we can find a place for him here."

As Michael recalled, it was those words from his wife months ago that had allowed his worthless grandson, if he really was his kin, to remain on the ranch. As he watched his ranch hands and Ivan Malone move off in the distance, he slowly shook his head from side to side as he recalled all of the instances when Malone had been at odds with Michael or his ranch crew. In the short few months that Malone had been on the ranch, the unpleasant instances were far too many to count. Yet, when he mentioned the conflicts to Sylvia, she only smiled and continued to say, "He'll come around, Michael. He'll come around."

Michael knew better. His opinion was that Malone was just plain evil, as on several occasions he had used verbal threats and his fists to beat on the weaker ranch hands when conflicts arose. There was not a cowhand on the ranch who could physically hold his own in a fight with Malone. He was just too big and strong. Thus, the man could get away with being a slacker and a bully. And it seemed to Michael that Malone had wormed his way into his wife's heart. Sylvia could not see the hard and evil side of her alleged grandson. But what worried Michael Conley the most was that his son Sean, who was already able to take over managing the ranch, worked alongside the ranch hands learning every aspect of the ranch and the men who worked here. Michael was rightly concerned with what might happen if Sean ever had a row with Malone. Michael was practical enough to know that Sean, as tough as any cowhand on the ranch, would be no match in a fight with Malone. Michael knew that if that ever happened, he would be forced to move Malone off the ranch at gunpoint, dead or alive, and that would not go over very well with Sylvia. As a result, he had told Sean to give Malone a wide range and stay away from him as much as possible. Michael turned from the barn and walked back to the house.

Michael was not alone in his feelings toward Malone. Lee Stark, the Lazy C ranch foreman disliked Malone from the first time he met him. With his hard work, Stark's ranch crew worked as a team, and he was reluctant to have Malone join the crew. After getting to know Malone, he had expressed his frustration to Michael, even more so following the departure of two long-time cowhands due to their intense dislike for Malone, and Stark's personal observation of the friction growing among the work crew.

Chapter Six

Lazy C Ranch

Her thoughts would give her no peace. No matter how many tasks she undertook to take her mind off the subject, it would not stop nagging at her. The words of Ivan Malone, whom she now presumed to be her grandson, had burned into her soul as the weeks rolled by. Ivan had alluded to her and Michael that their only daughter, Jane, had quite possibly died in Fort Worth. She continued to ask herself, what kind of mother would simply walk away from such news? Where had Jane died? Did she die of disease, as Ivan had led them to believe? Did anyone take care of funeral arrangements? These were some of the many questions that nagged at Sylvia.

As days passed, Sylvia made up her mind. Although she knew that Michael might not agree with her course of action, she was determined to ease her mind. Her first action was to set aside a day to drive her buckboard into Nocona, where she made contact with their long-time attorney. At Sylvia's insistence, the lawyer wired two hundred dollars to a law firm in Fort Worth with instructions to find out for sure if Jane was alive and if she was, give her the money and persuade her to come to the Lazy C. Sylvia was encouraged by her visit with the attorney, and her heart was lighter as she rode back to the ranch that day. At the end of a week of waiting, the attorney for the Conleys rode to the Lazy C and gave Sylvia a telegram that he had received from his Fort Worth attorney friend. The telegram read:

Believe we have located Miss Jane Conley. Have given her the funds per your request. Await your further orders. P. Willoughby, Esq.

The news in the telegram was of great joy to Sylvia. That evening, at dinner, she sat at the table with Michael, Sean, and Ivan. With dinner completed, she retrieved the telegram, carefully unfolded it, and read it to the men. Their reactions were not unexpected. Even though it was his own daughter whom they were discussing, Michael seemed somewhat indifferent about the situation. After all, hadn't Jane left the ranch years ago without so much as a fare-thee-well? He was not against Sylvia trying to bring Jane back to the family, but he did not want to see Sylvia disappointed or hurt. He did not have to be told what would happen next. He knew in his gut that his wife was going to pursue the search for their daughter, and he feared that she would be greatly downhearted if Jane did not want to join them at the Lazy C. Then he looked across the table at Ivan Malone and thought to himself that none of this would be happening if Malone hadn't suddenly appeared at the ranch weeks ago.

Sean was a bit more enthusiastic. After all, he and Jane had grown up together and had been playmates and confidants as only siblings can be. He had been disappointed when his sister had gone away years ago. But he was thinking more about his mother and could only hope that this news worked out favorably for her. Without getting his hopes up, he was very curious as to what had happened to his sister in the years she was absent from the ranch.

Ivan, on the other hand, was silent, yet managed to paste a slight, false smile on his face. He was seething inside. He was sure that he had killed his mother, as she had lain inert on the floor of her room after receiving a beating at his own hands, but now it appeared that he had failed in his attempt to put a gruesome closure on the matter, and there was a chance that his mother might be coming to the Lazy C. Ivan knew full well that his mother would not fit into his plans to wrest ownership of the Lazy C from Michael and Sean Conley. To himself, he thought that if his mother ever came to the Lazy C, she would reveal his treatment of her and would spoil the plans he had made for taking over the ranch. His long-range goal was not to be a nursemaid to a bunch of cows. His plan was that when he gained control of the property, he intended to sell the ranch and take the money for his own use. The presence of his mother would only derail that plan. Therefore, he would need to do everything possible to keep his mother from rejoining the family. His thoughts were interrupted by his grandmother.

"I'm going to catch the train the day after tomorrow in Nocona and go to Fort Worth," said Sylvia. "I will go see this Mr. Willoughby so that he can take me to see Jane. I'm certain that if I have some time together with Jane that she will come around and come back home with me."

"Now, Sylvia," said Michael. "I don't want you to go getting your hopes up too high. You haven't seen Jane in years, and she might have no interest at all in coming back here. If she wanted to come back, why did she send Ivan here to us, and her not come along? I don't think she's going to have any interest in coming back here, and I don't want you to keep thinking she might. I don't want to see you be disappointed when it doesn't work out."

"Well, Michael, I've got to find out for sure. I'm her mother, and I'm going to see her," said Sylvia. "Now, I will need one of you to take me to the train the day after tomorrow."

The grimy cog wheels in Ivan's warped brain began spinning an evil scenario. He knew what he would do. "I'll take you Grandma," he said.

"Good, then that's settled," said Sylvia. She refolded the telegram, rose, and walked away from the table.

When she was gone, Sean spoke up, "I can take her to the train, Ivan."

"No, no," said Ivan. "I'm going to look around town for a while after I drop Grandma off."

"Mmm," Michael grunted.

* * *

Two days later, Sylvia's luggage was loaded onto the ranch's buckboard and Ivan Malone shook the reins and clucked to the two-horse team. They were off to Nocona to catch the train to Bowie where she could catch another train to Decatur and then on to Fort Worth. It was a glorious morning for Sylvia as she could only think of how wonderful it would be to see her daughter after all these years. As they drove, Sylvia looked over at Ivan and naively said, "Won't it be nice to see your mother again?"

Malone, of course, would not answer that question truthfully. He had no intention of seeing his mother again, but dutifully answered, "Sure will, Grandma." To himself, he thought, *That aint' gonna happen.*

The buckboard had now reached the boundary fence of the Lazy C. They had traveled nearly two miles from the ranch house, nearing the road to Nocona. They were still on Lazy C property. Ivan knew this place and specifically selected it because of its seclusion. As they suddenly left the path, Sylvia did not have time to wonder what Ivan was doing before the butt of Ivan's pistol crashed to the top of Sylvia's head. She was knocked out cold and slumped on the buckboard seat. Stopping the buckboard, Ivan picked up the limp body of his grandmother and tossed her like a sack of potatoes into the back of the buckboard. Ivan then continued driving along the fence row and drove over a ridge so that he and the buckboard were completely out of sight of the ranch path and the road to Nocona. He then took the shovel from the back of the buckboard and began digging, perspiration dripping from his nose as he carried out his evil work.

Deep enough, thought Malone, and he laid the shovel aside. He retrieved the limp body of Sylvia Conley and carried her to the open grave where he callously dropped her into the crude dirt opening. Knowing that he was too far from the ranch house for any sound to reach it, Malone then shot Sylvia between her eyes, a few drops of blood soon appeared on the dead woman's forehead. He holstered his revolver and returned to the buckboard, picked up Sylvia's luggage, and threw the bags into the grave. He retrieved Sylvia's purse and removed the money she had been carrying. But his fingers also found the gold necklace with the inscribed horse pendant at the bottom of the purse. He put that in his pocket along with the cash, then he walked back to the grave and threw the purse into the opening. Using the shovel, he then scraped the dirt he had dug from the hole and covered his grandmother and her possessions. *She ain't likely to ever be found*, thought Malone. He returned the shovel to the buckboard, sat down in the shade of the wagon, and rolled a cigarette. He lit it and stayed by the wagon until the smoke was finished. When he judged enough time had passed for him to have driven to the Nocona train station and back, he climbed up on the buckboard and headed back to the ranch house. When he reached home, he unhitched the team and put the animals in the corral. As he was putting the horses back in the corral, Michael came to join him.

"Did you get her to the train depot all right?" asked Michael.

"Yep, sure did. Train was on time, too, so we didn't have to wait long," said Malone.

"Well, that's fine," said Michael and turned and walked back to the house. Michael could not see the smile on Malone's face as he turned the horses into the corral, and Malone could not see the lines of worry that crossed Michael's weathered brow.

Chapter Seven

Delta Hide Tanning Works
Lafayette, Louisiana

Atop the sprawling building, several rusty metal stacks gave off plumes of smoke and steam. The smoke rose from wood-fired boilers used to heat water to scalding temperatures needed to strip hair from hide. The steam rose from huge iron kettles where the hides soaked before moving to the stripping machines, also driven by steam. In addition to the flumes from the top of the building, the chemicals and dyes used to process cowhides into marketable leather gave off an unpleasant stench that hung in the air for several acres around the run-down processing plant. The factory had been in its present location for decades, and there was certainly a reason that the factory was located several miles outside of Lafayette proper. Even so, when the wind and temperatures combined to carry the sickening aroma away, the smell could be discerned in town, much to the dismay of the city residents. But the leather factory provided much-needed jobs, enabling factory workers to have cash that could help revitalize parts of Louisiana that had been devastated by the Civil War. The jobs were, for the most part, unpleasant due to the hard labor and constant odor involved in treating the hides. Laborers who returned to their homes in the evening undressed outside before entering and left their work clothes hanging on homemade racks in their back yards. The majority of the men lived in shabby, multi-family apartment houses, abodes that reflected the men's low wages. After doffing their odiferous clothing in the back of their respective apartment buildings, without exception, the men hoped that it would rain that evening to wash some of the stench from their clothes.

The following morning, they put on the same work clothes, wet or dry, and trudged back to the leather factory for another day's work.

Calvin Kahl pushed the loaded cart across the floor of the tanning factory. It was his job to move wet hides to a giant roller press, where the hides would have the excess water and chemicals squeezed from them as they moved through the press. It was back-breaking work pulling the wet hides from the hot vats and loading them onto the cart. Calvin was seventeen years old and had been working at the hide factory for three years, ever since he was old enough to push a broom around the trimming tables to sweep up the small pieces of leather dropped to the floor after the machines had made their cuts into the hides. He remembered the day he had walked into the factory with his father, Wilburn. Wilburn (Will) Kahl had decided that his son was old enough to push a broom and contribute to the family's meager income. Calvin had been so proud that day to walk to work with his father. It was not long before the illusion wore off, and mental and physical fatigue took its place. When he was a bit stronger and taller, Calvin had been moved from the sweeping crew to the job he now held. But lifting heavy hides and pushing a cart full of wet hides to the press area of the building was not Calvin's idea of a good job, even though he had received a three cent per hour raise in pay. But the job was not the only thing that was nagging at Calvin.

As he pushed the cart across the factory floor, Calvin paused in his thoughts and looked across the huge room where he could see the cutting and trimming tables. He could see his father, Will, working at one of the cutting tables. His father's job involved receiving the tanned and dried hides, now considered to be a sheet of leather, and cutting the hides into workable shapes needed by customers of the factory. Those customers might order just a neatly trimmed full hide or they might order custom shapes of leather pieces that would then be made into such things as shoes, harness ware, and other leather goods in the customer's own finishing factories. Will Kahl was at the top of the hierarchy of the factory jobs. It took skill and patience to do Will's job. In addition, it was dangerous. The giant, steam-driven, industrial-sized knives dropped to the trim table and effortlessly sliced leather into custom shapes and sizes, and if the operator at the trim table stepped on the floor pedal to lower the knives at the wrong instant, or did not have the leather properly placed, those same knives could slice an entire hand off the operator in the blink of an eye. As Calvin watched his father moving the leather sheet around on the cutting table, he could plainly see his father's hands. Thus, he could see that his father was missing the fourth and fifth fingers of his right hand, the result of an accident that had occurred a few years ago. Calvin shuddered slightly as he thought about how that must have felt to his father when the accident happened.

But it was not his father's hands that were giving Calvin cause to reflect. Instead, it was something that his father had said at home a few nights ago. Will Kahl had broken the news to his wife Matty and to Calvin that he was going to go away for a time. As he put it, he was going "to take a little vacation. I'm going to try my hand at gold prospecting." His wife, Matty, had nearly fainted and had to be helped to a chair.

"Have you lost your mind, Will?" said Matty. "What do you think that Calvin and I will live on with you gone? You're a bigger fool than even I thought." She was subtly reminding Will that he had had some zany ideas in the past and had earned a reputation among their friends of being a nice fellow but a bit daft in his thinking. Matty began weeping softly.

"I have to agree with Mom," said Calvin. "You can't just go off and leave us here."

"Now, now," Will responded. "I won't be gone long, and if there ain't no gold to be had, why, I'll just trot on back here to home. And Matty, you know that we've put enough money away to last you 'til I get back."

The discussion of Will's sudden interest in gold mining continued for the remainder of the evening, but no matter what argument was directed to him for staying home, Will insisted that he was leaving in just a few weeks. Back on the factory floor, Calvin recalled every word of the gold mining discussion. As he looked over at his father, Calvin slowly shook his head. When the discussion was being held, Calvin did not know whether to be mad at his father for leaving them or excited to await the outcome of his father's latest ideas. It soon became readily apparent that his father's leaving was having a detrimental effect on his mother.

Matty Kahl came from good stock. She was of German heritage, a hard-working woman who kept a clean home, such as it was, and stretched her husband's earnings to put passably tasty meals on the table for Will and Calvin and pay the rent for their four-room, second-story apartment. She was understanding of Will's foibles and daydreams and loved him just as he was. In Calvin, she had always dreamed that he would have a better life than she and Will had. But she recognized the limitations to achieving such a life for her son, especially now that he had taken his place among the workmen at the Delta Leather Factory. The future for such a working man was bleak, with low wages and hard work that never offered a glimmer of a better life. Will's announcement that he was leaving their home to go to Colorado was devastating news. It was profound, more so because Matty was keeping a secret.

Matty Kahl continued to harbor her secret from her husband. For months, Matty had been experiencing abdominal pain, mostly just a dull but angry pain, but sometimes the pain was sharper and more intense. Unbeknownst to Will, Matty had visited with a physician. After probing and pushing on her body, the doctor had offered an opinion. He had told her that she had a growth, a tumor he called it, that was growing inside her. He had given the growth a name, cancer. With the physician's scant knowledge of the disease, and certainly no known cure, the doctor had opined that Matty would not live to see her next birthday. With that knowledge held closely to herself, Matty was now faced with the surprise announcement by her husband that he would be leaving. Her concern of most importance was the effects of both situations on the life of her son, Calvin. His father was leaving the family for an unknown length of time, and he would soon lose his mother to an insidious disease about which no one seemed to know the true prognosis.

Matty sank into a melancholy depression. Will did not see the change in his wife. Matty kept up a good front for just that purpose. But Calvin saw through his mother's façade. He watched as she occasionally wiped tears on her apron, and he could see that she seldom smiled. Matty also seemed to slow down in her work around the house, and Calvin would sometimes see her staring out the kitchen window, lost in deep thoughts known only to herself. One day, when his father was away from the house, Calvin confronted Matty.

Calvin approached his mother and placed his hands on her shoulders. "What's wrong, Mom? Something is bothering you, and I would like to help you, if I can," he said.

Matty smiled slightly, recognizing that it was difficult to hide her melancholy inner feelings from her near-grown son. "There's nothing you can do to help me, Calvin. I'm just sad because your father is leaving us for a while," she said. She had no intention of telling Calvin about the insidious disease that was growing within her.

"Well, I guess we will need to depend on one another while he's gone," said Calvin. "But I sure wish he wouldn't go. Doesn't he think about us? Doesn't he think what this will do to us? Doesn't he care about us? I'll bet he won't find even one damn gold nugget."

"Don't swear, Calvin," said Matty. Then she chose her words very carefully. "Calvin, your father does care for us. In his own way, he loves us. But in his soul, he has a demon flaw. That demon causes your father to be a dreamer who finds it hard to settle down and be happy. And no matter how much we argue with him to stay, the demon inside him will not let him listen to us." She paused, then went on. "And you are right. We must depend on each other to get through this, and we should pray that your father comes back to us soon."

When Will returned home that evening, he was smiling. He disrobed, leaving his work clothes hanging outdoors. Calvin's work clothes were already hanging on the outdoor rack. Will came into the apartment. He stood in the kitchen in his union suit. He was waving papers in his hand. "You see what I've got here?" He got no response from Matty or Calvin.

"These are maps," said Will. "After supper, we'll sit down, and you can help me map out my route to Colorado." He laid the maps on the kitchen table and while still smiling, turned to the sink to wash up for supper.

Little was said while they ate. Matty and Calvin made a feeble attempt to dissuade Will in his plan to leave the family and go gold mining in Colorado. His mind was made up, and there was nothing more to be said. While Matty washed dishes, Will laid his maps out on the kitchen table.

"Lookee here, Cal," said Will as he motioned to his son to sit down near him at the table. Calvin did not want to, but he sat down by his father at the table. Will was moving his index finger slowly across the maps as he spoke excitedly. "I figure I'll head on up to Shreveport, then skirt around Dallas, Texas, then take this angled road through Denton and Decatur, on up to Wichita Falls, then up to Amarillo, then over to a place called Trinidad, New Mexico, and finally on up to Pueblo, Colorado. I've heard tell that they are doing some mighty good stream panning in those parts." Will grinned as he looked at his son. Though he was dead set against his father leaving, Calvin could not help but be somewhat mesmerized as he watched his father name the small towns that he would pass through on his trip west. The fact that he had never travelled outside of Lafayette caused a twinge of envy within him, which was quickly replaced by anger that his father was leaving the family behind.

"Well, what do you think, son? Your old man is going to be a gold miner," said Will.

Calvin did not respond. He shrugged his shoulders, rose from the table, and walked to his room where he lay on his back on his bed, his arms tucked up under his head. He loved his father but could not help but think that Will was betraying him and his mom. He did not like it one bit, but what could a seventeen-year-old do about it? Nothing, he reckoned. That did not stop his anger nor his worry for his Mom and himself.

The following morning, Calvin ate his breakfast with his mother, but his father was mysteriously absent from the table. As Calvin went about his work at the leather factory, he noticed that his father was not at his usual workstation at the cutting and trimming machine. Another man had taken his father's place. Calvin worried through the rest of his workday. *Where was his father? Had he left for Colorado?* At the end of the day, Calvin trudged home. But when he went to the rear yard of the apartment building to remove his work clothes, he came face to face with a horse and burro, both tied to the railing of the back porch. A pack tree and panniers were strapped to the burro. The horse was saddled and bridled. Both animals lifted their heads when Calvin approached them and stared at him as Calvin removed his work clothes. Calvin knew immediately why the animals were there, and his anger rose within. He threw his work clothes onto the rack and stomped into the house. His father was sitting at the kitchen table drinking a cup of coffee.

Will spoke quickly. "Did 'ja see my horse and burro, son?"

Matty was at the stove, making the final preparations for supper as Calvin began washing up at the sink. "Yeah, I saw them Dad. I guess there's no stopping you now since a new guy has taken your place on the cutting table at work."

Will simply laughed. "Yep, I plan to leave in the morning."

Conversation was again limited at the supper table. When they had finished eating, Matty made one more plea to Will. "We don't want you to leave, Will. But you know that. Is there anything we can do to make you change your mind?"

Will answered as he spread his maps out on the table again. "Now Matty, you know we have been over this many times. I'm going to try my hand at this gold panning. If it works out, we will have a nice nest egg. If it doesn't, well, I'll come on back home and get myself another job. I don't think I'll be gone all that long, and you and Calvin will get along just fine while I'm away."

Both Matty and Calvin doubted that they would get along just fine, but they held their tongues. Calvin looked more closely at his mother. It was then that he noticed that Matty did not look well. Her complexion had taken on a grayer appearance and her eyes seemed sunken. Calvin worried about her. He asked her, "Are you all right, Mother?"

Matty knew that she was not all right, but she rose from the table to return to the sink. "I'm fine, Calvin," she said. She continued. "Will,

I expect you to write to us at least once a week to let us know you are safe, and everything is all right with you. You'll do that won't you?"

"You can count on it Matty," Will replied.

The following dawn Will was up and loading the final gear into the panniers. He had not told Matty how much of their savings he had taken to purchase the horse, burro, and the supplies needed for his trip. He did not want to worry her more than she was already. It was not long before he hugged and kissed Matty, and hugged Calvin before mounting the horse. His final words were, "Take care of your mother, Calvin." As he rode away leading the burro from a rope attached to his saddle, silent tears rolled from the eyes of both Matty and Calvin. They could not help but think that they might never see Will again.

Chapter Eight

Lazy C Ranch

Only a few days after the brutal killing of Sylvia Conley at the hands of Ivan Malone, two strangers arrived at the Lazy C Ranch. When asked, they told the Conleys that they were out-of-work and down on their luck cowboys who needed jobs. Michael and Sean Conley knew that jobs for ranch hands were few and far between, with most ranch men never leaving their jobs, unless they got in trouble with their employers or had a lust for traveling and roaming from job to job. Lazy C hands generally did not leave their jobs, that is, until recently, when two hands had become injured. The Conleys were good people, men who tried to help their fellow cattlemen when it was warranted. Because they really did not need any new permanent hands, out of kindness, they told the two strangers they would keep them on for two months. By that time, the injured men should be able to return to work, and the short-term work would let the new men earn traveling money that they would need to move on. If the Conleys had only known the true nature of these two men, they would never have made them welcome on the Lazy C.

The two men who came upon the ranch were not strangers to Ivan Malone. Malone knew them from Fort Worth, where they had all frequented the same gin joints and houses of prostitution. Their names were Beryl Dunn and Matt Woods. The two men were the lowest of the low, with no redeeming qualities except a fast draw and a cold soul. They survived by committing criminal acts of armed robbery, beatings of innocent people for profit, and gunplay to intimidate their victims. Each had committed at least two murders. But while they may have been prime suspects for any number of crimes, their major crimes had never been solved by the police, and they had served time in the Tarrant County Jail only for petty crimes. While he had lived in Fort Worth, Ivan Malone had participated in several criminal ventures with the two men, so he knew their nefarious skills and their abilities to keep their mouths shut. In a fair gun fight, each of the two men could hold his own without being killed, but they made it a point not to get in a fair fight. They always found a way to stack the odds in their favor, with the predictable outcome of injuring or killing their opponents. Thus, they were murderers, gunmen for hire. And Ivan Malone had ensured that they gained a foothold on the Lazy C.

There was an ominous timeliness to the arrival of the gunmen. With the animosity of the Lazy C ranch hands that had developed toward him, Malone now felt that it might be in his best interest to have paid protectors living on the ranch and posing as out-of-work ranch hands. They were just the men he needed to watch his back and keep him from any sort of revenge by the cowhands at the Lazy C. After arriving at the ranch, the two thugs never left the side of Ivan Malone. The long-term ranch hands soon spotted Dunn and Woods as phonies, men who did not know the first thing about the hard work required on a ranch. It was also plain to see that the two men seemed to be favored by Ivan Malone who kept them close by most of the time. In addition, the ranch hands observed that every couple of days, the two new men practiced their gun skills when neither Michael nor Sean Conley were around the work crews. With Ivan Malone, Dunn and Woods would ride off a ways from the working crews and spend time practicing their fast draws and shooting at targets. This practice was unheard of among ranch hands, who were paid for their cattle sense, not their gun skills. Thus, it became more evident to the hard-working ranch hands that the two new men were paid gun hands. None of the ranch crew had any well-founded inkling as to why Malone had convinced the Conleys to hire them. But there was an uneasy rumor that arose as a result of the activities of the two new men, and their relationship with Ivan Malone. The rumor was that Malone and his friends meant to harm the Conleys. The ranch hands felt that it was not their place to question Michael or Sean Conley about the imposters they had hired.

Adding to the unsettling of the ranch crew, they had witnessed some of the brutality directed toward any cowboy who got sideways with Malone. In fact, two of the Lazy C crew had recently left the ranch to find other work after being on the receiving end of Malone's fists. And since the tenure of the two men was to be just a couple of months, the other men decided it was easier to keep quiet until Woods and Dunn departed. But the ranch was short of good cow hands, and shortages of good men put a burden on the ranch hands who were doing the daily work of the ranch.

As the days turned into weeks, it soon became apparent that the paid gunmen, who were protecting and being protected by Ivan Malone, had no intention of leaving the Lazy C. And with the two gunmen to back Malone's actions, life for the honest ranch hands became far less pleasant. Even though all the ranch crew agreed that the Conleys were good people to work for, it seemed that Ivan Malone was insidiously usurping the authority of Michael and Sean Conley. Talk among the crew took a turn to a subject never before discussed by the men. They began to quietly discuss when they might be able to quit their work and ride away from the Lazy C.

Chapter Nine

August
Lazy C Ranch

The ranch house, barn, and bunk house could not be seen from low rise where the men were working. They were nearly two miles away from those facilities. This morning, the air was still cool, and wispy clouds were taking on a pink hue as the sun perched on the horizon. The fence crew had been out since sunrise the previous day repairing and stringing new barbed wire where it was missing or broken. When they broke their overnight camp this morning, they had been given their assignments, primarily, where they would be working. The men all knew the work to be done. Fence work was a never-ending job on a ranch of five thousand acres, and it was especially less pleasant when the temperature was over ninety degrees. But today, the air felt that there might be a cooler respite for the men from the hot weather of the previous few days.

The ranch hands rotated their work assignments so that it was not always the same men who rode fences. On this day, there were four men assigned to the fence work. One man drove the wagon that contained their wire spools, tools, water barrel, food, and supplies while the other men rode to the side. When they reached a specific location, two men split from the group. Those two men carried one spool of barbed wire perched on a leather pad behind the saddle of one man's horse while the other man had a large leather satchel attached to his saddle horn. The bag contained all the tools necessary for their assignment. The wire and hand tools they carried, fencing pliers, twisting pliers, hammers, staples, and come-alongs were for repairing fence, not setting new fence. A one-thousand-pound steer can play havoc on fence as the animal leans against it while attempting to reach a tasty grass morsel on the other side of the fence. Hence, fence repair was an ongoing process on a cattle ranch.

Ross Simmons and Jack "Wobbly" Wilkins rode side by side, each studying the fence wires as they rode. They were soon out of sight from the other men of the fence crew. The men were best of friends, and they talked as they worked.

"I don't like it, I tell you. There's something going on, but you sure as hell don't want to complain about it," said Jack. "Elsewise, you could end up like old Jim Lester and that other fella. After Malone beat on him, Jim and his amigo hightailed it out of here. Didn't even say *adios* or nuthin'. Malone got all over him, just because he showed up late for breakfast. That don't make sense to me," said Jack.

The two men had now attached the come-along and were splicing a length of wire onto the ends of a broken strand. Taking several twists on each side of the break, they soon had the splice wired in and the strand back together and ratcheted the come-along before pounding new staples into the fence post. They disconnected the come-along and stowed their tools.

"I ain't so sure that being late to breakfast was the reason for Jim gettin' beat on," said Ross. "I've got a hunch that Malone means to run off any hands that he don't like. What's more, I ain't so sure that Sean Conley is man enough to stand up to the likes of Malone."

The two men remounted and walked their horses down the fence line to the next break they found. This one was much easier to fix since it only needed to be restapled to the mesquite fence post where the wire had been pulled from the post. Jack watched as Ross pounded in the new staples. When he was finished, he stood for a moment before speaking again.

"I'll tell you, Jack. I've got a hunch that Malone and his gun hands aim to take over the Lazy C, lock, stock, and barrel. And I don't think you and me fit into that scheme," said Ross.

"I reckon you're right," replied Jack. "It's a good thing this ain't the busy time here on the ranch, what with the shortage of hands. But we'll sure be short-handed come calving and brandin' time. And if Conleys let Malone hire more of his men, why shoot, there won't be anybody working from the old crew but you and me."

"I don't intend to stick around for that to happen," said Ross as he remounted his horse.

The men had reached the end of the fence line and spotted one more break near the corner post and its braces. It was a clean break of rusty fence, so both men dismounted to make the repairs. Ross walked to the corner post to make sure it was secure. He gave it a shake and found it to be solid. He then walked a few paces to the point of the wire break. But as he neared the break, he noticed that the weeds and grass were more sparse near a rectangular patch of dirt. He didn't think much of it until he walked on the bare patch and his foot sank sightly into the dirt. He stepped back and bent over to see that his boot had sunk into the dirt at least an inch. At first, he thought it must be evidence of moles or prairie dogs. But then he stepped on a different spot on the bare patch, and again his boot pushed the soil down. He stepped back off the bare patch, and then he saw it. At the bottom of his boot print, a spot of purple could be seen in the indentation.

"Jack, c'mere," said Ross as he bent down to get a closer look at the boot print.

Jack joined him as Ross got down on his knees. As Ross picked at the dirt to reveal more of the purple article, it soon became apparent that it was a small bit of cloth.

"Hmmph. What do you suppose that's doing way out here?" asked Jack.

"Don't know," said Ross. He continued scraping dirt away from the cloth. After a few minutes they had made the gruesome discovery. The purple cloth was the sleeve of a woman's dress, and there was an arm within the sleeve.

Both men stood up, mesmerized by the discovery. "Well, what do we do now?" asked Jack. The men stood still; their gaze locked on the purple clad arm.

"I don't guess we have any choice," said Ross. "Grab the hammer and we can use the claw end to loosen up the dirt and keep digging."

Using their hands and the claw end of the hammer, they dug for another ten minutes until they had cleared the dirt from the head of the body. They became frozen as the reality of the horrible scene became clear. In barely a whisper, Jack spoke. "My god, Ross, it's Miss Sylvia."

Indeed, the men had found the now decomposing body of Sylvia Conley. As they removed more of the dirt, they found the bullet hole in Sylvia's skull. The slain woman's purse lay on her body. Both men sat on their heels staring at the macabre scene.

"Who would do such a thing?" asked Jack.

But even as he asked the question, the two men looked at each other, both knowing the most probable answer to the question.

"What should we do?" asked Jack, as he became more agitated, looking around to make sure that nobody else was nearby watching them.

Ross was also extremely upset, although it did not show on his outward appearance. In his mind he turned over the situation. There was no single answer. He had seen the consequences of getting crosswise with Ivan Malone and his sidekick gunhands. He reasoned that he and

Jack were holding a losing hand. If they confronted Malone, they would be killed on the spot, with Malone telling the Conleys some outlandish story to cover their killing. If he and Jack told Michael or Sean Conley what they had found, and the Conleys confronted Malone and his gun hands, the Conleys would be shot down like vermin, when it was the human vermin in the form of Ivan Malone that should be killed. Then, with the Conleys out of the way, it would be a cinch that he and Jack would be next to be killed. Neither he nor Jack would stand a chance in a gunfight with Malone and his men. Ross and Jack both thought highly of the Conleys. They had always been treated fairly by the Conleys, who let their cowhands take the initiative to carry out their work without unnecessary oversight. But Ross reasoned that if he and Jack spoke with the Conleys, their bosses would be killed.

A shudder went through Ross Simmons. Staring at the fragile body of Michael Conley's wife, a picture of his own death formed in his mind. It was not a pretty picture. He turned to Jack and said, "We'd best not tell anyone what we found, or all hell will bust loose, and we will both be killed."

Ross paused and looked again at the body of Sylvia Conley. Like all the men on the Lazy C, he had a great deal of respect for the ranch matriarch. He had never seen anything so gruesome in his life. His hand reached out to touch the body, but he pulled it back before it made contact. He removed his hat and mumbled a prayer. Jack also removed his hat as he watched his partner. When Ross put his hat on his head, Jack did the same. Turning to his friend, Ross said, "Jack, we are dead men if we say anything about this. I'm countin' on you to keep your mouth shut. Promise me that you won't say anything to anybody. Can you do that?"

Jack Wilkins kicked a clod of dirt, looked up at Ross and said, "Yep, I can keep quiet. But it ain't right."

"I know it," said Ross. "But that's the way it has to be if we want to stay on the right side of the grass."

He looked back at the makeshift grave. "Let's get the dirt back in that hole, Jack." In a few minutes, the two men rode slowly back down the fence line to join the other hands working in another section of the pasture, the two men mulling a multitude of thoughts in their heads. Just before they reached the other men, Ross said, "Jack, the day is coming real fast when I pack up my kit and hightail it out of here."

"Just let me know when you're going," said Jack, "because I'm going with you." The men had no way to know it, but that day was coming faster than they thought.

Chapter Ten

On the Lazy C Ranch, near Spanish Fort

The morning sun cast a shadow of a horse and rider at the front of Will Kahl's horse. The intense heat of the day had not yet formed, and on this pretty, late summer morning, Will was still enjoying his travels. A man on a horse leading a burro can only go as fast as the long-eared burro wants to walk. Thus, his traveling was a bit on the slow, but Will did not mind. The topography of north central Texas was strikingly dissimilar to the verdant, flat land of Louisiana, and Will was enjoying each day that revealed new scenery and wildlife. At the present time, the scenery was a bit rough, with rocks and thorny mesquite trees causing him to pick his path carefully. He saw no cattle grazing in the area. He figured that was why he had not come across any fencing.

Some days ago, Will had been very tempted to change his travel route in order to pass through Dallas and Fort Worth to see the sheer size of those large cities. Instead, he had followed his planned route and had gone through Greenville, skirted around Dallas, then passed through Sherman and Gainesville days ago. As day turned to late afternoon, he was now nearing Spanish Fort, where he intended to cross the Red River. Some days back, after nearly being drowned, he had learned that it was best to cross rivers and streams in the daylight hours in order to select the best crossing sites for depth of water and solid footing. He decided that he would hold up overnight in a sheltered area before starting out again in the morning.

After searching, he found an acceptable place to shelter for the night. It was a limestone outcropping with a jutting overhang, much like the opening of a cave. He maneuvered his horse toward the opening and climbed down from the saddle. He gingerly rubbed his backside to get the blood moving in the sore spots. Although he had gotten over his saddle sores some days ago, he still had some discomfort in those areas. He unsaddled the horse and staked it near some sparse grass so that it would have sufficient grazing through the night. He lifted the panniers from the burro and staked the animal near the horse. He then went about gathering broken mesquite branches and other dead wood for his fire. Will soon prepared a small supper and boiled coffee, which he devoured in short order. He spread his blanket beneath the limestone overhead and placed his saddle where he could rest his head. Darkness soon fell, and as he gazed and wondered at the array of stars in the Texas sky, he fell into a deep and restful sleep. His naive dreams of finding gold nuggets in a Colorado stream filled his subconscious. The hardwood mesquite fire, while it had lowered in intensity, still continued to periodically throw sparks into the air, as is the nature of burning mesquite.

When he woke in the morning, Will reheated the leftover coffee and munched on a hardtack biscuit. He watched the horse and burro as they grazed on the sparse vegetation. He would need to water the animals as soon as he came upon some water. As he swigged the last of his coffee, he was lost in his own thoughts. As a result, he did not hear the riders approaching until they were upon him.

* * *

In the evening darkness the night before, Beryl Dunn had been sitting on the fence of the upper corral at the Lazy C. He was unable to sleep in the lingering heat of the day, and he had slipped out of the bunk house to have a smoke. This upper corral sat on ground that was a bit higher than the ranch house and bunk house. Therefore, it caught the night breeze more easily and was slightly cooler than the bunk house.

It was common for some of the ranch hands to sit on the top rail of the corral after eating their dinners.

After rolling and lighting his smoke, Beryl Dunn gazed out at the dark landscape. Something caught his eye. He turned his attention to faint bits of light in the black distance. As the small lights drifted upward and then died, Beryl knew it was the sign of a mesquite fire. It could only mean one thing. Someone was camped on the limestone ridge that could only be faintly seen from this upper corral. Dunn climbed down from the corral fence and walked back down the hill to the ranch house. He knocked gently and walked in. Ivan Malone was sitting in the main room with Michael and Sean Conley, but he saw Dunn and rose to meet him. The two men then went outdoors where Dunn told him what he had seen.

"Tell Matt to get two of the hands, and tomorrow at first light we will ride out to the ridge," said Malone.

The Following Morning

As the sun rose slowly to show the first rays of light at the eastern horizon, five men rode from the Lazy C. Ivan Malone, Beryl Dunn and Matt Woods rode toward the location of last night's mesquite fire sparks. Beryl Dunn had told Jack "Wobbly" Wilkins and Ross Simmons that they must come along with him. Jack and Ross had no idea why they were asked to go along with Malone and his two gunhands, but their worst fear was that they were going to be killed. They rode reluctantly to the rear of the group. Riding side by side, they could talk quietly to each other.

"What do you think this is about?" asked Jack. He was visibly upset. The nervousness plainly showed through his normally calm demeanor.

"I don't know, but I don't like the looks of this," answered Ross. "I hope you didn't do something to cause Malone to want to do us in."

Jack objected quietly. "Hell, no, Ross. I didn't do nuthin'. I don't even talk to Malone if I can help it."

Ross knew that to be the truth, as they both avoided Malone and his gunhands as much as possible.

"Do you figure he might know that we know about Sylvia Conley? He'd sure as hell want to kill us if he knew we knew about that," said Jack.

Ross rode in silence for a moment, then answered. "I don't think there's any way he would know that. We ain't said nuthin' to nobody about it, and we left the grave just like we found it. It must be something else."

While both men were troubled as to why they were accompanying Malone and the other men, they need not have worried. Ivan Malone was simply ensuring that he was not outgunned when he approached the strange campfire that was seen last night. He figured that five guns ought to be able to confront any strangers encroaching on the Lazy C.

By now the sky was lit with enough sunshine to be able to easily see the campsite of the stranger as they rode upon him. Malone was relieved to see that it was only one man sitting by a small campfire drinking from a tin cup. Will Kahl had now seen the five riders approaching and knew in his gut that five men coming toward him was not a good sign. He rose to his feet and greeted Malone and his men.

"Howdy gents. Beautiful morning, ain't it?" said Will.

Malone did not answer the stranger's comment. Instead, he replied, "What are you doing here mister?"

Kahl replied, "Just finishing my coffee, and then I'll be on my way."

"You're on my property," said Malone, who knew very well it was not his property. "This here is Lazy C ranch property, and you're trespassing."

Will Kahl was thinking fast, trying to figure out from the tone of the big man's voice which way this confrontation was going to go. "I don't mean no harm, mister. I only needed a place to bed down last night. I'll be getting on my way."

Malone now knew that this stranger was no match in a gun fight, nor in any type of fight. These were the odds he always looked for, a skirmish that he could win. He drew his gun and fired it at Will Kahl. The bullet hit Kahl in his left hip and knocked him to the ground. Malone was now smiling, as he brought the hammer back again on his pistol.

"You can't just go tramping across people's property," said Malone. He was re-aiming the pistol.

"I said I'm sorry, mister. I didn't mean to trespass. I didn't see no fences, so I thought it would be all right. Just let me get on out of here," said Kahl. Blood was creating a large red spot through Kahl's trousers at his hip wound.

Malone drew the pistol up, steadied it, and fired once more. This shot hit Will Kahl dead center in his chest. Kahl fell to the ground, blood flowing freely from his fatal wound. Matt Woods got off his horse and walked to Kahl's body. After seeing the life flow from Will Kahl, Woods looked up at Ivan.

"What did you go and have to do that for, Ivan?" asked Matt. "He meant no harm, and he would have been on his way in a few minutes."

Malone just laughed, but then became deadly serious. "Matt, you better shut your damn mouth if you know what's good for you. I'm tired of you not toeing the line with me. You want to end up the same way as this drifter?"

Matt looked down again at the stranger's body. He did not answer Malone.

Malone looked over at Beryl Dunn. "You and these boys drag the body under that overhang and let the buzzards take care of him. Get that horse and donkey stripped down and you can turn the donkey loose. We'll keep the horse. We can sell him with the next batch. I'm heading back to the house." Malone turned his horse and rode away.

Jack Wilkins was in a daze with what he had just witnessed. Malone had cold-bloodedly killed a man for no reason other than the man was just passing through. He looked over at Ross Simmons. He could see from Ross's face that he too, was in a state of disbelief, but both men dismounted and helped drag Will Kahl's body under the limestone overhang. The remoteness of the location would mean that nobody would find the body. They helped Beryl and Matt rummage through the panniers, and they pocketed anything they took an interest in. They unhitched the burro and put its harness and panniers next to the body, along with the saddle from the horse. They left the bridle on the horse in order to lead it back to the ranch house. When they were done, they were readying to get back on their horses, but Beryl Dunn stopped them. Dunn went to stand between Jack and Ross. He pulled his pistol from its holster, casually looked to make sure it was loaded, and then pointed it at Ross Simmons's chest.

"I'm going to give you boys a piece of advice. What you saw here today is never to be mentioned," said Dunn. "If you've got a hankering to run your mouth off to somebody, just remember that you will be disposed of just like this drifter. And you wouldn't be a pretty sight after Malone gets done with you." Dunn began pulling back the hammer on the pistol and then releasing it slowly so that the gun did not fire. Just the same, he was making his point perfectly clear.

"I don't know why the hell Malone decided that he needed the two of you to come along today," said Dunn. "But since he did, you better remember what I said. Do I make myself clear?"

Jack Wilkins and Ross Simmons nodded their heads slowly.

"Good," said Dunn. "Now let's get out of here."

The men mounted their horses and rode slowly away, leading Will Kahl's horse. The burro stood some distance away and watched the men ride away. He brayed one time, probably to express his confusion. In time, the burro would become feral and rely on the Texas prairie for its livelihood.

With Beryl Dunn and Matt Woods riding ahead, Ross and Jack rode some distance behind as they led the Kahl horse. "That was it, Jack," said Ross. "I'm gonna skedaddle tonight and get away from these killers. Are you with me?"

Jack Wilkins needed no encouragement. The scene that had unfolded only minutes ago had shaken him badly. "You bet," said Jack. "I'll be damn glad to be rid of the bunch of them. But I sure hate to think what might happen to the Conleys when Malone thinks that it's his time to take over."

"Yep," said Ross. "But I don't mean to hang around and find out."

At one a.m. the next morning, in a light drizzling rain, Jack Wilkins and Ross Simmons, with as much silence as possible, slowly rode away from the Lazy C Ranch and headed South. They would not be missed for several hours. Unbeknownst to them, and even though Jack and Ross knew information highly detrimental to Ivan Malone, Malone and his gunhands chose not to pursue the two ranch hands. Malone's ego continued to lead him to believe that he was above the law, could fight his way out of any threat, and was safe on the Lazy C Ranch.

Hours later, as Michael Conley emerged from the house, he knew something was afoot when he saw Lee Stark striding purposefully toward him. Lee removed his hat and slapped his thigh with it as he said, "Two more of our best men took off sometime during the night."

"Are you sure, Lee?" Michael replied.

"Sure as I'm standin' here, Mr. Conley. Wilkins and Simmons are nowhere to be found. Their horses and gear are gone, but nobody else in the bunk house seems to know anything about it."

"Well, what do you make of it, Lee?" asked Michael.

Lee knew exactly what he thought, but he did not want to be disrespectful to his boss. "Well, I figure it's all about your grandson, Ivan. He won't do a lick of work and keeps bullying the other hands to the point that they walk off. And those other two fellas that are Malone's friends are just as bad. They ain't cowhands, and they don't pull their share of the load at all."

Lee paused and was about to say more but decided that he had said enough. But then he said, "With all respect, Mr. Conley, we have got to do something about Malone."

Michael did not respond at first, but then said quietly, almost to himself, "I know we do; I know we do."

Chapter Eleven

Some Days Later
Lazy C Ranch House

The polished oak dining table had eight chairs. It had been several years since there had been that many people at the table. As he sat there, Michael's thoughts returned to fond memories of dinner parties when he and Sylvia were younger, and they had hosted large gatherings of friends and neighbors, warranting a full table. But those days had passed, as the tasks associated with such a large gathering were too much for Sylvia, and she had reluctantly given up on the large parties.

Presently, only three of the chairs were occupied by Michael and Sean Conley, along with Ivan Malone. Each man had a self-rolled cigarette wedged in his fingers as they finished up their mugs of strong coffee. Michael Conley seemed lost in his thoughts as he gazed first down the length of the old table, and then at the twilight-graying vista seen through the dining room window. He missed the old days, and he missed Sylvia. He turned to face the others. A look of grave concern covered his weathered face.

"I'm worried about Sylvia," said Michael. "Seems to me she's been gone far too long down there in Fort Worth, and she ain't even sent us word on how she's getting' along. I don't know what to make of that, and it has me a bit worried. What do you boys think?"

Sean looked at his father. "I agree, Dad. I didn't want to mention it a couple days back for fear of worrying you."

Ivan Malone made no comment. He knew exactly what had happened to his grandmother. He stirred his coffee, his spoon clanking against the mug.

"You have a thought on this, Ivan?" asked Michael.

Ivan did not answer right away. Instead, he turned to look at Michael and simply said, "Yeah, I guess I wonder too." Lies came easily through the lips of Ivan Malone.

Michael looked disdainfully at the grandson that he disliked intensely. If it were not for Sylvia, he would have rid the Lazy C of this no-account weeks ago. He had held contempt for Ivan from the first day he had stepped onto the Lazy C. While Malone claimed to be his daughter Jane's offspring, there was something phony about Ivan, almost an evil aura surrounding him. Michael gave a slight, outwardly unseen shudder and returned his gaze to the window. After a minute or two, the men had finished their coffee.

Michael rose from the table. "Sean, you and I are going into town tomorrow morning. I'm going to send a wire to that lawyer fella in Fort Worth and find out what's going on. I don't feel good about this whole situation."

Ivan was instantly alert. He knew that he could not allow Michael to send that telegram. It took only seconds before his thoughts churned out an evil course of action. It would require the help of his two associates, and with them, he could handle the situation.

"If you don't mind, I'd like to go along with you in the morning," said Ivan. "It'll do me good to see a bit of fresh scenery and maybe get myself a few supplies in town."

The last thing that Michael wanted was the company of Ivan Malone on a ride to town. But he could not think of any reason to tell Malone to stay at the ranch. He shrugged and said, "Suit yourself. I figure to be on the road near seven o'clock." He stared at Ivan, turned and walked away. Sean soon followed, leaving Ivan to think through the details of his plan.

Late that night, Ivan Malone met with Beryl Dunn and Matt Woods. After briefing them on his plan, Woods spoke up. "You know, Ivan, I ain't so sure that I signed up for cold-blooded murder when you hired me. Are you sure you want to do this?" He looked at Dunn for agreement, but Dunn looked down and did not say a word.

Ivan took a step toward Woods and glared at him. "Listen here, Matt," said Ivan, and he laid a beefy hand on Woods' shoulder. "I'm paying you good money to do exactly what I want done. If you weasel out on this job, you may not live to regret it. You get my drift?"

It was only a few seconds before Woods answered. "Yeah, Ivan, I get it." While he may have just agreed to carry out Malone's orders, Matt Woods had had a bellyful of Ivan Malone. Yet, he had no alternative for the time being. He knew that Malone was a powder keg, and it did not take much to light his fuse. He also knew that his days were numbered if he refused to carry out Malone's orders. For the time being, he was stuck, but Matt Woods was beginning to formulate his own plan. When he could screw up his courage at an appropriate time, he believed that there was a possibility that Ivan Malone could be killed, possibly by Matt's own gun. He would have to be incredibly careful, keep his thoughts to himself, and wait for the opportunity to arise. He also did not trust his friend Beryl Dunn enough to tell him of his disgust toward Ivan. He knew that one slip of the tongue by Dunn would probably mean that he would be killed on the spot. So, he kept his thoughts to himself. Reluctantly, with no alternative course of action conceived, he would need to help Malone carry out his plan.

The Following Morning

As autumn became more evident, the days had shortened to the point that at seven a.m. the full sun had not yet risen above the eastern horizon. Only a portion of the sun cast its light and heat onto the Lazy C as Michael, Sean, and Ivan finished saddling their horses. Seven a.m. was not considered early on a working ranch and work often times did not wait for sunrise. Because it would soon be full light, a few of the ranch hands were pulling supplies from the barn and loading a wagon for outlying chores. Those men shouted their morning greetings to the Conleys and went about their business getting ready to ride out.

Well before sunrise, Beryl Dunn and Matt Woods had saddled their horses and quietly ridden from the barn at the Lazy C. They were each heavily armed, with their handguns belted at their waists and a repeating rifle in a scabbard attached to their saddles. They were riding out early, following the instructions from Ivan Malone, who had told them where they were to be waiting to ambush Michael and Sean Conley. They were riding on the road to Spanish Fort, but they would soon leave the road. Matt Woods did not like Malone's plan and the part he would play in it, especially since he and Dunn would soon become murderers. They talked softly as they rode.

"Beryl, I know we've been friends for a long time, and we generally think alike when it comes to carrying out our petty crimes. But we have never murdered anyone. I have to tell you, I ain't real keen on killing the Conleys," said Matt.

Dunn did not reply right off. He was thinking to himself. The way he figured it, he was not ready to high tail it away from the Lazy C. Ivan Malone was paying him good money, and he pretty much did not have to do any work to earn his pay. And just maybe, his bond to Ivan Malone was a bit stronger than that with Woods. At any rate, he figured that he would carry out Malone's plan, and then watch where the chips fell before he decided to make himself scarce around these parts. He was not sure what he would do about Matt's reluctance to kill the Conleys. He sure as hell could not tell Malone, or he and Matt might both find themselves in shallow graves. He turned in his saddle to face Woods.

"I'll give you a little advice, Matt. First of all, you better not let me down shootin' the Conleys, or I'll turn my gun on you."

Dunn paused and then went on. "Also, if you let me down, I'll sure as hell let Malone know what you did. And from thereon, you're a dead man."

Woods could not believe he was hearing this from his longtime friend. He opened his mouth to reply to Dunn but could not find the words. It was at this point that the close friendship began to unravel. Matt knew that he could no longer trust his old friend, but it firmed his resolve that he would find a way to slip away from Beryl Dunn, Ivan Malone, and the Lazy C. Then he remembered why he and Dunn were riding out to set up an ambush. He shuddered as a chill ran through him, but he resolved that he would play along with the plan. He had resolved to himself that it would not be his bullets that killed either of the Conleys.

The two outlaws rode on until they left the road. Soon, they reached a grove of trees next to a slowly flowing feeder stream that joined the river some distance away. Dunn and Woods hid and tied their horses deeper in the grove where they would not be seen, then walked back toward the road. They took up positions behind some trees and brush where they had a clear view and gun sight line to anyone on the road. They would be able to get a clear shot at the Conleys as they rode by with Ivan Malone.

Thirty minutes passed as the men waited in the thicket. Woods idly slapped a mosquito on his arm, leaving a blood stain on his skin. He shuddered at the sight of his own blood. Neither man spoke. Just as it had to Matt Woods, it now occurred to Beryl Dunn that a firm friendship between the two men had been broken. But that fact had less impact on Dunn than it had on Woods. Beryl Dunn simply valued money more than friendship. He had a job to do, and he was being paid for doing it. The hell with Matt Woods.

The thoughts of both men drifted away as they heard approaching hoof beats. As they watched, the Conleys and Ivan came into view. Just as the horsemen passed, Ivan took a quick glance to the side and could faintly see his two criminal cohorts through the brush. He quickly turned his horse, putting distance between himself and the Conleys. Almost immediately, two shots rang out from the brush. At the first shot, Michael Conley slumped in his saddle. Sean Conley felt a searing pain as a bullet grazed his upper arm. Matt Woods had purposely aimed wide, knowing that his shot would not kill Sean Conley. Michael Conley had fallen to the side and slid out of his saddle. His body hit the ground, but his boot was firmly stuck in its stirrup. His gelding bolted and ran a few yards before stopping and turning its head to see Michael Conley lying next to him, his foot still in the stirrup. While that was happening, another shot from Beryl Dunn's rifle put a bullet in the back of Sean Conley, who then fell from his horse. He lay face down in the middle of the dirt road.

Michael Conley, the patriarch of the Lazy C ranch had quickly and quietly succumbed to his fatal wound. But unbeknownst to Dunn and Woods, Sean Conley clung to life. Ivan Malone rode to where Michael Conley lay next to his horse. Malone dismounted and walked to Michael's horse, where he wrenched Michael's boot from the stirrup. The leg fell to the ground with a thump. Both Dunn and Woods stood near the bodies, watching the blood pool from Michael Conley's wound. Dunn's bullet had entered Michael's back and exited his chest, ensuring that Michael Conley had no chance of survival.

The only sound from Ivan Malone was a "hmph." He remounted his horse and turned to Dunn and Woods. "You two drag the bodies to the river and throw them in. I'm headed back to the ranch." And with that, Malone turned his horse and trotted into the distance." The way he figured; a fine piece of work was now done. Nothing now stood in his way to take ownership of the Lazy C. His face twisted into a smile as he rode.

"Well, you heard him," said Dunn as he laid his rifle down on the road. He reached down, grabbed the ankles of Michael Conley and began dragging the inert body toward the feeder stream.

Matt Woods laid aside his rifle. He bent over Sean Conley and turned him over on his back. Quickly he cleared the dirt from Sean's nose and mouth, and it was then that he could see that Sean was breathing weakly. Glancing over at the receding figure of Beryl Dunn to make sure he was not being watched, he unstrapped Sean's gunbelt, and pulled off his boots. He then began to drag Sean to the stream at a location away from where Beryl Dunn was placing Michael Conley's body. He dragged Sean to the edge of the stream and waded into the water. He tugged Sean to the point that Sean's head and shoulders were face up and out of the water at the edge of the stream. He was out of sight of Beryl Dunn and quickly walked back to where he had left his rifle and Sean's gunbelt and boots. Seconds later, Beryl Dunn emerged from the brush leading his horse and returned to Woods' side.

"Did you take care of business, Matt?" asked Dunn.

"Yep," replied Woods. "I didn't get these wet pants and boots from walkin' in the woods. He's in the water."

Dunn looked down at the gunbelt and boots as he retrieved his rifle. "What the hell is this, Matt? Why'd you take Conley's gunbelt and boots?"

In truth, Matt Woods had taken the gunbelt and boots, hoping with less weight, Sean Conley might be able to float face up if it came to that. But he did not tell Dunn that. Instead, he answered. "Sean had a fine pistol. I thought maybe you might want to hang on to it for yourself. Same with the boots."

Dunn picked up the gunbelt and examined the belt and pistol. He turned the gun in his hand. He returned the pistol to its holster, wound the belt around the holster and put them in his saddlebag. He then picked up one of Sean's boots, turned it over to examine the sole, and decided that Conley's boots were nearly as worn as his own. He threw the boot into the surrounding brush and followed it with its mate. "Go get your horse and let's get out of here before anyone comes along," said Dunn. He remounted and waited while Matt Woods went back into the brush and retrieved his horse. The two men then rode toward the Lazy C.

Across the Red River

The shots that were intended to kill Michael and Sean Conley were heard by others. Across the river, Black Horse led a small hunting party to near the river's edge where they had killed a deer. After gutting the deer, they tied the dead animal to one of the horses and were nearly ready to leave the area when they heard the shots. The Indians immediately led their horses into a post oak grove to avoid being seen. Black Horse and one other hunter cautiously walked back to the river and hunkered down in riverbank vegetation where they could not be seen, but they could easily watch the road on the other side of the river. The scene unfolded to reveal Michael Conley with his leg hung up in his stirrup and lying in the road, as well as Sean Conley also lying in the road. Black Horse could easily see the other three men. The big man sat astride his horse, and the two other men stood over the bodies of the Conleys. It was readily apparent that the three men had killed the Conleys.

Black Horse and his fellow hunters continued to watch the aftermath of the shootings. The big man could be seen giving orders to the other two men before he rode away. The two men then dragged the bodies of Michael and Sean Conley to the edge of the feeder creek. The first man had then unceremoniously placed Michael Conley at the river's edge and rolled Michael's body into the water with his boot. Some distance away, the other man looked intently to make sure he was not seen while he placed Sean Conley carefully at the edge of the flowing feeder. Black Horse had seen how he was careful to keep Sean's head out of the water. He watched as the man shook his head and walked away. The Indians then watched as the two outlaws retrieved their horses and slowly rode off in the direction of the Lazy C ranch house. The hunting party gathered at Black Horse's side.

"Get your horses. We are going to cross the river," said Black Horse.

After reaching the other side of the river, Black Horse went directly to the body of Sean Conley. Leaning down above Sean, Black Horse could see that Sean was not yet dead, but he was concerned that Sean could soon die.

Because the Comanches were friends of the Conleys, in a highly unusual act, the hunting party quickly scooped out a crude, shallow grave for Michael Conley, placed Michael's body in the depression, and placed stones and tree limbs atop the shallow grave. If Sean lived, Black Horse would later tell Sean where his father was buried.

Black Horse was concerned with keeping Sean Conley alive. A hastily built travois was made from two long deadfall oak branches with shorter branches tied between the longer side rails. The travois was tied to the front and rear of two horses lined up in tandem. Sean was then carefully lifted and tied to the travois. Slowly, the Indians recrossed the river. This time, in order to keep the animals calm as they crossed the river, two of the hunting party swam and walked alongside the two horses that bore the travois. The Red River is normally shallow, and with a paucity of recent rain, it was easily forded. The river was shallow enough that the animals did not need to swim, and the travois remained above the surface of the water.

When they reached the other side of the river, the travois was removed from the rear horse, allowing the longer branches to drag their ends along the ground while Sean Conley rode the travois back to the Comanche reservation. At the Indian encampment, Sean was immediately cared for by native women who had gained valuable skills in the treating of bullet wounds, skills they had learned from long years of conflicts between the Indians and the U.S. Army and white settlers in the years before the natives were forced to a reservation. Their skills rivaled those of any white doctor. After delicate surgery and continued treatment by the native women, Sean Conley would live.

Ten Days Earlier
South of the Red River
Montague County, Nocona, TX

U.S. Marshal Nathan Wolf was dog tired. He had not slept well following his all-day trip from Decatur, in Wise County, to Nocona in Montague County. The road from Decatur to Bowie was well travelled, but after leaving Bowie, the twenty miles to Nocona had been mere paths in some stretches of the route. In fact, the road sometimes resembled game trails or old Indian trails, and he had lost his way twice before returning to the correct path. Nathan had cursed himself several times for not riding the train. Having just become a resident of the Lone Star State, he was unfamiliar with the sheer vastness of size in Texas. Compounding his weariness was his lack of sleep last night due to a worn and lumpy bed at a run-down hotel in Bowie.

Nathan was on his way north to meet with a rancher named Sean Conley, whose Lazy C Ranch stretched for five thousand acres near the Red River and the town of Spanish Fort. He was responding to a telegram from Sean Conley, the son of the ranch owner. Mr. Conley had requested that the marshal come to investigate the theft of several horses. By return telegram, Nathan had given Conley a time to meet at the post office in Nocona. Nathan had been led to believe that there was no law man in Nocona or Spanish Fort. Therefore, he was on his own in the investigation.

He watched the bobbing head of Wander, his sometimes-hard-headed horse. The gelding could still travel a good distance over the course of a day, but white hairs were beginning to be evident on the muzzle of the horse. Nathan figured that he should be able to keep Wander on the trail for a couple more years, at least. He reached down and stroked and patted his horse's neck. Wander had been foaled and raised in Kansas, and after his move to Texas, as he was being unloaded from the train's stock car, he was a bit skittish with the new smells and vegetation of the Lone Star State. But he had quickly become accustomed to the other animals and the surroundings on Nathan and Claire May's ranch, now known as the Wolf Ranch.

After having a telephone installed in his new office, Nathan was still settling into the county's combination jail and marshal's office in Decatur. It was while he was making improvements to the office that he had been shocked to see his first horseless carriage, a belching, roaring, and sometimes whining conglomerate of metal pieces being driven down the main street by a man who obviously had too much time and money on his hands. It was the talk of the town, and folks were calling the contraption a *Duryea*, but Nathan wanted no part of this new phenomenon. *He would keep Wander, thank you*, he thought to himself, as he had watched the foul-smelling contraption making a noisy retreat from the center of town.

The trail widened and became more worn as Nathan approached the edge of Nocona, and at the center of town, he quickly found the post office. With a bit of a groan, he dismounted and again patted and stroked Wander's neck. Nathan's back was barking its soreness, and he walked a bit to stretch his legs and loosen his back. Wander eyed him as he walked to the side of the horse. Because he was a bit early to meet Sean Conley, he walked to a nearby café and sat down to enjoy a cup of coffee. He took a seat where he could look out the window. After two swallows of the hot dark liquid, he looked up to see three riders bring their horses to a halt in front of the post office. Nathan continued to look at the men as they dismounted. He thought to himself that one of the men was as large as any man he had ever seen. His thoughts immediately flashed back to a similarly sized man whom he had been tracking in Kansas and who had nearly killed him. He shuddered and took a last gulp of the coffee. He left a coin on the table as he walked out of the café and made his way toward the strangers. To the big man, Nathan stuck out his hand and introduced himself.

"Marshal Nathan Wolf," he said. "Are you Sean Conley or is it one of these other gents."

The stranger gripped Nathan's hand. "Nah, I ain't Sean. My name's Ivan Malone, and I'm runnin' the Lazy C, and these are a couple of my hands. This here's Beryl Dunn and that's Matt Woods," said Malone as he pointed to the two men that were with him.

Nathan now looked at the other two men. He did not like what he saw. The men did not offer their hands and stood to the back and side of Malone. In Nathan's estimation, both men wore expensive pistol rigs, and they wore their guns too low. They did not have the look of ranch hands who worked in the hot summer sun and the winter cold. It was easy to speculate that these two men were hired guns working for Malone. He especially did not like the looks of Beryl Dunn. His eyes had the vacant look of a man who had no scruples, a man who could kill without a qualm, and he wore a perpetual sneer because of the downturn of his lower lip.

Nathan thought it was odd that Sean Conley had not kept his appointment. He asked, "I was supposed to meet Conley here. Where is he?"

Malone let go of Nathan's hand and stepped back to look Nathan over. He replied, "Don't rightly know, Marshal. We ain't seen him for a couple days and don't know where he might have gone off to, so I'm runnin' the place while he's gone."

Nathan's interest was piqued. Conley had sent him a telegram to meet with him, but he didn't show up for the meeting, and this Malone fella claimed to not know where Sean Conley was, even though he claimed to be running the Lazy C. "And you don't know where Sean Conley is?" asked Nathan. He was finding it hard to believe that Malone would not know where his boss was.

"Sean Conley sent me a telegram just a few days ago and wanted to meet with me about some missing horses," said Nathan. "Do you know anything about that?"

"Oh, sure, Marshal, I know about Mr. Conley's telegram. But we have cattle and horses disappear all the time. It ain't nothin' to worry about," said Malone. A sneer crossed Malone's face as he said, "Matter of fact, you can probably turn around and head on back to where you came from. I know who rustled that livestock, and I've taken care of it, don't you worry."

Nathan was starting to size up Malone, and he was getting a bad feeling about the big man. "Mr. Malone, it doesn't quite work that way. If a crime has been committed, you need to turn it over to me, and I'll look into it," said Nathan. "Also, I've worked around ranches for many years, and I know the disappearance of livestock from ranches is a big deal." Nathan found Malone's flippant attitude hard to stomach. This man was like no rancher Nathan had ever been around. Horses were the working stock on any ranch, and any time horses went missing, it was an issue of high priority. Nathan thought to himself that Malone was strangely unconcerned that his ranch had horses disappear.

Nathan continued, "Malone, you mentioned that you know who made off with your horses. Who do you think it was?"

Malone did not answer right away. Instead, he turned his gaze to a passing rider moving down the street before he turned back to Nathan. "I don't think you understood, Marshal. Yeah, we had some livestock go missing, but we handled the situation."

"Who rustled the horses, Malone?" Nathan asked again more forcefully.

After another pause, Malone finally said, "The damn Comanches, Marshal. I caught a bunch of them up on the corner of my ranch. They had a couple of our horses and were skinning out one of my steers. They had another steer that would have been butchered if I hadn't broken up their little party."

Nathan looked closely at Malone. He had a hunch that Malone wasn't telling the entire story. "Indians, huh," said Nathan. He already knew the answer to his next question but asked anyway. "I thought all of them had been pushed onto reservations. Aren't the Comanches up in Oklahoma?" he asked.

"Oh, yeah, they're supposed to stay up around Lawton. But they don't always stay put. They come down here, cross the Red River, and make themselves at home on my ranch. Then they act like they're still hunting buffalo and grab cattle and horses off of my property," said Malone. "This the second group of red thieves I've run off of my place;

had another group just a couple months back. The same thievin' Indian, Black Horse, was leading both groups."

Nathan thought to himself that it was odd that Malone had used the term 'my place,' and decided to nettle Malone. "Malone, is it your ranch or the Conleys' ranch." Nathan watched as Malone seemed to bristle at the question.

"Well, sure it's the Conleys' ranch," said Malone. "You know what I meant."

Nathan changed the subject and asked, "Do you know this Black Horse fella?"

"Yeah, John Black Horse; well, I don't know him personal like," said Malone. "But a couple of my hands know him because they've had to deal with him before."

"What do you mean? Have there been other meetings with the Indians before these two that you mentioned?" asked Nathan.

Malone was getting impatient. For his thinking, *this damn Marshal was asking too many questions.* But he answered, "Yeah, there were other run-ins with the Indians, but Sean Conley handled those. But since he disappeared, I got stuck with facing this last bunch of redskinned thieves."

"What did you do to the Indians, Malone?" asked Nathan.

"Why, we pushed 'em on out of here," replied Malone.

"What do you mean, you pushed them out of here? And what do you mean by 'we'," Nathan asked. "Was it just you, or did you have help?"

Malone did not reply quickly. It was as if he was trying to figure out the best story to tell the Marshal. The pause was not lost on Nathan. "Yeah, I had a few of my boys with me. You don't want to go out and meet Indians by yourself. And when they didn't want to just leave peaceful like, we had to shoot a few rounds at them, and that got them to movin'."

"Did the Indians fire back at you?" asked Nathan.

Malone hesitated before answering. Then he replied, "Now Marshal, you ain't one of those Indian lovers, are you?"

"I'll ignore that stupid question, Malone. I asked you a question," said Nathan.

"Hmm," replied Malone. "Well, hell yes, it was a regular shootout with them," replied Malone. "Like I said, it's all over now, so I don't see any reason for you to stay around. And if you ain't got any more questions, I think I'll head on back home." He turned to get back on his horse. His companions moved quickly to do the same.

"Just a minute, Malone," said Nathan.

Malone turned around. "What's the matter, Marshal? You have trouble understanding what I told you?" Malone's companions openly laughed.

Nathan took two steps toward Malone who had yet to mount his horse. "I understand completely what you told me, Malone. But could you clear something up for me?"

"Marshal, this is getting a bit tiring. Now what is it you want to know?" asked Malone.

"Malone, I'd like to know exactly where it was that you met up with the Indians. Can you give me some directions on where that might have been?" asked Nathan.

Again, Malone did not reply for a few seconds. "Well, Marshal, I don't see that that is any of your damn business. It was on my property," said Malone. "That's all you really need to know."

Once again, Malone had referred to the Lazy C as his property. With those words, Nathan took another step and was now just an arm's length from Malone. "You mean the Conleys' property, don't you?" This time, Malone's face became red, the anger showing.

"Well, Malone, you say this is not my business, but I'm going to make it my business. You see, that's what us marshals do. We keep digging until we get to the bottom of a story. So, I'd like to know where this fight with the Comanches took place." Nathan's face did not change. He was looking intently into the eyes of Malone. In seconds, he saw what he was looking for. Malone's eyes had flared, and his lips began to curl, but just as quickly, the big man's eyes relaxed.

"All right, Marshal, if you say so." Malone relaxed a bit and said, "We met them Indians about four miles southwest of Spanish Fort, right close to where they crossed the river. There's a feeder creek that comes out of a grove of oak trees there and then feeds into the river. It's easy to find. You aim to go up that way?"

Nathan answered, "I thought I might, but not today, maybe in a day or two."

"Suit yourself, Marshal. If that's all you want to talk about, I'll be on my way," said Malone. He turned and climbed up onto his saddle.

But Nathan was not through with Malone. "Are you sure you don't know where Sean Conley is?"

"I already answered that question, Marshal. I'm leaving." But as Malone reigned his horse, he turned it into Nathan, who had to take a step back so he would not be stepped on by the horse. The intent was not lost on Nathan. He watched as the three riders slowly rode away. Nathan was now sure of Ivan Malone. He classified Malone as a bully, a mean man whom he was sure he would meet up with again. And as Malone rode away, Nathan watched the big man being jostled from side to side on his horse. Nathan thought to himself as he watched, *Malone sure doesn't sit a horse very well.*

Two Days Later
Bound for Lawton, Oklahoma

After leaving Nocona, and following his meeting with Ivan Malone, Nathan decided that he would not yet investigate the site on the Lazy C where Malone had described his confrontation with a group of Comanche Indians. He reasoned that by the time he could find and examine the location, there would not be any clues of a crime, so for now, he would forego a trip to the edge of the Lazy C ranch. During the meeting with Malone, Nathan had developed a deep distrust of the large man. He had seen plenty of evil men in his job of bringing outlaws to justice, and Malone had all the makings of another such character. Just the fact that Malone had brought along two hired gunmen to their meeting in Nocona told Nathan that the big man was used to getting his way in any manner possible, but apparently, he occasionally needed help to do so. It was proof, confirming Nathan's thought that when confronted by force, Malone lacked the grit to follow through on his own, that is, unless he had additional help from hired gunmen. With years of experience listening to stories from criminal suspects that almost always turned out to be false or only half true, after meeting with and hearing Malone fill the air with a flimsy story, Nathan wanted to hear the other side of the story of Malone's meeting up with the Comanches. Therefore, after his meeting with Malone, Nathan had doubled back to Bowie, where there was a railroad depot. He spent the night in the same rundown hotel with the same lumpy beds, which resulted in another night of tossing and turning trying to get comfortable. The following morning after taking a seat in the hotel dining room for breakfast, he gave his order to the waitress who had already set a hot mug of coffee next to his plate. Nathan intended to make his way to Fort Sill in Oklahoma after he finished his breakfast. He idly stirred the coffee and looked around the room at the other breakfast patrons. His eyes stopped, and so did his stirring of his coffee. From across four tables a man with a toothy grin was watching him. "Well, I'll be damned," Nathan said under his breath.

Texas Ranger Ben Steele rose from his seat, picked up his coffee mug and his tan hat and came to Nathan's table. The men shook hands. Nathan had met Steele when he and Claire May had come to Decatur to look over the John Summers ranch that was left to Claire May in her Uncle John's will, the ranch where they now lived. Neither man had had the time to look up one another after Nathan and Claire May moved to Decatur.

"I reckon they'll just let anybody eat in this restaurant," said Steele, with a grin on his face.

"Yeah, I reckon so, Steele. After all, you're here aren't you," countered Nathan.

Steele laughed as they sat down. "Good to see you again, Marshal. I understand you took the transfer to Decatur. Did you and your wife get all moved in?

"Sure did," said Nathan, as he resumed clinking his spoon on his coffee mug while stirring the hot liquid. "The wife and I are happy to have our own place."

Steele said, "Well, that's good." He took a sip of his coffee as he asked, "So, what brings you up to these parts?"

The men kept up their banter while Nathan shoveled through a short stack of pancakes and a hunk of ham that the waitress had set down in front of him.

"I'm taking a look at a complaint of some missing livestock. Probably a minor case, but I got hooked by a couple pieces in the puzzle," said Nathan. "What about you? You're kinda far from home, too."

"Oh, I was a witness in a murder case here in Bowie that has been strung out over three years. It finished up yesterday," said Steele. "So, I'm going to head on back to Wise County. Where are you headed?"

"Fort Sill," said Nathan. "I want to go up and talk to a Comanche by the name of John Black Horse."

After the waitress returned and refilled their coffee, Steele looked over the rim of his steaming mug as he took a sip, then put the mug back on the table. "I know Black Horse. What's he up to these days?"

"I'm not sure," said Nathan. "But he may be rustling cattle and horses, and I want to talk with him. Listen, Ben, I'd like to talk with you some more, but I have to go catch the train." As he said that, Nathan stood up and was pulling some coins out of his pocket to pay for his breakfast. Steele rose from his chair and took the last sip from his coffee.

"Nathan, I'm not doing anything today except maybe a long hard train ride back to Decatur. So, if you don't mind, I'd like to tag along. 'Spose that would be all right?"

Nathan had no idea why Steele might want to tag along, but he thought he might enjoy the company. "Sure, c'mon along," said Nathan.

Both men had already checked out of their hotel rooms. They walked down the street to get their horses, then rode to the depot to catch the forenoon train to Wichita Falls, where they deboarded the train. They rode their horses to the crossing at the Red River, boarded a ferry, and crossed the river. After a short ride to the first rail head on the Oklahoma side of the river, they boarded another train to Lawton. With their horses safely in stalls in the stock car, they were on their way to Fort Sill to meet with the Comanches and the resident Indian Agent.

The train arrived in Lawton after dark, and after retrieving their horses, Nathan and Steele followed directions given to them by the train crew and made their way to a livery stable to bed down the horses for the night. After reaching the recommended hotel, Nathan had the first good night's sleep on a tolerable bed in several nights.

The following morning, the lawmen met for breakfast. As they waited for their food to arrive, Ben asked, "Have you ever been to an Indian reservation?"

"Nope," said Nathan.

"Well, not much to see, really," said Ben. "But I'm sure that Black Horse will fill in a few pieces in your puzzle. Don't be surprised, though, if you're met with a chilly reception." Nathan raised his eyes in question, but Ben offered no further details.

Their breakfast arrived, and their conversation paused while they attacked their plates. After the hot breakfast and stiff coffee, they asked for and received directions from the hotel staff. Following those directions, they were soon on their way to the Comanche reservation Indian Agent's office at Fort Sill. While they rode, they talked.

"Ben, did you ever know a man named Sean Conley?" Nathan asked.

"Yeah, I know him. I met him a time or two when he came into Wise County to buy cattle. He always came to town with his dad. He seemed like a real decent sort of fella."

Nathan turned in the saddle to face Steele. "They came all the way to Decatur to buy cattle? Seems odd to go that far to buy livestock."

"They could get a little better grade of stock at a larger sale barn," Ben replied. "I figure that's why they made the trip south."

Nathan asked, "You say he came with his father? I hadn't heard anything about his dad. You see, I got this telegram from Sean. He asked me to check into some horse rustling from the Lazy C. But then, when I went to meet him, he never showed up, and I ended up getting the snub from one of the ranch hands."

"Hmm," said Steele. "That doesn't sound like the Conleys. They're damn fine folks. It wouldn't be like them to not keep their word. Sean's dad is Michael Conley, and his mom is Sylvia Conley. They took over the Lazy C decades ago after Michael's father and mother, Morris and Patricia Conley died. The younger Conleys are really nice people. As I understand it, Michael and his wife, Sylvia, had two children, Sean and his sister Jane. Apparently, Jane was a bit peculiar, and she left the ranch years ago. Both Michael and Sylvia are still on the ranch, but Sean is of the age to take over one of these days when Michael gives him the go ahead. The Conleys are pretty well known in these parts. In addition to their success on the ranch, they have helped out a few of their neighbors when times are tough, so most everybody likes them. It doesn't seem to be their nature to call you out and then not show up."

The men rode in silence for a few seconds. Then Steele asked, "So, when Sean didn't show up, what did you do?"

"Well, instead of Sean Conley showing up in Nocona, this fella named Ivan Malone showed up," said Nathan. "I wasn't real happy about that, especially when he kept trying to get me to drop the case."

If he was not mistaken, Nathan thought that he heard a quiet chuckle come from Ben Steele. "Is something funny?" asked Nathan.

"Oh, yeah," said Steele. "I know Malone pretty well. He hasn't been at the Lazy C very long, but he's been making enemies seems like everywhere he turns up. I've run into him a couple times after some complaints of some cowboys getting beat up or knifed. He always seems to be in the center of it, but nobody ever wants to prosecute him. The rumor is that anyone who crosses Malone won't live to talk about it. Therefore, you can't even get a grand jury to sign on preliminary to any trial."

"Why did the Conleys hire this Malone fella at the Lazy C?" asked Nathan.

"Well, the story is that he just showed up at the ranch one day and claimed to be their grandson, the son of Jane Conley. Apparently, Sylvia Conley believed him, and Malone's been at the ranch ever since," said Steele. "I've heard some talk from cowboys who have friends at the Lazy C that Michael Conley does not like Malone but doesn't want to disappoint Sylvia by getting rid of him."

"Anybody know anything about him before he came to the Lazy C?" asked Nathan.

"Yep, one of my Ranger buddies stationed in Fort Worth knows Malone, and he sent me a telegram while I was camped out in your office before you got to town. He told me that he had heard that this Malone fella was headed my way, and he gave me some background on him. Seems Malone was always crosswise with the law, mostly for fighting and petty theft. This had gone on for years in Fort Worth. My friend also said that the local police told him that Malone even beat up his mom, Jane, a few times, but she would never press charges. She was scared to death of him."

Then it was Nathan's turn to chuckle. "I knew I had him pegged right. I figured him for a bully who would probably do anything to people who got in his way."

"Probably all true," said Steele. "My friend told me that he had beat on his mom again before he left Fort Worth. He told me that some of Malone's acquaintances told the police that he had lit out of town headed north on a stolen horse."

"Hmm," replied Nathan. "I guess one of these days we'll see that man in court or hanging from a rope."

They rode in silence a few more minutes before Ben Steele broke the silence. "You know," he said, "going onto the Comanche reservation ain't going to be like most of your visits to talk to suspects. What do you know about the Comanches?"

"I'll tell you, Ben," said Nathan. "I don't know much of anything about them except that they used to be a force to be reckoned with in these parts. Is that going to be a problem?"

Steele chuckled. "Yeah, a bit of a problem; I keep forgetting that you ain't from around here. So, let me tell you a bit about the Comanches."

Ben drew in a breath and began talking. "The Comanches came from up north in Wyoming and were related to the Shoshones. They came to the southern plains back in 1700 or so, to follow the buffalo and the wild mustangs. But they didn't all come at once. See, the Comanches don't have just one big tribe. They're made up of family groups, or bands, and each of the bands had their favorite hunting areas. Those bands would come together when there was a need for bigger war parties to rid their hunting areas of other Indian tribes or buffalo hunters who were rapidly killing off the buffalo."

"Well, when the groups all came together, how much land did the Comanches have?" asked Nathan.

"The Comancheria, that's the land they controlled, stretched from Kansas south through Texas and all the way into Mexico," said Ben. "They could control all that land because they were fierce warriors and the best damn horsemen ever on the plains. They were such expert riders and held control so easily that they earned the nickname *Lords of the Plains*.

"I guess it was the settlers that drove the Comanches off their hunting areas," said Nathan.

"Well, the settlers would never have been able to do that by themselves. The Comanches could just pick them off any time they chose. No, the U.S. Army and the buffalo hunters drove the Indians from their prairie," said Steele. "The last nail in the coffin was the buffalo hunters. They killed so many buffalo that there aren't many left even today. Those buffalo hunters were killing those animals just for their skins that they sent out East to the market there. And they would leave the dead buffalo meat to rot on the plains. That was meat and hides that the Comanches and other Indian tribes needed to survive."

Ben was quiet for a moment and then continued. "The buffalo was the center of the Comanche way of life. They depended on the buffalo for food and shelter. It got so bad that the Comanches damn near died off from starvation. Without food, they couldn't protect their hunting areas from the Army, the buffalo hunters, and all the settlers moving in, so they had no choice but to move to the reservation."

"And that's where they are today, huh," said Nathan.

"Yep, that's what became of the toughest Indians in Texas," said Ben. "They share their reservation with the Apaches and Kiowas." He paused and looked at the trail ahead. "They've had their share of problems while on the reservation. Years ago, there was a smallpox epidemic that hit the Comanches and killed a bunch of them; most likely brought to them by white trappers and traders."

They rode on for a few minutes in silence until Ben said, "Looks like Fort Sill is just down that long hill. The Indian Agent will be there, I reckon."

Even though a sometimes-difficult peace existed between the Native Americans and white settlers, after hearing Ben's story of the Comanches, the hair on the back of Nathan's neck tingled as he rode into Comanche territory. While he had had interaction with Indians several years ago when he lived in Iowa, those meetings had always been peaceful. He had never been personally involved in a fight with Indians and preferred to keep it that way.

The men spurred their horses and were soon allowed by the gate guard to enter the fort, where they tied their horses to the hitch rack in front of the Indian Agent's office. They stepped to the side to allow two Indians to exit the office, and then they entered. A small window on each side of the door let light into the dimly lit, one-room office. There was a worn counter inside the front door. Shelves along the back wall contained trade goods and merchandise for sale to the Indians. A U.S. flag was tacked to the wall above the shelves and an oil lamp hung from the ceiling in the middle of the room. Two desks were the only other furnishings. Two Indians sat across from each other at one desk. They were noisily playing a card game, slamming cards on the desk in turn. But they paused in their game and turned their attention to the two white men who had come through the door. A white man that Nathan judged to be no more than thirty-years-old rose from the other desk and approached the counter.

"Mornin' gents, my name's Jeff Keller. What can I do for you?" he asked.

Nathan pulled his vest aside to reveal his badge. "I'm U.S. Marshal Nathan Wolf." Turning slightly to Steele, he said, "And this here is Ben Steele, Texas Ranger." Steele showed his badge to Keller. Keller's lips pursed and his eyes narrowed a bit when he saw Steele's badge. The two Indians sitting at the desk quietly laid their cards on the desktop and turned their full attention to Nathan and Steele. They listened carefully to the conversation between the lawmen and Indian Agent.

Keller turned back to Nathan. "What do you want, Marshal?"

"Mr. Keller, I'm looking for a Comanche by the name of Black Horse. Do you know him?" asked Nathan.

"Sure, I know him," said Keller. "What do you want with him?"

"I just want to talk to him, Mr. Keller. I'm working on a case that he might have some information that would help me," said Nathan.

"I see," said Keller. "Can you tell me a little more about the case?"

"I'd rather not," said Nathan. "I only want to ask Black Horse a few simple questions."

"Hmm," answered Keller, answering neither yes nor no.

Nathan was getting the impression that Keller was not inclined to cooperate. "Mr. Keller, I don't know what your protocol is for access to one of the residents of the reservation. Is there something you need me to do? I want to talk to Black Horse, so do I need to get permission from the head chief of the tribe?"

Nathan thought that had been a rather straight-forward question. But he became confused when both Keller and Ben Steele began to laugh. He looked behind Keller and saw that the two Indians were also quietly laughing. "OK," said Nathan, I didn't know that I was that damn funny. So let me in on the joke."

Jeff Keller was still chuckling. "Have you been in Texas very long, Marshal?" he asked.

Nathan looked over at Steele, who still had a wide grin on his face. Steele answered Keller. "The Marshal is kinda new to the area, so just tell him what he needs to know, Keller."

Keller turned to Nathan and said, "Ever hear of a man called Quanah Parker, Marshal?"

"Don't believe I have," answered Nathan.

The Indian Agent then said, "Marshal, Quanah Parker is the chief of the Comanches. He was appointed by the Federal Government to lead his people."

Nathan interrupted, "Okay, so is he the man I need to see to speak with Black Horse?"

Keller chuckled again. "No, Marshal. You don't have to see Quanah Parker. And you probably couldn't see him even if you wanted to."

"Why is that Mr. Keller?" asked Nathan. He was getting impatient with Keller's slow commentary.

"Well, Marshal, that's why the Ranger and I were chuckling. Quanah Parker is of the *Quahadi* band but is head of all the Comanches. So, he's a rather big deal around here and up in Washington, D.C. Why, Theodore Roosevelt, the Governor of New York, has even been here to visit the chief. They're hunting buddies. And it looks like Roosevelt is going to be our next Vice President, since he's running alongside William McKinley. On top of that, Quanah Parker is running for deputy sheriff in Lawton and will probably win that office. And finally, Quanah Parker is great friends with Burk Burnett, owner of one of the largest cattle ranches that stretches from Texas to up here in Oklahoma."

"What's your point, Keller?" asked Nathan.

"My point, Marshal, is that Quanah Parker is a busy man and doesn't have the time or the inclination to talk to a visiting marshal," said Keller. "He may be head of the Comanches, but he has other chiefs that take care of the common tribal business, so he seldom meets with outside folks, except when it comes to issues that affect the entire Comanche nation. Then he gets real active."

Nathan had learned a quick lesson and was ready to humble himself to the Indian Agent. "Okay, Keller, I guess I understand. But you still have not answered my question about how I go about talking to Black Horse," said Nathan. "So, what do you suggest?"

"Marshal, John Black Horse is one of Quanah Parker's secondary chiefs. He's a war chief, a minor one, but still a chief," said Keller.

"I'll get a runner to go and ask him to meet me here in the morning. He can talk with you then."

Nathan thought to himself, *why didn't you just say that in the first place?*

"All right," said Nathan, still not liking the Indian Agent's stilted cooperation. "We'll come back tomorrow morning about ten a.m. Is that all right with you, Keller?"

"Sure. That's fine," said Keller. "I'll let John Black Horse know. But, one other thing," said Keller. "The ranger won't be coming with you."

This surprised Nathan. He asked, "Why not. Ben Steele is welcome to come along with me tomorrow."

"No, Marshal, he won't be coming with you," said Keller. "He knows why, and I'm sure he can tell you all about it on your ride back to town. Now, if you'll excuse me, I've got some paperwork to catch up on." Keller turned, left the counter, and walked back to his desk and sat down. The two card-playing Indians stared at Nathan and Ben Steele as the two lawmen turned and walked out the door.

As they returned to Lawton to spend the night, the two lawmen had time to talk about what had transpired in their meeting with Indian Agent Jeff Keller. "I can't say that I took a liking to Keller," said Nathan.

"Most white folks would say the same thing," Steele replied.

"What got into him saying that you could not come with me in the morning to meet with Black Horse?" asked Nathan.

Ben Steele continued to look at the trail ahead, and after a few seconds, he answered. "Keller doesn't like my Ranger badge."

He paused, and Nathan was almost ready to ask him the reason, but Steele continued. "You see, the history of the Texas Rangers goes back many years. Most of the Rangers' history is good, since the Rangers were one of the first outfits to bring law and order to Texas."

"Can't see where that would be a bad thing," Nathan commented.

The men rode in silence for a several seconds before Ben said, "You're right, that's a good thing. But it was the way that they did it that gave the Rangers a reputation for being heavy handed."

"What do you mean?" Nathan asked.

"The answer to that, my friend, goes back before my time and yours," said Ben. "You see, when the Texas Rangers first formed, they were all strictly volunteers, out to protect their homesteads and those of their neighbors. But in 1836, Texas began to pay the mounted men, and that is what us Rangers like to think of as our beginning. But the Rangers were scattered all over Anglo Texas and didn't always have the same group of fighters. That changed in 1839 or so, when a fella named Jack Hays got together a more formal group of volunteers in San Antonio. That group could be ready to ride out in short order when an alarm was sounded. They were sort of like the Revolutionary War 'minutemen'."

"What kind of an alarm would bring those boys out, Ben?" asked Nathan.

Steele chuckled. "It was almost always Indians or Mexicans that raided homesteaders and small towns. Those first Rangers' job was to follow the raiders and put a stop to them once and for all. When those men rode out, they travelled light and only carried what they could on horseback. They slept out in the open, no flags, no uniforms but as much firepower as they could manage. They would chase down the marauders and when they caught up with 'em, they showed no mercy. In most instances there was no jury trial. Justice was at the hands of the Rangers. In most cases the Indians or Mexicans were killed, with no witnesses left behind."

"That still doesn't tell me why Keller doesn't want you coming back to the agency tomorrow," said Nathan.

"I'll get there," said Ben. "You need to understand some of our Texas history. It'll help you in your marshalling down here." Steele laughed. Nathan did not.

"When Texas became a state in 1845, Senator Sam Houston asked Washington for money to pay Rangers so Texas would have its own peace keeping force. Washington didn't want to do that. They wanted to send a few Army boys down here, but Houston knew that wouldn't work. The Army was too rigid and had to answer to the Washington stuffed shirts. And since Washington wouldn't give up money for the Rangers, the Rangers remained a Texas state militia. Their job was to fight Indians and Mexicans in order to keep the Texas frontier safe for settlers."

Ben paused and looked at Nathan as their horses kept a steady walk. Nathan screwed up an eyebrow and looked back at Steele.

"All right, I'll get to the point," said Ben. "Over the years, a bunch of treaties were signed between the Indians and the governments of Texas and the United States, and damn near every one of them was broken by one side or the other, and the wars against the Indians continued to rage across Texas. A bunch of those battles were fought by the Rangers. Mind you, all of this took place before I became a Ranger, but the stories lived on. Remember I said that the Rangers didn't take prisoners. So, in the course of many of these fights, Rangers killed the Indian men, but also killed many women and children in the process of wiping out the warriors."

Nathan did not respond. He continued to look straight ahead, but he was listening keenly to Ben Steele.

"The Comanches were great fighters. They could outride the Rangers or any Army boys. The only thing that saved the Rangers or an

Army troop was the fact that they had guns where the Comanches, Kiowa, and Apaches relied on bows and arrows and lances," said Ben. "'Course there were always outlaws that sold guns to the Indians. But, over time, the Rangers and the Army wore down the Indians, who damn near starved to death because of the lack of buffalos for food and the need to keep moving their camps so the Rangers and Army would not know where they were. It finally got so bad that Quanah Parker had little choice but to bring his people to the reservation."

"So, my guess is that the Comanches still carry a grudge against the Rangers for losing the war on the plains," said Nathan.

"Nah, it goes deeper than that," said Ben. "Their bone to pick is the fact that along with their warrior men, the Rangers and the Army burned out entire villages and killed women and children in the process. Jeff Keller knows that, and he knows all that history was before my time."

"So, if he knows all that, why does he still insist that you don't come back?" asked Nathan.

"Because I'm a Ranger," Steele answered. "Remember those two Indians hanging around Keller in the Agency?"

"Sure," Nathan answered.

"Well, those two old boys are the eyes of the tribe. They pass their time playing cards or checkers in the Indian Agency office so that they can let the tribal leaders know about anything out of the ordinary, and that's me and you. We're not ordinary," Ben laughed as he said it. "They know that a Texas Ranger stopped by the Indian Agency office, and now the whole reservation knows it. And since Comanches have a long unpleasant history with the Rangers, Keller wants to avoid any trouble. That's why he doesn't want me back on the reservation. I'm not here to rile him and the Indians up on account of a case you're workin' on, so I'll just stay in town tomorrow 'til you get back."

Later that evening, after the two lawmen had finished their supper in the hotel, they moved to the hotel bar, nursed their bourbon, and told stories to each other as only fellow lawmen can do. By the end of two hours, they each had a pretty well-defined picture of the past life of one another. By eleven o'clock, Nathan was in bed and sleep came rapidly.

The following morning, as Nathan made his way back to Fort Sill, Wander was up to his usual practice of walking the trail while observing his surroundings with the intent to move off the trail to investigate anything to which he took a fancy. A minute ago, he had nearly come to a complete stop as he watched a hummingbird flit in and out of some purple prickly pear cacti blossoms. But a gentle rein reminder and boot heel nudge brought the gelding back on course. Nathan could see Fort Sill up ahead, and he wondered to himself how the day would unfold. When he reached the fort, he passed the sentry and found a shady spot within the walls of the fort and under a full-growth mesquite tree where he tied Wander.

When he entered the Indian Agent's office, Jeff Keller was standing at the counter, and the same two Indians Nathan had seen the day before were sitting behind him.

"Mornin, Keller," said Nathan.

"Marshal," was the only response from tight-lipped Keller.

Keller knew why Nathan was there, of course, and he slowly drawled, "He'll be along shortly."

Those words had barely left Keller's mouth when the office door opened and a lean, black-haired man entered. He was dressed in a mixed style of Anglo and Indian attire. His hair was decorated with a lone feather and was tied in two plaits on each side of his face. He wore a leather thong around his neck from which hung a stone that had been carved into a design that Nathan did not recognize. The Indian wore denim pants but wore hand-made, tooled leather shoes on his feet. The shoes had no laces but tied with a flap that wrapped to the side and held in place by a silver conch button. As he came through the door, he ignored Nathan and approached Keller. The two men spoke in the Shoshoni language, keeping their voices low. When they paused, the Indian looked at Nathan, and then back at Keller. A few more words were spoken between the men until finally the Indian looked more intently at Nathan. But at that point, Nathan was at a loss, not knowing whether the Indian spoke and understood English or whether he would need to have Keller interpret for him. But just then, the Indian spoke.

"I speak English," the man said. "I learned from the Bible people."

Nathan did not know exactly what Black Horse meant by Bible people, but he thought that he must be referring to the Christian missionaries who were commonly seen as they traveled between areas of Indian populations, attempting to bring Christianity and their form of socially acceptable behavior to people they deemed to be uncivilized.

Nathan moved his open hand forward to shake hands, but the Indian initially ignored the gesture and kept his hands at his sides.

"My name is Nathan Wolf, U.S. Marshal Nathan Wolf," said Nathan. "What is your name?"

The Indian looked closely at Nathan and then spoke. "My people call me *tuhubitu puuku*. White men call me John Black Horse," he said.

"May I call you Black Horse?" asked Nathan. He was determined not to embarrass himself or disrespect John Black Horse.

Black Horse nodded and answered that it would be all right.

Having seen a sturdy wooden bench just outside the door of the Indian Agent's office, Nathan asked Black Horse, "Mind if we go outside and sit a bit and talk?"

Black Horse nodded and followed Nathan outdoors where both men took a seat on the bench.

"You know why I'm here, don't you?" Nathan asked.

Black Horse nodded and replied. "Keller told me you want to ask me some questions."

"That's right," said Nathan, "and thank you for coming to see me today."

Black Horse merely looked at Nathan and nodded.

Nathan thought to himself that this might turn out to be a rather one-sided conversation. But he pressed forward. "Black Horse, do you know a man called Sean Conley?"

"Yes," answered Black Horse. "I know him."

"How did you meet Mr. Conley?" asked Nathan.

"I first knew the father of Sean. He was Mr. Michael Conley, and Sean would always be with Michael Conley when we met with him," said Black Horse. Somewhat furtively, Black Horse continued, "Some say Michael Conley is dead."

Unbeknownst to Nathan, Black Horse had first-hand knowledge regarding the death of Michael Conley, but Black Horse was not ready to divulge the information. Instead, he was testing to see what Nathan knew. He was still measuring this stranger, a U.S. Marshal.

Nathan did not know what to make of Black Horse's remark regarding Michael Conley. He paused momentarily, but then pressed on.

"Was it Michael Conley that started the Lazy C Ranch?" Nathan asked.

"No," Black Horse answered. "My grandfather knew the father of Michael, Mr. Morris Conley. He started the ranch on land that my people hunted on. My grandfather always told us, that even though your government took our land, Mr. Morris Conley was an honorable man, and he let us continue to hunt on his ranch. When Morris Conley died, Michael Conley still let us hunt on the ranch."

"What about Sean Conley?" asked Nathan. "Did he let you hunt on the ranch?"

"Mr. Sean Conley followed in the footsteps of his father," said Black Horse. "Sometimes I would see Sean Conley when I would lead a hunting party on his ranch. Many times, we talked, and he was never displeased that we were on his land. Sean Conley is an honorable man."

Nathan was a bit confused, which led to his question, "Why would a ranch owner allow you to come on his land, and what was it that you were hunting?"

Black Horse did not answer immediately. He looked away and then looked at Nathan. His demeanor gave evidence that he could not understand how this white lawman could be so naïve. He then answered. "Many years ago, our brothers hunted the buffalo on these plains. The buffalo provided everything that our people needed to survive. But then the white men came and killed all the buffalo. This was very bad for our people, and many people grew weak from hunger. And when our land was given to white people, we were sent to live with our brothers near this white men's Army fort. But we could still hunt for deer and prong horn antelope on Mr. Conley's ranch."

Nathan was beginning to think that Black Horse's story had no ending. He asked, "Didn't the government in Washington provide food for your people here on the reservation?"

Black Horse grunted his disapproval. "Yes, some food was provided, but many times the food was spoiled and could not be eaten. The food was strange and was distasteful to our people. Many times, the rotten food caused our people to become sick and die. We were forced to leave the reservation to hunt for food."

There was a long pause in the conversation between the two men. Finally, Nathan spoke, "Black Horse, I mean no disrespect to you, but are you sure that Sean Conley allowed you to hunt on his ranch?"

Nathan could tell from his demeanor that Black Horse did not like the question. "Marshal, I do not speak lies," said Black Horse. "You should ask Indian Agent Keller that question if you are not sure that I speak the truth."

Again, there was a lull in their conversation before Nathan asked, "Black Horse, do you know a man called Ivan Malone?"

Black Horse looked intently at Nathan and said, "I do not know the name, Ivan Malone. Who is this man?"

"He is a very large man who may be causing trouble at the Lazy C Ranch," Nathan answered.

Black Horse grunted and nodded. "I know of this Ivan Malone," he said. "He is the man I am going to kill."

Nathan was initially at a loss for words. Black Horse had just claimed that he intended to commit murder, and Nathan was not sure how to reply. "Black Horse, you know that you cannot kill anyone. Murder is a violation of law, and you would be hanged."

"It is white man's law, Marshal, not my law. It is my duty to kill the man you call Malone," said Black Horse.

"Your duty?" questioned Nathan. "Why do you say you must kill Mr. Malone?"

Black Horse did not answer the question. After a minute or two, he rose from the bench and asked Nathan to get his horse and come with him. Black Horse went to his own horse and swung up on the back of the horse, waiting until Nathan had joined him. The two men rode out of the fort and broke into a trot. After a few minutes of steady riding, Nathan could see a group of tepees mixed in with a few wooden cabins. Black Horse looked at the encampment but continued riding. At last, they came to the banks of a small river, where Black Horse turned and followed the riverbank. He soon dismounted and walked to an arroyo that was branched off of the river's path. The arroyo was dry, and its sides were stepped from erosion over many years of water flow. Nathan walked to the side of Black Horse as they reached the edge of the arroyo. Immediately, Nathan could see that on one of the upper steps on the arroyo's side, two decorated lances were standing, their shafts adorned with strips of colorful cloth. Between the two lances, a blanket-covered bundle in the shape of a human body, was peacefully reposed on the arroyo shelf. Nathan had never seen such a thing. He did not know that the Comanche practice of placing a body in an inaccessible location was common practice until a burial took place.

"Black Horse, I don't know what this is," said Nathan.

"Marshal, the brave warrior that you see resting is my brother. His name is *yupuhiwi puaka*. White men would call him Iron Arrow. He is preparing to return to the earth. He was killed while hunting on the Conley ranch with me. He was killed by the man you call Malone. That is why it is my duty to kill him."

So, it was now clear to Nathan that Black Horse intended to take revenge for the killing of his brother. "Black Horse, when did this happen?" asked Nathan.

"Five sunrises ago," answered Black Horse. "My brother lived for two more days before he died. Another one of my brothers has prepared *yupuhiwi puaka* to meet our great spirit. His body will be placed in the earth in one more day."

In his head, Nathan was putting together a timeline, and he came to the conclusion that the death of Iron Arrow would have been about the same time that Ivan Malone had said that he had had a gunfight with some Indians who Malone alleged were stealing cattle and horses.

"Was your brother killed on the Lazy C ranch?" asked Nathan.

"Yes," replied Black Horse. "We were collecting our gift cattle."

"What do you mean by 'gift cattle'?" Nathan asked.

"In exchange for living in peace, several of the white man ranchers who live on the land my people once occupied, pledged to give the Comanche people a yearly gift of cattle to help feed our people. Morris Conley and his son, Michael, gave us gifts of two steers two times during the year. They have done this for my grandfather, my father, and for me. We were on the Lazy C for our harvest time collection of two steers."

"Did Sean Conley know about this agreement between your people and the ranchers?" asked Nathan.

"Yes, he knew. In the past spring, he was there and helped us to get our two steers at that time," said Black Horse. "He gave us his good wishes as we led the steers back across the river to the reservation."

"Five days ago, when you had your fight with Ivan Malone, was Michael or Sean Conley there with Malone?" Nathan asked.

"No," said Black Horse, "only Mr. Ivan Malone and his evil spirit warriors."

Nathan took that to mean that Malone must have had his hired gun friends with him when he met the Indians.

Nathan was blunt in his next question. "Black Horse, did you steal any horses from the Lazy C when you were there?"

Black Horse curled his lips and his nostrils flared as he answered, "No, Marshal. We were there to gather only two steers. We have no need for white man's horses. We have our own horses that are far superior to those of the white men. Our horses are much faster and more suitable for chasing game."

Nathan immediately thought of his horse, Wander. Wander was a good trail horse but would be ill-suited for chasing game. However, as a thick-muscled quarter horse, Wander could probably hold his own in a short race with the Indian ponies, but would, indeed, lose to those ponies in a longer race. "Black Horse, I apologize if my question offended you," said Nathan. "But I need to ask many questions to find out what happened at the Lazy C."

Black Horse had calmed somewhat, and simply nodded his head in understanding of Nathan's apology.

"Black Horse, can you tell me more about what happened at the Lazy C when you were taking your steers?" asked Nathan. "What did Mr. Malone do?"

"When we crossed the river to get to the Lazy C ranch, we saw three riders in the distance. But we had gathered steers on that ranch many times and had no cause to believe that there might be danger for us. We lassoed two steers, and we were ready to leave when those three riders came to us. Their leader was the man you call Malone," said Black Horse. The Indian paused, and then continued.

"Malone told us that we must leave the ranch and that we must leave the two steers at the ranch. I argued with him and told him of our agreement with the Conleys, but Malone would not listen to us. Instead, he took his pistol from its holster and fired near my feet," said Black Horse.

"But he did not hurt you," said Nathan.

"Not with that shot," said Black Horse.

"What did you do?" asked Nathan.

"We had no guns with us, so I told my people and my brother that we must leave, and we took our ropes and began to mount our horses. But then, Ivan Malone began to laugh, and more shots were fired. This time his evil men also fired their pistols. But at first, they did not hurt us. But as we rode away, my brother was shot and another of our warriors was also hit. We rode quickly away and returned to our home. My brother died two days later. The warrior who was shot will live to hunt again." Black Horse gazed into the distance, as if reliving the incident in his head. He then turned back to Nathan.

"So, you can see, Marshal, I must avenge my brother's death. I will kill Malone," said Black Horse.

Nathan replied, "Black Horse, I understand everything you have told me. But you know that killing Ivan Malone would be against the law, and that you could be hanged for murder if you kill him."

"Hmph," snorted Black Horse. "That is white man law, not Comanche law."

Nathan decided that there was no point in talking more about Black Horse's intent to kill Ivan Malone. Instead, he simply warned Black Horse that killing Malone would only bring more trouble to him and his people. He decided to change the discussion.

"Black Horse, does Indian Agent Jeff Keller know about the arrangement with the local ranchers and the 'gift cattle'?" asked Nathan.

"I cannot speak for Mr. Keller," said Black Horse. "You must speak to him about these things."

Having witnessed Keller's habit of being slow to answer direct questions, Nathan asked, "Well, Black Horse, will Keller tell me the truth?"

"Yes. Even though he is part of the white man's government, a government that is not a friend to the Comanche people, Jeff Keller has always told us the truth. We have grown to trust him," said Black Horse. Black Horse turned his head and looked back across the arroyo. "Now we must leave my brother in peace."

The men walked back to their horses and mounted. They wheeled their animals and began walking away from the arroyo. Neither man said anything. In his head, Nathan was trying to put together all the pieces of the puzzle of Ivan Malone. How in the world did Malone become the face of the Lazy C Ranch? Where were Michael and Sean Conley? He now had the impression that everyone he had met while digging into Sean Conley's complaint of missing horses on the Lazy C had more knowledge about the case than he did, but they were holding back information. It was readily apparent that Ivan Malone cast an evil shadow that caused disruption, and it was certainly understandable why Black Horse wanted to see the end of Malone's life. But Nathan was also convinced that he did not yet know all the answers to the questions regarding the Lazy C and how Malone fit in the picture. Most of the time when he was tracking down details of a criminal case, the pieces of the puzzle fell into place more easily, but not so in this case. Suddenly, Nathan was wrested from his musings.

"Marshal Nathan Wolf," said Black Horse. "I want you to come with me." Black Horse had stopped his horse within sight of a group of tepees and other Indian shelters.

Nathan was not sure if Black Horse was trying to lure him into some sort of trap, but quickly dismissed the thought. After all, Black Horse's story had seemed plausible enough and could be checked out further. He turned Wander and walked to the side of Black Horse. "Where are we going, Black Horse?"

"You will see," replied Black Horse. In the moments before, Black Horse had formed an opinion and made up his mind. He was convinced that he could trust Marshal Wolf.

The two men approached the tepees, dismounted, and a young boy came quickly to take the reins of Wander and the hackamore of the Indian pony. The boy walked the horses to a shady spot at the side of the tepee and sat down in the grass.

"This is my home, Marshal Wolf. Come inside, I want to show you something," said Black Horse.

The men entered the dimly lit tepee. The smoke vent allowed light to enter from the top of the dwelling, affording Nathan an opportunity to take in his surroundings. He was struck with the roominess and neatness of the tepee's interior. Skins covered the floor and possessions of the family that lived there lined one side of the tepee. The smell within the tepee was a blend of human odors and cooking smells, all mixed with wood smoke. Skins and blankets were stacked neatly to one side of the tepee to be used as sleeping mats, but near that stack was an additional sleeping mat. A man, a white man, sat cross legged on that mat carefully watching Black Horse and Nathan. The man was wearing a pair of pants but had neither shirt nor shoes. Pieces of cloth strips of various colors were wrapped around his upper torso, apparently to cover a wound. His hands lay peacefully in his lap. A native woman sat nearby, seemingly to look after his wound and the well-being of the man.

"Marshal Wolf, this is my friend, Mr. Sean Conley," said Black Horse.

Needless to say, Nathan was taken aback. He looked at the white man and asked, "You're Sean Conley?"

"Yep, I'm Conley. Who are you?" said Conley, as he stuck out his hand to shake.

"I'm Marshal Nathan Wolf. I'm the guy that you sent the telegram to and asked me to meet with you in Nocona."

"Conley wheezed as he said, "Didn't show up, did I." His face was stoic, until a grimace of pain crossed his face and his face paled.

Conley recovered in a moment, but Nathan could see that he was still in pain. "What happened? How come you weren't in Nocona?" Nathan asked.

"I would have been there. But two days before we were to meet you in Nocona, my dad and I started out from the ranch early that morning. We were going to Spanish Fort to the telegraph office. My mother went to Fort Worth, and we wanted to send her a wire to make sure that she was all right. That goddam Ivan Malone was with us."

Sean paused and coughed lightly, his face showing the pain caused by coughing. When he recovered, he continued.

"As we approached the river near Spanish Fort, we got bushwhacked by Malone's friends." Conley took a couple of pained deep breaths, and then said, "I got shot in the back. Then I got dragged to the river, dumped in, and left for dead. Black Horse told me that Dad was killed and also got dumped in the river. Thank God that Black Horse and a couple of his friends happened to be hunting and running their trap lines a bit farther downstream and found me and brought me here. Black Horse and his friends buried my dad." Conley went on to describe the location of his father's burial site as it had been told to him by Black Horse.

Black Horse looked away from Sean Conley. He had formed a mental picture of the killing of Michael Conley and attempted murder of Sean, and the death of his own brother. The images were replaced by the white-hot flames of the need for revenge. He turned back to observe Nathan and Conley.

Sean continued his recollection. "Black Horse's woman dug two slugs out of me," said Conley. "If they hadn't rescued me, I probably would have drowned or bled to death and become food for the river catfish."

"Do you have any idea who did this to you and your dad?" Nathan asked.

"Sure, I know who did it. And one of these days when I am up and able to ride again, I'm going to kill the son of a bitch," said Conley.

It only took a few seconds before Nathan said, "Let me guess. Ivan Malone?"

Conley did not answer, but nodded his head. Another wave of pain was crossing his face, and he groaned. Black Horse helped Sean Conley straighten out his legs so that Conley could lie on his stomach. As he lay down, Nathan could see that the bandages across Conley's back showed both dried blood and small areas of fresh blood. Nathan could not help but wonder to himself whether Conley would live to tell more of the story. The native woman moved to Sean's side and examined Sean's dressings. She frowned as she looked up at Black Horse.

"Sean needs to rest," said Black Horse.

Before the two men left the tepee, Nathan leaned down and faced Conley. "Conley, I would like you to come to Decatur as soon as you are able. I don't think it would be very wise for you to return to your ranch right away. If it was Malone who did this to you, he might just want to finish the job. When you come to see me, I would like for you to tell me all the details of how you came to have two slugs in your back and your dad's disappearance. Will you promise me that you will do that?"

Conley remained inanimate and did not answer right away. Finally, he said, "Yeah, I'll come to see you when I am able to travel. But I won't promise you that I won't take my revenge on the man that shot me and killed my dad."

"I understand," said Nathan. "Just remember, you promised to come and see me before you take the law into your own hands."

Sean Conley was too weak to answer. He simply nodded his head.

"All right, we've got a lot to talk about," said Nathan. "So, I will see you in Decatur when you're up and about. Please don't try to do anything that might get you killed until we have a chance to talk. I'll see you then."

He and Black Horse left the tepee. "Black Horse, I must leave you now," said Nathan. This time when Nathan put out his hand to shake, Black Horse took his hand in his own.

"I know you don't think much of the white man's law, but give me some time to take care of bringing Ivan Malone to justice. I'm sure you don't want to spend time in prison for killing Malone. Don't take the law into your own hands, Black Horse. I know you want revenge, but let me take care of bringing justice to Ivan Malone," said Nathan.

Black Horse did not respond. Nathan turned and as he did so, the young Indian boy led Wander to him. He mounted and told Black Horse that he had enjoyed meeting with him. "We'll meet again," said Nathan. He waved, turned Wander and trotted away. He wanted to stop one more place on his way back to town.

After a short ride, Fort Sill loomed ahead. Nathan showed his badge to the gate sentry and walked Wander to the front of the Indian Agency office where he dismounted and tied the horse to the hitch rack. When he entered the Indian Agent's office, Jeff Keller was at his desk, and two Indians sat at the desk near him playing checkers. Keller looked up, nodded, and simply said "Marshal."

"Afternoon, Keller," said Nathan. "If you've got a few minutes, I'd like to ask you a few more questions."

Keller got up from his desk, stretched his arms over his head, and walked to the counter. "Are you learning a few things, Marshal?" asked Keller.

Nathan was not sure if the question was meant to be derogatory or whether Keller was just making conversation. He answered, "Yeah, it appears that I am."

Nathan paused and then went on, "Keller, what can you tell me about some of the North Texas ranchers allowing the Comanches to come on their land to hunt?"

Keller seemed unfazed by the question. "It's true, Marshal. Those are pretty much verbal agreements, but there are several ranchers in Texas and up here in Oklahoma who allow the Indians to hunt on their ranch ranges. The ranchers figure that if the Indians take some deer or pronghorns, it leaves more grass for their cattle."

Nathan now knew that Black Horse had told him the truth about having permission to hunt on the Lazy C, but he would need to confirm that with Sean Conley when he had a chance to talk with him. "Keller, have you ever heard anything about 'gift cattle'?" asked Nathan.

Keller chuckled quietly. Then he spoke, "It is not really called gift cattle," he said. "Gift cattle is the term the Indians use. The government reasons that the payment of a small number of herd cattle is considered part of an old lease agreement that went into effect when settlers were allowed to settle on the hunting grounds of the Indians. The agreement was that a specified number of beef cattle were to be given to the Indians two times per year as a good faith gesture for the use of the land." Keller paused, choosing his words. "Of course, we know what has transpired since that time. The Indians have been forced off the land and moved to reservations like the one here at Fort Sill. The land no longer belongs to the Indians, but rather than open old wounds, the giving of the gratuitous cattle remains in effect."

"How do you keep track of the ranchers who still honor that original agreement?" asked Nathan.

"Most of the time, it's not hard," said Keller. "Those ranches don't change hands very often. Most of them are still owned by the families of the original homesteaders. So how do we keep track of them?"

Keller turned back to the shelves next to his desk and retrieved a well-worn, green, cloth-covered ledger book. He brought it to the counter, opened it, and turned the pages of the journal until he found what he was seeking. He turned the book around so that Nathan could read it.

"Each page of the journal is a separate document for an individual ranch. As you can see, this is the entry page for the Bar Lazy C Ranch. The agreement allows the Comanches to hunt wild game on the ranch and if you read down farther, the agreement also states that two head of cattle will be given to the Comanches twice per year."

Nathan looked to the bottom of the sheet and saw handwritten signatures. "Are these Conleys' signatures?"

"Yep," answered Keller. "Those are the signatures of Morris Conley, the original homesteader and his son, Michael."

"Is Morris still alive?" asked Nathan.

"Naw, he passed away quite a number of years ago," said Keller. "But since Michael is still living, the agreement remains valid."

Nathan was recalling what Black Horse had just told him and Sean Conley. Michael Conley was dead, but Nathan would keep that fact to himself. "Keller, what would happen to that agreement if Michael passed away."

"Well, it would become null and void without a valid signature. But since Sean Conley is still living, all that needs to happen is for him to come in my office and add his signature to the agreement, and it would remain in effect since he is part of the original family. I haven't seen Michael or Sean for quite a spell, but I assume they are both still alive," said Keller, with a questioning look crossing his face. But Keller knew more than he was revealing.

"Yep, I've seen Sean recently, so I know he is still alive," said Nathan. He was not quite ready to share the location where he had seen Sean just hours ago.

"It's kinda funny that you are asking about this, though, Marshal. I had a man come in here not many days ago and asked those same questions. He claimed he was from the Bar Lazy C. He didn't tell me why he was asking the questions, though, but I told him the same things I've just told you."

"Was he a rather large fella?" asked Nathan.

"Nah," replied Keller. "He was a kinda skinny man, not out of the ordinary, except he wore a fancy pistol, kinda low slung on his hip."

Nathan knew that it must have been one of Ivan Malone's hired guns who had come to the fort, no doubt following instructions from Malone.

"Keller, I appreciate you showing me that ledger," said Nathan. "That pretty much lets Black Horse off the hook for being on the Lazy C and gathering his two steers. But I still need to figure out the details of Sean Conley and Ivan Malone alleging that there were horses stolen from the Lazy C. Of course, Ivan Malone alleges that Black Horse and his friends stole them. I don't think I believe him, but I still have to get to the bottom of it." Nathan shook hands with Keller and was almost ready to walk out the office door when he turned back to Keller.

"Say, Keller, Black Horse told me that someone at the Lazy C Ranch killed his brother, Iron Arrow. Is that a fact?" asked Nathan.

"You need to remember, Marshal, on a reservation there isn't much that goes on that I don't hear about," said Keller. "Yeah, I heard that Iron Arrow had died from his injuries. I understand that he is to be buried tomorrow. But I haven't heard who shot him. The rumor is strong that it might have been that Malone fella at the Lazy C. And one more thing, Marshal. As for the allegation that Black Horse and his party stole any horses at the Lazy C, why, that's just loco. The Indians don't need any ponies. They raise their own. And if there were any new horses brought onto the reservation, I would most likely hear about it. There aren't many secrets in our community. Therefore, I think the rumor that Black Horse stole some Lazy C horses is just so much hogwash."

"I'm beginning to think the same thing," Nathan said, "but I'm going to need to do some more digging to get to the truth." The fact that Keller said he knew most of the happenings on the reservation caused

Nathan to take a stab in the dark. "One more question, Keller. Did you know that Black Horse has a white man recuperating at his tepee?"

"You mean Sean Conley," Keller said rather matter-of-factly. "Yes, I know he's there. Like I said..."

"Yeah, yeah, nothing goes on around here that you don't know," answered Nathan. "Strange how you kept that fact away from me just a minute ago when you told me you hadn't seen Michael or Sean for quite some time."

Keller responded, "No, Wolf, it's a fact that I have not laid eyes on Michael or Sean in quite a spell."

"Hmm," Nathan murmured. It was all he could do to remain calm while continuing to talk to the obfuscating Indian Agent. "Keller, I would like you to have a talk with Black Horse and try to convince him that it would not be a good idea to go after his brother's killer. It will only get him in trouble with the law and could start a flare up of a range war between the Indians and the ranchers."

Keller seemed to pause to think. Then he replied, "I'll do that Marshal."

"Thanks," said Nathan. "I'm going to head on back to Decatur, but I will be back as soon as I dig out a few more facts in the case." He stuck out his hand and Keller shook it, then turned and walked out the door of the Indian Agent's office.

But Nathan did not return to Decatur immediately. Instead, he rode south, reaching the Red River after several hours. He crossed the river just north of Spanish Fort and found his way to the northern edge of the Lazy C ranch, and the site of Malone's altercation with the Comanches. After spending a half hour searching, he found what he was looking for. A fresh mound of dirt was cleverly hidden among some scrub bushes where it was not easily seen. It was the site of Michael Conley's grave, just as it had been described by Sean Conley. He quickly left the area and headed back to the road to Nocona.

Chapter Twelve

Wise County
Decatur, Texas

Beryl Dunn spent the night in the Chisholm Trail Hotel after arriving in Decatur late the previous evening. He had caught the last train from Nocona to Bowie with the late-night connection to Decatur. After checking in to the hotel, he found a local bar and joined a card game where he lost a few dollars. He did not care, as he was finally able to spend some of the money that Ivan Malone was paying him to hang around and protect Malone's back side in case of an uprising by the cowhands on the Lazy C Ranch. But now, Malone had given him another piece of work, and this time it included murder. Dunn was not too keen on getting himself into another killing. As it stood now, he had followed Malone's orders and shot one of the Conleys and watched as Malone had killed a prospector who just happened to be passing through Lazy C property on his way to Colorado. He was also with Malone when he had shot two of Black Horse's hunting party. He was pretty sure that one of those Indians had died from his gunshot wound. The way he figured, it would only be a matter of time before the law caught up with Malone and him and Matt Woods. But right now, Malone was paying him good wages, and he was not yet ready to hightail it away.

Before he had gone to sleep last night, Dunn's mind wandered to two days before, when Malone had pulled him aside and wanted to talk with him. The two men held a discussion on the front porch of the ranch house.

"Beryl, I've got a job for you," Malone had said. He went on to say, "I overheard one of our fence crew yakkin' with some others. He said that he had seen that damn U.S. Marshal nosing around out by the place we shot up Black Horse and his boys."

"So what?" answered Dunn. "He said he might go out there and have a look around. Don't mean nuthin' to us. He won't find anything to chew on."

"Maybe not," answered Malone. "But just the same, he also said that he would keep looking around until he was satisfied that there was no rustling going on at the Lazy C. And I'm damn tired of having to look over my shoulder to make sure that jackass Marshal isn't anywhere around to mess up my plans."

Dunn gave Malone a blank look. He was afraid of where this talk was going, and sure enough, Malone soon filled in the blanks.

"So, here's what I want you to do," said Malone. "I want you to head down to Decatur and find out where this Marshal Wolf lives. Then I want you to go on to his place and kill him. Ambush him, or wait until after dark, whatever you think works best, but I don't want to ever see him again."

Dunn had been afraid this was what Malone wanted done as soon as he had begun talking about the Marshal. "You want me to go out and kill a U.S. Marshal?" asked Dunn, incredulously. "By God, Malone, you really are crazy."

Malone did not for one minute think that he was crazy. In fact, his ego told him that he was the only sane person around these parts. He took two steps toward Dunn and wrapped his huge hands around Dunn's neck. "Dunn, I don't want to hear any more sass out of you. I'm paying you good money, and I expect you to carry out my orders." Malone then shoved Dunn backwards. Dunn stumbled but did not fall down.

Dunn answered Malone. "I hear you, Ivan. But if you're so hell fire convinced that the Marshal has to die, why don't you do it yourself?"

"You know damn well why I don't do the messy jobs. I've got to stay out of prison so I can run this ranch. That's why I hired you and Woods," answered Malone. "And if you don't take care of this little project, why, you might find that our friendship takes a nasty and fatal turn. You get my meaning, don't you?"

Dunn knew exactly what Malone meant. If he did not carry out Malone's wishes, he would be a walking dead man. He had little choice, yet he was going to take a gamble. His plan meant that he would take care of Malone's business, but he was also thinking of a plan to extricate himself from the clutches of Malone.

"Ivan, I'll make you a deal," said Dunn. "I'll take care of the Marshal, but you know that I'll be a wanted man for the rest of my life."

Malone just laughed. "Maybe, but then if no one knows who killed the Marshal, how will you ever get tracked down?"

"You'll know, Malone. And I don't trust you any farther than I could throw you. You'd sell out your best friend, if you had one, just to save your own hide," said Dunn.

Malone chuckled. "That might be," he said. "But I wouldn't sell you out, Beryl, since you are helping me get what I want. I want the Lazy C."

"I still don't trust you, Ivan," replied Dunn. "So, here's what I want. I want a thousand dollars cash up front. Then I'll go hunt down and kill the Marshal. And then, you'll never see me again, because I plan to be long gone after killing the law man."

Malone hesitated before answering. He knew that he had to get the U.S. Marshal out of his business, but now he was faced with losing one of his bodyguards. He was reasonably certain, though, that if Dunn hightailed it, he would keep his mouth shut. And since the Conleys never had much use for banks, he knew that the strong box in the ranch house contained enough cash money to meet Dunn's demand. But he did not want to appear too eager to accept the terms set out by Dunn.

"Now Beryl, a thousand dollars is a pile of money. I'm not so sure that I've got that much cash on hand," said Malone.

"Don't give me that trash, Ivan. You know I've seen you playing around with that cash from the strong box when the Conleys were away from the house," said Dunn. "There's enough money in that box to choke a horse. I figure I need to have half the money up front, and then I'll come back to get the other five hundred after I take care of business."

"All right, all right," replied Malone. "But you better take care of this problem, and you better not even think about weaseling out on me. If I pay you half up front and you decide to make off with the money, I'll come lookin' for you and set things straight. You got that?"

"Sure, Ivan, I got it," said Dunn, all the while smiling to himself and thinking that Malone couldn't track down a buffalo on a wide-open prairie because Malone had lived in the city all his life. There would not be any danger of Malone finding him if he decided to vamoose. Still, thought Dunn, I won't renege on the deal.

Chisholm Trail Hotel
Decatur, Texas

Dunn woke up with a pounding headache. He had stayed up too late the evening before while playing cards and drinking whisky. He stumbled over to the washstand and splashed some water on his face, then got dressed. He then walked to the livery stable, retrieved his horse, and walked back toward the hotel. After hitching his horse to a rack at the rear of the hotel, he was now ready to leave after breakfast.

Last night Dunn had seen a café next door to the hotel, so he came back around the corner to the front of the Chisholm Trail Hotel and made his way to the next-door café for something to eat. He walked in and found an empty table near the back of the room. He looked around the room and was satisfied that there was no one there who knew him, but his eyes rested on a man sitting a few tables away from him. The man was drinking coffee and reading a newspaper. An empty plate in front of the man gave evidence that the man had finished his breakfast. *Lawman,* thought Dunn. While he had no evidence, Dunn prided himself on being able to spot an adversary.

Beryl Dunn's hunch was spot on. Texas Ranger Ben Steele had just finished his breakfast and was casually drinking his third mug of coffee, while scanning a three-day-old Dallas paper. As he turned the page of the newspaper, he furtively glanced around the dining room. For a mere two seconds, his eyes rested on Beryl Dunn. And just like Dunn was able to spot a lawman, Steele could spot an outlaw in the same manner. Steele saw that Dunn wore a gray, flat-topped Stetson, and that he sported an expensive gun rig worn a bit lower than normal. He had the look of a paid gunman.

A waitress came to Dunn's table. "What can I get you, hon?" she asked.

"Need my coffee mug filled," said Dunn. "And gimme a couple scrambled eggs and some fried bread and a chunk of ham."

"Okay," said the waitress. "I'll be right back with your coffee."

In just a few minutes, Dunn's food was delivered to his table. But before the waitress left again, Dunn questioned her in what he thought was a quietly subdued voice.

"Have you got a Marshal here in Decatur by the name of Wolf?" he asked her.

The waitress poured coffee into Dunn's mug. "Yeah, I think so. He's kinda new, so I'm not sure of his name. But it seems I recall Wolf as his name."

"Is his office close by?" asked Dunn.

"Sure, right down the street. No telling if he's there, though," she said. "Seems like he travels a lot." She then looked toward Ben Steele and suddenly remembered that Steele shared the office with the Marshal.

"Say, you might…" She stopped in mid-sentence. She was looking at Steele and could see that he had made a gesture of a finger held up to his mouth, signaling to her that she should not mention him. She looked back down at Dunn's coffee mug.

"What were you saying?" asked Dunn.

"Oh, nothing," said the waitress. "I was just thinking that you might have to wait for the Marshal to get back from one of his trips.

"Mmm," Dunn responded.

Even though Dunn had spoken quietly, Ben Steele had overheard everything that had been said. He had nothing pressing on his schedule for the day and wondered why this stranger might have business with the Marshal. He aimed to find out. *Think I'll hang around this character today and see what he's up to,* thought Ben.

Ben Steele could not help but think that the rest of the day had been a waste of time. The stranger walked up and down the street several times. Each time, he looked in the window of the Marshal's office. Ben was having second thoughts about his surveillance of Dunn. For one thing, it meant that he had to stay out of the office because he did not want to reveal to Dunn that he was a Texas Ranger. Second, he had to find a nice shady spot where he could remain and keep an eye on the stranger. He decided that he would sit at the end of the street in the door of Brown's livery stable. So, he took up a chair next to Leonard

Brown, the blacksmith proprietor, who was having a rest between customers, and for the rest of the day, he watched Dunn, who had taken up a spot on a sidewalk bench outside the Marshal's office. But finally, Dunn decided that he had waited long enough. He rose from his bench and buttonholed the first man that was walking past. Steele observed that he spoke briefly to the man and then walked back to the hotel. Steele quickly rose and walked to catch up with the man who had spoken with Dunn.

"Hey mister," called Steele.

The other man stopped. He knew Steele and spoke to him. "Mornin' Ranger. How in the world are you?"

Steele now recognized the man as somebody he knew and called him by name. "Mornin' Bob. Do you know that man you were talking to a couple minutes ago?"

"You mean the fella that was sitting outside the Marshal's office? Oh, beg pardon, I guess it's your office too."

"Yeah, that's the man. Do you know him?" Steele asked again.

"Nope, never saw him before in my life. He asked me if I knew where the Marshal lived."

Steele now had a good idea what the stranger might be up to. "Did you tell him where Marshal Wolf lived?"

"Sure. You know, it's the old John Summers place. Didn't see any harm in it. Did I do somethin' wrong?"

"I don't know, Bob. Did the fella say why he wanted to see the Marshal?' asked Steele.

"Nope, nope, he didn't."

Steele unconsciously scratched at his cheek. "Hmm," he grunted. "Well, anyway, Bob, thanks for the information," said Steele, and he walked away.

Bob scratched his head and then continued walking down the sidewalk.

Ben Steele quickly walked back to the livery stable and asked Leonard Brown to saddle his horse, and Steele again sat in the chair just outside the livery stable door. He waited for Dunn to come out of the hotel. An hour passed, and Steele rose and walked over to the hotel. He saw no one in the hotel lobby except the desk clerk. He walked over to speak to the clerk.

"Have you got a fella staying here that wears a fancy gun rig and a flat top gray hat?"

"Sure, Mr. Steele. That gent stayed with us last night," answered the clerk.

"What's his name?" asked Steele.

The clerk looked down and turned a page in the register. "His name's Smith, Arnold Smith."

"Smith, huh," said Steele. "Ten to one that's not his real name. What room is he in?"

"Well, Ben. He ain't in any room," said the clerk. "He checked out over an hour ago."

"Dammit," replied Steele, and he rushed out through the door of the hotel. He sprinted down the street to the livery, checked to see that his rifle was in its scabbard, and swung up into the saddle. He turned his horse and loped out of town to head northwest to the Wolf ranch.

Afternoon
The Wolf Ranch

Claire May's painting project had seemed to take on a life of its own. She had finished giving a coat of paint to the chairs from the cabin and had now begun working on the small tables. With Pablo Carillo's help, she had dragged the tables out to the back yard next to the covered porch. Her gold blonde hair was tied at her nape, and she wore a bandana as a hair scarf. A paint-spotted apron covered her blouse and skirt. Her bronzed arms continued to pull the paint brush across the surface of the table that she was completing. Claire May had just fed Bobby, so he was contentedly babbling in his basket on the porch. Claire May was tired, and sweat beads had formed at her temples. She had been painting since morning, so perhaps it was because she was tired that she was not paying attention to the excited barking of Sparky, the ranch dog that came with the ranch when she and Nathan had moved there. The barks became more frenzied to the point that Claire May now took heed of the noise. She stopped her painting, and just as she laid down her paint brush, the stranger on horseback came around the corner of the cabin. Sparky continued to bark, but he soon stopped while still regarding the stranger.

Claire May was instantly on alert. As a general rule, strangers did not come onto another person's property without hollering out their approach. She looked at the man, taking in his rough facial hair, the flat gray hat, and the sidearm the man was wearing. She did not like the looks of this stranger.

Beryl Dunn slowly dismounted and waited while Sparky came to him and gave Dunn's boots the once over with his nose. Dunn reached down and patted the dog's head. It was apparent to him now that the dog was not aggressive. He walked slowly toward Claire May, and touched his fingers to his hat brim, but he did not remove his hat. Dunn wore several days of beard growth on his face, his clothes were dirty, and his boots showed considerable wear. Dried and crusted mud gave a dirty border to the boot soles. The man wore a gun belt low on his hip with a tie-down on the bottom of the pistol's holster. As he neared Claire May, she could smell the rank odor emanating from Dunn.

"Afternoon, ma'am," said Dunn.

Claire May gave no response. She was now certain just by the stranger's looks that he was not a friend, nor a rancher, and probably not an acquaintance of Nathan's. This stranger would have to be watched closely.

Dunn looked over to the porch. "Is that your little baby there?" he asked. Dunn pointed with a crusty, filthy finger to Bobby's basket on the porch. He made a false smile cross his face, revealing his stained and yellow teeth. One of the front teeth was black with rotting decay.

In that instant, Claire May's instincts kicked in. She was now alarmingly convinced that this was a man who intended harm to her or Bobby. She would be on guard to every move the stranger made. Her heart was pounding, and she was trying to keep her fear at bay and make no outward appearance of alarm. As she further studied the stranger, her fear grew to the point that she was now on the verge of hysteria, but she was still able to reveal no outward sign of her fear.

"What do you want, mister?" asked Claire May, her voice nearly cracking.

"Just bein' friendly, ma'am. Are you Mrs. Wolf?"

"I'm Mrs. Wolf. Now what do you want?" Claire May repeated.

"I'm lookin' for your husband, the Marshal. Is he around?" asked Dunn.

Claire May was now stuck in a difficult situation. Out of fear for herself and Bobby, she did not want to reveal that Nathan was not at home. Yet, there was no point in trying to lead the stranger on by saying that her husband was home, when it would quite quickly be proven to be a lie.

"The Marshal is not at home right now," said Claire May. "I expect him at any moment, though. He usually comes home at about this time. Tell me your name, and I'll tell the Marshal you want to see him." In truth, Claire May did not have any idea when to expect Nathan, as he sometimes stayed on the trail for several days. Beryl Dunn did not answer her with his name and continued staring at her.

"My name isn't important, missy," said Dunn, sneering at her.

"Now, if you will excuse me," said Claire May, "I need to continue with my painting, but I will tell the Marshal you were here." She reached over and picked up her paint brush and put it in the paint to fill the brush.

Oh God, she thought. *Let him get home quickly.*

Dunn cleared his throat and spat to his side. He then quickly took a step toward and grabbed Claire May by the shoulders. "Now if the Marshal isn't here, well, why don't you and me have ourselves a little fun," said Dunn, and he leaned his face into hers. The odor was overpowering, and Claire May was immediately disgusted by Dunn's rancid breath and discolored teeth. She struggled and managed to wrench her arm free, and she quickly used that hand to slap her full paint brush into the eyes of Dunn. Dunn dropped his grip on Claire May and stepped back, wiping the paint from his eyes with the backs of his hands and his shirt sleeves.

"You little bitch, you're going to pay for that," said Dunn as he spat paint out of his mouth. He then grabbed Claire May again. This time his hands were on her upper arms, and his grimy fingers clawed painfully into her arms. Claire May did her best to endure the pain. Dunn then moved a hand to the front of Claire May and ripped downward. His effort tore Claire May's apron and blouse away from one shoulder. "Now, we'll see who likes to play rough," said Dunn, his mouth in a sneer that revealed his dirty and rotting teeth.

But as he leaned toward Claire May again, she managed to wrench her arms free, and she swung a fist upward from her waist and connected solidly to Dunn's jaw which snapped shut causing him to bite his tongue. He then released his grip on Claire May and took two steps backward. He used his shirt sleeve to wipe again at the paint around his eyes and nose.

"Well, Mrs. Wolf, if your old man ain't here, I can't kill him. But I can take second prize. You'll have to do," said Dunn as he drew his pistol from its holster. "And after I'm through with you, that little kid of yours is going to follow you." Dunn raised his pistol, slowly took aim, and the quiet of the Wolf Ranch was shattered by the explosion of gunfire.

Minutes Later

Ben Steele was urging his horse to maintain a fast lope, but the horse was nearly played out from the ride from town to the Wolf Ranch. The animal was still making the effort to continue but was near to the point that it would not go much further. Ben figured that they were only a quarter mile or so from the ranch. The sun was nearing the end of its westward path, but dusk would still be another hour or more. But then he heard gunfire. It was a single shot, and Ben knew that it had come from the Wolf Ranch. *Oh God, don't let me be too late,* thought Ben. He stopped his horse just as he was turning into the lane to the Wolf cabin. He pulled his revolver, checked the loads, replaced the pistol, and checked his rifle. He kept the long gun in his hands as he urged his horse to walk the lane to the cabin. When he reached the cabin, he dismounted. Climbing the front porch steps, he peered into the windows of the dimly lit cabin. He saw no one. He slowly moved to the side of the cabin, keeping his rifle at the ready. As he grew closer to the rear of the cabin, he could hear someone talking, a man and a woman's voices. Interspersed with their voices, he could hear a child crying.

Sparky now heard the clicking noise as Ben Steele chambered a shell into the breech of the rifle. The dog began barking and moved cautiously to the corner of the cabin. Ben knew now that he had been detected. He came quickly around the corner to the back of the cabin where he saw a man holding a rifle. Almost immediately, he recognized Claire May standing next to the man, but he was not sure of the identity of the holder of the rifle.

"Drop the gun, mister," Ben called out loudly.

Claire May turned and recognized Ben Steele and shouted to him, "It's all right, Ben. This is our hired man, Pablo."

Just to be safe, Pablo Carillo dropped the rifle he had been cradling in his arm. Ben took four steps toward Claire May, but nearly tripped over the body lying near Claire May's feet.

Ben looked down at the body and then looked at Claire May, who was doing her best to hold up the front of her blouse with a free hand and hold Bobby in her other arm. He then looked around the back yard and asked, "Where is Nathan, Claire May?"

A tear then trickled down Claire May's cheek. She struggled to wipe it from her cheek while maintaining her hold on her dress. "He's not home, Ben. I – I'm not sure when he will be home."

Ben looked down at the body of Beryl Dunn. "Do you know this turkey?" he asked Claire May.

"I've never seen him before. He came here to kill Nathan," she said, and then the tears began to flow.

Ben did not know Claire May well enough to physically comfort her, so he set his rifle on the ground and reached to take Bobby. "Why don't you go in the house and fix yourself up a bit, and then come back and tell me all about what happened. I'll hang on to Bobby for a minute."

Claire May placed Bobby in Ben's waiting hands, went up the steps, and disappeared into the cabin. Ben turned to Pablo. "What the hell happened here?"

"That fellow on the ground attacked Mrs. Wolf." Pablo was pointing to the inert body of Beryl Dunn. "He was ready to kill her, and I could not let that happen," said Pablo. "So, I shot him."

Bobby began squirming in Ben's arms. It was evident that he did not like being held by a stranger. He began to whimper and wiggle even more before Pablo took the toddler from Ben. Bobby knew Pablo and settled down, but he still looked around for his mother. But it was only another minute before Claire May emerged from the Cabin. Repairs to her clothing were made with the help of a trio of metal safety pins. She took the wriggling toddler from Pablo and sat down on the edge of the porch with her feet dangling toward the ground.

Ben came and sat down on the steps near her. He did not say anything, he knew that she would tell him the story in her own good time. And she did, the words spilling from her as she described the horrific incident. She shuddered several times as she told the story. At last, she stopped. She was talked out.

"He told me he was going to kill me, Ben. And then he said he would kill Bobby when he was through with me," she said. "I was sure I was going to die, and my child would be killed." She began to sob. She hugged tightly to Bobby until she stopped crying. With a free hand, she lifted the hem of her apron and wiped her eyes and nose. "All right, it's over," said Claire May. She rose from the porch, walked down the steps, walked to Pablo's side, and kissed him on the cheek. Ben joined them.

"Thank you, Pablo. I owe you my life," said Claire May, and she kissed him again.

Ben spoke up then, "Pablo, do you have a buckboard?" Pablo said that it was in the barn. "Help me get this body down to the barn and loaded in the buckboard. One of us will need to take it into town to the undertaker," said Ben. The two men carried Dunn's body to the barn and returned a couple moments later. Pablo retrieved his rifle and cradled it in the crook of his arm.

Claire May was waiting for them. "Let's sit up on the porch, and I'll go in the house and get us something to drink. They moved up onto the porch, where she put Bobby in his basket and placed it at Pablo's feet.

In a short time, Claire May returned to the porch. She had changed her dress and was carrying a tray with three glasses and a squat bottle with a cork stopper. Setting the tray on a table, she poured three fingers of the clear liquid from the bottle into the glasses. "I warn you, Ben, just sip this very slowly," said Claire May. When she took her seat on a chair between the two men, she raised her glass and turned to Pablo. "To Pablo. He saved my life and the life of Bobby. And here's to friends, may we have many."

"To Pablo," Ben echoed.

The three of them clinked their glasses. "Remember, Ben, very small sips."

They each took a sip of the liquor. "Yikes," said Ben. "You weren't kidding. What is this stuff?"

Claire May and Pablo laughed. "Tequila, Ben. It's homemade. Pablo gets it from one of his friends," said Claire May. "It's pretty powerful, so we don't do seconds on it."

They became quiet as dusk turned into early darkness. They were lost in their thoughts, remembering the terror caused by an unhinged outlaw. The long shot of tequila had calmed their nerves, and they began reveling in the quietness of early evening. The only sounds were the tree frogs, crickets, and an owl that sat in an oak tree in a distant grove.

That Same Evening

Nathan sat up and groggily rubbed his eyes. The monotonous rhythm of the clacking train wheels crossing the rail joints had put him to sleep a few hours ago, but it had helped that the conductor had let him stretch out on a settee in the smoking/bar car, as there were few passengers on the evening train moving south to Decatur, and he would not be disturbing anyone with his nap. As he sat and slowly woke up, the conductor came through the car.

"Just a few more minutes to Decatur, Marshal," the train man said.

"Thanks. Guess I'll go check on my horse," said Nathan.

Wander turned his head as Nathan entered the livestock and baggage car. Nathan went to the horse's stall and stroked the gelding's nose. "Hope you had a nap, boy. We'll be on the trail in just a bit."

Screeching brakes signaled the train's arrival in Decatur. Nathan climbed down from the train car as the train came to a halt with a subsequent blast of excess steam from the locomotive. He walked to the side of the livestock and baggage car and unlatched the hasps on the car's side ramp and let the wooden slab door down to the ground. In a few more minutes, Nathan sat astride Wander, and he waved at the conductor as the man was refastening the hasps on the side ramp of the livestock and baggage car. The conductor returned the wave. Nathan turned Wander and headed off into the night. Twenty minutes later, Wander trotted up the lane and started to the barn where Nathan would unsaddle, brush down, and feed the horse. But he was stopped by the barking of Sparky, and then he saw Claire May running to him and Ben Steele and Pablo standing on the back porch. He dismounted and opened his arms as his wife came crashing into him.

"Whoa, girl," said Nathan as he laughed and hugged his wife. After kissing her, he noticed that she was shivering. "Are you cold?" he asked.

Claire May snuffed her nose. "No, I'm not cold. I've just missed you so much." She laid her head on his chest.

Pablo had come to join them. "Let me take Wander, Mr. Nathan."

"Okay, sure," said Nathan, and he handed the reins of the horse to Pablo. Pablo turned and led Wander toward the barn. Nathan turned to Claire May. "Did you get along all right while I was gone?"

She replied in almost a whisper. "No."

"Uh, oh," he said. "What happened? Seeing Ben, here, makes me think it was something big."

Claire May did not answer his question. Instead, she stepped back, and went to the porch and picked up Bobby.

"Well, aren't you going to tell me what happened?" Nathan asked.

She came back to him, and with her free hand, she took him by the hand and began walking to the barn. Ben Steele followed them.

Pablo was working in the barn. Lanterns cast shadows on the interior walls. Pablo was brushing down Wander when the trio entered. The buckboard rested in one corner. Claire May walked to the buckboard and stood at one side of the wagon.

"This is what happened," she said. "You and Ben can talk about this while I go up to the house and make us some sandwiches." But before she turned to go, she leaned over the side of the buckboard and spat in the face of the body of Beryl Dunn. And then, she did it again. She turned and walked out of the barn.

"Sweet Jesus!" said Nathan. "I've never seen Claire May like this. What the hell happened here?"

Ben stood by Nathan as they looked into the buckboard. Pablo brought over a lantern and stood by their sides. "Do you know this jackass?" Ben asked.

Nathan glanced at the body once more. He already knew who it was. "Yeah, I know him. He's one of Ivan Malone's gunhands. His name is Beryl Dunn. But what the hell is his body doing here in our barn?"

"Well," said Ben, "It appears that he's dead." Ben turned his head and smiled at Nathan.

"Ben, it's not a time for jokes. What happened here?"

"Your friend, Mr. Dunn came here to kill you," answered Ben.

"What?" cried Nathan. "What are you talking about?"

"Like I said, from what this buzzard told Claire May, he came here to kill you. But since you weren't home, he decided he would kill Claire May and Bobby instead. That is, until Pablo here, put an end to that plan. One shot from Pablo's rifle put an end to Mr. Dunn. Got him smack dab in the pumper, quite a shot."

"You shot him, Pablo?" asked Nathan.

"Yes, sir. He was hurting Mrs. Wolf and tore her dress. He said he was going to kill her and Bobby," said Pablo. "I couldn't let that happen. Did I do the right thing, Mr. Nathan?"

"You're damn right you did the right thing, Pablo. Did he hurt Claire May?" Nathan asked. He put an arm on Pablo's shoulder and shook his hand.

Ben spoke up, "I don't think she was hurt other than a bruise or two. But I think she had her pride hurt, thinking that it was her fault that this happened."

Nathan stood staring at the body of Beryl Dunn. Finally, he spoke. "That goddam Ivan Malone. He's behind this. He wants me out of the way and sent his gunman to make sure I don't get to the bottom of his operation."

"Well, that about sums it up," said Ben.

"You know," said Nathan. "I've met several people that want that Malone character dead. Well, I just joined the list. I'm going to kill him."

"Whoa, partner. You can't do that. You're a lawman," said Ben. "You can't take the law in your own hands. That silver badge you wear says you will do things according to the law."

Slowly, Nathan reached inside his vest and unpinned his badge. He held it in his hand momentarily, then tossed it onto the dirt floor of the barn. "You heard me, Ben. I'm gonna kill Malone." Nathan turned slightly. "Now, I'm going up to talk with my wife."

After he had left the barn, Ben picked the Marshal's badge off of the dirt floor, shined it a bit on his pants, and put it in his vest pocket. As he left the barn, he could see that Pablo was hitching the team to the buckboard. Even though darkness had fallen, he would soon take Beryl Dunn's body to the undertaker in town, even if it meant that he had to wake up the undertaker. Pablo had emptied Dunn's pockets and set his pistol and gunbelt aside in the barn.

Just as Ben was about to leave, Pablo called out to him. "Mr. Ben, wait. I need to show you something."

Ben came back into the barn and walked to where Pablo was standing. He looked down at the gunbelt, pistol, and a wad of money, all which Pablo had removed from the body of Beryl Dunn. "What should I do with these things, Mr. Ben?" asked Pablo.

Ben picked up the pistol. It was a standard 1895 Colt double action revolver. "Pablo, the pistol and gun belt are yours. Neither Nathan nor I have a need for it. Keep it or sell it, it doesn't matter."

Ben looked at the wad of paper currency. "My God, there's over five hundred dollars here. Well, that tells me that this Dunn character was getting paid to kill the Marshal. Hmm. Pablo, I figure you need to keep two hundred dollars of this money. Consider that a reward for taking care of this outlaw and saving Claire May's life. The rest of the money will go to a couple families that I know that are desperately trying to pay their bills. And Nathan and I will use a hundred dollars of this money to make some repairs on the office we share in town."

Ben peeled off two hundred dollars and handed it to Pablo. Pablo seemed stunned as he looked down at the money in his hand. "Thank you, Mr. Ben. I will use the money to help some of my family."

Ben asked, "Family, huh. Are you married Pablo?"

"No sir," Pablo answered. "But I have brothers and sisters. My wife died many years ago. One of my sisters needs help, and I can help her with this money. She and her children are my closest relatives. They live in San Antonio. But I also have a cousin who lives in town. She is raising two little ones by herself. She can use some help, too."

"I'm sure they will appreciate it, Pablo." He clapped a hand on Pablo's shoulder. "I better get on up to the house," said Ben. He turned and walked out of the barn and made his way to the cabin where he joined Nathan and Claire May. As he came through the door, he could see that Nathan and Claire May were locked in an embrace.

Quietly, Claire May spoke to Nathan. "You can't do that, Nathan. That would be the same as murder, and you would probably go to jail. Where would that leave me and Bobby?" It was obvious that Nathan had told Claire May his plan to kill Ivan Malone.

Nathan did not respond to her. Even now, in the arms of his wife, his temper was beginning to cool down. But Claire May's question had made perfect sense to him. It forced him to think, *if he was convicted of killing Malone, what would happen to Claire May and Bobby?* The answer to that thought caused him to shudder. As much as he would like to put a bullet in Malone's head, the consequences of that action could have disastrous results for his family. Reluctantly, he simply could not let that happen. "I'm just so damn mad that someone could come to our home and do that to you. If it hadn't been for Pablo, you would have been killed along with Bobby."

"Look at me, sweetheart," said Claire May. "I'm not dead, and Bobby and I are perfectly fine. Yes, we had a scare, but everything came out okay. So, I want you to get the idea of killing Malone out of your head. Will you do that for me?"

Nathan released his hold on his wife and looked down at the floor. He would do anything for Claire May, and he could never say no to her. At last, he looked at her again. "All right, I'll track him down and see him hang."

Claire May grabbed and held Nathan again and kissed him. He returned the hug and kiss, after which Claire May was smiling.

Ben approached them, held out his hand, and said to Nathan, "I think you dropped something out at the barn. You need to be more careful with this thing," and he handed Nathan's badge back to him. "You got a bottle of bourbon handy?" asked Ben. Nathan could not help it, he looked at Steele and smiled.

Claire May poured them each a three-finger glass of bourbon, and they went to sit on the back porch. In a few moments, Pablo drove the buckboard from the barn and stopped as he came by the porch. "I should be back in a couple hours," said Pablo.

"Tell the undertaker to plant him deep," said Nathan. "We never want to see that snake again."

Pablo laughed. "Okay, Mr. Nathan. I'll tell him." He clucked to the team, and the wagon continued around the cabin and out to the road.

There was not much conversation among the three of them. They each seemed to be reliving the events of the evening in their heads. Ben told Nathan and Claire May about the money that Pablo had found on Beryl Dunn.

"Only one reason Dunn would have that much money in his pocket. He was getting paid to kill you, Nathan. And since he works for Ivan

Malone, it seems reasonable to presume that Malone is the person who paid him."

"And you two keep telling me that I shouldn't kill Malone," said Nathan as he turned his head from side to side. "I sure do want to see that varmint swing on a gallows."

"I don't think we have any problem with that," said Claire May.

Ben then told Nathan and Claire May what he was going to do with the money that Dunn had been carrying. He told them that he had given Pablo part of the money as a form of reward for his part in getting rid of Dunn, and he told them what he was going to do with the remainder.

"That's great," said Nathan. "Maybe we can buy a filing cabinet, so you stop rooting through my desk drawers."

Ben laughed. "Believe me, I have no intention of rooting through your drawers."

They all laughed at Ben's crude humor.

As it was getting late, Ben finally asked, "If it's okay with you, Nathan, I think I'll bunk down in the barn with Pablo tonight. I don't feel much like making the ride to town this late."

"Help yourself," Nathan replied.

"Well then, I'll go on down and get my horse bedded down. I may not see you in the morning, 'cause I want to hit the road early." Ben led his horse, walked away, and entered the barn.

"I'm glad he was here tonight," said Claire May.

"Yeah, me too. He's not such a bad fella once you get to know him," said Nathan. "Even though he is a Ranger."

They both chuckled.

"I'm going to bed," said Nathan. Claire May answered, "I'd better feed Bobby again and then I'll join you."

Chapter Thirteen

The Following Morning

Ben Steele had risen early, saddled up, and ridden to town. Nathan and Claire May were on the back porch enjoying a second mug of coffee. Pablo had come up from the barn to join them. The three adults watched Bobby as he sat chewing his fingers on Claire May's lap, his blue eyes taking in his surroundings. With a full tummy, he was perfectly content with listening to the sound of the birds and the talk of the adults, while gurgling his own small sounds. The sun was above the horizon, cardinals and blue jays kept up a steady chorus of challenges to each other, and the black crossbreds, which were kept separated from the smaller purebred Hereford herd, could be seen grazing near the tank. The blackface bull kept to himself, grazing apart from the steers and heifers; he was not interested in the heifers until they came into season. It was an idyllic country setting.

Claire May gave no indication of the fright that she had been subjected to the previous day. She was strong. A ranch-raised girl has to be strong. Nathan gazed at her and smiled, knowing that there was an inner strength and drive harbored within his beautiful wife. Her hair was tied back with a colorful ribbon holding the hair at the nape of her neck. She wore a clean apron over her dress, but Bobby had already seen to it that it would need to be washed again soon. With her husband and son at her side, she was as content as she could be and had placed last evening's events away in her least recalled memories. The life on her new ranch would go on.

Pablo broke the silence, "There are about eight steers that are ready for market, Mr. Nathan. Should I go ahead and arrange to get them picked up for the sale barn in town?" asked Pablo.

"Sure, go ahead," said Nathan. "We could use the cash right now to pay off some bills, and I want you to have the money from two of those steers."

"I don't need that money, Mr. Nathan."

"After what you did for our little family last night, you deserve even more," said Nathan. "So, you take a fourth of the money from the sale of the steers for yourself. No argument, please."

Pablo shrugged his shoulders, smiled, and stepped off of the porch to head back to the barn.

Nathan turned to Claire May. "I'd better hit the trail to town. I've been out of the office for several days. I want to talk with Ben Steele about my meetings up at Fort Sill."

"Will you be home tonight?" asked Claire May.

"I hope so, sweetheart."

Nathan rose from his chair and walked back into the cabin, followed by Claire May who was holding Bobby. Nathan used the toilet, then gathered up his pistol belt and rifle. He kissed Claire May and walked to the barn to get Wander. In twenty minutes, he was on the trail to town. After another fifteen minutes, he left Wander at Brown's Livery Stable where he could be fed and held in the corral until Nathan came for him in the afternoon.

Nathan left the livery stable and began walking toward the low, one-story stucco building that served as his office. Nathan thought back to the months prior when he and Claire May and her brother Will had come to Decatur to see the town where their ranch was located. They had walked around the town square, and they had seen the squat, low building with the barred windows, but they had not entered the building at that time. It had needed freshening up, as the color had almost all faded from the stucco. A sad, painted sign was mounted at the top of the flat-roofed building. It read, *U.S. Marshal* with a line below that reading *Wise County Jail*. After their move, Nathan had hired several of Pablo's friends to come to the small building to restore the stucco, paint the interior of the building, and repaint the sorry-looking sign over the front entrance. They had also repaired the furniture inside the building and built a second desk from scrap lumber they found behind the building. Nathan had requested that second desk because he was quite certain that he would need to share the office with a deputy, if he hired one, or the Texas Ranger, Ben Steele who lived in the area. The work crew had done a great job, and the little building now seemed to glow in the sunshine as Nathan drew near to it.

He was not surprised when he saw Ben Steele's horse tied to the hitch rack in front of the office. Nathan had concluded that since the Rangers would not pay for an office for their local Ranger, Steele had seen fit to hang out at the marshal's office in between bouts of Texas Ranger business. Some of Dunn's ill-gotten money would go to improving the office and jail for the two lawmen.

"Mornin', Marshal," said Ben Steele as Nathan entered the office. "Coffee's on the stove."

"Mornin', Steele. How's the Ranger world treating you?" asked Nathan, as he poured himself a mug of the steaming brew.

"Can't complain," answered Steele.

Ben was cautious as he asked the question. "I felt real bad about Claire May. How's she holdin' up?"

"Probably better than me," Nathan answered. "She's pretty tough and seems to be able to put the scare behind her. I don't like to think what might have happened if Pablo hadn't been there."

Ben nodded his head. "Hmm." He paused, then casually asked another question for which he was anxious to have an answer, "How'd you make out up at Fort Sill after I left? Not that I really care, you understand. Just curious."

Nathan knew that Ben Steele would not have asked the question in the manner that he did if he wasn't very curious. A case of alleged missing horses had now turned the corner to become the murder of Iron Arrow and Michael Conley and the attempted murder of Sean Conley. So, for the next 20 minutes, Nathan briefed Ben Steele on all of the details of his meeting with Black Horse, the death of Black Horse's brother, Iron Arrow, the murder of Michael Conley, and the discovery of Sean Conley in the home of Black Horse. He also briefed Steele on his additional talks with Indian Agent Jeff Keller. He also told Ben that Sean Conley had promised to come to Decatur as soon as he was physically able, in order to brief him on the details of his father's murder and nearly losing his life at the hands of Ivan Malone and his gunmen.

When Nathan was through, Ben said, "You know, that Malone fella has only been around the Lazy C for a short time, and already he's buried in a mountain of cow patties. We need to corral that hombre, but we need to think on what's the best way to do it, so we don't get ourselves killed in the process."

"All right, so I think we need to get our heads together and figure out the charges that we can prove. Then, I think it's about time we go pay Mr. Malone another visit and bring him in to face a judge," said Nathan. "Even though you know I'd just as soon save the taxpayers the price of a trial."

Ben chuckled. "But your pretty wife said you need to be a good boy and get that notion out of your head." He laughed again. Nathan did not. He just glared at Ben.

"Oh, and by the way, what is this 'we' stuff?" asked Ben. "I thought this was your case."

"Well, it is," Nathan replied. "But have you seen the size of Malone? He's bigger than a horse. And Lord knows how many more gunmen he might have on the payroll. So, I'll ask nice, would you like to tag along on this one, just to cover my back?"

"Yep, thought you'd never ask," Ben replied.

So, for the next couple of hours, the two lawmen hashed and rehashed their charges and the best way to go after Malone. When they thought that they had made up a feasible plan, they just needed to decide when they would carry out their business of arresting Malone. They would first need to obtain an arrest warrant signed by the local judge. But it would not be today. Nathan's stomach was talking to him.

"I'm hungry, Ben. Let's go get some dinner," said Nathan. "You've lived here for a while. What's a good place for real food?"

"Got just the place," said Ben. "You ain't gonna' believe this place, but a guy I know has a hole in the wall joint that's near to falling down. But he's got a real oak wood fire going behind the place, and he cooks up the best damn steak you've ever had."

"What are we waiting for," said Nathan.

The two men left the office. "We've got a little walk. The *Second Chance* is a ways down the street," said Ben. With Ben leading the way, the two men walked briskly down the board sidewalk until it ended. They continued down the road toward their destination.

Chapter Fourteen

At the Edge of Town

Calvin Kahl was dozing in the saddle. For fifteen days, he had been traveling and talking to strangers along the way, and he was dog tired. But sleep was a premium that was often elusive. He had the money to sleep in hotels along his route, but he chose to save his money. Thus, he was rough sleeping every night and living on short rations. His body ached from sleeping on the hard ground, and he lightly dozed, being mindful not to fall from his horse. His travels had a purpose. He was searching for his father, Wilburn (Will) Kahl. Calvin was following the same route his father had taken on his way to Colorado to try his hand at gold prospecting. It was not hard to follow his father's footsteps, as Will had shown his son the maps he had purchased and from those, the route he would take to Colorado. But because his father was not drawing attention to himself as he traveled, it was sometimes difficult to find people who had seen a man riding a horse and leading a burro laden with prospecting supplies. Yet, through perseverance, Calvin had spoken to people along the trail who remembered his father, and sure enough, Will had taken the trail that he had previously shown to Calvin.

He swayed in the saddle as his horse plodded along the trail. The rhythmic cadence lulled Calvin, and his mind rambled as it brought memories to Calvin's thoughts. Those memories included the day that his father had left their home in Lafayette, Louisiana. Calvin had stood with his mother on the back porch of the apartment house where they had lived. The memory was more bitter than sweet, watching his father smiling and waving as he departed for Colorado. But the bigger shock in his life turned out to be the death of his mother. Matty Kahl never did tell Calvin about the cancer that was growing within her. Along with her illness, Matty's heart had broken when Will had left home, and she had died only a few days after Will had gone. Her death had left Calvin on his own. Calvin had been shocked to learn from his mother's doctor that Hatty had died of cancer, a condition that his mother had never revealed.

With no other family, Calvin decided to pursue the whereabouts of his father. He gave notice at work and told the landlord, who insisted that Calvin would need to clean the apartment and rid it of his parent's possessions, a task that Calvin had reluctantly completed. But in the throes of that cleaning, he had discovered a cigar box hidden under his parent's bed. Inside the box he found an insurance policy taken out on his mother's life. There was an identical policy on his father, and in both policies, Calvin was listed as the beneficiary. Therefore, with this windfall from his mother's death, Calvin had the funds to purchase a horse and other items needed for his trip. Calvin could have remained in Lafayette to work at the tanning factory, but with no other family in the area, he decided that he would strike out on his own and find his father. It was a daunting task for a young man who had only days before reached his eighteenth year, but one that exhilarated the young man every time he thought of setting out on his own.

The horse had stopped. They had reached a fork in the road, and the horse wisely paused. This brought Calvin from his shallow sleep. He looked up to see buildings in the vista along with a hand-carved road sign that pointed to the path of one of the roads that would lead into Decatur, Texas. The other road turned north to Alvord. Several miles back, after conversations with strangers who had small businesses along the road, Calvin had confirmed that his father had been riding in this direction. He meant to go into Decatur and ask about the whereabouts of his father, and to see if anyone had seen him. He turned the horse's head and gave the animal a nudge in his ribs. They were headed to Decatur.

When he reached the Decatur town square, he dismounted, stretched his whole body, and began the tedious task of going into businesses, the livery stable, and asking strangers if they might remember seeing a man riding a horse and leading a burro pass through town some weeks ago. After hearing the same answer to his questions, he passed an office window and did a quick turnaround. *Marshal's office* thought Calvin. *It's worth a try.* But when he stuck his head in the door and called out for the Marshal, there was no answer.

Next door to the Marshal's office, a man was sweeping dirt from his shop onto the sidewalk, then pushing it into the street. He turned to look at Calvin. "Who you lookin' for, kid, the Marshal or the Ranger?"

Calvin was taken aback. "Well, I guess the Marshal."

"He ain't here. Him and the Ranger went to dinner. Looked like they were headed down to the *Second Chance Saloon*," the man said.

"Oh," said Calvin. "Can you tell me where that is? I'll try to find him."

"About four blocks down the road here, and then go past where the sidewalk ends and pretty soon, you'll see it on the right. You can't miss that old shack. *Second Chance Saloon,* it's called." The man pointed with his broom in the direction to follow.

"Much obliged, Mister," said Calvin, and he began walking in the indicated direction.

That Same Morning
Second Chance Saloon
Wise County, Texas

The warm Texas sun was near to reaching its noontime zenith and had begun sending its yellow and orange rays through the oak treetops on the wood shingled roof of the run-down clapboard building that sat at the edge of town. The sorry-looking building had been hastily constructed some twenty years back by whomever had owned the property at the time. The building's condition was evidence that little had been done to the establishment over time. Rather than fall down on its own, hastily made repairs had kept it standing for the past few years.

The old street-front property still served the original purpose for which it had been built. It was a seedy bar that served low-quality liquor and beer to low-standard, down-on-their-luck men. Few women would ever dream of crossing the dirt threshold of such an establishment. That is, of course, unless they were willing participants in the alternate thirst of the establishment's male patrons. In addition to the mainstay alcohol choices available to its patrons, the *Second Chance Saloon* also served up chuck wagon style food to its dinner time visitors. An open oak or mesquite fire that glowed under an open grill was the means to grill steaks and bake potatoes. Patrons said to their friends that once you had a steak char-grilled at the Saloon, that you would return another day for a second helping.

The noon-time sunlight attempted to push its way through the two, grime-darkened windows occupying space on each side of the worn front door that hung slightly askew at the front of the building. Those same dirty tobacco-tarred windows allowed filtered light to enter the dingy bar area. Cast-off tables and chairs that had seen better times occupied space on the hard-packed dirt floor. To one side of the room, a larger round table and chairs served as a cigarette-burned and stained gathering place for those patrons anxious to lose any spare change in a shady game of cards only loosely observed by the bar's owner.

A wood-planked bar with a metal pipe foot rail stretched nearly the width of the back wall. A few of the bar-top boards still had printing and drawings on them signifying that they had been part of shipping cases before being disassembled to make splinter-coated planks for the bar top. A small assortment of bottles with imaginative labels sat beckoning the boozers as they stood at the bar nursing their strong drinks. While the bottles might be adorned with colorful labels, only the bar owners knew how many times those bottles had been refilled from cheap moonshine liquor jugs that were kept out of sight in a back storage room. Not one patron had ever thought to ask why none of the labeled bottles ever disappeared or why they were never replaced by new bottles. It made little difference to the hard-core drinkers who were dependent on the taste of alcohol even though a booze bottle seemed to stay forever on the shelf. They only cared that there was some form of alcohol in the bottles and in their glasses.

On a second shelf just below the liquor bottles, a row of assorted well-worn glasses rested upside down on their rims in readiness for serving the afternoon and evening patrons. To the side of that shelf, a crudely made wooden rack held a keg of beer. Unlike the liquor bottles on display, the keg contained a legitimately crafted beer, kegs of which were purchased periodically from nearby German farmers whose side business was producing and fermenting old world, tried and true recipe beers and then providing kegs of refreshing ale to drinking establishments in the area.

This sorry excuse for a drinking establishment had only recently been purchased by Ross Simmons and his partner, Jack (Wobbly) Wilkins, the same two ex-cowboys who had discovered the frail body of Sylvia Conley in a hastily dug, shallow grave at the Lazy C Ranch while they were at work mending fences. That gruesome discovery could only mean one thing. Ivan Malone and his cohorts had murdered Sylvia Conley, and Ross and Wobbly had discovered Sylvia's remains. In addition, they had witnessed the murder of a passing prospector at the hands of Ivan Malone. They also knew that telling anyone about either event would ensure their deaths at the hands of Malone and his gunmen. As a result, the two men had sworn each other to secrecy. They knew that if they uttered one word about Sylvia Conley's death at the hands of Ivan Malone they would not live. True to their word, they had told no one about their discovery. The way they figured it, they had moved far enough away from the Lazy C Ranch that Ivan Malone and his gunslinger henchmen would not come looking for them if they kept their mouths shut. With the working conditions at the Lazy C becoming intolerable due to the treatment of the ranch hands by Ivan Malone, Ross Simmons had planned to leave the Lazy C as soon as he could. Discovering the body of Sylvia Conley moved his departure date to the forefront.

Two days after finding the body of Sylvia Conley, Ross and Jack had planned to leave the ranch during the night. But as they were saddling their horses to ride away from the Lazy C, Ivan Malone saw them in the corral as he was returning from the back outhouse. Malone was dressed in a night shirt and carried no weapon, but he confronted the two cowhands at the corral.

"Just where the hell do you two think you're going?" asked Ivan Malone when the two cowboys told him they were leaving.

In his best attempt at bravado, Ross had replied. "Not sure yet, but we figure we might head on out to Colorado," he had said. "Might like to see some of them mountains, and we heard that there might be some gold to be dug up out there." Ross and Jack had no intention of going to Colorado, but they sure did not want Malone to get any idea that he might be able to track them down if it ever came to that.

The look that Ivan Malone gave the two cowboys could have melted an iceberg. He had already had two other men leave the ranch, and now, here were two more ranch hands telling him they were leaving. If this kept up, he would not have anybody left to carry out the real work of running the Lazy C. Malone did not like it, and immediately took out his wrath on Ross and Jack.

"You two can go to hell as far as I'm concerned. Neither one of you are of any use to me anyway. Now, get the hell off my ranch," shouted Malone.

Ross Simmons and Jack Wilkins knew that the Lazy C did not belong to Ivan Malone, and they resented the fact that Malone called it his ranch. But they sure were not going to argue with Malone, especially when he had already had his hand in at least two murders. They were especially grateful that Malone was not armed, as they felt he probably would have killed them on the spot where they stood. The two cowboys needed no more encouragement to make tracks. In the bunkhouse, they gathered their bedrolls and everything else that belonged to them and made their escape. They headed south.

"I gotta tell you, Ross, I didn't think we were going to get away from there alive," said Jack.

Simmons shuddered as they continued to spur their horses. "I know what you mean, Jack. I'm sure as hell glad to be away from there. Don't ever forget what we agreed on. We ain't telling anyone about what we know."

No one from the Lazy C ever ventured as far south as Decatur, so the two men figured they were safe from the reach of Ivan Malone. As Simmons and Wilkins had made their way south, they had seen the broken-down saloon as they travelled through Decatur. They had stopped, and perhaps against their better judgement, decided that they were up to the challenge of resurrecting the old saloon. Five days later they had signed the papers and given away their last bit of money. They had decided to become the owners and proprietors of the *Second Chance Saloon,* a broken-down storefront on the edge of Decatur, Texas.

Ross and Jack, with the last of their meager funds, had purchased the sorry excuse of a bar, and were running it themselves. The two men only hoped that their endeavor was far enough away from the Lazy C that they would not be confronted by the likes of Ivan Malone and his henchmen. So far, they were pleased that they had not experienced any follow up from Malone.

* * *

Although it was approaching noon, it was still a bit early in the day for the regular clientele or for passing travelers to be in the bar. It would not be long, however, before the lunch customers began trickling in. As a result, Ross Simmons, the owner of the *Second Chance Saloon*, was taking the daily lull in business as an opportunity to make crude repairs to the bar. During the prior evening, two rowdy cowboys from a nearby ranch had decided to test their drinking stamina, and when their alcohol saturation was high enough, they had proceeded to bust up the bar in the course of their roughhouse fisticuffs. It had taken both Simmons and Wilkins to forcibly remove the two inebriated cowboys from the bar, but not before the drunks had broken a section of the stand-up bar and laid open a cut above Simmons' eye. This morning, Simmons was making cursory repairs by hammering nails into planks on the bar top while sporting a hunk of tape above his eye. With each blow of his hammer, the noise was near-deafening in the confines of the shack and was accompanied by puffs of years-old dust that rose from the boards. But the loud noise of the hammer blows did not seem to affect the only other person in the bar.

At a small table in a dark back corner of the bar, an unkempt man sat bent over, his shaggy-haired, full-bearded head resting on his arm on top of the table. His clothes were dirty, and an unpleasant odor hung in the air near his person. Dried tobacco juice adorned the man's beard at the corners of his mouth. His appearance told the casual observer that this man simply did not care what other people thought of him, and in truth, it was fact. The man quietly snored as his partially open mouth drew wheezy breath after breath. He and Ross had had a late night the night before, and his morning work was now caught up, so he was having a short nap. The noise of Simmons' bar repairs did not rouse Wobbly Wilkins from his slumber.

Wobbly Wilkins was not the man's real name. Jack Wilkins was the name given him by his mother over four decades earlier. But unkind fellow ranch hands had thrown the Wobbly moniker on Wilkins in years past, and it had stuck. The nickname, Wobbly, had been given to Wilkins because of his odd manner of walking. Wilkins seemed to lean side-to-side as he walked, giving the appearance of a man who had drunk a bit too much firewater. It was easy to see how folks who did not know the background of Jack Wilkins simply assumed that Jack was drunk as he walked down one of the town's wooden sidewalks, and they had given him the nickname, Wobbly, while they put a comfortable distance between themselves and the unsteadily-walking man. As for Wobbly being drunk, it was simply not the case.

During the previous two hours, Jack had built the mesquite fire at the back of the saloon and scrubbed the few tin plates that he had not cleaned up last night. He would soon need to rouse himself to go out to the underground vegetable cellar to bring up a bucket of raw steaks. He had already placed a few potatoes at the edge of the fire so that they would bake and be ready for the noontime customers. It was Jack's job to do the cooking and cleaning of the tin plates and eating utensils, which he washed at the outdoor, hand-pumped water well. Because he was part owner, Jack Wilkins spent untold hours in the *Second Chance,* but he never had a yen to partake in drinks for himself. In fact, even though he was the co-owner of the bar with his pal, Ross Simmons, he was very seldom inebriated. The exception to this condition was when his sister, Justine, sent him a bit of cash on his birthday or at Christmas. In her younger days, his sister had been a pretty thing with beguiling ways, and she was smart. She had the good sense to take an interest in a handsome Yankee Army Officer who had come to the Texas territory at the close of the Civil War to finish up the time remaining on his Army commitment. During his stay in Texas, the young officer had succumbed to the wiles of comely Justine, and he and Justine had married and moved to Ohio after the officer's term of enlistment expired. The cashed-out Army officer soon took over his father's manufacturing business, giving him and Justine the wealth that set them apart from the mere commoners. But Justine was not in the least cold hearted. She remembered her brother Jack fondly, as Jack had always looked after her when their own parents took little interest in their offspring. And knowing Jack's physical limitations, she felt that it was her duty to render a bit of periodic financial aid to her older brother. Jack generally spent the money she sent, quietly celebrating his birthday by having a bit of bourbon that he shared with his buddy Ross.

Wobbly's physical limitations, of course, had no connection whatsoever to his part ownership of the *Second Chance Saloon*. But his frequenting of the saloon led casual observers to believe that Wobbly remained on a near-permanent drunk. Such was not the case. While bar owners, Ross Simmons, and Jack "Wobbly" Wilkins were longtime friends and co-owners of the bar, that friendship had played a great part in the reason for Wilkins' compromised physique. The poor fellow's strange manner of walking was the result of a near-death goring and trampling by a bull from which Wobbly had fared poorly in his attempt to distract the cantankerous animal during a ranch rodeo. Ross Simmons had just been thrown through the air by that same bull as he had attempted to ride it. Simmons had lain unconscious in the rodeo arena dirt after landing on his back. The hell-fired brahma bull then decided that the inert fallen rider was worth a stomping and goring. At that instant, Jack Wilkins jumped from the arena fence and ran in front of the bull in order to divert the bull's attention to himself and save his friend from being stomped. But the reward for his selfless act to save his friend was that the bull turned its attention on Wilkins. The outcome was disastrous. Jack was gored in his upper thigh and thrown through the air, blood streaking from the injured cowboy. Fortunately, Jack could be patched up, but he would have a permanent limp, hence his wobbly gait. Even with this impairment, he could still do a man's work on the ranch, and the Conleys had allowed him to stay on even though Jack sometimes had to work at a bit slower pace than the other hands. That incident produced a further lifetime bond between Ross Simmons, and Jack "Wobbly" Wilkins.

As the first lunch time customers entered the door of the saloon, Jack roused himself, snuffed his nose, wiped his eyes, and shuffled out the back door where he washed his face, head, and hands at the water pump. Then he retrieved the steaks and spuds and loaded up the grill.

* * *

"I told you it didn't look like much," said Ben.

"Yeah, but you didn't tell me that the place was near to falling down," Nathan laughed as the men entered the *Second Chance Saloon*.

Ross Simmons laid aside his hammer and began walking from table to table, keeping track of orders with a pencil stub and a piece of paper. He got to the lawmen's table.

"What'll it be, Ben?" Simmons asked. Ross knew the Ranger but had not been introduced to the Marshal. His only knowledge of Nathan was that he had overheard Ivan Malone cursing the fact that the Marshal had been nosing around the Lazy C.

"Two that still moo," Ben replied, "and two beers. Say, Ross, do you know the Marshal, here?"

"Don't believe we've ever met," said Simmons.

Ben introduced them, and the men shook hands. After a few words, Ross turned and walked out the back door to where Jack Wilkins had thrown a few steaks onto the grill. Ross gave him the slip of paper with the orders on it and went back into the saloon. He filled a few beer orders and took them to the tables. As he served the tables, he only partially listened to the conversations of the patrons before he turned back to the bar.

In a short time, Jack began bringing loaded tin plates to various tables and put a knife and fork next to each diner's plate. Nathan and Ben dug into their steaks. "Didn't I tell you that the steaks were great here?" said Ben.

Nathan was blissfully chewing a bite of sirloin. "Yep, pretty darn good and done just right." He sliced his baked potato in half and put a clump of butter on each half before he cut off a chunk of the spud and put it in his mouth.

At the bar, Ross Simmons lifted a wet rag from a bucket on the floor behind the bar and did his best to wipe off the top of the bar. His rag snagged a couple of times on nail heads that still protruded from the boards on the bar. When he was done, he threw the rag back into the bucket. The open front door that allowed a bit more sunshine to enter the bar caught Ross's attention. His eyes turned toward the door of the saloon as a young man entered. That young man was Calvin Kahl. Calvin walked up to the bar.

"What'll it be?" asked Ross.

Calvin was too unsure of himself to order a beer, so he answered, "I'll take a ginger beer, if you have it."

Ross set a bottle on the bar in front of Calvin. "That's a nickel if you've got it."

Calvin reached in his pocket and put a nickel on the bar. "Say, mister, I'm looking for the Marshal. Is he here?"

"Ross nodded his head toward the table where Ben and Nathan were sitting. "Right over there. He's sitting with the Ranger."

In the background Jack Wilkins could be heard crying out, "I've got two rares and a medium rare." Patrons held up their hands, and Jack put their plates on the table in front of them.

Calvin looked over at Ben and Nathan's table and took a sip of his ginger beer. He picked up the bottle and cautiously walked to their table.

"Say, Marshal, could I talk to you for a minute?" Calvin asked.

Nathan looked up but kept chewing his bite of steak. When he swallowed, he said, "Sure. Pull up a chair."

Calvin dragged over a chair from an empty table and sat down. "I don't mean to disturb your dinner, Marshal."

"I can talk and eat at the same time," said Nathan.

"Yeah, he can. I've seen him do it," said Ben. Nathan glared at his friend and continued chewing.

"What's on your mind, young man?" Nathan asked. Nathan soon finished his steak and potato and set his fork and knife on the plate.

Ben also placed his utensils on his plate, took a swig of his beer, and burped. "Oops," he said, and he pushed the plate to the middle of the table.

Calvin began to tell Nathan his reason for seeking him out. He told them of his father's departure from Lafayette, Louisiana, to travel to the gold fields in Colorado, the death of his mother, and his subsequent continuing search for his father. He also told them that his father had shown him the maps he was going to use, and he had shown him the exact route that he was going to follow on his trip to Colorado. All the while that Calvin was talking with the lawmen, his stomach was telling him that it was empty. The smell of the charbroiled steaks that permeated the *Second Chance* did not help the situation of Calvin's hunger.

Trying to be as inconspicuous as possible, Jack Wilkins went about his business of picking empty plates from the diner's tables. But as he stood near the table occupied by Nathan, Ben, and Calvin, he paused, trying to give the impression that he was rearranging the empty plates that he was carrying on his arm. But when he overheard the story told by Calvin Kahl, he was disturbed enough that he dropped two of the plates with their eating utensils onto the floor. He hurriedly picked them up and moved to the bar, where Ross Simmons stood shining a beer glass with a not-so-clean rag.

Quietly, Jack said to his partner, "Ross, you ain't gonna believe what I just heard."

Ross turned his attention to Jack. "Okay, what did you hear?"

Keeping his back turned to the table of lawmen, Jack told him. "See that young fella sitting with the Marshal and the Ranger?"

"Sure, I see him. What about him?" Ross asked.

Jack asked Ross another question. "You remember that prospector that Malone shot dead out at the Lazy C?"

"Jack, keep your voice down," Ross admonished. "Sure, I remember. What about it?"

"Well, that kid over there with the Marshal is the prospector's son, and he's come to town looking for his dad." Jack's eyes blinked rapidly several times, a sure indicator that he was upset.

Ross stopped running the rag around the inside of the beer glass. "Oh, criminy. Are you sure you heard them talking about that?"

"I'm damn sure, Ross. The kid was asking the lawmen if they had seen his dad," said Jack. "Seems the kid has been tracking his dad to find him and lost the trail up north of town. And we sure as hell know why, don't we?"

The two men became silent as a bar patron came to the bar to request a refill of his beer glass. Ross drew the glass of beer and handed the glass back to the customer, who walked back to his table.

The men then continued their quiet conversation. "Well, there ain't much that we can do about it. Remember, if word gets out that we talked, we could be next on Malone's list," said Ross.

"I don't know, Ross. I just thought you should know about the kid, that's all," said Jack. He turned and left through the back door to take his soiled plates to the wash tub out back. He put the plates and utensils in the water-filled tub, then returned to the bar to collect the remaining dirty plates.

"So, you see, Marshal," said Calvin, "I have followed his trail this far, and everywhere that I go, I ask people if they have seen a prospector on horseback and leading a burro loaded with prospecting gear. Most of the time I'm able to find someone who has seen him. But the trail sort of dried up around these parts, so I thought I would ask the local Marshal if you had seen such a man."

It took Nathan only a second to answer. "I wish I could help you, kid, but I haven't seen your dad. How about you, Ben?"

"Me neither," Ben answered. "Where did you lose his trail?"

"Up north of here," said Calvin. "The grasslands up there are so thick that there are no trails, and hardly any folks living up in those parts. So, there was nobody to ask about him, and I decided to double back to here to ask around."

Jack Wilkins had returned to picking plates from diner's tables, and edged toward the tables near to Nathan, Ben, and Calvin, where he could better overhear their conversation.

Ben had been mulling over what Calvin had told them. "You say you lost your father's trail north of here. Why were you looking for his trail up that direction?"

"Because he told me that he was going to avoid towns as much as he could," said Calvin. "He told me he would avoid Decatur and head north just before he came to Decatur."

"Well, if you head north from here, you will eventually come to the Red River, which, depending on how much rain we've had, can sometime be a little tricky to cross," said Ben. "Did your dad mention where he was going to cross the river?"

Calvin had to think for a few seconds. "Yeah, he told me, but I'm not sure I remember the name of the town. Hmm. It had the word 'fort' in it, I believe."

"Only one town up there that has the name fort in it. That's Spanish Fort," said Ben. "Is that where your dad meant to cross the river?"

Calvin lifted his eyes. "Yes," he said. "I'm fairly sure that's the name of the town Dad showed me on his maps. Spanish Fort, yeah, that's it."

Nathan and Ben looked at each other for a few seconds.

"You know," said Ben, "if you are going overland instead of sticking to the trails, you would need to cut across the Lazy C Ranch to get to Spanish Fort."

The two lawmen continued to look at each other, and almost simultaneously they discreetly nodded to each other.

Once again, Jack Wilkins hurriedly carried a stack of plates to the bar.

* * *

"What now, Jack?" Ross asked. "You look like you've been hit by lightning."

Jack was pale and visibly shaking so badly that he was in danger of dropping the plates he was carrying.

"Here, let me take some of those plates," said Ross. The two men walked together out the back door. After setting the plates he had been carrying into the wash tub, Jack turned to Ross.

"They know, Ross. They know," cried Jack.

"What the hell are you talking about, Jack? Who knows what?"

"That kid in the bar, Ross. He told the lawmen that his old man was headed to Spanish Fort to cross the river there," said Jack. "And somehow the lawmen put two and two together. They knew that to get to Spanish Fort, if you ain't using the trail, that you would have to cross part of the Lazy C. I tell ya, they know, Ross."

Ross stood still for a few seconds before he said, "Jack, they don't know anything, except that the kid's old man might have crossed the Lazy C. That don't mean nuthin."

With a crash, Jack dropped the remaining tin plates he was holding into the wash basin. He then stood still for a moment before turning to face Simmons. His face was contorted into a frown that appeared that he was on the verge of crying. His eyes glistened as they teared up.

"I know what we promised each other, Ross. I know I'm not supposed to open my mouth. But I can't do this anymore," said Jack. "I have nightmares about seeing poor Missus Sylvia layin' in that dirt grave. She needs somebody to revenge her murder."

"I think you mean avenge her murder, Jack," Ross replied.

Jack became more agitated, waving his arms and pointing at his partner. "Goddamit, Ross, I don't need no damn language lesson from you," said Jack. "I'm telling you we are not doing the right thing by keepin' our yaps shut. We've got a U.S. Marshal and a Texas Ranger inside, and we damn well need to tell them. We owe it to that kid in there to tell him how his old man died. What if it had been your dad that was murdered? Wouldn't you like to know?"

"Don't get all lathered up on me, Jack," said Ross. "You know why we haven't talked to anybody. If that murderin' Malone ever heard about us talkin', he might come lookin' for us. I don't aim to be a dead man anytime soon."

But Ross had listened to his friend, and in his gut, he knew that Jack was right. Yet, he had a real concern about Ivan Malone. He would never admit that he was afraid of Malone, but deep down, he held a fear of the big man's wrath.

Jack's arms dropped to his sides as he looked down at the ground. He raised his head and spoke to Ross. "Ross, we're pards, and you're just like a brother to me. But I don't aim to go to prison for not telling those lawmen what I know. I'm fairly sure you can be arrested for not letting the law know what we seen."

Ross had never thought about that aspect of their witnessing crimes committed on the Lazy C. He guessed it was probably true that withholding evidence could be a crime all by itself. And when he thought long and hard on it, he knew that keeping that secret for all these weeks had been eating at him, too. It wasn't right that Missus Sylvia had no one to talk for her. He gave a deep sigh and turned his eyes to the back door of the bar. With great reluctance, he said, "All right, we'll tell them."

Ross and Jack walked back inside the bar. But as they approached the table where Nathan and Ben sat, the lawmen began to get up to leave.

Ross spoke up, "Marshal, could we have a word with you?"

"Sure, I guess so," said Nathan. "Ben, if you want to, you and Calvin here can probably go back to the office."

"No, Marshal," said Ross. "I think the Ranger and the kid should hear what we have to tell you."

Ben and Calvin sat back down at the table. Nathan thought that Ross's request was a bit odd. After all, Calvin had only just come into town. Why would he need to stick around? But he replied to Ross, "Okay, they will stay. Now what's this all about?"

"You tell 'em, Ross," said Jack.

Ross and Jack had pulled up two more chairs to the lawmen's table. Ross squirmed a bit as he began to speak. "Marshal, Ranger Steele knows that Jack and me, we used to work at the Lazy C before we bought the *Second Chance*."

Ross looked at Ben, who nodded his head in acknowledgement.

"Well, things out at the Lazy C got so bad for the ranch hands that me and Jack just had to get away from that place," said Ross.

Nathan asked, "What do you mean, they got so bad? What got so bad?"

Ross's thoughts returned to the day that he and Jack had witnessed the murder of the prospector, and the manner in which Beryl Dunn had made it clear that unless he kept his mouth shut, he and Jack would be the next people to be killed. He shuddered at the thought of facing Dunn or Ivan Malone. Jack had to prod his friend.

"Tell them about Missus Conley, Ross," said Jack.

"Dammit, Jack, I'll tell the story, or do you want to?" Ross barked.

Ross's demeanor shut down his partner. "No, no, you tell 'em what we saw," said Jack.

By this time, Nathan and Ben Steele were getting a bit impatient to know what this was all about. But the mention of the Lazy C had certainly piqued their interest.

"Ross, get on with it," said Nathan.

"Yeah, yeah, Marshal. Do you know a fella named Ivan Malone?" asked Ross. At the mention of Malone, Nathan's focus was now locked on Ross.

"Oh, yeah, we've met him," Nathan replied.

"Well, then you know what kind of fella he is. Nobody wants to tangle with him and his hired guns."

"Um, hmm," replied Nathan.

Ross paused again before he spoke. It seemed as if he was screwing up his courage to go on with the story. "Well, what we seen, umm, we seen Ivan Malone kill this kid's dad," said Ross, and he pointed his thumb toward Calvin Kahl.

"What? You say you saw Ivan Malone kill a man," said Nathan. "How did you see him do that? Were you there when he shot this man?"

At this point, Ross Simmons and Jack Wilkins did not know whether they were going to be in trouble with Ross's next answer. Ross hesitated, but then went on. "Well, what happened, Marshal, was that one morning, Malone's gun hand, Beryl Dunn, came and got me and Jack and told us that we needed to go somewhere with him and Malone. Jack and me, we didn't know what to think, except that we were afraid that Malone was going to take us out somewhere and kill us to keep our mouths shut permanent like."

"Okay, so you went with Malone," said Nathan. "Then what happened?"

"Well, we rode out to the edge of the Lazy C where there was this limestone outcropping. And there was this fella who appeared to be a prospector. He had a donkey all loaded with prospector gear," said Ross. "He wasn't aimin' to stay on the Lazy C. He had just camped for the night and was gonna' move on."

"How do you know that?" Nathan asked.

"Ivan Malone told him he was trespassing on Lazy C property," said Ross. "But the prospector told Malone that he would be moving on and didn't mean any harm by camping overnight. He just wanted to get on his way."

"Did Malone send the man on his way?" asked Nathan.

"Nah," answered Ross. "After Malone told the man that he was trespassing on the Lazy C, he shot him in cold blood. Killed him."

"And you saw all this?" Nathan asked.

"Yep. Jack and me were sitting our horses right near Malone and his gunmen."

"Did you bury this prospector fella?" asked Ben.

Ross turned toward the Ranger. With his face reflecting his shame, Ross answered, "No, Ben. Malone told us to drag the dead man up under the outcropping shelf. He said to just leave him for the buzzards. After that, we turned the prospector's burro loose, and we took his horse back to the ranch with us. But before we left that outcropping, well, that's when Beryl Dunn told us to keep our mouths shut or we would be killed, too."

Initially, no one seemed to notice that tears had begun to drop from Calvin Kahl's cheeks. He made no sound, but his heart was breaking because of what he had just heard from Ross Simmons. It certainly seemed to him that his father had been killed at the hands of an evil man named Ivan Malone. All the while that he had been trailing his father, he had been afraid that an accident or other mishap would injure his father or something more serious would befall him. He was convinced that he had heard his fears come to fruition.

Nathan turned and saw Calvin's heartfelt reaction to Ross's story. He could not imagine what the young man must be thinking. His heart went out to him.

Quietly, Nathan said, "Calvin, we don't know that the man that was killed was your father. It could very well be an unknown stranger."

Calvin made no reply. He merely nodded his head, as if affirming Nathan's attempt to console him.

"Ross, tell 'em about Missus Conley," said Jack, "Go on, tell 'em." Jack was anxious to tell the lawmen what he and Ross had found, "You know, what we seen out at the Lazy C."

"Hold your horses, Jack. I'm getting there," Ross replied. He paused for a few seconds and then looked at Ben Steele. "Sylvia Conley is dead!"

"What?" exclaimed Ben. "I never heard anything about her dying."

"And you won't," Ross replied. "She didn't die of any natural causes. She was murdered."

"How do you know such a thing?" Nathan asked.

Jack piped up, "We done found her body, while we were mendin' fence out at the Lazy C. She was buried by whoever shot her."

"Ross, you better explain," said Nathan.

"Well, like Jack said, we were out mending fence, and I was workin' on one of the fence posts when my boot sunk down in the dirt. When I pulled my foot back, there was this little piece of purple cloth that was showing in the boot print."

"How did a piece of purple cloth show up in the dirt on your fence line?" Ben asked.

Ross continued. "That's what I wanted to know. But when I bent down to pick it up, why, it turns out it was part of the sleeve of Mrs. Conley's dress. I called Jack over and we dug her up. Well, I should say, that she was in a shallow grave, and we could see her plainly."

"It was her all right," said Jack. "And she had a bullet hole in her head. Somebody shot her, and I figure we know who, don't we Ross?"

"Um, hmm," was Ross's reply.

"Well, wait a minute, boys," said Nathan. "Are you thinking that it was Malone that killed Mrs. Conley?"

"Damn right," said Jack. "He made it pretty darn clear around the hired hands that they would soon be working for him. It makes sense that he would need to get the Conleys out of the picture, and Mrs. Sylvia was the easiest one to pick off first. If I was a bettin' man, I'd bet everything I own on Malone being the killer."

"You feel the same way, Ross?" Nathan asked.

"I don't know who else it could be," Ross replied.

"I don't have any reason to disagree with you," said Nathan. "But we don't have any proof that he was the killer."

"Well, there's one more thing," said Ross.

"What's that?" Nathan replied.

"Well, everybody at the ranch knew that Miss Sylvia had left the ranch to take a trip to Fort Worth to see if she could find her daughter," said Ross.

"Wait a minute," said Nathan. "You mean the Conleys had a daughter?"

Ben interrupted Nathan. "I thought I told you about that. Conleys had a daughter named Jane, who left the ranch several years ago and hasn't been back since."

"Yeah, I guess you told me, but I forgot," said Nathan. "Ross, go ahead with your story. Mrs. Conley left the ranch to go to Fort Worth?"

"Yep," Ross replied. "But to get to Fort Worth, Sylvia was going to go by train. And the morning that she left, Ivan Malone was driving the buckboard to take her to the Nocona train depot."

Jack then interrupted. "And she ain't' been seen since."

Ross turned his head toward Jack. "Jack, just shut up. I'll tell the story."

Jack grumbled a quiet response. "Seems like you're kinda slow at it."

Ross turned back to Nathan. "Like I said, Marshal, Ivan Malone left the ranch with Sylvia Conley, and we never saw her again. That is, until we found her in a shallow grave at the edge of the ranch. She had a bullet hole in her head, so somebody killed her. And we figure it could only be one man, the last person to see her alive."

"And that's Ivan Malone," said Jack.

The conversation around the table in the *Second Chance* came to a halt. No one seemed to know what he could add at this point.

Nathan broke the silence. "How come you boys didn't tell me or the Ranger about what you found?"

Jack and Ross looked at each other. "Because we like livin'," said Ross. "There's no tellin' how many people that damn Malone has shot or killed, and we didn't aim to be added to his list."

"I understand," said Ben.

Quietly, Nathan said, "Four murders."

Ross spoke up. "Four? We know of the prospector, this kid's father maybe, and Sylvia Conley. Who are the others?"

"Ross, do you remember the Comanches coming to the ranch for their gift cattle?" Nathan asked.

"Sure," Ross replied. "We were with Sean Conley a couple times when the Comanches came."

"Do you remember a Comanche named Black Horse?"

"Yep. He was with his hunting party when they came to the ranch for their steers," Ross replied.

"Well, it seems that Ivan Malone had a hand in killing the brother of Black Horse, Iron Arrow, the last time they came to the ranch to get their cattle," said Nathan. "So, we have Black Horse up at Fort Sill, vowing to kill Ivan Malone if he ever gets the chance."

"Black Horse isn't the only one that wants to kill this Mr. Malone," said Calvin.

"Oh, no, not you, too." Nathan groaned. "I think everyone in two counties wants to get a bullet into Malone."

Nathan was quiet for a moment, and then said, "Ross and Jack, there's something else that you don't know. Ivan Malone also killed Michael Conley."

"My God," cried Ross. He and Jack looked at each other with their mouths open. They could not believe what they had just heard.

"How do you know that?" asked Jack.

Nathan thought for a moment, then said, "I'd rather not say right now. But believe me, Michael Conley died at the hands of Ivan Malone, and I aim to bring him to justice for all of these murders, along with the attempted murder of my wife. So, I've got a good reason to get to Malone and see him tried and hung."

"I'm thinkin' you might need a little help with that," said Ben.

"You might be right, Ben. He's the most evil man I ever ran across, I believe," Nathan answered.

"You mentioned your wife?" said Calvin and Ross almost simultaneously. Ross continued, "How did that happen? She never came out to the Lazy C."

Nathan was hesitant to tell the story, as it seemed too close to his heart.

"She didn't need to," said Ben. "Malone sent one of his hired guns to the Marshal's ranch. A man called Dunn. He meant to kill the Marshal, here, but when the gunman found out that Nathan was not home, he decided to kill Mrs. Wolf."

"Oh, Lordy. We know Dunn," said Ross. "Well, what happened?"

"Let's just say that the gunman met his end," replied Ben.

"Jumpin' Judas," said Ross. "Four murders." He looked over at Jack. "I'm damn glad we got out of there when we did."

Ross didn't see the tears welling in Jack's eyes, as Jack kept his head down. "Michael Conley was a great boss," he said. "And Sylvia was the nicest lady I ever did meet."

Again, the table became quiet until Nathan finally stood up. He extended his hand to both Ross and Jack and they shook hands. "I'm glad you told me about this. I have a special interest in seeing Malone at the end of a hangman's rope, so you can figure I'll keep working on this to get Malone in front of a judge and jury." He turned to Calvin Kahl. "Calvin, let's go on back to my office, and we can talk a little bit more about your dad."

Ross Simmons stood up to leave, but before he walked away, he said, "Marshal, our lunch customers are gone, so we're going to be closing up here shortly."

"Okay," said Nathan. "We need to be getting back to the office anyhow," and the men all rose from the table.

Calvin spoke up, "Marshal, I'll come back to your office. But if it's all the same with you, I need to stop at that café by the hotel and get something to eat. I've been a whole day without vittles," said Calvin as he looked at the Marshal.

"Sure. I'll wait for you at our office," said Nathan.

At the Lazy C Ranch

Every time he thought about that louse, Beryl Dunn, the hair on the back of Ivan Malone's neck raised. Dunn had been gone for days, leaving Malone to believe that Dunn had simply taken the five hundred dollars that Malone had paid him up front and run off with it. Dunn was supposed to get another five hundred after he killed U.S. Marshal Nathan Wolf. Malone figured that since Dunn had disappeared, it was only logical that Dunn had taken the money and run. *Dunn is a dead man if I ever run into him again* Malone thought to himself. Malone had no way to know that Dunn truly was already dead, killed at the ranch of Nathan and Claire May Wolf. A well-placed rifle shot by Pablo Carillo, their hired man, had silenced Beryl Dunn for eternity.

Though Dunn was missing, Malone was not without resources for carrying out his evil intents. One of his original cohorts in crime, Matt Woods, was still working for him, albeit reluctantly. Unbeknownst to Malone, Matt Woods was tired of taking orders from Malone, and knew that his life was not worth a plug nickel if he told Malone that he was through working for him. Woods believed that he only had one choice. He was biding his time, waiting for just the right opportunity to kill Malone and leave north Texas. Matt Woods was certainly not the only individual who wanted an expiration date on the life of Ivan Malone. The list was long, and now it had added another individual, Woods.

Malone was not so stupid that he did not know that there were individuals who wanted him dead. After he had killed the Comanche at the edge of the ranch, he was sure that in the days following he would be hunted down by the Comanches who wanted their revenge. So far, that had not taken place. Then there was that damn prospector that was passing through. In hindsight, he had killed that man only to impress Dunn and Woods and those other two cowards, Ross Simmons and Jack Wilkins, and throw a scare into them. He figured that little show must have sufficiently scared Simmons and Wilkins, because they had lit out for parts unknown. *Well, good riddance to them,* thought Malone. In hindsight, Malone thought that he probably should have just beaten up the prospector, robbed him, and sent him on his way. And then there were the Conleys. Too many of the ranch hands suspected that Malone had had something to do with the disappearance of first, Sylvia Conley, and then Michael and Sean Conley. It didn't much matter, because none of the ranch hands could prove what they might be thinking, and the only two men who knew anything about killing Michael and Sean were Dunn and Woods, and he didn't figure they would flap their yappers. He now wished that he had not taken Simmons and Wilkins along when he shot the prospector. Someday, that might come back to bite him. But for now, he did not figure that those two would ever return to the Lazy C, and if they did, he would kill them.

All the same, a gritty case of paranoia had set itself upon Ivan Malone. Knowing that it was a good bet that the U.S. Marshal might start snooping around again, and the Comanches might pay him a visit, Malone had tasked a couple of ranch hands to go into town a couple days ago to bring back a load of lumber and other supplies. He had then helped those same ranch hands as they nailed planks across some of the windows, leaving only enough space between the planks to shoot through. Malone was delusioned enough that he now believed that the Lazy C was his. With the Conleys gone, and no other relatives to stake claim on the ranch, Malone would never leave the ranch. *Oh sure,* he thought to himself, *his own mother probably had a right to the ranch, but she would never come back. And if she did, he would kill her too.* And if there were any other persons who disputed his ownership, he intended to defend himself, boarded up inside the ranch house for any gun fight that might ensue. He did not think that he would need to remain at the Lazy C for more than a few months. By that time, the Spanish Fort attorney that he had hired would have the rights of ownership straightened out through the court, giving him sole ownership of the ranch. It was then that he planned to sell the entire property and be on his way, set for the rest of his life. He was not certain where he was going to go, but he knew that he had to get far away from north Texas, just in case the law ever did catch up to him.

At the present time, Malone was waiting for his two hired cowhands to return to the ranch. Early this morning, the two men had left the ranch leading a string of eight Lazy C horses. They were headed for Spanish Fort, where they would sell the horses and bring the money back to Malone. Those animals were the last of the sizable Lazy C remuda, which Malone had been furtively selling off in small groups ever since he arrived at the Lazy C. He believed that he was so successful in his horse stealing that Michael Conley had never suspected him. But Sean Conley had noticed the dwindling size of the remuda, and rightly suspected Malone was at the bottom of those disappearances. Malone had panicked when Sean asked him about it and was further agitated when Sean had contacted that nosy U.S. Marshal. Still, he had managed to get the Conleys out of the way and sell the remainder of the herd right under the noses of the ranch hands and the ranch foreman. The horse thefts had given Malone a sizable amount of ready cash, and he also held the cashbox that belonged to the Lazy C.

When Beryl Dunn vanished with his upfront payment from him, Malone had managed to persuade two of the Lazy C cowhands, the same two men who had helped him board up the ranch house, to begin working for him full time. Money talks, and when Malone offered the men a salary that was twice what they had been making, they reluctantly agreed to work for him, much to the disgust of the ranch foreman, Lee Stark, who had also witnessed and become wise to the demise of the ranch remuda at the hands of Ivan Malone.

Lee Stark was a dyed in the wool cowman. He had been raised on a ranch as a boy, had worked his way up on several ranches, and had been hired by Michael Conley shortly after Michael and Sylvia Conley had taken over the Lazy C from Michael's parents. Lee Stark looked the part and walked the walk of a ranch leader. Stark wore a neatly trimmed beard, with multiple specks of white hair mixed in with the auburn color of his hair. In his younger days, he would have kept up with the hard-drinking and whoring of his fellow ranch hands but had learned hard lessons that changed his perspective on life. Now that he was older, he seldom drank to excess, and when he was in town with some of his ranch hands, he stayed away from the women of the night. He was known to occasionally partake of a fresh chunk from a plug of tobacco but had even cut back on that when his gums began to ache from the brown vice. From his weathered, sweat-stained Stetson, his Nocona boots with the well-worn heels, and his heavily calloused hands, Stark looked the part of a seasoned cow hand. Flashing brown eyes, a weathered cross-hatched skin that was holding on to the ruddy face and beard, gave evidence to his many days in the hot Texas sun. He was a well-respected leader in great contrast to the fresh, unlined faces of the young men he helped to mold and mature. But in the beginning, it had not been easy. Being the foreman of a cattle ranch carries with it a great deal of learning and savvy, but the hardest part of growing into the job had been to establish himself as the leader of a pack of high-spirited young cow hands. He had succeeded beyond his initial trepidation, and he was held in high esteem by the Conleys and the rough-house ranch hands.

Stark felt that he owed the Conleys a great deal. They had taken a chance on him and stood by him as he had gotten his feet on the ground and learned how to ramrod the day-to-day operation of the Lazy C. The young men who worked the ranch had learned the ways of the Lazy C and the Conleys' way of doing business right along with Stark. Long ago, the generous and fair-minded Conleys had made Stark feel that he was part of their family, and inwardly he preferred to believe that he was a pseudo-relative of the Conleys. And with that state of mind, Stark had quickly read Ivan Malone as a slick-talking threat to the Conleys and the very life of the Lazy C Ranch. And now, Malone had hired two of his ranch hands right under Stark's nose. Stark was angry and disappointed in the two ranch hands. But, at least for the time being, aside from giving the men fair warning, there was nothing he could do about it.

Lee Stark would do anything for the Conleys. For the past few weeks, he had witnessed the startling erosion of the Conley family ranch and its associated values. He was of the opinion that the Conleys did not seem to perceive that Malone was a threat to them or the ranch. But, in truth, he was wrong on that assumption, because Michael Conley had seen the danger lurking in Ivan Malone the minute Malone stepped foot on the ranch. It was Sylvia Conley who had a soft spot in her heart for the no-account Malone. She was convinced that Malone was her grandson, and therefore, she held a faith that Malone would become an asset to the Conley family. And, because he thought the world of Sylvia Conley, Stark was forced to get along with Malone as best he could.

Lee Stark had been keeping a watchful eye on Malone whenever possible, and he was especially alert some months back after Malone had furtively hired two men, Beryl Dunn and Matt Woods, who turned out to be Malone's personal bodyguards. Lee Stark was not necessarily afraid of Ivan Malone or his two gunhands. In his line of work, he had handled many an ornery and tough cowhand who had thought they knew just as much or more about running a ranch than Stark. He had always managed to prevail and turn the young men around in their attitudes. But he had no illusions to the fact that Malone would never put himself in a position to go head-to-head with him. Malone would always stack the deck in his favor by having an extra gun guarding his back. But Stark also knew that if it ever came down to it, he would always support the Conleys, even if it meant that he would endanger his own life and face a most difficult adversary in the form of Ivan Malone.

Never in a hundred years would Lee Stark have thought that he would plan to kill another man. In all his years, he had managed to distance himself from any fracas that held the potential of gunplay between opponents. His opinion was that other folks' lives held no concern to him unless those other folks' actions hurt him or his friends. And by now, it had become glaringly apparent to Stark that Ivan Malone was interfering with him and most of the ranch hands. But most importantly, Ivan Malone's actions were detrimental to the Conleys and the Lazy C. And for the first time in his life, Lee Stark felt the bubble of revenge within himself. The idea of killing Ivan Malone to save the Conleys and the Lazy C was an idea that would not cool within Stark. Especially now that Sylvia had gone to Fort Worth, and Michael and Sean had not been seen for days. His mind churned various scenarios on how to rid the Lazy C of Malone. None of those ideas warranted action as of yet, but Stark continued to seethe and was certain that he would reach a formula that worked. And when that happened, he would pray that he had the physical and mental strength to carry out the plan. The recent disappearance of Beryl Dunn was a curious happenstance, a fortuitous situation that pleased and emboldened Stark. With one less gun to contend with, he was even more determined to rid the Lazy C of Ivan Malone.

Chapter Fifteen

Earlier in the Day
Decatur, Texas Rail Depot

Jane was nearly too afraid to step off of the train, her stomach roiling at the thought. Jane Conley told herself that there was nothing to fear. She was still a considerable distance from Spanish Fort, and there was no one here who knew her, as she had left the area years ago. She was perfectly safe. Yet still, her anxieties and feelings of insecurity gave her trepidation. But if she were to carry out her plan, she had no choice. The train sat idling, periodically releasing gusts of steam, while the engineer waited for the last of the passengers to disembark. The engineer would move the train to a siding overnight in order to allow freight trains to pass on the same line. The passenger train was stopped over in Decatur for the night, and the next passenger train to Bowie and Nocona would not leave until the next morning.

She would need to stay overnight at a local hotel. As fate would have it, the Chisholm Trail Hotel carriage sat at the edge of the train platform. Its driver rested atop his seat, legs crossed and casually smoking his pipe, patiently waiting to carry passengers to the hotel. Jane stepped from the train car and walked to the carriage. After a short ride to the hotel, she registered at the front desk. Her inner fear of a chance meeting with someone who might know both her and her son caused her to give thought to signing in under a false name, but then she calmed, took a deep breath, and registered under her true name, *Jane Conley*. She was then shown to a comfortable room on the second floor, where she opened her travelling bag, splashed water on her face and dabbed it dry with a towel. From within, the first of her hunger pangs reminded her that she had merely picked at her breakfast on the train. She decided that she would walk to the café she had seen a few doors down from the hotel.

In Fort Worth several days ago, when the attorney had come to her room and explained that he was giving her two hundred dollars, and that the money had come from her mother, Jane could not believe him at first. But then he also explained that Sylvia had intended that Jane should use the money to return to the Lazy C, her home that she had left decades ago. After the attorney's departure, Jane had spent hours of mental anguish as she gave a great deal of thought to her mother's wishes. On the one hand, she was just too embarrassed to carry out her mother's plan. She felt that her life had turned into a great, horrible catastrophe, one that she had brought upon herself, and that she wished to share with no one else, especially her own mother. But on the other hand, for years, she had missed her mother deeply, and missed her brother, Sean. And finally, she had a gut feeling that her mother, her father, and her brother were in danger. For some odd reason, after discovering that the necklace that had been given to her by her mother years ago was missing, she believed that her son, Ivan Malone, had made his way to the Lazy C. She could not explain why she felt this way, only that she knew her son well and knew him to be a conniving opportunist, a man with no soul. She would later learn that her hunches were spot on the mark.

After much consideration and thought, she mustered the courage to visit a low-cost ladies' dress shop in Fort Worth, purchasing a few items for her trip. In addition, she visited a hardware store, where she purchased a .32 caliber handgun that she could easily carry in her handbag. She then walked to the railway depot where she bought a ticket to Nocona, Texas. In her mind, her pathway was clear. She was on her way back to the Lazy C, where she was certain that she would act on her plan to kill her son. Her trip had begun without incident but was presently paused. The train had now stopped for overnight routine maintenance in Decatur, Texas, where she would stay overnight with other passengers waiting for tomorrow's train to Nocona. After settling into her hotel room, Jane walked to the nearby café for what she hoped would be a late lunch.

* * *

Jane sat at the only table available in the café that was completely full of seemingly happy, conversing patrons. It was a table for two in an inconspicuous corner, where she had just given her order to a frazzled waitress, who had quickly brought her a cup of coffee while she waited for the rest of her meal. Her eyes roamed around the small café. The clientele seemed jovial and appeared to be honest, plainly dressed working people from the downtown area. She smiled slightly, thinking that it would be nice to be in their positions, happy with one's life, having friends, and having a nice job to go to every day. Her thoughts were interrupted when she noticed that her waitress was talking to a young man who had entered the front door. They spoke to each other for a few seconds, and then the waitress looked back at Jane, but continued to speak with the young man. Then both the waitress and the young man looked squarely at Jane at her table. Jane thought to herself, *no, no, don't do this. Don't bring him back here.* But the waitress and her charge came walking back to Jane's table.

"Sweetie, you seem to have the only chair available in the whole place. You won't mind if we put this young fella down with you, will you?" said the waitress. She had already put a menu at the empty place at the table. Jane did not respond. After a few seconds of awkward silence, the waitress departed. "I'll be back to take your order in just a moment," she said as she walked away.

"Sorry, ma'am," said Calvin Kahl, as he removed his hat, pulled the chair from the table, and took a seat opposite from Jane. After sitting, he shoved his hat beneath his chair to have it out of the way. Jane quietly stirred her coffee with a spoon, keeping her eyes down at the coffee mug. Calvin studied the menu, made his selection, and placed the menu back on the table.

"Kinda crowded in here today, ma'am," said Calvin.

Jane merely murmured in reply. She was determined not to get into a lengthy conversation with this young man. Yet, she did not want to seem rude. She lifted her head and saw that Calvin was watching her. His face carried nothing but a mild curiosity.

"Your coffee looks good. I guess I will order a mug when the waitress comes back to take our order."

"I've already ordered," Jane quietly responded.

The two strangers were quiet, while Calvin's eyes roamed the restaurant. But then he spoke. "You know, this is the farthest west I've ever been."

"I see," said Jane. And then she did not know why she said it, but added, "And where are you from?"

"Lafayette, Louisiana," said Calvin.

Jane merely nodded in reply, and silence returned to their table. But the quiet was soon interrupted by the waitress who returned to take Calvin's order. "What'll you have, hon?" she asked.

"I'll have the open roast beef sandwich and a cup of coffee," Calvin replied.

"Comin' right up," said the waitress, who then looked at Jane. "You want a refill on that coffee, ma'am?"

"Yes, thank you," Jane answered.

The waitress hurried away, her flat shoes slapping the wood floor as she walked.

Calvin remembered his manners and stuck out his right hand. "My name's Calvin, Calvin Kahl."

Jane was somewhat taken aback; it had been so long since anyone had introduced themselves to her. She hesitatingly held out her hand. "My name is Jane Conley."

"Pleasure to meet you, ma'am," Calvin responded, and then continued.

"I've come to Texas lookin' for my dad," said Calvin. But as he said it, he turned his eyes away and seemed to speak wistfully.

Jane merely nodded and stirred her coffee again. She was hesitant to carry on a conversation with Calvin, but she was still watching him, mildly interested, and had caught the small change in Calvin's demeanor.

Calvin spoke again. "See, he left home some weeks ago. He was going to head for Colorado to search for gold. When my mom died, I decided I'd try to find my dad," said Calvin. "I ain't got any other kin." Jane now noticed a near tear welling in Calvin's eyes.

"Did you find him?" Jane asked quietly.

"Nah," Calvin responded. "I've kinda lost track of his trail hereabouts, but I talked to the Marshal and a Texas Ranger, and they kinda think they know where he might have ended up."

"What do you mean, 'ended up'?" Jane asked.

It took a few seconds for Calvin to answer, and in that time, the waitress brought a steaming plate and set it in front of him. She had a coffee pot in her other hand and pulled a coffee mug from her apron pocket. She quickly filled Calvin's mug and refilled Jane's, then hurried from their table to fill other nearby customers' coffee mugs.

Jane waited for Calvin to continue, but he took two quick bites of his roast beef, slowly chewing the savory beef and its fat bark. Only after swallowing did he continue his story. "I went lookin' for the

Marshal earlier to see if he might have seen my dad passing through town. He was eating dinner down the road a ways at a place called the *Second Chance Saloon.* He had a Texas Ranger with him. When I asked the Marshal, he said that he hadn't seen my dad." Calvin paused to take another large bite of bread and roast beef.

After swallowing, he went on. "But there were two fellas there that ran the saloon. They told the Marshal and Ranger that they had worked at a ranch somewhere near here." Calvin's voice became noticeably quiet. "They claimed that they had seen a man kill another man who might have been my father."

After saying that, Calvin set his fork on his plate and rested his head in his hands, his hands covering his face. Jane watched and could now see Calvin's shoulders shaking in the rhythm of his silent sobbing. Jane's heart ached for the boy. Her thoughts nearly screamed at her in her head. In front of her was a young man who loved his father enough to follow his trail from Louisiana to find him; only to find out that his father might have been killed. And yet, here she was, on her own mission that was diametrically opposed. She was aiming to kill her son. She swallowed hard and watched as Calvin drew a soiled handkerchief from his pocket and wiped his eyes and quietly blew his nose, then returned the handkerchief to his pocket.

"I'm sorry, ma'am. I didn't mean to do that, but I truly miss my dad," said Calvin.

Jane again swallowed an emotional lump in her throat. Her emotions seemed to be playing tricks on her because she reached out her hand and laid it on top of Calvin's. Nearly as quickly she withdrew her hand and placed both hands in her lap.

Sheer hunger had driven Calvin to finish his dinner, even though it had now lost its appeal. He could not stop thinking of his father and the story that Jack Wilkins and Ross Simmons had told the Marshal.

Although there was no proof at this time that the prospector who had been killed was his Father, Calvin had a gut feeling that this would, indeed, turn out to be his dad. His thoughts were interrupted again by Jane speaking.

"Did the Marshal and the Ranger have any idea where that killing might have taken place?' Jane absent-mindedly continued to stir her coffee with her spoon.

"They mentioned something about a ranch called the Lazy something," Calvin replied. "Maybe it was the Lazy C. Yeah, that was it, the Lazy C."

Jane's hands involuntarily jerked, spilling the remainder of her cold coffee on the table. Her eyes grew large as she stared at Calvin, and she made no move to wipe up the coffee spill with the napkin that was lying in her lap. Almost in a whisper, she said, "Lazy C?"

"Yep, pretty sure that's what they said," Calvin responded.

Jane's heart was racing. She knew that her father and her brother would never kill a stranger that was simply crossing the ranch in his travels. That is, unless their characters had changed so much over the years that their hearts had hardened. She did not think this was likely. No, more likely, she thought to herself, was that Ivan was at the ranch and had somehow put himself into a position whereby he could kill a stranger traveling across the Lazy C without suffering consequences. And this only made him that much more dangerous. That knowledge made her goal of killing him more hazardous, but it did not dissuade her. She was, however, more fearful that something may have happened to her parents and her brother.

Calvin continued watching Jane's reaction to what he had told her. Jane had gone pale, and she stared at the spill that she had made on the table. Calvin used his napkin to wipe up the puddle of coffee. He slowly put the napkin to the side of the table and looked up at Jane. "Did I say something wrong?" he asked her.

Jane slowly brought her chin up and looked at the young man sitting across from her. "No, you didn't say anything wrong. I was just lost in my own thoughts." She managed a thin, partial smile, and she was nearly afraid to ask Calvin a question, but she calmly and quietly asked, "Was there anything else that those men at the saloon said?"

Calvin had now finished eating. He had not cleaned his plate. His appetite had seemed to wane as he thought of his father while speaking with Jane.

"Those men; I think their names were Jack and Ross," said Calvin. "They also said something about a woman that had been killed. I think they said that her name was Sylvia, and they said they thought it was the same man that had killed her and maybe my dad."

The cold reality of her mother's death pierced Jane's soul. To make matters worse, Jane knew in her heart who had killed her. Her emotions were so raw that Jane could not form the words to ask her next question. Tears were streaming from her eyes as she pulled a handkerchief from her handbag. Her shoulders shook as she silently cried. This time it was Calvin who laid his open hand on the table in front of Jane. She responded by grasping his hand while wiping the tears away with her free hand.

"I didn't mean to make you cry," said Calvin. "What did I say to make you so sad?"

Jane could barely control her quiet sobs and spoke in a whisper. "Sylvia was my mother."

"Oh, my God," said Calvin. "The Marshal and the Ranger talked about a woman named Jane being the daughter of the woman that got killed. Is that you?"

Jane slowly nodded her head, and whispered, "Yes."

Calvin thought for a moment, then said, "So the same man may have killed your mother and my father."

They held onto one another's hand while silent tears ran from their eyes. It was a few moments before they released their hands.

Jane had one more question for Calvin, but it was another moment or two before she could compose herself. While gathering her thoughts, the waitress returned to their table. She began gathering their plates.

"Will there by anything else for you two?" she asked.

Rather abruptly, Calvin answered, "No."

The waitress looked at him, her face held in a questioning look. She then turned her attention to Jane. She seemed to sense that both Calvin and Jane were experiencing unknown troubles, as each of them appeared to have been crying. She tore off two tickets from her order pad and laid them on the table. "I hope an angel looks over you two and helps your troubles go away," she said, and then walked away, carrying their dirty dishes.

At last, Jane summoned the courage to ask Calvin another question. "Did the Marshal have any idea who might have killed my mother and your father?"

"Well, the Marshal, the Ranger, and those two fellas in the saloon all seemed to think that it might be a man named Malone," Calvin responded.

Calvin's answer did not upset Jane nearly as much as the news of her mother's death. She had loved her mother and always admired her kindness. Through the years, she had received letters from Sylvia attesting to the love for her daughter, and her wish that Jane would return home. Instead, she had not answered her mother's pleas and had taken up with no-account bums, one of whom had sired what appeared to be the devil himself in human form. At that very moment, Jane wished that there was a quick way to kill herself. She held herself responsible for the death of her mother at the hands of her son. Her hand wavered as she thought that she could reach into her handbag and retrieve her pistol, then put herself out of her misery.

Jane's thoughts settled. Her wish to commit suicide eased. Instead, her resolve to rid herself of Ivan resurfaced as cold steel. She would not be dissuaded. She would go to the Lazy C and kill Ivan. Only then would she feel relief for the evil things that her son had done. She would avenge her mother's death.

Calvin had let go of Jane's hand. "The Marshal said I needed to come to his office as soon as I finished eating. I reckon I ought to go. What will you do, Miss Jane?"

Jane gazed at Calvin. The look on her face and the intense stare of her eyes nearly startled Calvin. But he waited for Jane's answer.

"Calvin, I believe that I will come along with you to the Marshal's office," said Jane. She picked up her handbag, reached into it, and placed some coins on the table. "Let's go." They rose together and walked out of the café.

* * *

Nathan was alone in his office. Ben Steele had left for the day, telling Nathan that he had some Ranger business to work on. Nathan looked up from his desk as the door to the office opened. He was expecting to see Calvin Kahl, but Calvin was accompanied by a woman he had never met. He rose and asked, "Could I help you with something, ma'am?"

Remembering his manners, Calvin spoke up, "She's with me, Marshal. I think you might want to talk with her?"

"Yes, ma'am," said Nathan as he stuck out his hand. "I'm Nathan Wolf."

Jane extended her hand. "I'm Jane Conley, Marshal. I'm the daughter of Michael and Sylvia Conley."

Almost hesitatingly, Nathan shook hands with Jane. To himself, he was thinking, *what am I going to say to her? Does she know about her mom and dad?* "Pleased to meet you, Miss Conley." He did not know what more he should say.

In her own manner, Jane broke the ice. "Marshal, I have just learned from Calvin, here," as she turned her face to Calvin, "that my mother has been killed by my son, Ivan Malone."

"Oh, my God," blurted Calvin. "That Malone character is your son?" he asked.

Jane nodded to Calvin.

Nathan, of course, knew the story behind the heretofore missing Jane Conley. But, though he had also been told that Malone was Jane Conley's son, it had never been truly verified. Now he knew the truth. He moved to the small table in the office. "Why don't you folks have a seat over here, and we can talk about Mr. Malone, among other things."

After they were seated, Nathan went to the wood stove and lifted the coffee pot. "I just made a fresh pot, and I'm going to have a cup of coffee. Shall I fill three mugs?"

Jane mumbled her assent followed by Calvin nodding his head. When they all had their coffee mugs, Nathan sat down at the table.

Nathan began to speak, "Miss Conley…"

He was interrupted by Jane. "I would prefer that you call me Jane, Marshal."

"Yes, ma'am." Nathan paused. He was not sure where to start. "Jane, what brought you back to North Texas?" He hesitated, then added, "I'm mighty glad you are here."

Jane took a sip of her coffee, collecting her thoughts. "To tell you the truth, Marshal, I came here to see my mother. She had sent me some traveling money so that I could came back to the Lazy C. Are you familiar with the Lazy C?" she asked.

"Yes, ma'am," Nathan answered.

Jane continued. "But then," and Jane's lips quivered before she blurted out, "I come here and find out that my mother is dead. Is that right, Marshal?"

"I'm afraid it is, Miss Conley. We have learned from two former Lazy C ranch hands who found your mother's body. She had been brutally murdered and hastily buried at the ranch."

Nathan paused to take a drink of his coffee. "Miss Conley..." Nathan began.

"Jane, Marshal."

"Yes, ma'am. Jane, why do you think that your son might have killed your mother? Nathan asked.

"Marshal, I have seen some mighty rough men in my life. But I sincerely believe that my son, Ivan, is the most evil man I have ever had the misfortune to know. He was evil as a child, and even meaner as a man. I have been beat up innumerable times at his hands."

"By your own son?" Calvin interjected.

"Yes, Calvin, by my own son," Jane answered.

For a moment, they were each trying to assimilate what had happened, but then Calvin spoke. "Marshal, I figure this Malone person also killed my dad. So, what are we going to do about it?"

Nathan hesitated, then answered, "I don't believe *we* will be doing anything about it. I intend to bring Malone in to stand trial."

"Can't we go along with you when you go to arrest him?" Calvin asked.

"If Malone is as dangerous as we think he is, I don't believe that would be a very good idea," answered Nathan. "Rest assured that I intend to get up to the Lazy C and bring him back to stand trial. There's not much doubt that he will be found guilty and hung for his crimes."

Jane and Calvin looked at each other. It was as if they read each other's minds.

"When will you be going up to the Lazy C?" asked Jane.

"I am not sure," Nathan replied. "Before I can arrest Malone, I have to get an arrest warrant from the County Judge, and that could take some time because we have several charges to describe to the judge. I also want to make sure that our Texas Ranger, Ben Steele, is available to go along with me. From what we know, Malone has a couple of gun hands always hanging around him for protection. So, it may not be just a one-man job to bring him in."

Once again, it was as if each of them was mulling over the situation in their respective minds. Their thoughts were disturbed by the opening of the front door of the office. They all looked up to see a stranger coming through the door. But with the sun at the man's back, it blinded Nathan, Jane, and Calvin. No one recognized the man until he had moved closer. Nathan immediately rose from his chair and extended his hand.

"Sean," said Nathan. "So good to see you up and around."

"Howdy, Marshal," said Sean.

"Sean, I believe you know this lady here at the table."

Sean Conley turned his head and looked at the woman. "No, no, I don't believe we have met."

"Sean, it's your sister," said Nathan.

Sean studied Jane's face again, and suddenly, he realized that he was looking at his long-absent sister. "Jane. Jane, is that you?"

Jane Conley rose quickly from her chair. "Oh, Sean," she said and rushed to her brother's outstretched arms.

"I had given up hope, Jane. I never thought I would see you again," said Sean.

"I wasn't so sure you ever would either," said Jane, and she managed a smile as she looked into the face of Sean. "Just look at you. You have grown so tall."

Sean laughed. "Well, it's been a few years. Where have you been all this time, Jane?"

"That's a story that is long, boring, and very sad. I will tell you about it sometime when we have a quiet moment," said Jane.

"Are you here to stay?" Sean asked.

"If you will have me back at the ranch," said Jane.

"Of course," said Sean. "You're going to take your place at the ranch as another Conley. I am thrilled that you are back."

Nathan interrupted. "Sean, I am so glad to see you well again. The last time I saw you up at Fort Sill, I was not sure you would pull through."

Sean chuckled. "I wasn't too sure I was going to make it either."

"What's he talking about, Sean?" asked Jane.

"Well, that's another long story," Sean replied.

Nathan interjected, "Before we sit down to talk about your parents and what is happening at the Lazy C, Sean, I don't believe that you have met this young fella here." Nathan pointed to Calvin. "Sean, this is Calvin Kahl. He's passing through Decatur looking for his dad, and we think there might be a connection to what has been happening at your ranch."

Sean and Calvin shook hands. Sean did not know what to make of what Nathan had just said. But before he could ask a question, his thoughts were interrupted as Nathan said, "Have a seat here at the table, Sean. I want you to tell your sister and me what happened."

In the next few minutes, Sean told them about the day he and his dad left the ranch to go to Spanish Fort to send a telegram to their attorney in Fort Worth to check on Sylvia, who had recently gone there to find Jane but had been gone a bit too long.

"Mom was on her way to Fort Worth to find me?" echoed Jane.

"Yes," said Sean.

Jane began crying again. "You don't know, do you."

Sean was confused. "What do you mean? What did I say?"

Jane blurted it out, "Mom is dead."

"What," cried Sean. "Oh, no. This can't be true." But inwardly, Sean knew it must be true. His mother had left the ranch some time ago to visit Jane in Fort Worth. Yet Jane was here, and she had made no mention of seeing their mother.

"You tell him, Marshal," cried Jane.

Nathan gathered himself. "I have two pieces of bad news. Both of your parents have been killed at the hands of Ivan Malone. Jane, when Sean and your dad were leaving the ranch to go to Spanish Fort, they were ambushed by Ivan Malone and his crony gun hands. They killed your dad, and almost killed Sean. Sean was severely wounded by a bullet in his back. That's why Sean has been laid up for a while and is only now getting around again."

Turning his face to Sean, Nathan continued, "And Sean, your mom was killed even before she got off the ranch to go to the train station for her trip to Fort Worth. Again, it was Ivan Malone who killed her and threw her in a shallow grave at the edge of the Lazy C."

Jane leaned her head on Sean's shoulder and continued to cry, periodically wiping her eyes with a handkerchief. Tears leaked from Sean's eyes as he comforted his sister. He wiped them on the back of his hand.

"So, what are we going to do about all of this, Marshal?" Sean questioned.

"I think I said before," Nathan replied, "*we* aren't going to do anything. I intend to get an arrest warrant and go arrest Malone and bring him here for trial. There's no doubt that he will get what he deserves."

"Hmph," Sean snorted. "A slow painful death, and a fast trip to hell is all that Malone deserves, and the quicker the better. I believe that I can hasten his trip."

"Now Sean, I understand how you feel, but you can't take the law into your own hands," Nathan said. "You just can't do this by yourself. That man is far too dangerous for one man to handle. Did you forget that he has already tried to kill you?"

"He won't be alone, Marshal," Calvin spoke up. It seemed that Calvin Kahl had come to realize that there was only one way to avenge the death of his father. His intentions were clear. He would help Sean in any way he could to put an end to Ivan Malone.

"Calvin," said Nathan, as he turned to the young man. "We don't know for sure you're your dad was killed by Malone. Don't you get yourself mixed up in this mess."

Calvin shrugged his shoulders. "I'm betting that it was Malone that killed my dad."

"Now listen, you two," said Nathan. "You can't do this. You can't play vigilante, or I'll be forced to bring you to trial also. Don't make this matter even worse by adding another killing at your hands. I won't allow it." Nathan's words sounded hollow, even to him. He thought that if he was in their shoes, he would probably say the same thing. He remembered that he had, indeed, said the same thing after he heard what had happened to Claire May at the hands of one of Malone's henchmen. There was no way he could block their actions, aside from locking them up for their own protection, and he knew that he could not legally do that.

Nathan's thoughts were interrupted. "Well, you might as well add me to your list of criminals, Marshal," said Jane. "I'm not afraid of Ivan, especially if I have Sean and Calvin for company."

"Dammit," shouted Nathan as he loudly slapped his hand on the table. "You intend to back their play, Jane?"

"I won't be backing anybody, Marshal. I may even send the first bullet myself, toward the stone-cold heart of Ivan," she said. "You simply have no idea how miserable he has made my life and the lives of other people who have had contact with him over the years. It's time that it stops for good."

The room grew quiet. There was nothing left to say. Nathan did not want to get into an argument with three people bent on killing an outlaw. He could only repeat himself, saying again, "I am advising you not to do anything foolish. If you approach Malone, one or all of you could end up dead. I promise that tomorrow, I will go see the county judge for the arrest warrant and then go to the Lazy C and bring Malone back to stand trial. I don't want to have to arrest any of you in the process."

"We want to go with you when you arrest Malone, Marshal," said Calvin. The others nodded their head in agreement.

"I don't think that's a good idea," Nathan responded. "You would be putting me in a position of having to look out for your welfare. If I'm hunting a man down, I don't want those distractions. I would strongly suggest that you set yourselves up in the hotel and wait until I get back from the Lazy C in a couple days. Will you please do that?"

There was no response from Sean, Jane, or Calvin. Sean rose from his chair. "Jane and Calvin, let's go over to the hotel like the Marshal says." With that, the three of them rose from the table and walked out of the office. Nathan watched them out of the front window of the office as they made their way to the hotel. He hoped that they would take his advice.

It had been an unusual day, and Nathan was tired. *Where the hell did Steele run off to* thought Nathan to himself. But he was not going to dwell on his whereabouts. It was also too late in the day to go search out the county judge to get a warrant. Nathan had not had any dealings with the judge, and he did not want to get off on the wrong foot with him by showing up after working hours. He would go search him out in the morning. For now, he was going to close the office, go to the livery to get Wander, and head for home. He looked forward to the normalcy of his own family and home, even if it was only for the evening, knowing that he would need to return to town in the morning. In only a few minutes, he was riding the trail out of town as the sun's rays became dimmer to the west.

* * *

As they sat in the lobby of the Chisholm Trail Hotel, they had already discussed some of their options. None of those options involved staying in Decatur, the course of action requested by Marshal Wolf. Sean, Jane, and Calvin had made up their minds that they would be going to the Lazy C Ranch to end the life of Ivan Malone.

"You two wait here. I'll be back in a few minutes," said Sean.

"Where are you going?" asked Calvin.

"I'm going over to the railroad depot. I seem to remember that there is a north bound freight train that comes through here later this evening, and I aim to get us on that train for Nocona," said Sean.

He turned to go out of the hotel lobby, but then he turned around and came back.

"Do either of you have any money?" asked Sean. "I only have a few dollars in my pocket since I have not been back home yet."

Jane and Calvin each gave him a few more dollars, and Sean left the hotel. When he reached the depot, the night agent was on duty, and the man looked up from his desk behind the ticket window and watched Sean approach the window.

"We're closed, mister," said the agent.

Sean neared the window, where he could see that the station agent was reading what appeared to be a police story magazine. Obviously, the man had little to occupy him on the night shift.

"If I remember correctly, don't you have a freight train that comes through here at night?" Sean asked.

The clerk was slow to answer, but finally said, "Yeah, there might be, but how would you know that?"

"Well, you see, I live on a ranch up north of here, and when we would go to town to get our supplies, our mercantile man in Nocona would tell us about new merchandise that had come in on the previous night's freight train."

"Where 'bouts is your ranch?" asked the clerk.

"It's the Lazy C, up between Nocona and Spanish Fort," Sean replied. "Maybe you've heard of it."

"Yeah, I've heard of it. Last I knew that ranch was owned by a fella named Conley. I seem to remember his name was Michael Conley. You any relation to them Conleys?"

Sean wondered how this railroad freight agent would know of the Lazy C. But he answered, "Yes, my name is Sean Conley. Michael is my dad. How do you know of the Lazy C?"

"Well son, before I got put into this night station agent job, I used to ride the rails as a freight clerk on the freight trains," answered the agent. "I remember that when we would pull into Nocona, your dad would be there waiting with the mercantile man sometimes, if he was anxious to get his supplies. I met him on one of those runs." The freight clerk chuckled. "Anxious, he was. How is your dad getting along?"

"He's dead, mister," replied Sean. "He was murdered recently, and I need to get back to the ranch pronto."

"Well, what the hell are you doing down here in Decatur?"

"It's a long story, mister," answered Sean. "My dad was killed, and the killer almost got me. I'm down here talking to the Marshal, but I've got to get back to the ranch as soon as possible."

"Well, what's that got to do with me?" questioned the agent.

"I need you to let me ride that freight train tonight. Me and my sister and another fella; we all need to get up to the Lazy C," said Sean.

The station agent scratched the stubble on his cheek. "You got animals?" asked the agent.

"Yeah," Sean answered. "We got my horse and the other fella's horse."

"Hmm," the agent appeared to be thinking about it. "You got any money?"

Sean had known that at some point, the underpaid station agent would be asking for a payoff for himself. It just seemed to work that way.

"I only got a couple dollars, but I figure we could ride in the freight car, or even the stock car with the horses if that would be okay," said Sean.

"What do you mean by a couple dollars," the agent asked.

There it was, thought Sean. The payoff. "I've got three dollars, a dollar for each of us."

"Mmm," noised the agent. "I reckon I could let you ride in the baggage car, but then, you've got those two horses. And the railroad ain't in the business of shipping horses for free."

"Yep, I don't suppose you are," answered Sean. But he knew that his request had nothing to do with the railroad and its rules. It all hinged on the freight agent being able to pocket a couple dollars under the table. "I'll give you another dollar to put the horses in the stock car," said Sean. "Do we need a ticket or anything?"

"Nah," said the agent. "Train usually gets here sometime around nine or ten o'clock. You just need to be here before nine o'clock tonight. I'll flag the freighter down and get you on."

"I appreciate it," said Sean. "We'll be here before nine." Sean was just about to turn around and walk back to the hotel, but he was stopped by the freight agent.

"That's four dollars," said the man. "You need to pay me in advance."

Sean was not surprised. In fact, he was expecting it. The freight agent was pocketing the money for himself. Sean did not mind. He only cared about getting on the northbound freighter. He paid the man the four dollars and walked from the depot as he shouted to the agent, "We'll see you tonight."

Jane and Calvin were still in the hotel lobby when Sean returned. "We're leaving tonight," he said. He then looked at Jane, then at Calvin. "How much more money do we have?"

After counting out their money, Sean said, "That will be plenty. Jane, we need to go to the mercantile and get you some travelin' duds, and I need to get a gun before the store closes. Jane, we'll need to get you a horse when we get to Nocona."

"I have a gun," said Calvin.

"Well, that's fine, Calvin. Have you ever used it?" asked Sean.

"Well, no," said Calvin.

"We better buy you a shotgun, Calvin. No offense," said Sean.

"I have my own pistol, Sean," said Jane, "and I know how to use it."

Sean chuckled. "Nothing surprises me about you, sister. Let's go." They walked to the mercantile store.

Later, the train depot's night-shift freight agent kept his word and flagged down the late-night freighter. He and the surprised baggage car agent helped Sean and Calvin get the two horses into the stock car, after which the train began rolling once more with the trio comfortably bedded down on a mat of discarded potato sacks. In a few hours, just prior to daybreak, they would arrive at Nocona.

Chapter Sixteen

Wolf Ranch
Decatur, Texas

Nathan and Claire May sat next to each other on the back porch of the cabin, listening to the chorus of frogs at the tank, cicadas singing their strange song, and crickets keeping time in the nighttime chorus. Claire May's hand was nestled in Nathan's larger hand. In Nathan's other hand was a nearly empty glass of diluted bourbon.

"Peaceful, isn't it," said Claire May.

"Mm, mm," was Nathan's sleepy reply.

A light shown from the barn where Pablo was finishing a few chores before he turned in for the night. Claire May had fed Bobby earlier, and the child was sleeping soundly in the small bed in the couple's bedroom. An hour earlier, the couple had finished a catfish dinner, catfish courtesy of their tank. Pablo had caught and cleaned the fish in the afternoon, and Claire May fried them in corn meal for their supper. Pablo had joined them for the catfish supper, and then retired to the barn.

"I've got to take off in the morning, and it looks like I might be gone two or three days," said Nathan.

"Marshal business I presume," Claire May replied. "Or do you have some girlfriend that I don't know about?" She was teasing.

He returned the teasing, "I'm too tired to have a girlfriend, but I keep my eyes open." Claire May playfully slugged Nathan in the shoulder.

"Mr. Wolf," she said. "I think we need to head for bed and get the twinkle out of your eye."

A little over an hour later, they lay in bed, with no night wear gracing either of them. Nathan lay on his back, his mouth slightly open, quietly sleeping after their love making. Claire May had her arm across Nathan's chest, and she smiled at the husband she dearly loved as she drifted off to sleep.

Earlier that Same Day
When he had left Nathan earlier in the day, Ben Steele did have Ranger business to attend to. He had gone over to the telegraph office and sent a familiar telegram to Ranger headquarters in Austin. It was the same telegram he had sent to his old friend and cohort on previous occasions when he knew he was going into a dangerous situation. The telegram read:

To: Captain Bill McDonald, Texas Rangers Headquarters, Austin, Texas
Headed into trouble, Bill. As usual, if the good Lord takes me, all my worldly goods should be given to my sister Betty in Waco.
Regards
Steele

Ben Steele had lost track of how many times he had sent this identical wire to his senior agent and old friend in Austin; he reckoned a dozen at least. He was no fool. He knew that Ivan Malone was pure and evil danger. But Steele had been a Ranger for so long that he firmly believed in the old Ranger adage, "One Riot, One Ranger," a complete over-exaggeration of the capabilities of the Texas Rangers. While the Texas Rangers were a formidable force on the plains of Texas, they were only human, and over the course of history, plenty of Steele's fellow Rangers had been killed in the line of duty.

After leaving the telegraph office, Ben boarded the afternoon northbound train that was headed for Nocona. Ben Steele was determined that he would bring Malone to justice even if it meant stepping on the toes of his friend, Marshal Nathan Wolf. The source of this whole sordid business dealing with Malone had sprung from a telegram to Nathan from Sean Conley. Conley had alluded to there being a mysterious disappearance of horses belonging to the Lazy C Ranch. Therefore, it was Wolf's case. And Ben was quite certain that Nathan would not necessarily agree with Ben's strategy regarding Malone. Steele meant to get himself to the Lazy C Ranch, confront Malone, and put the outlaw in his grave. The Ranger was not such a stickler for the rules of law when there was a clear menace to society on the loose in the form of a serial murderer, Ivan Malone.

Hours later, the northbound train arrived in Nocona. After off-loading his horse, he looked up at the sky. As it was late afternoon, he decided to stay overnight in Nocona and start out for the Lazy C in the morning.

The following morning, after eating breakfast, he retrieved his horse from the livery where the horse had been left the evening before. In a short time, Ben was riding toward the Lazy C Ranch. He shifted in his saddle, trying to get a more comfortable position. After starting his day so early, he knew it was going to be a tiring ride. He also knew that a lawman's business always took long methodical days, and it would be late afternoon when he reached the Lazy C. He would be tired at the end of this day.

Later, being as furtive as possible, Ben rode, following a creek bed that bordered the Lazy C. The shadows were lengthening, and he was hoping to use the coming darkness to his advantage. Off in the distance, he could see the topmost rooftop of the Lazy C barn. The barn was his destination in the oncoming darkness. Turning his horse into a grove of post oaks, he dismounted and found a place to rest until full darkness had enveloped the countryside. But even the best plans can run afoul. Unbeknownst to Ben, he had been seen by one of Malone's henchmen who had been riding a slow picket on the same side of the ranch now occupied by the Texas Ranger, and he quickly retreated to ride back to the ranch house where he reported his discovery to Malone.

"I don't know who he is or what he wants, but if he's hunkered down in the trees by the creek, I don't figure he will come knocking on the door," said Malone, when he heard the news. "Only two ways he can get close to the house without being seen; either behind the barn or behind the back of the house. The brush behind the house is pretty thick, so I'm figuring he'll wait 'til dark and come up behind the barn. We'll be waiting for him."

* * *

As dusk descended, the cicadas began their nightly mating game chorus. Above Ben's head in the tree, he swore there must be a dozen of those critters trying to beckon girlfriends for mating. Three hours later, when dark had fully descended and the lights in the ranch house had been extinguished, Ben thought that it was time to go pay a visit to Ivan Malone. He did not climb onto the saddle of his horse, but instead, led the animal quietly from the oak grove, through the weedy grass to the back of the barn where he tied him off on a loose board. He drew his pistol and crept around the side of the barn until he had just reached the main door. He cautiously peered inside but could see nothing in the black darkness within the building. He began to cross the doorway on his way to the house. It was then that he was struck on the head from behind with such force that he slumped to the ground in a state of unconsciousness.

Ivan Malone and his ranch hand henchman had been waiting within the barn, just inside the barn's entry door, careful to stay in the darkest places possible. The moment Ben walked in front of the open barn door, they rushed to ambush the intruder and put him out cold. It was then that they noticed Ben's Texas Ranger badge.

"This ain't that marshal, it's a damn Texas Ranger," said Malone. But Malone and his partner had been up all day and now half the night waiting to ambush whoever pursued them. And because he was tired, Malone made a mistake. With Ben Steele out cold, he told his cohort, "Drag him into the tool room, tie his hands and feet and take his gun. Make sure you latch that tool room door. We can deal with the Ranger in the morning."

Malone's hired man carried out his boss's orders, dragging Ben into the barn and into the tool room, where he tied Ben's hands and feet. He then took Ben's pistol and closed and latched the door to the toolroom. He examined Ben's pistol and decided that it wasn't any better than the one he owned, so he tossed the pistol onto the top of a wood barrel outside the toolroom, a careless action on his part. He left the barn and walked to the ranch house.

In his unconscious state, Ben's mind was playing tricks on him. As he was dragged across the floor of the barn, the smell of the hay on the floor brought a picture of Ben enjoying a hayride with a lost love of his youth. In the tool room, his mind shifted to the smell of leather and steel of the tools that he had used in his youth to help his father on their small farm. It would be some time before Ben returned to reality.

Hours Earlier
Nocona, Texas

Sean, Jane, and Calvin arrived in Nocona in the dark of early morning. After off-loading Sean and Calvin's horses, they sat on a wooden bench outside a café on the main street of Nocona, waiting patiently until the owner made her appearance to open the door. Above the door, a weathered sign attested to the fact that this was the aptly named *Main Street Café*. The café owner allowed them to come inside while she and the other arriving help bustled about preparing to open their door to the public. She asked a waitress to serve three mugs of steaming coffee to the travelers.

The sassy waitress had a few words for them. "My, oh, my," she said. "You three look like you just woke up in the woods." She had noticed the bits of straw and dirt clinging to their clothing from sleeping on the floor of the baggage car.

Although her remarks were a bit on the rude side, Sean and Calvin smiled and nodded their heads.

As she placed the steaming coffee mugs on the table, she said, "I'll be back in a minute to take your orders." She then went back to her duties to help ready the café for customers. Once again, the three travelers had to pool their money to pay their breakfast bill. They then led the two horses and walked to the livery stable.

Sean recognized the livery owner as he and his father had had business dealings with the man in the past. Likewise, the livery owner recognized Sean and stuck out his hand and welcomed them. "You're Sean Conley, ain't you?" the man said.

"Yep, I'm Sean," he replied, as the men shook hands.

"Sean, you're a sight for sore eyes. I haven't seen you in quite a spell," said the livery owner. He conversed with Sean for a couple more minutes. Then Sean introduced him to Jane and Calvin.

"My Lord a'mighty," said the livery man. "Miss Jane, I remember many years back when your dad would bring you and Sean with him to town." The man's curiosity got the better of him, and he asked, "Have you come back to stay with us?"

Jane smiled slightly, but she did not remember the man at all. She had been too young to remember coming to the livery stable as a child. "I haven't made up my mind yet" she answered.

The livery man turned to Sean. "Say, it ain't any of my business, but why did your dad sell the ranch? Is he all right? I haven't seen him for quite some time. He used to come in once in a while with a horse or two to sell," said the livery owner. "Is he gettin' along all right?"

Sean was astounded at the livery man's rather personal question and was not sure how to answer, but he said, "We have not sold the ranch. Whatever would make you ask that question?" And in answer to the man's other question, Sean answered, "Dad died recently, accident at the ranch." Sean did not believe that the livery man needed to know the specifics of the murder of his Father.

"Oh, my," was the livery man's answer. "Sorry to hear that. He was a good man, and always treated me fairly."

Sean just nodded his acknowledgement, then spoke, "My sister, here, needs a horse. We aim to ride on home to the Lazy C, but I'll tell you up front that I don't have any money. I need you to put it on account, and I'll pay you later."

The livery man scratched his whiskery cheek. "Yep, Sean, I can do that. I figure you'll pay me as soon as you can. Let's go take a look at what I've got out in the corral."

They all walked out to the side of the livery and back to a corral, where four horses turned their heads to watch the four people as they approached the holding pen. The hair on the back of Sean's neck tingled. He was looking closely at the four horses. As he got nearer to the animals, he walked to the fence and swung a leg between the fence rails, went on through the fence and walked slowly to the horses. He examined two of the horses more closely, a roan and a gray, running his hand down the side of the horses, and looking intently at the brands on the left rear hip of the animals. He ran his fingers over the brand on each horse. He saw what he was looking for. The brands on the two horses had been modified. An older branding scar showed a different color next to the more recent brand overlay. The Bar Lazy C had been overbranded to look like a "T – O." But Sean recognized the two horses as belonging to the Lazy C remuda, and his suspicions were proven out by his examination of the brands.

Sean turned to the livery stable owner. "Do you have any idea who owns the T bar O?" "I don't rightly know," the livery man responded. I think I bought those two horses at auction here in Nocona."

Sean looked at the livery owner and did not see any initial sign that the man was lying. "I reckon that if you bought them at auction, you should have the bill of sale on them. Ain't that right?" Sean asked.

The livery owner hesitated a moment, then replied. "I'd have to look through my papers in the office. Sometimes those papers get lost. You know how it is."

Sean scowled and stepped back through the fence rails. He approached the livery man. "You got bills of sale for them, or don't you?"

"Sure, I've got the papers on them. And I remember for sure that I got those two at the Nocona livestock auction a few days back. Let's go see if I can find the papers."

"Yes, I'll look at them," Sean replied, "but I'm telling you right up front, those two out there that I was looking at are my horses. I don't know how you got them because I never sold them off my ranch."

The livery owner immediately took offense. "Are you trying to tell me those horses are stolen? Why, I don't ever deal in stolen livestock." He stuck his chin out and stared at Sean.

"I'm not *trying* to tell you; I'm telling you outright that those two horses are stolen. Let's look at your paperwork."

In the office of the livery stable, Sean was soon looking over several sheets of paper regarding the sale and ownership of the two horses in question. For each horse, there was a signed copy of a paper giving the seller the right to act as an agent and sell the horses that had previously been owned by the Lazy C. They were signed by the agent and the alleged owner. Sean recognized the signatures. The acting selling agent was a ranch hand at the Lazy C. The authorizing signature was none other than Ivan Malone.

The livery owner interrupted Sean's thoughts. "I guess you can see why I thought you had sold the ranch. I don't know this Malone fella, but since he was the person authorizing the sale, why, I figured that he was the new owner of the Lazy C."

"Mister, you ain't thinkin' real clear,' Sean said. "You know that the Lazy C is owned by us Conleys. And you know that only the Conley's would have the right to sell stock off of our ranch." Sean was getting angry again. "Seems to me like you were a party to horse rustling from our ranch."

"Well, I reckon you might be right," said the sheepish livery man. "But I swear, I thought maybe your dad sold off the ranch. I didn't know any different."

Sean was cooling off. Maybe the livery man was being truthful. Sean decided not to pressure the man any further. He simply wanted his horses returned to him so that he could be on his way.

Sean had known for quite some time that horses were mysteriously disappearing from the ranch. But at that time, he did not have any inkling on how they were being lost. Yet, he had a niggling suspicion, since the disappearance of the animals began to occur after Ivan Malone had moved onto the ranch. But he did not have proof that Malone was involved, and that is why he had contacted the U.S. Marshal weeks ago. His thoughts went back to the day when he had sent a wire to Nathan Wolf, asking for his assistance in an apparent horse rustling incident at the Lazy C. The bills of sale that he had just seen proved his suspicions. Sean now had proof and knew the rustlers involved in the disappearances from the ranch remuda. The horses were being secreted from the ranch by Ivan Malone and his cronies, no doubt in order to pocket their ill-gotten loot. Just the thought of Malone's crooked dealings caused Sean's temper to raise once more. He was seething within, and his countenance showed it.

"Mister, I still own the Lazy C, and I did not sell any horses from my ranch." Sean's face was crimson. "What you've got here is a worthless bunch of paper. Those horses are still mine, and I will be taking them with us when we leave. You go on and saddle and tack the gray and put the saddle and tack on account. If you have a problem with this, then I think we can get the Marshal involved. But I'll remind you, that dealing in stolen horses can put you at the end of a noose." Sean let his glaring eyes and stinging words sink in on the livery man.

"Nope, nope, we don't need to get the Marshal involved," the livery man stuttered, then lifted his head. "But I want you to know, I didn't know anything about those horses being stolen. Seemed like to me that the paperwork was in order when I bought 'em."

"Sean's temper cooled a bit. "Hmm. Maybe so. But it seems to me like you should have been able to see that the brand on the horses had been changed."

"I knew by looking at the brands that they had been changed, but that happens all the time when livestock changes hands. But I gotta admit that I never heard of the T bar O. But I didn't have cause to doubt it being legit. Brands get changed all the time."

"Yeah, I reckon they do," said Sean. "Just go ahead and get the gray saddled up, and I'll lead the roan. We gotta make tracks for home."

Wolf Ranch
Just Outside Decatur, TX

It was still near dark, as a light struggled to break the horizon at the Wolf Ranch. "Time to get up, sleepyhead." Claire May bent over and kissed Nathan, who was trying his best to ignore her while pulling the bedsheet closer to his neck. If he could, he would pull the sheet over his head. It seemed to him that he had just fallen asleep, and yet, here was Claire May rousing him to get up. He was not having any of it.

Claire May had gotten out of bed thirty minutes ago to get dressed and feed Bobby. She knew what she would do, and she turned and walked out of the room, only to return quickly with a bundle of squirming toddler in her arms. She placed the baby next to Nathan and watched as Bobby crawled over to his daddy's face. Bobby began pulling on Nathan's nose and gurgling while he chortled his happiness.

"That'll teach you to ignore your wife, Marshal," she teased. "Bobby will wake you up for sure," said Claire May, and laughed as she turned to leave the room.

Nathan groaned, but it was a happy groan as he pulled his arms from under the sheet and clasped his son in his arms. "You're up kinda early, aren't you, big boy?" Bobby jabbered in response. Nathan continued to give attention to his son. He still marveled at the miracle of birth and the fact that he had his own small person to love. After another minute, Bobby became restless. He wanted to know what had happened to his mother. Slowly, Nathan rose from the bed and gathered up Bobby. He walked to the kitchen, where the toddler spied his mother and chuckled. Nathan placed the baby on the floor so that Bobby could crawl over to his mother. Nathan went back to the bedroom to dress and shave.

As he shaved, Nathan's mind wandered to the previous day, and he suddenly became alert as he remembered that Sean Conley, Jane

Conley, and Calvin Kahl were waiting for him in town. He had a premonition that he might find that they had not waited for him, and he now felt that he needed to get to town as quickly as possible.

"Just some toasted bread and a cup of coffee, sweetheart," said Nathan as he came to the kitchen. "I need to get back to town."

Claire May's response was a "Hmph." But she laid two slices of bread on the top of the stove to toast. Nathan had already told Claire May most of the gist of the drama surrounding the Lazy C, and of the danger inherent with the outlaw Ivan Malone.

In many ways, Claire May was just as astute as Nathan in her understanding of human nature. This was born out in her question, "Do you think the Conleys and that prospector's boy will still be in town waiting for you?"

Nathan was slathering butter and jam on his toast as he answered. "Hope so. I don't want them going out to the Lazy C on their own." He devoured the toast and gulped down his coffee, ignoring the fact that the coffee was a bit too hot for that sort of drinking. He left the kitchen, went to the bathroom, then came back and kissed Claire May, who was holding Bobby in her arms. Nathan lifted the toddler and gave him a buzzing, noisy kiss on his cheek. The baby laughed as he was given back to his mother.

"Be careful, Nathan." Claire May reached out and grabbed Nathan's sleeve, drawing him closer as she kissed him again."

She watched from the back porch as Nathan finished saddling Wander. Nathan waved at her as he fast walked the horse down the lane to the road. At the road he spurred Wander and the horse and rider disappeared from view at a loping pace. "Lord, look after him," whispered Claire May.

* * *

When he arrived in town, Nathan did not see Ben's horse tied to the hitch rack, nor was Ben in the office. He then inquired at the livery stable, and Leonard Brown told him that Ben had not been there either. Nathan had a suspicion about where his friend might be.

As Nathan finished his second mug of coffee, he sat at his desk looking out the front window and growing ever more impatient. He glanced up at the old Regulator wind-up clock, loudly ticking away the seconds. He was waiting until nine o'clock when he would ride to the home of Judge Wilford Shelby to get an arrest warrant for Ivan Malone. He had never met the local county judge but had heard stories that the Judge was a bit eccentric and hard-headed. He finished his coffee, picked up his saddlebags and his rifle, and locked the office door as he left. He stowed his gear on his saddle and climbed up on Wander. He rode to the east side of town where he had been told the judge lived. A sign on the front gate leading to the house attested to the fact that it was the judge's home. It read *Wilford Shelby, Esq., Wise County District Judge and Justice of the Peace.* The sign was black with bright yellow lettering. *Rather pretentious,* thought Nathan. He dismounted and walked to the Shelby front door, where he rapped softly. In short order, the door opened to reveal a near-bald, spectacled, and owl-eyed, rotund man. Nathan guessed him to be in his late fifties or early sixties.

"Yes, state your business," said Judge Shelby, his bushy eyebrows keeping time with the cadence of his words.

"Are you Judge Shelby?" Nathan asked.

"Yeah, yeah, I'm Judge Shelby, who are you?" Shelby responded. His eyes opened even larger than before as he waited for a response.

Nathan put his hand out, saying, "I'm U.S. Marshal Nathan Wolf."

The judge accepted Nathan's hand, shook it twice, and dropped his hand.

"So, you're the new Marshal, eh. Well, we've not had much to recommend our previous lawmen," said Shelby. "I hope you're better than they were." He paused, as if looking Nathan up and down for flaws. "Well, why are you here?" The judge did not ask Nathan to step inside.

"Judge Shelby, I need an arrest warrant," said Nathan. "I need to go pick up a man for murder."

"Murder, you say?" Shelby said it as if he doubted Nathan. "I haven't heard about any murder around these parts. I reckon you better step inside here and tell me the particulars on why you need this warrant." He stepped back from the doorway and allowed Nathan to enter. "Follow me," he said. He led Nathan to a room at the side of the house. It was obviously the Judge's office. A matching set of lawbooks as well as other books lined several shelves behind an overly large desk that was strewn with papers and files. The room smelled of burnt cigars. Nathan thought to himself that the whole room could use a good cleaning and straightening. Apparently the disarray did not bother Judge Shelby in the least. He casually picked a cigar stub from an ash tray full of ash and cigar butts and lit it. Nathan wondered how he kept from lighting his eyebrows on fire.

"Have a seat, Marshal," said the Judge as he sat his ample girth on a chair behind his desk. The chair seemed to creak its protestation. "What's this talk about a murder?"

Nathan tried his best not to cough amidst the rancid cigar smoke being blown around the room by the Judge as he related the story of the evil works of Ivan Malone. He purposefully left out the story of one of Malones henchmen coming to the Wolf Ranch and harassing Claire May. He figured that was irrelevant to getting a warrant for murder. After telling most of the details of the happenings at the Lazy C to the

Judge, to Nathan's surprise, the Judge seemed to have knowledge of some of the key players in the scenario.

"When I was just a young pup starting out in the law business, I helped out on a case of boundary disputes. There were lots of them in the old days. Anyhow, in my research, I seem to recall a large ranch up in Montague County that belonged to the Conley family," said the Judge. "Is that the ranch you are talking about, Marshal?"

"Yes, that's the one, Judge. It's the Lazy C."

"I don't believe I've ever heard of this Malone fella," said the Judge. "Is he from around these parts?"

"No Judge, he recently came up here from Fort Worth," Nathan said.

"Oh, Fort Worth, huh. There's a whole passel of outlaws down there just waiting to rustle some cattle or rob the cowboys and workin' folks," said the Judge. "I get a few of them in my court if the law ever catches the scoundrels. So, why is this Malone fella up here?"

"Apparently Judge, he may be the grandson of the current owners of the Lazy C. He was taken in by the Conleys because he is their grandson and is now doing everything he can to take over the Lazy C, even if it means killing the present owners, his own grandparents. Like I said, Judge, we have witnesses to corroborate the murders of the prospector, Michael Conley, and Sylvia Conley at the hands of Malone."

"And you say he killed a Comanche up there too?"

"Yes, sir," Nathan answered.

"Oh, criminy. All we need is another flare up from the Comanches," said the Judge. "I 'spect the Indian Agent up there in Lawton is fit to be tied," said the Judge. "He's liable to bring some buffoon out of Washington into the picture and mess everything up."

Nathan had to chuckle. Before he answered, he watched as a clump of cigar ash dropped down onto the front of the Judge's rumpled shirt.

"No, I don't think so, Judge. The Indian Agent is more likely to just let the Comanches track down Malone, take their revenge, and settle the problem right fast."

"Well, that would solve the whole problem. But then again, Marshal, the people pay us to keep the peace and bring criminals to justice, don't they?" the Judge stated.

"Yes, sir, they do," Nathan answered.

Judge Shelby straightened up in his chair and leaned over to open one of the desk drawers. As he shifted his weight, his chair creaked ominously. He retrieved a blank warrant, filled in the pertinent lines on the form, and handed the warrant to Nathan.

"After you arrest this Malone character, are you going to bring him here to Wise County, or hand him over to the authorities in Montague County?" the Judge asked.

"Well, I hadn't given that much thought, Judge. But, I figure since I'm based here in Decatur, I guess I thought I'd bring him back here," said Nathan. "And from what I understand, there isn't any full-time lawman in Montague County. What do you think, Judge?"

Judge Shelby's eyebrows danced for a few seconds before he said, "I look forward to seeing this Malone character in my court room." The Judge pulled himself up out of his chair and stuck out his hand to Nathan.

The men shook hands. Shelby's parting words were, "Good luck, Marshal."

Nathan trotted Wander back to the center of town and tied up in front of the Chisolm Trail Hotel. He expected to see Sean Conley, Jane Conley, and Calvin Kahl waiting for him in the lobby. He saw no sign of them when he walked toward the front desk. He had a sick feeling in his stomach as he caught the attention of the desk clerk. The man looked up from the newspaper he was reading.

"Hello, Marshal. What can I do for you?" the clerk asked.

"I think you have a fella named Sean Conley and his sister Jane and another fella that were supposed to meet me here in the lobby. Have you seen them?"

"Yes, sir, I saw them, Marshal," said the clerk. "I asked them why they were hanging around my lobby. They said they were waiting for you. But they didn't stick around or stay here last night. They headed on out of here yesterday, late afternoon. Said they couldn't wait for you and had to get on back home. Probably just as well. Didn't seem like they had the money to stay here overnight."

"What makes you say that?" asked Nathan.

"Well, I saw the one fella asking the other two for money. Don't know why," said the clerk. But it didn't seem like they had enough money to stay here overnight. Moot point, though, since they up and left."

Nathan shook his head. "Dammit," he mumbled.

"Beg your pardon?" the clerk asked.

"Oh, never mind, mister. Thanks for the information." Nathan walked out of the hotel. He headed for the railroad station and soon looked across the counter at the ticket agent.

"Need a ticket, Marshal?" the clerk asked.

"Maybe," Nathan replied. "First, though, do you know if you sold any tickets late yesterday afternoon to two fellas and a woman, all travelling together?"

The ticket clerk seemed taken aback by the question. He stammered a bit and said, "Well, I'm not sure. What's this about, Marshal?"

"They're not in any trouble, mister. I just need to catch up with them,"

"Mmm. Well, we're not supposed to do this, Marshal, but my night relief man told me that he had let two men and a woman ride the night freighter to Nocona last night," said the clerk. He said they rode in the baggage car and had a couple horses with them that went in a livestock car."

"Does that happen very often?" Nathan asked.

"Mmm, it ain't supposed to, Marshal," said the clerk. "But now and then, we clerks can make an extra dollar or two if we let someone ride the freighter. And my night man gave me a buck to keep my mouth shut so the station master doesn't find out."

"Okay, not my concern," said Nathan. "But what time did that train leave last night?"

"Not sure, Marshal. It usually comes through here between nine and eleven. Then the night clerk had to flag them down and get the horses loaded. So, they might not have left until eleven or midnight."

Nathan pursed his lips, thinking how he had let the trio leave right under his nose. "When is the next train to Nocona?"

The clerk looked up at the clock on the side wall of the office. "I think you're in luck, Marshal. The northbound should be here within the next hour. Want me to write you a ticket?"

"Yes. I've got to water my horse and then bring him around back. We'll wait on the platform," said Nathan, and he turned to go get Wander.

*** * * *

The train arrived in Nocona in the late afternoon. It was supper time, and Nathan's stomach told him that he had not had lunch. He would take care of that when he went into town. Nathan had been able to have a nap on the train between Bowie and Nocona, but the purpose of his trip weighed on him as he unloaded Wander from the stock car. He stroked the horse's neck.

"Hope you had a little nap too, boy. I'm thinkin' it's going to be a long tough night."

On the train ride north, Nathan had been playing out scenarios in his head regarding the arrest and capture of Ivan Malone. Any way he mulled it over, he knew he was on the way to meet unpredictable evil. It seemed that Malone had no moral framework to make him hesitate before killing another man.

After arriving in Nocona, Nathan pushed thoughts of Malone out of his head as he led Wander away from the train platform. Another sight brought him to a standstill. Three horses were tied to the hitch rack at the side of the rail station and as he glanced into the station windows, he groaned to himself. Staring back at him from inside the depot were the trio of Sean Conley, Jane Conley, and Calvin Kahl. Nathan tied Wander to the hitch rack and went into the station.

"Howdy, Marshal," said Calvin, innocently.

Nathan did not respond to Calvin, but instead said, "I thought I told you three to wait for me at the hotel in Decatur."

The three remained quiet for a few seconds until Sean spoke. "Well, you see, Marshal, you did, indeed, ask us to wait. But the thing is, we didn't have the money to stay overnight in the hotel. So, we just decided that we would keep heading for home."

Nathan curled up a side of his lips and shook his head from side to side. "What do you think you're going to do up here?"

"Well, we are going to go on up to the ranch, Marshal," Sean answered.

"Now, just a damn minute," said Nathan, as his temper began to rise.

"Now, now, Marshal," said Sean. "As you can see, we didn't move on. We decided that we would wait right here for you. We knew you would be along shortly. You see, we are going to ride out to the Lazy C with you. Four guns are better than three."

Nathan was not going to put up with their plan. "I told you back in Decatur that I did not want you coming up here with me. I can't be responsible for you if things get dicey at your ranch. And I'm pretty certain that Malone isn't going to go peacefully."

An awkward silence followed. Nathan was about to turn around and go outside to get Wander and ride away from the three of them. But then Sean broke the silence. He spoke in a very quiet, yet forceful tone.

"Marshal, you can say what you want, but you know you can't keep us from traveling to the ranch. After all, it's the Conley ranch, and Jane and I are Conleys. You can't keep us from going to our own home."

"And I'm still looking for my dad, dead or alive," Calvin added.

"I ought to throw the three of you in jail in Nocona for safe keeping until I get back from the Lazy C," said Nathan.

Sean smiled. "Now Marshal, you know you can't do that. We haven't broken any law by coming up here. We're just travelers returning home, and you can't stop us from going home."

Nathan knew he was beat. He thought to himself that if Jane and Calvin were not here, he might just put Sean in jail for safe keeping. But he certainly did not think he could do that to Jane. "Are the three of you armed?" he asked, even though he knew the answer to the question.

Sean and Jane confirmed that they were each carrying a pistol and Calvin volunteered that he had a shotgun out on his horse.

"Hmmph," Nathan grunted. Then he remembered again that he was hungry. "Well, before I do anything else, I've got to get some grub. You want to come along?"

Nathan made a move to leave the depot but noticed then that the trio was not making a move to follow him. "Did you already eat supper?" he asked.

"Could we impose on you to buy us a plate, Marshal? After getting a saddle for Jane and a shotgun for Calvin, we're a bit strapped for money."

"Oh, my aching back side," said Nathan. "Not only do you want to go along with me where you should not be going, but you want me to feed you, too." He shook his head again and looked at Calvin who was foolishly grinning at him. "C'mon," he said and turned to walk out the door of the depot. The trio followed him, and they made their way to a café on the main street of Nocona.

* * *

Two hours later, Nathan, along with the Conleys and Calvin Kahl, was making his way along a heavily wooded creek that ran across the Lazy C. They wished to arrive at the ranch as inky darkness fell. With scudding night clouds, they would need to worry about being spotted in the occasional full moonlight. Sean knew the ground well, so he was leading the group. They paused as Sean spoke.

"There are only two ways to approach the ranch house without being seen," said Sean. "One is in a direct line to the back of the house, but there are two windows at the back of the house, and we risk being seen in the moonlight. The other way is in a direct line to the back of the barn, where we can't be seen from the house. I think we should take the route to the barn."

"I agree," said Nathan. "Lead on. But, if at all possible, there should be no more talking. Malone might have a roving patrol out here away from the house."

They moved slowly through the brush and trees. Where the creek took a turn, they would now have to be in the open as they made their way through the prairie grass toward the barn. They had dismounted and were leading their horses. Although it took only a few minutes to cross the open area, it seemed like a much longer time that they were subject to being seen in the moonlight and shot at from the house. They considered themselves incredibly lucky to reach the back side of the barn without incident. They ground tied their horses next to Ben Steele's horse that was still attached to the loose board at the back of the barn.

Sean whispered to Nathan, "Whose horse is this, do you know? I don't think it's one of the Lazy C's."

"Can't say for sure here in the dark," said Nathan, "but I think it might be Ben Steele's horse."

"Steele, the Ranger?" Sean asked.

"Yep," Nathan answered.

"Well, what's he doing here?" Sean asked.

"Same thing we're doing," Nathan answered. "But it looks like he got here before us."

Just then, one of the horses blew through its lips and shook its reins, making a sound that seemed much louder in the quiet night than it really was. Somebody else had also heard it. No matter how quiet people think they are being, small noises carry in a still night setting. And Ben Steele had heard the sounds outside the board wall of the back of the barn. His head felt like it had been caved in by the blow of a gun butt in the hands of Ivan Malone. He was not sure if he was hearing things or there really were sounds outside. He decided to risk making his own sound. He began to rotate his tied ankles to tap his foot against the back wall of the barn.

"What's that?" whispered Sean. Nathan and the others listened to the gentle tapping on the barn wall.

"Stay here," Nathan hissed. "I'm going to find out what's making that noise."

The trio did as they were told and remained with the horses. Nathan left them and slowly walked around the side of the barn that was away from the house. He reached the main door of the barn and stood listening again before he cautiously put his head into the doorway. He could not see anything, it was just too dark inside the barn, but the tapping noise continued. Nathan hurried back out of the barn, around the side, and back to where the horses and Sean, Jane, and Calvin waited. Moving to Wander, he opened a saddlebag, reached into it, and retrieved a box of matches that he kept for when he was traveling on his own and needed to sleep outdoors and build a campfire.

"What did you see?" whispered Sean.

"Nothin'," Nathan replied. "It's too damn dark. Now stay here and be quiet."

Nathan hurried back to the barn door and entered. He stumbled into a wheelbarrow, painfully barked his shin, and cursed under his breath. He lit a match, while being ready to draw his pistol, if necessary. He then got his bearings while looking around the inside of the barn. His match grew low, and he blew it out. He lit another match, and then saw an oil lamp hanging on a peg on a support post. He took it from the hook and put a match to the wick. He murmured *thank God there's oil in it*. With the lamp in one hand and his pistol in the other, he soon determined that the noises they had heard were coming from behind a door in the corner of the barn. Cautiously, he moved to the door, listened for a moment, then removed the hasp pin that was holding the door closed.

Standing to the side of the door while he slowly opened it, he heard a voice say, "Is that you, Nathan." He thought he recognized the voice and confirmed his suspicion by holding the lantern above the prostrate figure on the floor of the tool shed.

"Well, well, Steele. Got yourself in a pickle, I see," teased Nathan.

"Yeah, yeah. I hate to say it, but I'm mighty glad to see you," said Ben. "Help me get these ropes off of me."

Nathan untied his friend. Ben tried to stand too quickly and nearly went back down due to light-headedness. "Damn, my head hurts," he said as he rubbed the back of his head and rubbed his wrists where the ropes had been. He stomped his feet to get the blood circulating.

"Hate to disappoint our friend Malone," said Ben, "but I won't be his morning murder victim, thanks to you, Nathan. Malone and his gun toters were going to come and get me in the morning to end my days."

"Ben, I believe we agreed that it should be the two of us together to come after Malone," Nathan reminded his friend.

"Yep, you're right. My Ranger badge got the best of me," said Ben. "Say, you wouldn't happen to have an extra pistol, would you?"

Nathan shook his head from side to side. "Let's get out of here." But as he turned, Nathan's lantern lit the area ahead of him, and the light danced off of the steel of Ben's pistol that still rested on the top of a barrel. Nathan picked it up, turned, and handed it to Ben. "It's your lucky day."

"Mmm, thanks," said Ben.

Nathan blew out the oil lamp and set it on the barrel. The two lawmen then cautiously made their way out of the barn and back to where Sean and the others waited. As his eyes adjusted to the darkness, Ben said, "I guess we meet again, Calvin." He turned to the woman and said, "You must be Jane Conley," and to Sean, he said, "I thought you were supposed to be dead." Ben meant that to be a joke, but no one laughed.

"Just a rumor, Ranger. Just a rumor," said Sean.

But at that instance they all heard a noise. The sound of footsteps could be heard slowly coming toward them. In the dim light, the form of a man was soon seen. Nathan had drawn his pistol and said, "Stop right where you are, mister, or get yourself shot."

"No, no, don't shoot, Marshal. I'm Lee Stark."

"Who's Lee Stark?" Nathan asked the group.

"Lee, is that you?" Sean asked.

"Sean? Sean Conley?" Stark asked.

Sean turned to Nathan. "He's our ranch foreman. Don't shoot."

Stark joined the group. "Sean, I am so glad to see you. When you disappeared, I thought sure that Malone had killed you. Is your dad all right?"

"No, Lee. Malone killed Dad and nearly killed me. I'll tell you all about it later," said Sean. "Right now, we've got a rattlesnake to kill."

Only seconds later, two shots split the night. They thumped into the barn boards near the group. Neither shot hit anyone, but it sent them all to the ground as they looked for the shooter. Seconds passed as they heard running footsteps receding towards the ranch house.

"He's gone," said Stark. "That was Shorty Thomas. Malone hired him away from us, and I saw him on night patrol earlier."

"Shorty Thomas?" Sean said incredulously. "He was a good hand. How did he get mixed up with Malone?"

"Money. Malone paid him more than we did, and he jumped," said Stark. "Malone also hired Ike Croft. Him and Thomas got hired by Malone at the same time. So, those two are somewhere looking out for Malone."

"And Croft," said Sean resignedly. "He was a good hand, too, and had been with us for several years."

Two more shots rang out. Both hit near the group. Running footsteps were again heard.

"We're sitting ducks here," said Nathan. "We need to spread out and cover the front and the back of the house. Sean, you and I will take the front. Ben, you take Lee and Calvin and cover the back. First light will be coming soon, and we need to all be under cover when the shooting really starts. Let's hold our fire until we can see what we are shooting at."

"Marshal, Jane comes with us," said Sean. "She's a Conley, and this is the Conley Ranch."

Nathan saw no point in arguing. Inwardly, he agreed with Sean. "Suit yourself, but for crying out loud, stay under cover." It was all he could think of to say.

In minutes, they were all behind cover of the oak trees and deadfall timber around the house. The front and back doors were easily seen by the group, leading them to believe that no one would be able to leave the house unseen.

* * *

Inside the Conley ranch house, four men, Ivan Malone, Matt Woods, Shorty Thomas, and Ike Croft waited. The others watched as Malone repetitiously paced from the front door to the back door. Shorty Thomas had returned to the house and had told him that there was a group of people behind the barn. He told Malone that he was relatively sure that Lee Stark was part of the group, but he had not been sure of the identity of the others.

In the course of the past few days, Ivan Malone had turned a corner in his grasp of reality. In his mind, the Lazy C was now his ranch. The attorney he had retained in Nocona had told him that since he was the only living relative of the Conleys, the ranch was his by law. Malone had told the attorney that the Conleys had packed up and left Texas, which, of course, was a bald-faced lie. But the lawyer did not know that and assumed that the Conleys had abandoned their claim to the land. As a result, the attorney was proceeding to file the proper paperwork to transfer ownership of the Lazy C to Malone. Thus, at this point, Malone was only waiting for the Montagne County Recorder to change the county records and put the deed to the ranch in his name. As soon as that was completed, Malone would sell the ranch and leave Texas, thereby making good his escape from the law.

When Malone had been told that Lee Stark was with a group of people, it could mean only one thing. Stark and other people had come upon the Lazy C to stop him from taking over the ranch. The thought of the people he had caused to be murdered never crossed his mind.

"Stark, huh," Malone had said. "I should have taken him out of the picture a long time ago. I never liked him from the first day I met him. Well, we'll just take care of that right now. Matt, you and Ike take the back door, and Shorty and I will be at the front. We'll just bide our time and pick them off one by one."

Malone moved to the front of the house and squinted through small portions of the windows and through the gun slits he had left open between the boards when he nailed the planks across the front and back windows of the house. He could not see anyone, but he was certain that morning light would soon reveal the identities of his pursuers.

A hazy false dawn sent the first light rays into the sky in the east. The faintest stars soon disappeared in the growing glow in the sky, and in less than an hour, the first full rays of the sun broke over the horizon as Nathan, Steele, and the others watched the front and rear doors of the house. Nathan thought it was time to move this standoff along.

"Malone," Nathan shouted. "This is U.S. Marshal Nathan Wolf. We know you're in there. You need to come out with your hands up."

Inside the house, Malone recognized the voice from outdoors. "It's that damn nosy Marshal," he said quietly. "He can't stop me."

Malone looked intently through the spaces between the planks. He saw no one, that is until he saw a small bit of color showing from behind and to the side of one of the trees. Malone correctly assumed that it was a bit of cloth worn by one of his pursuers. Malone had no way of knowing that the bit of cloth was part of the sleeve of Jane Conley's shirt. He took slow, careful aim, and fired one round at the bit of color. The bullet bit off a bit of tree bark but missed the piece of cloth. Jane quickly pulled her arm closer to her side. From the house, the piece of cloth disappeared.

"Sean, could you see where the shot was fired from?" Nathan asked.

Sean was lying on the ground behind a fallen tree, and he was taking careful aim. "Yes, and I'm going to fire a few rounds into where I think it came from." With that, he fired four rounds in quick succession. His shots were answered by a group of answering shots from the house. Malone and Shorty Thompson had now revealed from where they were firing, and Nathan and Sean answered with their own fusillade of shots. As the quiet returned to the front of the house, shots could be heard from the rear of the house.

Ben and Lee Stark had also seen the location of shots being fired between planks nailed to the back of the house. In answer, they shot the locations, reloaded and fired again until their pistols were empty. As they began reloading, Ben looked up and shouted at Stark. "Lee, watch out. There's one coming out the back door."

Indeed, a figure had opened the rear door and was running toward them. But instead of shooting, he was holding his hands above his head as he ran. Lee quickly shouted, "Don't shoot, Ben. It's Ike Croft, and it looks like he's surrendering."

But as Croft ran, two shots were fired from inside the house. The first shot was wild and passed above Croft's head. The second shot met its mark and struck Croft in the leg. Croft stumbled and fell, but quickly regained his feet and continued his run until he reached the safety of the trees and lay down near Lee Stark. He was pressing his hands on his open wound to stem the flow of blood.

Stark bent down and roughly removed Croft's neck kerchief. He then removed his own bandana handkerchief from his back pocket and tied the two kerchiefs together. Then he tied them around the wound in Croft's leg.

"You'll live," said Stark. "You've got a bucketful of explaining to do, cowboy."

Stark then turned his attention back to the house. He and Ben continued to fire at the openings in the wood planks until they needed to reload again. But after they were ready to resume firing, they realized that the ranch house had become eerily quiet. No one was shooting at them. From the front of the house, they could hear Nathan shout again.

"Malone, come out here with your hands up, or we're coming in to get you," said Nathan. There was no response. Nathan watched as the cloud of gun smoke wafted away on a gentle breeze.

Nathan turned to Sean and said, "Sean, can you make it around to the back of the house to where Ben is?"

"Sure, I think so. If I stay low, I can make it."

"Tell Ben to wait for my single shot. That will be the signal that I am rushing the front door, and he should do the same thing at the back door," said Nathan. He watched as Sean holstered his gun and removed his hat.

"Here goes," said Sean. And with that, Sean took off at a sprint while remaining in a crouch. As he made his way across the front of the house and around the side to the back, no shots were fired from the house. Both Nathan and Ben thought that this was highly unusual. After receiving instructions from Sean, Ben waited for Nathan's signal.

One shot rang out from the front of the house. Nathan ran to the front door of the house, where he paused beside the door. He took two deep breaths, then turned and put his full weight behind a kick to the door. The lock broke from the door jamb and the door partially opened. Nathan kicked it again and the door flew open. Nathan crouched to the side of the door, waiting for shots from within the house. From where he crouched, he could hear a crashing sound from the rear of the house. *Good,* he thought. *Ben's coming in the back.* Nathan's stomach tightened. He now had to get inside the house and face a known, cold-blooded killer. A wave of fear passed over his body, but quickly passed. Taking another deep breath, Nathan sprang from outside the door to the inside of the house. He remained in a crouch as his eyes quickly scanned the large front room. The body of a man lay near the location where he and Sean had been aiming their shots from outdoors. Nathan crept to the man and kicked him over with his boot. The man did not move. How could he, there was a bullet hole just above his right eye. Nathan looked around the room. There was no place for anyone to hide in the room, so he knew Malone was not here. He stood and moved through the room. Suddenly he heard a sound behind him. He spun around with his pistol held high. For a fleeting second, he almost pulled the trigger to shoot the figure that appeared in the doorway. But in an instant, his brain told him not to shoot. Jane Conley was standing at the door.

"My God, Jane. I almost shot you," said Nathan.

"Sorry," she responded.

"Well, stay behind me and keep low," said Nathan, and he began to continue to walk through the house. He met Ben with Lee following close behind.

"I've got one dead fella in the front room," said Nathan.

Ben replied, "Another one at the back door. Stark says it was Matt Woods, one of the first hombres hired by Malone."

Lee walked to the front room and looked at the inert body lying on the floor. "This one is Shorty Thomas. He used to be a fair hand until he deserted us and went to work for Malone."

"Hmm, that leaves only Malone," Nathan answered. "Guess we better find him."

Nathan, Ben, and Lee continued their search through the house. The house contained a large kitchen, another sitting room, an office, and three bedrooms, along with a maid's quarters. That room seemed not to be used. A stairway led up from a hallway. They peered up the stairs that led to a closed door at the top of the stairway.

"Lee, do you know what is up there?" asked Nathan.

"It's a storage attic, I believe," Lee answered.

"Mmm. Lee, you wait here," said Nathan. "Ben and I will do the dirty work."

Lee stepped back and quietly said, "Be careful."

The two lawmen looked at each other. Ben grinned and whispered, "After you, sir." He held his arm out in mock servitude.

"I'll remember this, *amigo*," Nathan whispered.

As quietly as they could manage, the two lawmen walked up the stairs. At the top, Nathan silently tried the doorknob. To his surprise, the door was unlocked. "You ready?" he whispered to Ben. Ben nodded with his pistol at the ready. Nathan turned and quickly opened the door, and then, without hesitating, dove headfirst into the upper room, his pistol held out in front of him. Ben charged in after him and took a squatting position to the front of Nathan. With their hearts pounding, they listened. They heard nothing but their own heartbeats. They both scanned the room. There was no sign of Malone.

In a few moments, they finished their search of the attic and the house, with no sign of Malone, and the three men walked back toward the kitchen. Then Nathan looked around.

"What happened to Sean and Jane?" Nathan asked. "I want to ask them if there is a basement storm shelter somewhere under the house."

Ben walked out onto the back porch but returned quickly. "They're not out there."

Nathan and Ben looked at each other, and almost simultaneously asked, "Where's Stark?"

Suddenly, their conversation was interrupted by a series of muffled gunshots. The two lawmen looked at each other as if questioning the location of the sounds. Then a voice cried out, "Marshal, back here." It was Lee Stark calling to them.

The lawmen walked quickly back through the house to the ranch office. But as they made their way toward Stark, they both looked down at the floor. Droplets of blood left a trail on the floor. That trail was leading to Lee Stark. As they joined Stark, the ranch foreman was standing at a location in the office where the blood trail seemed to end. More shots rang out, but they were muffled.

"Is that your blood on the floor, Lee?" asked Nathan.

"No, it's not mine," Lee answered.

"Hmm," Nathan answered.

Their attention was quickly turned after hearing more muffled shots.

"Where in hell are those shots coming from," Nathan asked.

"I think I know," said Stark. "I've always heard that the Conleys built an escape room when they originally built the ranch house. They did this because at the time they built, there were still occasional flare ups with marauding Indians, primarily the Comanches. Settlers in these parts built escape rooms in case they were attacked by the Indians. But for the life of me, no one ever told me where the escape room was."

"Is that where the gunfire sounds are coming from?" Nathan asked.

"I think so," Stark replied. "See where those blood drops end?"

"Yeah," Nathan replied.

"Well, watch this," said Stark. He put both of his hands on a piece of wood trim that edged a piece of wood paneling that was next to a bookcase in the office. He then pulled the trim piece, and the wood panel came away from the wall. The men now could see a stairway leading down under the house.

"How did you find this, Lee?" asked Nathan.

"When I came back here to the office, I could see that that door panel was standing slightly open. As I opened it further, the gunshots became louder. I closed the door again and called for you. Marshal, I think Sean and Jane and that Kahl kid are down there in a gunfight with Malone."

"Oh, lordy," said Nathan. "Let's go, Ben." Nathan began descending the stairs but turned back to Lee.

"Lee, there's an oil lamp on the corner shelf. Can you grab it for us?"

Stark brought the lamp to Nathan, and Nathan drew the matchbox from his pocket. He lit the lamp and drew his revolver. He again began descending the stairs with Ben closely following.

"What the hell are you getting me into, Wolf?" Ben asked. He was quite certain he did not want to go down into a blind basement.

When they reached the bottom of the stairway, they could see that the room had a tunnel leading away from it. There were wooden shelves on each side of the passageway. Dusty jars were on a few of the shelves. "Canned food," said Ben. Ahead of the shelves, the tunnel narrowed, and the ceiling dropped several inches. It appeared that the tunnel was added after the cellar had been dug.

The light from their lantern reached ahead of them as they took only a couple tentative steps. But they suddenly stopped when they saw a light ahead of them. The light seemed to be dancing in air as it swung to and fro. The lantern then seemed to speak, "Don't shoot Marshal, it's me, Sean." He was accompanied by Jane and Calvin.

"Marshal, our tunnel curves slightly before it comes back up to the surface," said Sean. "Jane and I used to play down here when we were little. Malone is holed up just past the curve and we can't get to him without getting ourselves shot. Jane is already injured."

In the light from the two lanterns, Nathan could see that Jane's shirt was bloody near her left shoulder. "I think a bullet grazed her, and I need to get her upstairs to bandage her up," said Sean.

In the confusion and adrenaline rush, Nathan had missed something that Sean had said. But as he was thinking, a gunshot rang out. Malone had fired a round at them. In the confines of the tunnel, the sound was near deafening. Malone's bullet smacked into the top of the stairway behind them. Both Nathan and Ben answered Malone's shot with a volley from their pistols.

Quietly, Nathan said, "Everyone up the stairs. Quickly now!"

When they were all safely above, Sean took Jane to the kitchen to get her wound dressed. The two lawmen, Lee, and Calvin stood at the top of the stairway peering down into the dark tunnel.

"How do we get him out of there without being a target ourselves?" Calvin asked.

No one seemed to have an immediate answer.

Suddenly, Nathan blurted out, "Wait a minute. I seem to remember something that was used in a labor riot in St. Louis back when I lived in Iowa." He turned to Lee.

"Lee, do have any old glass bottles in the barn?"

Lee thought for a minute. "Yep, I think I know where there are a couple."

Nathan added, "Do you have any coal oil or kerosene in the barn, and maybe some rags?"

"Sure," said Lee. "We always have those on hand."

"Let's go to the barn," said Nathan. "Ben, I don't think I need to tell you what to do if you see Malone trying to come back up these stairs." Ben just grinned.

In the barn, Nathan and Lee found two old glass bottles. They appeared to have contained horse liniment at one time. Nathan filled both bottles with kerosene, then stuffed rags tightly into the neck of the bottles.

"What do you call these contraptions, Marshal?" Lee asked.

"They're called fire-bombs, Lee. The only reason I know about them is that when I was a sheriff up in Iowa, we heard about rioters in St. Louis years ago using these things to slow down traffic in a labor dispute."

Nathan gently shook the bottles, then felt the rags stuffed into the bottle necks. "Okay, Lee. Let's go smoke out a rat."

They went back to the house and returned to the mouth of the stairway leading to the tunnel. Ben saw the bottles in Nathan's hands.

"Got yourself a couple fire-bombs?" Ben asked.

Nathan wondered how he knew about firebombs, but he did not ask.

Ben continued. "Yep, some years back, some KKK crazies used those things to throw at our Ranger headquarters in Austin. Pretty effective. 'Course they didn't live to talk about it later."

Nathan turned to Lee and asked, "Are you pretty good with a lasso throw?"

Before Lee could answer, Nathan asked, "Can you make an underhanded throw with a lasso?"

Lee started to laugh. "Now Marshal, you're talking to a cowboy who has worked around cattle all my life. I can throw a rope overhead, sideways, and underhand. But why do you ask?"

"Because you're going to do the throwing," Nathan answered.

As quietly as they could, Nathan and Lee Stark lowered themselves down the stairway. They took a few steps until they were at the point that the tunnel narrowed.

"Are you ready, Lee?" Nathan whispered.

"I reckon," Lee answered.

Nathan put one of the bottles on the floor of the tunnel and gave one bottle to Lee.

"When I light the rag, I'll step back," said Nathan. "Then you take the best underhand throw you can. We want to get the bottle up to the bend in the tunnel. Think you can do it?"

"I'll try," said Lee.

Using his matches, Nathan lit the rags in the bottle neck that Lee was holding, then stepped back.

Lee took two more steps, then wound up his arm and gave a mighty heave. The bottle flew down the remaining length of the tunnel and thudded on the floor of the tunnel. The rag in the neck of the bottle loosened slightly and kerosene formed a small flaming puddle around the bottle. The bulk of the kerosene was still in the bottle.

"Mmm," Nathan grunted. "Good throw, Lee, but we need to hit the wall where the curve is. We want to shatter the bottle if we can. He picked up the remaining bottle and handed it to Lee. Then he lit the rags and stepped back. Lee seemed to study the situation for a few seconds and once again gave his arm a spin before letting the bottle fly. This time, the bottle went a bit farther, just far enough to shatter against the wall of the tunnel at the point of its curve. Glass shards and flaming fuel shot from the breakage.

"Oww." A loud scream was heard from around the corner of the tunnel.

"Sounds like we may have hit Malone," said Lee.

"We're not done yet," Nathan replied. He drew his pistol and leaned against the side of the tunnel to brace himself. He then took a two-hand grip on his pistol, carefully aimed, and fired. The bullet smashed into the bottle that was laying on the tunnel floor, spreading glass pieces and flaming kerosene drops around the tunnel's curve.

"Let's get up the stairs before Malone decides to fire back at us," said Nathan. He quickly followed Lee up the stairs. When they reached the top of the stairs, Sean and Jane were waiting for them.

"Did you get him, Marshal," Sean asked.

"I don't know, Sean. But I do know that we made it a bit hot for him down there," Nathan replied.

Sean seemed to clear his throat before he spoke. "Marshal, I forgot to tell you something about the tunnel."

Nathan turned his head to face Sean. "Okay, what is it?"

"Well, there's an opening out of the tunnel at the other end. I guess it was there so that my grandparents would not be caught in the tunnel if they were attacked."

"Oh, no, Sean. You mean that Malone might have gotten away?" asked Nathan.

Sean did not answer, while Nathan wagged his head from side to side. He was sure that he had failed to get Malone, and he was sure that Malone must have made good his escape.

"Do you know where the tunnel comes out?" Nathan asked.

"Sure," said Sean. "Like I said, me and Jane used to play in the tunnel when we were kids."

"Let's go. Take me there," said Nathan. "Ben, can you stay here just in case Malone is not gone, and decides to come back to this stairway?"

"Yep, I'll stay," Ben answered. "Calvin, you stay here with me. I may need the help of your shotgun." Calvin nodded.

At the other end of the tunnel, Ivan Malone was, indeed, crawling his way out of the exit opening. Having been shot during the gun battle while he was in the house, he knew he was badly wounded. But in his befuddled mind he was certain that he could make his getaway from the Conleys and the lawmen. He thought to himself, *I just need to get myself out of here and get to the horse*. He was carrying the metal cash box and shoved it through the brush that had nearly choked off the tunnel's exit. He then began struggling to get himself through the small opening. As he pulled himself through, he thought to himself that he would soon need to find a doctor who would accept cash to fix him up and then keep his mouth shut.

Malone may have thought he could make a getaway, but he did not know how badly he was wounded. In the darkness of the tunnel, he had not been able to see the amount of blood on his clothing. It was only minutes until the loss of blood would begin shutting his body down.

Malone's head, arms and chest were now out of the opening and into the daylight. It took his last bit of energy to pull himself out of the tunnel. He was on his hands and knees, gasping for breath. It was then that he saw the amount of blood on his clothing and noticed that the wounds were still dripping blood. Malone was dying. Just before he expired, he imagined that he heard hoofbeats. He tried to make out where the sounds were coming from. As he lifted his head, the Indian pony was nearly on top of him. From the corner of Malone's eye, he saw the colored streamers fluttering toward him as the head of the lance slammed into his back, flattening him to the ground. With his last bit of energy, he turned his head just enough to see the Indian, Black Horse, sitting astride the horse that had nearly trampled him. Malone's eyes closed and his head lolled back onto the ground. He was dead. His reign of terror while attempting to fraudulently usurp control of the Lazy C Ranch was over. Black Horse dismounted, removed his knife from his belt, and completed his final action to the body of Ivan Malone. Black Horse remounted and moved his horse into the shade of a nearby tree to wait.

The group hurried from the house. Sean and Jane led Nathan and Lee to the side of the house away from the barn and toward a patch of overgrown bushes. Those bushes were backed up to a small oak grove. Sean stopped abruptly. "This place has changed," he said. "That small corral was never there before." He was pointing to a small corral, more the size of a pen. He turned his head slightly and looked at Lee.

"Yeah, I saw Malone's boys build this pen," said Lee. "But I didn't know why."

Sean's eyes looked away. "There's Black Horse," said Sean. "What's he doing here?"

Next to a large clump of bushes, Black Horse sat on his horse with both of his legs on one side of the horse, much as you would sit on a chair. The horse's head was near the ground as it tore at and chewed the prairie grass. As they walked toward Black Horse to greet him, they suddenly saw the body of Ivan Malone at the edge of the tunnel's exit opening. Wisps of smoke emanated from Malone's blackened and burnt shirt. In addition, the body seemed to be covered in blood, and an Indian lance protruded from the corpse. The lance was decorated with various colors, and feathers and colorful streamers hung from a leather thong at the top of the shaft. The killing end of the lance was in Malone's back at a downward angle. It was apparent that the spear had been loosed from above Malone. Sean continued on to shake the hand of Black Horse. Nathan then joined him and shook hands with the Comanche.

"Did you kill him, Black Horse?" asked Nathan.

Black Horse scoffed. "I think you are smarter than that, Marshal Wolf. Go look at the evil white man. He was breathing his last breath when he crawled out of the ground like a poisonous snake."

It was then that Nathan noticed a bloody piece of flesh hanging from the belt of Black Horse. He almost asked the Indian about it but decided to examine Malone's body first. He walked back to the body, bent down, and then pushed the body over to its other side, with the lance still protruding and lying nearly level with the ground. Malone's shirt still gave off wisps of smoke from the kerosene fire that had struck him. After the body had been rolled, a metal box that Malone's body had been lying on top of was revealed. Nathan put the box aside and continued looking at the body. Getting down on his hands and knees, Nathan could see that in addition to the Indian spear, the body had several bullet holes, every one of which had contributed its share of blood to the crimson-covered body. Nathan decided that one wound was most interesting. A bullet had entered Malone's neck near the jugular vein. Nathan speculated that a bullet had found its mark through the planks at the front of the house. In all likelihood, that was the mortal wound, and the loss of blood would also have been enough to kill any man. With the number of wounds, there was really no way to determine who had fired the fatal bullet, or whether the Indian spear had finished off Malone's futile and evil life. Nathan had already seen that Malone had been scalped, and one ear was missing from the head of the body. He now knew what was hanging on Black Horse's belt. As he looked up and was about to rise from his hands and knees, Jane was looking at the body of her son. A look of sorrow was on her face, but it was not the face of grief. No tears came from her eyes. In seconds, she walked away from the body to stand at Sean's side.

Nathan rose from the ground and picked up the metal box. He handed it to Sean. "Does this belong to you?"

"Hmm. I guess that answers a question," said Sean. "Yes, this is the ranch's cash box. It is always kept in our safe. I'm guessing that Mom gave Malone the combination to the safe." Sean opened the lid of the metal box and whistled.

"Geez," said Sean. "We never kept this much cash on hand. Where did Malone get all this money?"

Lee Stark stood to the side of Sean. "I know where he got the money, Sean. Malone sold off most of our remuda. We only have a few horses left, and not a stallion in the bunch."

"Mmm," Sean mumbled. "Reckon we will need to invest this money in a few more horses, along with making repairs to the house and anything else that Malone managed to destroy."

Nathan walked back to Black Horse. "Did you have to scalp him and take his ear?" Nathan asked.

Instead of answering the question, Black Horse simply responded, "My brother, Iron Arrow, is avenged, Marshal Wolf."

"How did you know that Malone would be here?" Nathan asked.

"Because Sean Conley is my friend, I have watched his house and ranch. I have seen things that the evil man Malone has done," said Black Horse. "I knew that this day would come when I would avenge my brother's death. I knew that evil man Malone would die, either at my hands or some other man's hands. My friends who were watching told me that you came to the ranch in the night, so I come here, and I waited."

"How could you know that Malone would be here today, Black Horse?" Sean asked.

"I saw his men build this pen," said Black Horse. "There was only one reason to build such a pen. Evil man Malone would keep a horse here so he could escape when he was finally trapped. Two days ago, Malone put a horse in the pen, and the horse was still here this morning. So, I came here and waited."

"What happened to the horse?" asked Nathan.

Black Horse responded, "I would not let Malone have the horse. So, I took the horse from the pen, and I waited. Look in those trees, behind those scrub bushes," and he pointed to a small oak grove. Sure enough, one of the Lazy C's horses stood already saddled and bridled. The horse was contentedly chewing on a mouthful of prairie grass.

"I would kill Malone before he could get the horse and make his escape," said Black Horse.

"Hmm," said Sean. "Guess he won't be stealing any more of our horses."

Jane remained standing next to Sean. Sean turned to her, and then back to Black Horse. "Black Horse, this is my sister Jane. She has come to live at our ranch."

"Mmm," Black Horse mumbled. "You are the child that went away from here many years ago."

Jane managed a small smile. "Yes, but I am back to help my brother on the ranch."

"That is good," said Black Horse. "I will leave you now. I must get back to my people." He swung his right leg back over his horse's neck and nudged the horse near to Malone's body, where he retrieved his lance. Turning his horse, he soon disappeared from sight as he rode north.

"Oh, hell," said Lee. "I just remembered that I left Ike Croft behind the barn while we were shooting it out with Malone and his men. Sean, I'll go get him and take him to the kitchen in the house where we can patch him up, if that's all right?"

"Sure, go ahead. Do you need any help?" Sean asked.

"Naw, Ike's kinda scrawny. I can handle him," Lee answered, and he turned to head back to the barn.

"Tell the Ranger to come out here with us," Nathan shouted. "And tell him to bring some shovels from the barn." Lee responded by waving his hand as he trotted away.

Nathan turned back to see Sean with his arm around his sister. Jane continued to wipe tears from her eyes as she spoke softly to Sean.

"Oh, Sean. Seeing Ivan dead has made me realize how badly I have messed up my life." She began to cry. "My life is a disaster, and I don't think I want to live any longer," she said. "I can't help but think that I had a hand in the deaths of Mom and Dad, and I don't think I can live with that. After all, it was my son who killed them."

Sean continued to console his sister. "Jane, I don't believe you should look at the situation like that. None of this was your fault. Ivan was a particularly evil person, and that was not your fault."

"Perhaps not," Jane replied. "But I can't help feeling the way I do. If I had stayed here years ago, none of this would have happened."

Sean put his hands on his sister's shoulders. "Look at me, Jane. This is not your fault!" said Sean. "Both of us lost our parents, and we need to put that unpleasantness in the past. We are Conleys, and we are together. I am so happy that you have come back to the ranch. And together, we are going to continue to run our family's ranch." Brother and sister continued to lean on each other until Ben Steele and Lee Stark walked to them and interrupted them. Each man carried a shovel.

Sean turned to Lee. "Did you get Ike taken care of?"

"Sure did," Lee replied. "His wound was an in-and-out through a small part of his thigh muscle. We washed it out and dosed him up with sulfa powder and bandaged it up. He'll be down for a week or two and limping before he is completely healed but should be up and helping us out soon. He and I had a long talk about him being so stupid and bitin' the hand that feeds him. He knows he was wrong to fall for Malone's gab about money. I think he's sorry and all that, and he didn't shoot anybody, so if it's okay with you, we'll put him back on the payroll when he's able to do some work."

"If you're okay with it, Lee, then I am too," Sean answered.

Lee turned to go, but then turned back around. "Where do you want Malone planted?"

"I would just as soon throw him in the river like he did to my dad," said Sean.

Ben spoke up. "Nah, Sean, we don't want to do that. People down river see a corpse floating by and they start asking a wagon load of questions. Lee and I can drag him off and get him in the ground. You okay with that?"

Sean nodded his head in agreement. Then he walked over to Malone's body with Lee and Ben. He spoke with them in a low tone. "Ben, I don't want to know where you bury him. If Jane ever asks me in the future, I can tell her truthfully that I do not know where he is buried. I'll take Jane up to the house and leave you fellas to take care of burying Malone."

"Okay, Sean," Lee answered. "Oh, and by the way, the bunkhouse cook was working in the kitchen. I think he's got dinner ready, and Ben and I will be up in just a bit."

Ben and Lee watched as Nathan and the Conleys walked back to the ranch house. Ben then turned to Lee. "What are we going to do with this pile of cow dung?" he asked, referring to the body of Ivan Malone.

Lee responded, "I figure we can drag him behind that grove of oaks and bury him. No one will ever know where we put him."

The men went about their grim business. The soil yielded easily to their shovels, and within an hour and a half, they were done. Lee leaned on his shovel, perspiration dampening his shirt. "It's for damn sure the good Lord doesn't want him, so hell gets another resident."

"Amen," said Ben. "Let's go get some grub."

The men put the shovels on their shoulders and walked toward the barn to stow the tools before washing up at the outdoor water pump and going into the house to eat.

* * *

When it is made the right way, with care and proper ingredients, good beef stew has a comforting quality, along with satisfying one's hunger. The man they simply called Cookie was in fact, the man who did the cooking for the ranch hands in the bunkhouse, when they stayed out all night on the vast ranch, or when the ranch hands took the cattle overland to market, usually into Wichita Falls. The man knew his way around a cooking fire or griddle, as evidenced by the quiet at the big kitchen table, aside from the sound of metal spoons on metal bowls. A heaping basket of fresh-baked biscuits made its way around the table only twice before it was empty.

Jane Conley sat between Sean and Calvin Kahl. Her face still reflected the sorrow she felt within, yet she too was slowly devouring her hearty bowl of stew. In truth, it had been a long time since she had eaten a balanced meal sitting at a table with friends and relatives. The situation was helping to wash away some of her helpless feelings. When she finished eating, she slowly rose from the table, took her dishes to the sink, and told Cookie that she would help him with cleaning up.

"Are you sure you want to do that, Miss Jane?" said Cookie. "I can manage by myself."

"No, I'd like to help," Jane answered. "I've washed a few dishes in my time. It will do me good to do a bit of work."

"Yes, ma'am," said Cookie.

Jane turned and began collecting the empty bowls and spoons from the table, along with the drinking glasses. The men remained at the table.

Ben Steele was scratching at his teeth with a toothpick but paused to ask, "Well, Nathan, are you satisfied with the outcome of this case? It turned out to be a bit more serious than just a few missing horses."

Nathan was hesitant to continue this line of conversation. He knew that Jane, Ivan Malone's mother, was standing only a couple feet away, and he did not want to appear callous to the death of her son. But, just then, everyone heard Jane say in a noticeably quiet and solemn voice, "I'm satisfied."

Her remark caught everyone by surprise. Everyone except Sean. Jane had told him of her horrific treatment at the hands of Malone, so he understood that there was a distinct lack of mother's love in Jane's heart.

In a similar, quiet voice, Sean said, "Jane, if you are satisfied, we are all satisfied."

Nathan agreed. It had been a dangerous and volatile situation that could have played out in several different scenarios. "The fact that evil did not prevail, and we are all still alive certainly is satisfying to me."

Nathan turned to Ben. "Ben, we have one more thing to do before we are through here. There is the matter of the body of the prospector who might, or might not, be Calvin's father. We will need to go out and check it out before we head back to Decatur."

Sean quickly stood up, and rather loudly said, "No, no, no. You two aren't going anywhere. You are staying here with us, and we are going to enjoy ourselves for a few hours. We'll give Cookie and Jane a little time to straighten things up here, and then we can all sit on the porch and watch the sunset, and maybe drink a little wine or bourbon."

Cookie gave out a whoop. "I'll tell all the boys."

"I'll tell them, Cookie," Lee said. "We need to bring up a few chairs out of the bunkhouse, too. I'll help them with that."

"Lee, don't I recall that one of the boys has a fiddle?" Sean asked. "And doesn't Ike Croft play the mouth organ?"

"Yep," said Lee. "I'll put a couple of chairs together so Ike can stretch out his leg while he's sitting on the porch." Lee actually clapped his hands together. "By golly, it's been a long time since any of us have had a little fun around here."

Later, as the sun set, the last of the chairs had been arranged around the perimeter of the large back porch and adjacent yard of the ranch house. A small table in the corner held several bottles of wine and whisky, and tin drinking cups. Cookie had also made a batch of fried pork rinds and fried tortillas. As oil lamps were lit and set at the edges of the patio, the ranch hands began gathering together. Those few hands who had remained with the Lazy C needed no encouragement to come up to Sean and Jane and shake their hands and express a warm welcome. They all knew that Ivan Malone was dead, thereby lifting many spirits. One or two of the men had friends who had left the ranch. Those men promised Sean that in the coming days, they would reach out to their friends to come back to the Lazy C, now that Malone's reign of terror was over.

After a couple belts of whisky, the music started. The fiddle player turned out to be a pretty fair musician, and Ike Croft was able to follow the fiddler's lead. With Jane being the only woman, she certainly had a work-out dancing with various cow hands as they twirled her around the patio. The fact that there were no other women was not an insurmountable problem, as the cowboys with the pent-up energy began dancing with each other. Everyone laughed at their antics as they strutted around the patio laughing at their own dance steps. After Jane finally sat down to rest, Sean happened to look over at her sitting in the corner of the patio. Lee Stark was by her side. Lee and Jane seemed to be in happy, animated conversation. *Could be there was a connection between those two,* thought Sean. They were nearly the same age, and Lee had lost his wife to the flu several years ago. Sean chuckled under his breath and turned back to the dance floor.

It was nearly one a.m. before the men started drifting away to the bunk house. Each of them took a bunk house chair with him to get the clutter off of the ranch house porch. Quiet began to descend on the Lazy C.

The two lawmen sat with Sean, Jane, Lee, and Calvin on the patio.

"I'm worn out," said Jane. "I haven't danced in years."

"The boys gave you quite a work-out," said Sean.

"I think the boys really enjoyed themselves, Sean," said Lee.

"Indeed, they did," Sean replied. "They're liable to have some headaches when the sun comes up. I'm not sure how much work you will get out of them."

"I think it's worth it, and I'm glad you did this," said Lee.

He smiled at Lee's remark, then said, "There is so much to be done to correct Malone's messes. I'd like to get all of those ugly boards off of the house and repair the windows."

"I'll take care of that," said Lee. "I'll send a man into Nocona tomorrow to get some glass panes and glazing compound while the rest of us get the planks taken off the walls," said Lee. "We'll have it back to its pretty face in no time."

"You're a godsend, Lee. I know why Mom and Dad thought so much of you, and so do I," Sean said.

Calvin Kahl felt content. He was the same age as a couple of the ranch hands and had watched them as they enjoyed themselves. Inwardly, he carried a sadness. He had lost both of his parents and had no family and good friends. He was at a loss as to what he would do now. He did know, however, that he did not want to go back to the smelly, back-breaking work at the tannery in Lafayette. But right now, he had something else on his mind.

"Sean and Lee, would it be all right if tomorrow we went to the place on the ranch where my father was killed?" Calvin asked.

Softly, Sean replied, "Yes, I think so." Turning to Lee, he said, "Lee, you remember Wobbly Wilkins and Ross Simmons, don't you?"

"Sure," Lee replied.

"Well, we met up with them when I went to Decatur to see the Marshal. They bought an old run-down bar, and they're doing their best to make a go of it," said Sean.

Lee initially laughed. Then he said, "Well, they're good workers, so they'll probably make a living."

"Yep," replied Sean. "Anyway, they were with Malone when he killed a prospector who was passing across the northeast corner of the ranch; you know, where that limestone outcropping is?"

"Oh, yeah," Lee said.

"Well, that's where Malone killed that man," said Sean, "and we think that the prospector may have been Calvin's Dad."

"Oh, no," was Lee's only response, as he shook his head from side to side.

Sean turned to Calvin. "We'll go there after breakfast, Calvin. Maybe we can settle whether or not the man that was killed was your dad."

The group grew silent, each occupied with his respective thoughts. Finally, Nathan spoke up. "Sean, would it be all right if Ben and I bunked down in the barn for the night? It's too late to head into town."

"Nonsense," Lee cried out. "You can sleep with us boys in the bunk house. We've got a couple extra bunks. You too, Calvin."

"Makes sense to me," said Sean. He rose from his chair and stretched. "I'm beat. I'm going to bed. Jane, you take Mom and Dad's room. You'll be comfortable in there. Breakfast about seven," he said as he walked away.

Nathan suddenly remembered. "Oh my God," he said. "We left the horses tied behind the barn all day. We need to go get them, brush 'em down and feed 'em. Lee, can you get us fitted out with grain for them?"

"Sure, let's go."

Thirty minutes later, the men's horses as well as Jane's horse were brushed down, fed and watered and led into stalls in the barn for the remainder of the night. When the work was completed, Lee, Calvin, and the two lawmen began walking toward the bunk house. Calvin walked just behind the older men, lost in his thoughts. In the bunk house, Lee pointed out some empty bunks for the men. The ranch hands were nearly all asleep, sonorous heavy breathing emanating from the inebriated men. Lee's bunk was behind a partition, a bit of privacy to recognize his position as the leader of the hands.

"All right, gents, see you in the sunshine," said Lee and he slipped behind his partition. In minutes, Nathan, Ben, and Calvin had stripped down and were soon sound asleep.

What a day, thought Nathan. Pictures and thoughts of Claire May and Bobby crossed his mind as he drifted off to sleep.

* * *

Nathan, Ben, Sean, Jane and Calvin sat at the kitchen table drinking coffee. They were watching Cookie scramble a dozen eggs to go with the pancakes that were rising on the griddle. Chunks of pan-fried ham and potatoes rested in bowls that sat on the warming shelf of the wood-fired stove.

"You know," said Sean. "I never learned to cook. I spent years watching Mom cook and Cookie doing his brand of cooking, but I never learned much about it."

Cookie laughed. "It ain't too late to learn."

It was Sean's turn to laugh. "You know, Cookie, there are just some old bulls that won't learn no matter how many times they get lassoed. I'll leave the cooking to you."

The scrambled eggs were soon done, and Cookie set the bowls of food on the table. "Dig in before it gets cold," he said.

Bowls were passed around the table, portions taken, and soon the table was quiet save the clinking of silverware on plates and spoons stirring sugar into their mugs of coffee.

Calvin was nearly finished before the older people. He set his fork on his plate and took a swig of coffee. "I guess I'll have to learn how to cook," he said. "With my mom and dad both gone, I'll need to fend for myself."

"Well, I've got a plan for that," said Sean. "We can talk about it later. But right now, you wanted to ride out to the limestone outcropping, so I figure we ought to get saddled up before the sun gets too hot." Sean turned to Cookie. "Do you want to go along with us, Cookie?"

"Naw, Sean. I've got to get this mess cleaned up and then I've got some chores to take care of in the bunk house," said Cookie. "I've got to clean that place up and make some repairs."

"Okay," Sean answered. He had known ahead of time that the cook had chores he would be working at but thought he would ask anyway.

"Sean, if you don't mind, I'll stay here and help Cookie clean up the kitchen," Jane said. "He can always use a little help."

"Suit yourself, Jane," Sean responded.

But then another voice was heard. "I've got a couple of the hands that I need to check on, Sean," said Lee. "I'll stick around here to make sure they get their chores done."

Sean could not help but chuckle to himself. It seemed to him that his ranch foreman was making an excuse to stick around where his sister was. He could not help but toss out a disguised barb. "Are you sure you've got everything under control, Lee?"

Stark smiled. "Yep, everything's fine."

Nathan, Ben, Sean and Calvin soon left the house, retrieved their horses, and saddled them. After Nathan and Ben each tied a shovel to the saddle cantle of his horse, they were soon riding to the northeast. Wander seemed happy to be back on the trail. He held up his head as the riders walked their horses, and he looked from side to side at the new trail.

Nathan was riding next to Sean. "I'm not sure I know what a limestone outcropping is, Sean," Nathan remarked.

Sean laughed a bit. "It has something to do with the fact that Mother Nature carved out these hills, and wind and water tore away some of the topsoil, and that revealed these hills of limestone. Jane and I used to play on this one we are going to. We would see who was fastest to climb to the top of it."

"So, it's tall?" asked Nathan.

"Well, not exactly," answered Sean. "But with the surrounding soil eroded away from the limestone, it stands above the surrounding ground. But to us kids, it was like a stone mountain, and we had fun climbing up on it."

Sean looked back at Ben and Calvin riding together. "I think we need to pick up the pace, gents. It's still a ways up ahead."

For the next quarter hour, they kept the horses at a trot, until finally they reached and entered a draw. It was not long before they reached the limestone outcropping.

Nathan could see that below the top part of the limestone, the stone seemed to recede, almost creating a small cave. It was just like what Jack Wilkins and Ross Simmons had described days ago at their saloon. But something else caught his eye, just as it had for the others. Within the limestone alcove lay what was left of a human body. The men all dismounted. Nathan and Ben strode to the form and bent down for a closer look. The man's body was not a pretty sight. The food chain of Mother Nature had been processing the body. Larger carnivores had fed on the meat, as well as crows and buzzards. The clothing had been ripped and torn by those scavengers. Bones shone in the light where flesh had been torn from them. The face of the body was unrecognizable, and the odor of decomposition was nearly unbearable.

For a few moments, Sean and Calvin stayed back several feet. But then, overcome with curiosity, Calvin came closer to the body. Nearly immediately, he became sick and quickly walked away to vomit. He then walked to his horse, retrieved his canteen, and rinsed his mouth with the water. He put the canteen back in his saddlebag. Walking back to the body, he bent down and gently lifted one arm of the corpse.

Almost whispering, Calvin said, "It's my dad." He gently laid the arm back on the ground. He then moved to the back of the alcove where the panniers lay where Malone's men had thrown them. He started to open them when Ben spoke up.

"Careful when you open those, Calvin," Ben cautioned. "Watch for scorpions and spiders. They love to make themselves at home in strange dark places."

Calvin took Ben's advice and opened the panniers slowly. He retrieved several sheets of paper and studied them. "These are the maps that Dad showed me. He had marked his route to the Colorado gold fields on here. His writing is on the edges of the maps."

Calvin reached his hand into the pannier again. He then held up a photograph, with worn edges. The paper was brittle and near to cracking. Calvin held it and looked at it for several seconds before carefully putting the picture in his shirt pocket. It was a picture of his mother, father, and him. It had been taken some time ago, but apparently his father had cherished it so much that he had carried it with him. Calvin finished his look into the panniers. "Nothing else here that I want," he said and walked away from the group. He was soon seen leaning against the side of his horse, crying. The other three men watched him with a lump in their throats.

Nathan walked to the side of the young man. "Calvin, I know this is hard for you, but I have to ask the question. "Are you positively sure that the body over there is your dad's?"

Calvin lifted his head and looked at Nathan. Quietly, he answered, "I'm sure Marshal. Go look at my dad's right hand. There are two fingers missing from his hand. He lost those fingers in an accident at the leather factory in Lafayette. It's him, all right."

"Mmm, okay," said Nathan, and he left Calvin and walked back to the corpse where Ben was waiting. Nathan bent down and lifted the right arm of the body. Sure enough, the two smallest fingers of the right hand were missing.

Nathan looked up at Ben. "Calvin said his dad was missing those two fingers on his right hand."

Somewhat subdued from his usual persona, Ben said, "I guess this pretty well clinches it."

"Bones don't lie, I reckon," said Nathan.

* * *

Sean had moved to Calvin's side. "Would you like us to bury your dad?"

"I, I, I guess so," Calvin responded.

Sean asked Calvin if there was any place that he preferred that his father be buried. Calvin told him that since his father was travelling this route to Colorado, could he be buried close to here. Tears welled in his eyes.

"I think my dad would like this spot to be buried," said Calvin. "We can go up to the top of the hill where there is a wonderful view of the valley and prairie. He would like it there."

Sean squeezed the young man's shoulder and walked back to the other men.

"I'm figuring there should be a patch of softer ground over next to those scrub oaks on the top of that hill," said Sean. "Let's go dig the grave, and then we'll come back for the body."

Sean and Nathan each grabbed a shovel, and Ben walked with them to the trees. They talked as they took turns with the shovels.

"That has to be really tough," said Ben. "Losing your dad who wanders off to go search for gold, and then losing your mom. Now the poor kid has no one to call family."

Nathan leaned on his shovel for a moment. "And then to find out that your dad died at the hands of an evil man who left the body to scavengers. I only regret that we didn't have the legal cause to come after Malone earlier." Nathan continued digging.

Their work was slow, as there were plenty of rocks in the soil where they were digging, but with perseverance, they finished their task. In a low voice, Sean said, "And now for the unpleasant part."

They walked back to the body. Calvin joined them. "Can I help?" he asked.

"You don't need to," said Nathan. "But if you want to, yes, you can help."

As gently as possible, the four men lifted the odiferous corpse and slowly walked to the open grave. All the while, Nathan was dearly hoping that the body would not fall apart in their hands. Miraculously, the ligaments and tendons held together, and they slowly lowered the body into the grave. Calvin took one of the shovels and began shoveling dirt on his father's body. Sean joined him as they refilled the hole. When they were done, Sean asked, "Calvin, would you like me to say a prayer?" Calvin was intermittently crying again. He shook his head in assent.

The men removed their hats. "Heavenly Father," Sean began. "Please shine your face down on the spirit of Mr. Kahl. Take his spirit to your heavenly kingdom. He was killed by evil, but your hand can rectify and save the spirit of Mr. Kahl. We thank you, Lord. Amen."

Their work was done at the limestone outcropping, and the men retied the shovels to their saddle cantles and began the ride back to the ranch house. Calvin rode next to Sean, and the two lawmen rode behind them. Alternating between a trot and a walk, they talked when the pace was slower.

Sean spoke to Calvin, asking him, "Do you have any plans for the future, Calvin?" Sean knew the answer to the question before he asked. He knew a young man with no family was certainly cast adrift. Sean surmised that Calvin had no idea how he would spend the rest of the week, let alone the rest of his life.

"No, sir, I surely do not," Calvin answered. "With both Mom and Dad gone, I don't know what I'm going to do."

"Calvin, look around you. Do you like our ranch?" Sean asked.

"Oh, yes sir," Calvin responded. "It's beautiful here, not like the dirty city that I am used to."

"Calvin, my sister Jane and I would like you to stay here with us on the ranch. Would you like to do that?" Sean asked.

Calvin did not answer right away. Finally, he said, "Well, sir, that would be wonderful. But, sir, I don't know how to do anything on a ranch. And I don't know anything about cows."

Sean laughed. "Sometimes I think half our ranch hands don't know enough about cows. You need not worry. All of us had to learn the ranching business from the bottom up. We can teach you."

"Okay, I would like that," said Calvin. "What would I be doing?"

"Do you remember at breakfast you said that you would have to learn to cook?" Sean asked.

Calvin hesitated a bit. "Yes, I remember."

"Well, the first thing you are going to learn is how to cook. Cookie will be your teacher," said Sean. "Most of the ranch hands have had to work a bit with the cook of the outfit. We do that to test you and see if you can stick it out and earn your way. When you have learned that, we will start teaching you how to be a ranch hand, a cowboy. You will live in the bunk house with the other men. Oh, they'll give you a good teasing all the time while they teach you, but they're good boys and started out just like you. What do you think?"

"I guess all I can say is thank you," said Calvin. "I will do my best to learn the ranching business."

"Good. Then, that's settled," said Sean. "Lee Stark, the foreman, will take you under his wing and make sure you get your feet on the ground."

Chapter Seventeen

Lazy C Ranch

When the men reached the Lazy C ranch house, the first order of business was taking care of the horses. Sean and Calvin quickly unsaddled their animals and led them into the corral to throw some hay to them. Nathan and Ben left their mounts saddled and led them into the pen. Nathan tossed a few forkfuls of hay into the pen. Sean watched Nathan and Ben and looked at them quizzically until Nathan said, "We're going to try to catch that late afternoon southbound out of Nocona. You have everything under control here, so Ben and I are no longer needed. And I've got a wife and young'un I haven't seen for a few days."

"I understand, Marshal. But you need to come inside and get something to eat before you leave," said Sean.

Ben looked at Nathan and grinned.

Sean saw the grin and asked, "What's funny?"

Ben then laughed. "The Marshal, here, was hoping you'd say that. See, Sean, he's got this hollow leg and seems to be forever hungry."

Sean and Ben laughed, and Nathan had to smile.

As the men made their way to the house, Lee Stark came from the barn.

Sean stopped and pulled Lee aside to speak with him. "Lee, I've got a job I want you to do."

"Sure, boss," said Lee. "What do you need me to do?"

"First thing tomorrow, I need you to go into town and see the undertaker," said Sean.

Lee looked at Sean with a serious face but said nothing.

"Tell him we need him to bring two coffins and three head stones, two for Mom and Dad and one for Calvin's dad. We'll leave Calvin's dad right where he lies. He will need to dig up the bodies of Mom and Dad. We're going to give my parents a proper funeral and bury them in the family plot next to my grandparents," said Sean. "I'll write you a note with instructions for the head stones. Tell him I would like to have this taken care of as soon as he can. And when he's ready to come out, tell him to bring the Methodist preacher with him. We'll hold a service for Mom and Dad and Calvin's father. The undertaker can bring the bill, and I'll pay him when he and the preacher are done."

"Sure thing, Sean. That sure needs to be done, and I'll go into town tomorrow right after breakfast," Lee assured him. Lee then hesitated, "Umm, what about Malone? Should he be dug up too?"

"Hell no," said Sean. "The sooner the worms get to him the better. Let him rot in hell!"

"Yep," Lee replied. "I'll check in with you later, Boss. Right now, I need to go check on the hands to make sure a little work gets done around here." Lee walked away to retrieve a fresh horse from the barn.

Later, the group sat at the kitchen table. Empty plates that had previously held open-faced roast beef sandwiches with beef gravy sat in front of them, a reflection of the gastronomic skills of Cookie.

"Calvin. We are going to head back to Decatur," said Nathan. "Do you want to come along with us?"

Calvin glanced quickly over to Sean and then back to Nathan. "No, sir. Sean and Jane have asked if I want to stay with them. And Lee has told me that he will make a cowhand out of me. So, I am going to stay here at the Lazy C."

"Hey, that's great news," said Nathan. "I think you've got the makings of a good ranch hand. If Sean hadn't offered you a job, I might have done the same thing."

"I think you'll do fine," said Ben. "You're a tough kid, the kind that Sean and Jane need around here."

A broad smile was in place on Jane Conley's face. She would never reveal her feeling to anyone else, but in the actions and demeanor of Calvin Kahl, she saw a young man who, if fate would have dealt her the proper hand, she would have been proud to have as her own son. Calvin would give her another chance to nurture a young man into responsible manhood. She was very pleased that he was staying on at the Lazy C.

Nathan and Ben rose from the table and shook hands with Sean, Jane, and Calvin as they said their good-byes. Sean sincerely thanked them for their help in ridding the Lazy C of its evil interloper in the form of Ivan Malone.

"Keep in touch, Sean and Jane," said Nathan. "Don't hesitate to contact me if you have any other problems."

The lawmen walked from the ranch house, retrieved their horses, and made their way to Nocona to catch the southbound train.

* * *

The afternoon train to Decatur had few passengers. Not surprisingly, the railroad did not seem concerned, as they made more money hauling mail and cargo, which essentially made the run profitable. The rhythmic bumping and clacking of the train wheels had put both Nathan and Ben to sleep. They were stretched out on bench seats in the passenger car. They both needed the rest. After Nathan had put Wander into the stock car in Nocona, he sat down in the passenger car. He thought to himself that he had spent far too much time in the saddle in the past few weeks. It would be good to be home. He had then lain on the bench and promptly fallen asleep. When the train stopped briefly in Bowie, the lawmen did not stir. The train then continued on through Sunset and Alvord before finally reaching Decatur. Nathan and Ben were awakened by the conductor shaking one of each of their booted feet.

"End of the line, gents," said the Conductor. "We're in Decatur." He then moved on to rouse the other passengers.

Nathan looked over at Ben Steele as he sat up on the bench. Ben's hat was laying on the floor, and as he rose, his hair seemed to stick out in several different directions. "You look like hell, Steele. Glad I don't have to wake up every morning looking at you."

"The feeling is mutual, partner," said Ben, as he grinned and attempted to smooth his hair.

When the train came to a standstill, the lawmen unloaded their horses from the stock car and shook hands. "Don't look for me at the office tomorrow, Ben," said Nathan. "I need to stay home for a day or so with Claire May and Bobby."

"I may show up late at the office tomorrow myself," replied Ben. "*Adios*, Marshal," said Ben as he began to ride away.

"*Adios*, Ben," Nathan replied and nudged Wander in the ribs. "Let's go home, boy." Wander had followed this route before, and when he heard the word home, he turned his head to the trail. He knew the way and kept up a steady lope until his breathing indicated that he needed a rest. Nathan brought him to a fast walk, which Wander could keep up for extended periods. In another ten minutes they were home. As he passed the house on his way to the barn, he gave a yell.

"Hello in the house," Nathan shouted as he continued to the barn. When he reached the barn, Pablo came out to meet him.

"Welcome home, Marshal," said Pablo. "You go on up to the house. I'll take care of the horse."

Nathan knew that Wander was in good hands. Pablo had a gift with animals. He would give Wander a good brush down and feed. But he could not resist saying, "Make sure he gets a good feed, Pablo. He's been on thin rations the past few days."

"Yes, sir," Pablo answered. "I'll take good care of him."

Wearily, Nathan walked up to the house. He could see Claire May standing on the porch waiting for him, and he grinned. As he climbed the steps up to the porch, she quickly came to him and put her arms around him while they kissed. "Hello, darlin'," said Nathan.

"Nathan, I've missed you so much, and Bobby has missed his daddy." She moved back away from him for a bit as she continued. "You know I love you to death, but I've gotta tell you, you don't smell so good."

Nathan chuckled. "Yeah, I suppose that's a fact. That's what too many days on the trail will do for you."

"And," Claire May continued as she grinned from ear to ear, "I've got a surprise for you." She walked ahead of him as they went into the house. As his eyes became adjusted to the interior light, he saw her.

"Well, I'll be darned," said Nathan, and he quickly hung his saddlebags, gunbelt, and rifle on the wall pegs by the door. He walked swiftly to Virginia Summers and gave her a kiss on the cheek. Virginia was holding Bobby in her arms, and when the toddler saw his dad, he began squirming. Virginia handed the child to Nathan.

"Hello, big man," said Nathan, as he kissed his son and squeezed him. Bobby giggled and pulled at the hairs on Nathan's face. "I've missed you, little buddy."

"Mom's come to stay with us for a few days," said Claire May.

"Gosh, it's good to see you, Virginia," said Nathan as he turned his attention to his mother-in-law.

Claire May took Bobby from his arms and gave him back to Virginia. "I'm going to put a bucket of hot water into the tub, and you're going to get cleaned up while I make us some dinner."

Nathan grinned. "Yes, ma'am," he said and kissed Claire May again before he made his way to the bedroom to get some clean clothes, and then went to the bathroom where he began to draw water into the tub. He was nearly undressed as Claire May made her way into the bathroom carrying a bucket of hot water. She closed the door, poured the hot water into the tub, set the bucket down, and grabbed Nathan around the neck. They kissed a lingering kiss.

"I've missed you so much, Nathan," she said.

"I think about you every hour that I'm on the road," Nathan said.

The couple embraced and kissed again, before Nathan gently pushed her away. "If you want me to get clean, you better let me get in that tub."

"Well, if Mother wasn't here, you would find that two people can fit in the tub," Claire May said quietly. She picked the bucket off of the floor and slid out of the door before reclosing it. She joined her mother in the main room.

Bobby was on the floor contentedly playing with toys and crawling from place to place. When he reached a chair or table, he hoisted himself into a standing position and jabbered before he plopped back down on his bottom to quickly crawl to a new spot. When he spied his grandmother on the loveseat, he could see that she had something interesting, so he quickly moved over to her and stood up next to the small couch. Virginia was busily sewing, but when Bobby came to her, she put the needle and sewing box aside to pick him up.

Virginia looked at Claire May at the kitchen counter.

"Has Nathan lost some weight, Claire May?" Virginia asked. "He looks so tired."

Claire May turned to her mother. "No, I don't think he is any thinner. But these road trips really take it out of him. He doesn't get enough sleep, and he sometimes does not get good food while he travels. I worry about him."

"Is he still meeting up with dangerous people? That's what I worry about," said Virginia. "He's been nearly killed in the past."

"Uh, huh, he is. It gets bad enough that it can even spill over to me and Bobby," said Claire May.

"What do you mean?" asked Virginia.

For the next few minutes Claire May told her Mother about Ivan Malone's hired gunman, Beryl Dunn, coming to the ranch to kill Nathan. But when he learned that Nathan was not at home, he had threatened to kill Claire May and Bobby. The situation had scared Claire May greatly; not so much for herself, but just at the thought of a hired killer harming her child. Claire May shuddered after telling the story to her Mother.

"And you say that your hired man killed that outlaw?" Virginia asked.

Claire May nodded her head.

"Well, thank God for Pablo," said Virginia.

Just then the ladies heard, "Claire May, do I have any clean socks?"

The women laughed. "Honestly, he can't find anything," said Claire May as she walked from the room. She returned in a moment, with a smile on her face. Nathan had known exactly where his clean socks were. He had simply lured her into their bedroom to grab her and give her a proper kiss. She was also happy that he smelled better after his bath.

Nathan came to join the women. He sat at the kitchen table and Claire May put a roast beef sandwich on a plate in front of him. "Mmm," mumbled Nathan as he quickly devoured the sandwich.

"Now, we're going out on the porch, and I'm going to give you a haircut and shave," said Claire May.

"Well, that sounds interesting. I'll come along," said Virginia.

Claire May got Nathan's shaving mug, soap, razor and scissors, and they moved to the porch. Bobby had finally worn down and was peacefully sleeping on the rug in the main room. They left the back door ajar so that they could hear him if he fussed.

Nathan sat on a chair on the porch with an apron tied around his neck. Virginia asked as she laughed, "Are you sure you want her to do this, Nathan?"

"Oh, sure. She's my usual barber," Nathan answered. "No use paying a barber in town when my wife can do just as good of a job."

Claire May had added some water to Nathan's shaving mug along with some soap flakes. Then she stirred the shaving brush in the mug, working up a lather. When she was satisfied, she began brushing the lather onto Nathan's face until half of his face was white with lather. Holding the sharp razor in one hand, and stretching Nathan's facial skin with the other, she expertly transformed Nathan into a clean-shaven man.

"Geez, Claire May," Virginia remarked. "There's no end to your talent. I can't wait to see the haircut."

"Oh, the haircut is easy," Claire May answered. "I just hack away until my hand gets too tired." She was smiling, but Nathan uttered a playful growl. Virginia laughed at their playfulness.

It was not long before hair clippings encircled the floor around Nathan's chair, but the final product was, indeed, just as good as any professional barber's. "Do you think he'll pass muster, Mom."

"I would say so," Virginia answered.

"What do you mean, 'pass muster'?" Nathan asked.

"Well, Marshal Wolf," Claire May began, "the day after tomorrow is Sunday, and we are going to church."

"We are?" he responded.

"Yes, and you need to look presentable to the congregation," said Claire May. "After all, you will be standing up in front of everyone."

Nathan was truly confused. First of all, they seldom went to church, and second, why would he be standing up in front of everyone. Claire May observed the blank questioning look on his face. "Honestly, Nathan, you have forgotten, haven't you?"

There was no response from Nathan as he tried to remember any conversation dealing with going to church.

"I will remind you that we talked about this a couple weeks ago," said Claire May. "We are taking Bobby to get him baptized."

"Oh, sorry, Claire May. I've had a few things on my mind for the past few days," Nathan replied.

"I know you have, sweetheart. Just remember," said Claire May, "Sunday we go to church."

Later that evening, after they had eaten supper, they sat on the back porch. The sun remained above the horizon, lending plenty of light for Virginia's project.

"What are you working on, there, Virginia?" Nathan asked. He held a glass in his hand that contained three fingers of bourbon.

"It's Bobby's baptismal gown," Virginia answered. She held up the fancy lace and white gown.

When he looked at it, Nathan was a bit confused. "It's a dress," he said. "Is Bobby going to wear a dress to get baptized?"

The women laughed. "No silly," said Claire May. "Boy and girl babies all wear gowns that look alike."

"Hmm," Nathan mumbled. "Well, I hope you're sewing a pair of britches onto the gown."

The women laughed again.

"I declare," said Nathan. "My boy is getting baptized in a dress." And he wagged his head from side to side.

Claire May looked at him and said, "That's enough Nathan. For your information, both my brother Will and I got baptized in that gown. And now, Bobby gets to use it too. I think it's wonderful."

"Well, how come you're sewing on it?" Nathan asked.

Virginia looked at him and said, "Bobby is a bit bigger than most babies who are getting baptized, so I'm letting out the seams a bit so that it will fit him." Her implication seemed to be that Nathan and Claire May had been a bit negligent in getting their child baptized at an earlier time.

"Mmm. Pretty sunset, ain't it," said Nathan. With two women in the house for the time being, he figured he just needed to change the subject.

Later, as evening turned to darkness, and with Virginia sleeping in her own bedroom, and Bobby soundly asleep, the couple made love to the sounds of tree frogs and singing cicadas, the pleasant sounds coming through their open window. Nathan's eyelids were heavy in the afterglow of lovemaking, and he was nearly ready to nod off to sleep. But just before that happened, an elbow nudged him in the ribs.

"What," Nathan grunted.

"Are you awake?" Claire May asked.

"Mmm. I guess so," Nathan mumbled.

"Are you in a good mood?" she asked.

Uh, oh, Nathan thought. *What's this about?*

"Well, are you?" she asked again.

"Yes, Claire May. I'm in a wonderful mood," Nathan replied. *I'm in a good mood to just go to sleep,* he thought.

"Good," she said, "because I have something to tell you."

Nathan rolled over to face his wife. "Okay, what do you need to tell me?" He yawned as he asked the question.

Claire May placed her hand on Nathan's chest and playfully pulled a strand of the few hairs on his chest.

"Well, Marshal, I believe you have me in a family way," Claire May teased and laughed at her remark.

Suddenly, Nathan was awake. "Are you saying what I think you're saying?" he asked.

"Yes, silly. Bobby is going to have a brother or sister," she answered.

"Oh. Oh, my," was all Nathan could think to answer. "Umm, it's good, isn't it?"

Claire May just laughed. "Yes, it's good. But you know it's your fault," she said. "You get me in all these compromising positions, and this is the consequence." She was still smiling.

"Oh, bunk," said Nathan. "It takes two to tango."

They both laughed as Nathan drew his wife into his arms and kissed her. "Another baby," he murmured. "How 'bout that."

"Yeah, how 'bout that, Marshal. Now you can go back to sleep," she said, and kissed him again before rolling away to her side of the bed. She was still chuckling as she drifted off to sleep.

Nathan did not go back to sleep immediately. Instead, he lay on his back for a while thinking what a miracle it was that babies came to life at all. "Well, how 'bout that," he murmured again and rolled over to his side to go to sleep.

The Next Morning

Pablo Carillo joined them for coffee and cinnamon short bread on the back porch. It was late August, and the final cutting of hay had already taken place. Pablo had hired a few of his friends to come on to the ranch to cut and pile the hay for use as winter feed for the cattle. The early summer rains provided the moisture to get three cuttings from the hay field, assuring them that they would have ample cattle feed through the winter.

The sun was just above the horizon as they sipped their coffee and enjoyed the sweet treat. It was nearly time to tackle some lingering chores around the ranch. As always, there were fences to mend, weeds to pull in the garden, and deadfall tree limbs to saw for the firewood pile. Wander needed his hooves trimmed and a new set of shoes, but Nathen was not sure he was capable of that job. He would probably leave it for the blacksmith in town on Monday. Nathan would work with Pablo the entire day to complete as many tasks as possible. The time spent completing ranch chores gave Nathan a sense of satisfaction. It was work quite unrelated to his day-to-day law enforcement job, and as strenuous as it was, he liked it. He took pride in his work, as it meant that he was contributing to make the Wolf Ranch a wonderful oasis in his sometimes-stressful work as a lawman. As he worked alongside of Pablo the men talked.

"Do you have children, Pablo?" Nathan asked.

"No, Mr. Nathan. My wife died before we could have children," said Pablo, "and I never found another wife. I have lots of nieces and nephews, so I am *tio* to all those kids."

Nathan asked, "Did Claire May tell you that she is going to have another baby?"

"Oh, no," Pablo exclaimed. "That is *muy bueno*. Soon we will have little *ninos* running around the house."

"Well, we might have a *nino* and *nina*," said Nathan.

"Ah, yes," Pablo answered. "That would be good, too. This will be a blessing for you and Mrs. Wolf."

The two men continued their work through the rest of the day, interrupted only when Claire May rode her horse to join them. She had brought them a basket of sandwiches, cold fried chicken, and mason jars of cold well water. The men paused their work and walked a short way to the shade of some oak trees, where they sat down to eat their dinner. Claire May had dismounted and sat next to Nathan as he ate.

"Nice and cool here in the shade," she said.

"Mmm, much better than standing in the sun, stapling fence wire," Nathan said as he continued to chew his food.

Soon, Claire May stood up. "I've got to get back to put Bobby down for his nap. Can you bury your chicken bones when you are done, and I will take the basket back with me to the house?"

"Sure, and thank you darlin' for bringing our dinner to us," said Nathan. He leaned over and kissed his wife, then grabbed her offered leg to help her swing up onto her saddle.

"See you at supper," she said as she rode away.

"She's a nice lady," said Pablo.

"Yes, sir, she is," Nathan replied as the men went back to their work.

*　*　*

After supper, Nathan, Claire May, and Pablo sat on the back porch to enjoy the evening. They each had a glass of wine in one hand.

"Mmm, that was a good supper," said Nathan.

Virginia and Claire May had fried filets of bass, fish that Pablo had caught in one of the ranch's tanks the previous day. They had rolled the fish portions in corn meal and fried them in a skillet with bacon lard. They had also baked cornmeal muffins to be slathered with butter and strawberry jam. The jam was home-made and sold at the local farmer's market in Decatur. Fresh-picked wild asparagus rounded out the main course, before Virginia's fresh baked apple pie was savored for dessert. The wine was provided by Pablo, whose friend made several varieties of home-made wine.

"Those cicadas certainly are loud," said Nathan.

"What do you expect," said Claire May. "They're all boys trying to call a girlfriend."

"Is that so," Nathan scoffed.

"Yes, mister. The females don't make any noise." Claire May stopped, and then said, "Uh, oh. I think I hear another boy calling." She had heard Bobby crying inside the house. "Guess he woke up hungry. I'd better go feed him." She placed her wine glass next to her chair on the floor and went inside. In a moment, Bobby's crying suddenly stopped. Obviously, he was getting fed.

Nathan took a sip of his wine. "Ooo," he said. "This stuff seems pretty strong, Pablo. What's it made of?"

"My friend that makes it calls it juniper berry wine," Pablo replied. "He always tells me not to drink too much of it." Pablo laughed.

"Well, I can understand why," said Nathan. "One little glass of your juniper wine is enough for me, I think." Pablo laughed again.

Claire May joined them after overhearing their conversation regarding the wine. "It has an interesting taste, though," she said.

Pablo rose from his chair. "I think I will go to bed," he said. "I am tired after our work today."

"Okay, Pablo. We'll see you in the morning," said Nathan. "Remember, you're going to church with us tomorrow."

"I remember," Pablo answered. He turned and walked down the porch steps and on to the barn. He waved at them before going into the barn.

Nathan and Claire May, sat in silence, listening to the Cicadas, tree frogs, and an occasional low moo from a member of the cattle herd. In the waning light, Claire May watched her husband. She took a match from her apron pocket, stood, and lit one of the oil lamps on the porch.

"A penny for your thoughts, Marshal," she teased.

Nathan chuckled. "Oh, I was just daydreaming, wondering what it will be like to have two little kids to watch over."

Claire May stood up and slid her chair over next to Nathan. "Are you having second thoughts about another baby?" she asked. "Because if you are, it's just a little bit too late for second thoughts." She playfully jabbed him in the ribs.

Nathan had to laugh. "No, no, sweetheart. No second thoughts. I was only wondering how much work it would be for you since I am gone so much of the time. I mean, Bobby keeps you awfully busy by himself."

It was Claire May's turn to laugh. "Indeed, he does. But, Nathan, it's a happy kind of busy. I have always wanted to have children of my own. Besides, Bobby needs a playmate. Don't worry, it's all going to be fine." She leaned over and kissed Nathan on the cheek. In turn, he turned his head and kissed her.

"I really have a great wife," he said.

Claire May laughed. "Of course, you do."

"Ugh," Virginia mumbled as she joined them on the porch. "I think I need to go to bed before it gets embarrassing out here. Claire May, light that other lamp for me, please."

Claire May struck another match, lit the other lamp, and handed it to her mother. "All right, you two, I'm going to bed. Behave yourselves," said Virginia as she walked back into the house. Nathan and Claire May laughed.

"See you in the morning, Mom," said Claire May.

Virginia smiled to herself as she made her way to the spare bedroom. She thought to herself, *I so wish you were here with me, Robert. You would enjoy seeing how much your daughter has grown and how she has a good man who loves her dearly. It reminds me so much of you and me when we were young.* She sighed heavily as she closed her bedroom door.

* * *

The following morning, Virginia rose early and gathered eggs at the hen house. She stoked the wood stove and went to the cold root cellar to retrieve a small slab of bacon. She then cut several slices of bread from the loaf on the kitchen counter. Sliced bacon strips were placed in the cast iron skillet and began sending off their tantalizing aroma by the time Nathan and Claire May came to the kitchen. Claire May had heard her mother get up, but rather than join her right away, she had fed and changed Bobby, then nudged Nathan awake before going to the kitchen

"You're up early," Claire May said to her mother.

"The early bird, and all that…" said Virginia. "The coffee should be ready on the stove."

Nathan walked sleepily to the stove and filled a coffee mug before sitting at the kitchen table. He thought again how nice it was that Claire May had her mother to talk with during her mother's visit.

Just before putting a half dozen eggs into the hot pan that had been used for the bacon, Virginia placed the slices of bread on the heating griddle of the stove. The bread would be toasted by the time the scrambled eggs were done.

"I don't know how you do it, Virginia," said Nathan, "but your coffee always tastes better than mine."

While they ate their breakfast, Virginia talked about what was going on at Summer Prairie Ranch in Kansas, the Summers family ranch that Will Summers now managed.

"I don't know what I'm going to do with Will," said Virginia. "Do you know that he and Alice Morgan have still not set a wedding day?"

"I thought I understood him to say he was going to take care of that just before we moved down here," said Claire May.

"Well, he didn't," Virginia replied. "He keeps telling me that he's just too busy to get married. Hogwash! And I want to tell you, it's getting a bit embarrassing. Why, the other day when I was in town I ran into Dave Morgan, Alice's dad. He asked me 'when was Will going to finally get around to setting a wedding date with Alice?'" Virginia was shaking her head, then she paused to take a swig of coffee.

Claire May had to grin. "What did you tell him, Mom?"

"I told him I would have a talk with Will, but you know your brother," said Virginia.

"It went in one ear and out the other, didn't it?" laughed Claire May.

"Of course," Virginia said and sighed. "I guess they will set the date when he gets good and ready, whenever that is. Anyway, the ranch is doing well. We had good spring rains and calf season produced a bumper crop. Will was preparing to sell off the yearlings when I got ready to come and see you. He's a good manager, but maybe not the greatest material for a husband."

"I think he's scared to get married. He's a chicken, and you can tell him I said so," said Claire May. "But, having said that, I think my brother would make a good husband and father. Maybe Alice needs to put her foot down and tell him to set the date or forget it."

"I think you're right," Virginia answered. "But right now, by your mantel clock, it looks like we probably need to get ready for church."

Claire May looked up at the clock. "Oh, golly. We need to get ready and get on the road to town."

Later, Nathan and Pablo rode behind the buckboard that was driven by Claire May, with Virginia sitting at her side holding Bobby on her lap. Nathan rode up to the side of Claire May.

"I swear, Nathan, the way this buckboard bangs around it might just knock my hat off," said Claire May.

"I promise to pick up your hat if it flies off," answered Nathan, laughing as he said it.

"Well, here's what I think, smart guy," Claire May answered. "We need to get a nice carriage that is big enough for us and the children. After all, the U.S. Marshal should ride in something nicer than this hard-bouncing buckboard."

"Hmm. Do you think she's right, Virginia?" Nathan asked.

"I'm 'fraid I do," said Virginia. "I think my teeth are rattling. And, as you know, Claire May is always right, isn't she?"

Nathan looked at Virginia, who was doing her best to hold back a smile, then looked away wagging his head from side to side as he slowed Wander to fall back with Pablo. The two women began laughing gaily at their pressuring of Nathan. It did not bother Nathan and he smiled and winked at Pablo, who was also smiling. When they arrived at the Decatur United Methodist Church, Claire May parked the buckboard a short distance away from the nicer carriages. Nathan came to her and tied a line to the horse buggy weight and set it on the ground. Then he helped Claire May to the ground, walked to the other side and helped Virginia after she handed Bobby to Claire May. They walked up the steps of the church, entered, and found an empty pew.

Later, Claire May had to nudge Nathan, who was nearly asleep. His head came up quickly. "C'mon, sleepy. They have called us up front."

Nathan held Bobby as he, Claire May, and Virginia walked down the aisle and up two steps to the sanctuary to join the pastor, who was saying, "Mr. and Mrs. Nathan Wolf have brought their son to us today for holy baptism."

The pastor then opened his black bound book and found his place in the text. He stood next to Nathan who was holding Bobby and read through his text. In a moment he was finished reading and placed his text to the side. He held out his arms, and Nathan placed Bobby in the arms of the pastor.

"What name have you given your son?" asked the pastor.

Claire May answered, "Robert Summers Wolf."

"And do you bring Robert Summers Wolf freely before God?" asked the pastor.

"We do," said Nathan and Claire May.

As the pastor spoke, Bobby was finding this whole situation rather interesting. Here was a man who sounded a little like his father but was not his father. And the man wore glasses, something that Bobby found fascinating. He reached up with his small hand and pulled the glasses from the man's face. Laughter erupted in the church audience. The pastor was able to pry his glasses from Bobby's hand and continued. The pastor then dipped his hand into the baptismal font and put his wet hand onto Bobby's head. Bobby blinked a few times, but he tolerated the water. However, his eyes again focused on the spectacles on the face of this strange man. He reached up to grab the glasses again, but he could not quite reach them. Instead, his small fingers locked onto the septum in the nostrils of the pastor's nose. From that point forward, the pastor spoke in a distinct nasal twang.

With his free hand still on Bobby's head, he could not free his nose from the toddler's grip, and his words came out, "Mobby Summers

Woolf, I maptise you in duh name of duh father, son, and hoody speerid."

The audience burst forth with laughter. Nathan was laughing out loud. Claire May was laughing, but she was trying to keep a straight face. Virginia had pulled a handkerchief from her pocket and was using it to dab her eyes as her shoulders shook in laughter.

With Bobby's hand still locked firmly on his nose, the pastor then capped it all off by saying, "Led us sing oour negst hymn. 'Duh Hoady Spirid Haas a Hode on Me'." The laughter got even louder until the church organist launched into the opening notes of the hymn.

Nathan retrieved Bobby from the arms of the pastor and shook hands with the clergyman. Claire May, Nathan, and Virginia quickly moved back down the aisle to return to their seats next to Pablo. Singing faces with beaming smiles turned to them as they walked. Although they may have been a bit embarrassed, the four of them could not help but continue to chuckle as they took their place standing in the pew.

At the conclusion of the hymn, the pastor raised his hands for the benediction.

"What a wonderful day," he said. "Children are God's gift to us. And now, may the Lord bless you and keep you and make his face shine down upon you all of your days. Go in peace. Amen."

Later as the buckboard bounced its way down the road to home, Nathan was in high spirits. "I never knew going to church could be so much fun." He laughed loudly.

"Oh hush," said Claire May. "Everybody in town is going to know their Marshal now, and it won't be for a good reason."

"Oh, Claire May," Virginia said, "you have to admit, that was something you don't see every day," and she laughed.

Suddenly, Nathan burst forth in loud song, his own made-up song; *"Oh, the holy spirit's got a hold on me, hold on me, hold on me. Oh, the holy spirit's got a hold on me, and he won't let go."* They all laughed as they rode down the lane to the Wolf ranch house.

Later, after supper, with Bobby fed and tucked into his bed, Nathan, Claire May, and Virginia sat on the back porch listening to the song of the cicadas and tree frogs. It was nearly dark, and they had an oil lamp sending out its comforting yellow light. Pablo had gone to bed early and his light in the barn had already been extinguished.

"Well, it was a nice day, all in all," said Nathan. He had consumed a nightcap of three fingers of bourbon and began to yawn.

"Bobby was so funny," Claire May giggled.

"Well, I will offer a piece of advice. Don't wait so long for this next baby to be baptized," said Virginia. "Maybe he or she won't be able to give the pastor such a hard time."

"Mother!" Claire May said loudly. "How in the world do you do that? How did you know?" Claire May had not told her mother that she was pregnant.

Virginia just shrugged her shoulders. "I knew when I first saw you at the train depot when you picked me up. You have to remember that I've known my daughter all of her life."

"Sounds like hocus-pocus to me," said Nathan. He yawned again. "If you ladies don't mind, I need to get to bed. Sadly, I have to go back to work tomorrow."

Claire May looked up at him as he rose from his chair. "I have enjoyed having you home for two days."

"I've enjoyed it too, sweetheart." He leaned down and kissed Claire May. "I'm off to bed."

"I'll be there in a bit," Claire May answered. She and her Mother watched Nathan carry his drink glass into the house and disappear from sight.

"I worry about him, Mom," said Claire May. "He doesn't always tell me about all the things that happen to him when he is away. For instance, I know that he told me he was going after the most evil man he had ever met. But he didn't tell me all the details of what happened up by Nocona."

"Maybe it's better that he doesn't tell you all the details," Virginia said. "You would probably worry even more if you knew all the things that happen to him."

"Yes, I suppose that's true. But he did tell me that the outlaw he was going to arrest got killed in a gunfight, and you know what that means," said Claire May. "The outlaw was probably shooting at Nathan."

"Goodness, Claire May. That's the life of a lawman in this day and age," said Virginia. "And somebody has to go after the criminals, and lawmen can get hurt in the process."

"Well, you remember how he was nearly killed in Kansas. If he hadn't been taken in by those Amish folks, he would have died," said Claire May.

Virginia answered her. "Nathan is a smart man, Claire May. He will not put himself in a position where there is no escape. My advice to you is just love him for the way he is. He loves you, and he adores Bobby. He's a good man, and sometimes those are hard to find. Now, if you don't mind, I'm going to bed."

"Good night, Mom," said Claire May.

Claire May took the oil lamp into the house and went to her bedroom. She checked on Bobby in his bed, then changed into her bedclothes. Before she blew out the lamp, she looked at Nathan and then back at Bobby. "My boys," she whispered, then blew out the lamp and crawled into bed.

*　*　*

    She couldn't help herself. It was habit. Virginia Summers had been the matriarch of Summer Prairie Ranch for decades, and as such, she had always risen early to get breakfast ready for Robert, Claire May, and Will, her own family. Even though Robert had died years ago, and Claire May had moved to Texas, she still rose early to get breakfast for herself and Will. She also knew how taxing it can be to take care of a toddler, so she felt that she was helping Claire May and Nathan by getting their breakfast. Today, she was making pancakes. Slices of ham would share the breakfast plates with those pancakes.

    Breakfast was nearly ready when Claire May came to the kitchen carrying Bobby. Virginia quickly came to Claire May and patted Bobby's chubby cheeks. Then she kissed her grandson on the cheek.

    "He's just too cute, isn't he," said Virginia.

    Claire May laughed. "Oh, yeah, he's a cutie all right."

    Virginia then began removing pancakes from the griddle. "Where's that Marshal of yours?"

    "Right behind you," Nathan said as he laughed.

    Virginia was dishing up the plates. "Well sit down, you two. I'll take Bobby while you eat. Is Pablo down in the barn? I'll take a plate to him when we are done."

    "No, he's not there, Virginia. He left early this morning to go into Decatur. He wanted to get to the sale barn and talk to the owner. He is lining up the transportation and selling off half a dozen or our yearling steers," said Nathan. "He should be back for lunch."

    They sat at the kitchen table while Claire May fed bits of pancake to Bobby. The toddler's cheeks resembled those of a chipmunk, his jaws eagerly chewing the maple syrup coated pancakes. After a time,

Claire May washed the crumbs and syrup from Bobby's face as Nathan rose from the table.

"I reckon I'd better hit the trail to town," said Nathan. "Never know what strange problem I'll run across today." He left the ladies in the kitchen while he finished getting ready to leave. After kissing Claire May good-bye, he headed for the barn. In a few minutes he rode Wander past the house and waved at Claire May, who was standing on the back porch watching him.

Chapter Eighteen

Decatur, Texas

Wander's habits had not changed with time. His interest in his surroundings meant that he was always curious about insects, flowers, scents, and anything else that caught his attention. As a result, Nathan had to make periodic rein corrections to keep the horse on the road. Nathan did not mind, as he was used to the horse's idiosyncrasies. He and Wander had put many miles in their travels together, and they were used to each other. It did not take them long to reach the edge of town.

Nathan soon reached Main Street and nudged Wander to turn the corner onto the seemingly deserted street. But just as Wander began to turn the corner, Nathan and Wander encountered a great deal of noise. A motorized automobile came careening around the corner one block away. What with all the noise it was making, it appeared to Nathan that the automobile was travelling at a high rate of speed, but then, in truth, Nathan had not had any dealings with automobiles, so he would not know for sure what a high rate of speed would be with such a contraption. The automobile tore down the street heading directly for Nathan and Wander. The machine roared as it came to them and passed within inches of hitting Wander. The horse was terrified and literally jumped straight up in the air, seeming to jump from all four legs simultaneously. Nathan was unprepared for such an action from the horse and only by quickly grasping the saddle horn was he able to regain his seat on the saddle. Wander was still jumping and skittish as the automobile continued past them.

Nathan was furious. It was all he could do to get Wander under control, and Nathan was not about to let the incident go. Instead, he spurred Wander, and they began chasing the automobile. While the roar and noise of the automobile made it seem that the vehicle was moving fast, it soon became apparent that the auto was not as fast as it appeared. Wander's quarter horse speed was quickly moving him and Nathan near the automobile. The automobile was a brilliant, shiny black color that glistened in the sun. On the side of the car's hood was the lettering, *St. Louis Motor Carriage.* As the horse ran at the side of the auto, Nathan drew his pistol and fired three quick shots into the hood of the car. In doing so, one bullet struck the water hose running from the car's radiator to the engine. The water hose blew up causing the hood of the car to pop free of its clasps and be thrown upwards against the glass wind screen. A second bullet hit the spark distributor, which was immediately disabled. With no spark distributor, the car came to a halt. With no wind to hold it up, the hood then flopped back to its normal position with a loud clang of metal on metal. The third bullet had hit the back side of the car's radiator. Steam gushed from the radiator and escaped all around the hood. The car was completely disabled.

Nathan could now get a good look at the man who had been driving the automobile. On his head, he wore a brown fedora tilted slightly to the back. His face was distinctive because he had a scar on one of his cheeks, and he wore a thin, dark mustache on his upper lip. In addition, even though the temperature was high that day, he wore a matching set of coat and pants with a white shirt beneath the coat. Usually, the wearer of such an outfit would also sport a tie, even if nothing more than a string tie. The stranger wore no tie. Nathan could see that the man did not have the roughened hands of a worker. Nathan guessed that the man might be a gambler. He dismounted and stood next to the automobile.

After his initial shock, the driver opened the door of the auto and began shouting at Nathan. He then made the mistake of drawing his own pistol from beneath his coat. Not knowing that Nathan was a U.S. Marshal, the driver shouted, "You damn fool. You've ruined my automobile. I'll get you for this." The man began to raise his pistol to take aim. When the gun was up, the man fired. The bullet missed Nathan but went behind him and hit the saddle horn on Nathan's saddle. This spooked Wander a second time, and he bolted and ran. He had not gone far, though, before he stopped and looked back at Nathan.

"Throw the gun on the ground mister, or I shoot," Nathan said. "I'm U.S. Marshal Nathan Wolf."

But the man did not put the gun down. "I don't care if you're Robert E. Lee. You can't ruin my automobile," said the man as he raised his gun hand again.

Nathan's pistol barked loudly, and a bullet hit the driver's chest on the side above his gun hand. The shot spun the man to the side and his pistol flew from his hand. Nathan holstered his pistol and walked to the man who was now sitting on the running board of the car. "It pays to listen to a man who's pointing a gun at you."

"Go to hell," the man replied.

Nathan retrieved the man's pistol, turned, and told the man to remain where he was. "If you get up off of that contraption, I'll shoot you again." He then walked to Wander, talking gently to the gelding as he approached. He put the man's pistol in his saddlebags, retrieved the reins from the ground where they had fallen, and led Wander back to the automobile. From a saddlebag, Nathan retrieved a set of handcuffs. He walked to the man, leaned down, and pulled the man to a standing position.

"Turn around," said Nathan.

The man did so, and Nathan fastened one of the cuffs. "Get your other hand back here,"

Instead, the man spun around. In his free hand the man held a knife with a four-inch blade which he had hidden up his sleeve as he sat on the running board of the automobile. The man lunged at Nathan, but Nathan managed to turn slightly, and the blade of the man's knife only caught a sleeve of Nathan's shirt. In an instant, Nathan had retrieved the blackjack that he carried in his back pocket. He swung the blackjack, striking the man's knife-wielding fist, cracking bones in two of the man's fingers. He dropped the knife in pain and then bent over to pick it up with his other hand. But while he was bent at the waist, Nathan's blackjack connected with the man's head with a resounding 'thunk'. The man wilted to the ground.

Nathan looked at the pathetic figure lying in front of him, then placed his blackjack into his back pocket. He picked up the man's knife, looked it over, then put it in his saddlebags. It might be needed as evidence. He was about to turn back to the man, but he happened to see a horseman riding quickly toward him. *Oh no, what now,* Nathan thought. He then recognized the man. He was the owner of the general store on Main Street, Claude Nelson. Nelson was loudly yelling, his white apron flying to and fro as he galloped.

"Hold on to that man, Marshal," cried Nelson. "Don't let him get away."

Nelson brought his horse to a halt and quickly dismounted.

"He's..., he's the man," Nelson stammered while pointing to the prostrate man on the ground.

"Calm down, Claude," Nathan said. "What's this all about?"

"That man right there," said Nelson, still pointing to the prone figure. "He just robbed my store."

"Robbed your store, huh." Nathan was not sure whether or not to believe the over-excited storekeeper. He looked inside the man's automobile but did not see anything in the way of store merchandise. "What is it that you think this man took?"

"Guns, Marshal! He took two rifles from my gun rack while I was helping other customers," said Nelson. "I didn't even see him do it. Another customer saw him do it and yelled for the man to stop. But of course, he didn't."

Nathan looked inside the man's automobile again but could see no sign of any guns. He turned to face Nelson. "Claude, I don't see any guns in this automobile, but let me question this fella for a few minutes. In the meantime, I need you to go fetch the doctor. This fella has got a slug in him, and I don't want him to bleed to death before we get to the bottom of this. Now hurry on over to the doc's and tell him to meet me at my office.

"Well, all right, Marshal. But I'm telling you, he has those rifles somewhere in that contraption." Nelson remounted and trotted his horse down the street.

Nathan reached down and lifted the driver of the automobile to his feet, where he stood slowly rolling his head from side to side. "Ohhmm," he moaned.

"You'll live," said Nathan. "The doc's on his way."

Nathan led the man to the rear of the car and handcuffed him to the rear bumper. Then he walked back to the side of the car. He didn't see a man walking up to the car on the other side.

"Well, what the hell have you gotten yourself into this time, Marshal?" It was Ben Steele, who had walked up the street from the Marshal's Office when he heard the gun shots.

"Howdy, Ben. Don't know for sure, but Claude Nelson told me this fella stole two rifles from his store," said Nathan. "But I don't see any sign of any guns. I had to put a slug in him after he took a pot shot at me."

Ben walked around the car for a moment, saw the bullet holes in the hood of the car, watched the last of the steam rise from the car's radiator for a few seconds before he said, "You know, Nathan, I don't believe I've ever heard of any lawman ever killing an automobile. I think you've got yourself a first in the annals of law enforcement. Heck, not even a Texas Ranger has ever killed an automobile. Wait till they hear about this." He started laughing, but then walked to the rear of the car. He looked down at the man, then reached down and grabbed a handful of the man's hair and yanked the man's head so that Ben was looking directly into the man's face.

"Ohhh," Ben wailed. "I think I know this jackass."

"Is that so?" Nathan asked.

"Don't know his name, but I would recognize that scar on his cheek and the little dandy mustache," said Ben. "I think I've got a wanted poster with his ugly mug on it."

Nathan had moved to one of the rear side doors of the auto. "Ben, what do you make of this?" he asked. "Don't these contraptions have a back seat in them?"

Ben moved to his side to look. "Search me. I've never been this close to one of these noisy things. But I would think it should. See how the back part there is padded and upholstered, but there aren't any seats."

"I made it into a kind of wagon so I could haul things in it." The lawmen turned their attention to the rear of the car, from where the handcuffed man had spoken.

"Hmm. Well, what did you go and do that for?" Nathan asked. "What kind of things do you need to haul?"

"Whatever I damn well want to haul," the man replied.

"Kind of a smart mouth fella, ain't he," said Ben.

"Yeah, a real dandy," Nathan replied.

Nathan had crawled into the back seat compartment and was looking at the wooden platform on which he was kneeling. He crawled to the rear of the platform and put his hands down behind it. He felt nothing out of the ordinary. That is, until he went from side to side on the back wall. His hand ran into another object. His fingers traced the outline of what he had found. He moved his hand across the back wall and his fingers ran onto an identical object.

"Hinges," he muttered.

"What's that you said, Nathan?" asked Ben.

"Hinges," Nathan answered as he crawled back out of the car and stood to the side of the open back doors. Nathan tried to lift the wooden floor on which he had been kneeling. It budged slightly, but it did not lift. He walked around to the other side of the car and again tried to lift the back floor. He had the same result; it could not be lifted. He scratched his cheek while he thought about the situation. He took off his hat and laid it aside on the front seat of the car, and once again, he leaned into the back door of the car. This time, he pushed his head against the back of the front seat and looked down at the space between the front seat and the floor in the back seat. He could not see anything.

"Marshal, you need to come back here and take these bracelets off of me. I ain't done anything wrong and you need to let me go." The driver of the automobile was clanking the handcuffs over and over on the rear bumper of the car.

Ben walked to the back of the car and promptly slapped the driver. "Shut up weasel."

"You need to let me go. You can't hold me here," said the driver.

"I think the Marshal will hold you as long as he sees fit," Ben replied. "I've got a feeling you might take up residence in our jail for a while." Ben laughed, but then he looked more closely at the man. "Did you say you put a bullet in this turkey?" he asked.

"Yeah, I did," Nathan answered. "After he took a pot shot at me."

"That's mighty strange, Marshal," said Ben. "There's a hole in his fancy coat, but only a small hole in his shirt."

Nathan's curiosity was piqued. He walked to the back of the car to join Ben. Just like Ben, he could see the hole in the man's coat, a small tear in the shirt.

"The son of a bitch is a ghost," said Ben. "He ain't got any blood."

"Mmm," Nathan mumbled. Nathan then pulled the man's coat further to the side, where he could then see that there was a pocket on the inside of the coat, and the pocket bulged from the coat.

Nathan reached his hand into the pocket while he said, "Well, what do you think I'll find in here, mister?"

"Go to hell, lawman," the man replied.

Nathan pulled his hand from the coat pocket. In his fingers he held a thick rectangular packet, all neatly wrapped and taped closed. Protruding from the back of the package was the head of a bullet. Obviously, the bullet never got through the packet and into the man. Nathan then tore the wrapping from the package and looked at the thick stack of money bills.

"Well, well, would you look at that," said Nathan. "Where did a punk like you get a wad of cash like this?"

"My Uncle gave it to me before he died," said the man as he sneered at Nathan.

"That's your story, huh," said Nathan.

"Yep," the man answered, "and you can't prove otherwise."

"We'll see," Nathan answered. He threw the money packet on the front seat of the car and went again to the back door of the car. He again ran his hand between the back of the front seat and the wooden floor built into the back seat area. Near the corner of the wooden platform, he found it. A small metal knob protruded from the upright board that formed the front edge of the floor. He attempted to pull the knob forward from the board. It did not budge. But when he moved the knob from side to side, the knob moved, and Nathan heard a distinct click sound.

"Hey, Ben, c'mere," said Nathan.

Ben walked to the back door of the car and watched Nathan as he pulled the corner of the floor upward. Beneath the floor was a four-inch-deep wooden box, built to nestle under the frame of the floor. Within that box lay several rifles and pistols. All appeared to be in new or like-new condition.

"Well, well," said Ben. "It appears that our little automobile driver has himself a small arsenal."

"Yep, and I'll bet that Claude Nelson's stolen property is here," Nathan answered.

It was just at that moment that the storekeeper came walking up to the automobile. "Hey, Marshal," he said. "The doc is waiting for you at your office."

"It appears we don't need the doc," said Nathan. "But come over here, Claude. I want to show you something. But first, tell me what kind of guns were stolen from you."

"I believe that I had a Sharps rifle 1848 and a Springfield 1873 model," Claude answered. "Mind you, I'm not positive on that, but that's what I think was taken."

Nathan pulled the wooden floor upward again and rested it on his back as he rummaged through the rifles within the hidden box. He handed a rifle back to Ben, who was standing next to Claude Nelson.

"Springfield 1873," said Ben.

Nathan handed him another rifle before he backed up and lowered the automobile's wooden floor.

"Sharps 1848 model," said Ben.

"Looks like we found your rifles, Claude," said Nathan, as he handed the two firearms to the shopkeeper.

"Thank you, Marshal," Nelson replied.

Just then the automobile driver shouted again. "Those are my guns. You can't take them from me."

"I told you to shut up, weasel," said Ben, who had walked to the rear of the car. "How can you say they are your guns when we have an eyewitness who saw you steal them from our general store? You just ain't any too smart, are you, knucklehead?"

The handcuffed man glared at Ben and then attempted to spit on Ben. The spittle fell harmlessly in front of the man.

"You really are a weasel," Ben said and then walked back to join Nathan.

"Claude, do you know your customer that saw this character take the guns?" Nathan asked.

"Sure, he's one of my regular customers, lives right here in town," Nelson answered.

"Good," Nathan replied. "We will probably need him as a witness at a later trial. You can head on back to your store.

"Okay," Nelson said. "I'll walk back to your office and fetch my horse." He turned and began walking back to the Marshal's office.

"Ben, can you take the prisoner down to our jail. I'm going to get this contraption off the street."

Ben soon had the prisoner unhitched from the rear bumper of the car and walked him toward the Marshal's office.

Nathan retrieved his hat from the front seat of the car, jammed it down on his head, and moved to the side of Wander, where he retrieved the lariat from his saddle. He led the horse to the front of the automobile, where he tied one end of the rope to the front bumper of the car and the other end to the slightly damaged saddle horn. Then he picked up the horse's reins and led the horse forward. When the slack was out of the rope, he coaxed the gelding to take a strain on the rope. Just as Nathan had hoped, the automobile moved forward until it sat at the edge of the road. Nathan patted Wander's neck. "Good job, Wander. Good boy." Nathan untied the lariat from the car's bumper and his saddle horn and coiled the rope. After retrieving the wad of money from the front seat of the automobile, he walked and led Wander to Brown's livery stable where he handed Wander's reins to Leonard Brown.

"Get him fed and watered, Leonard. I'll pick him up this afternoon."

"Sure thing, Marshal," said Brown. "See you had a little excitement out there this morning."

"Yeah, never a dull moment, Leonard," Nathan replied. "Never a dull moment." He walked down the street to the office and entered to find that the prisoner was sitting in one of the two cells, and Ben was at his desk leafing through wanted posters.

"Coffee is on the stove," said Ben. A grin was on his face. "Then come see what I found."

Nathan filled his tin mug and moved to look over Ben's shoulder.

Ben held up one of the posters. "Does the picture look familiar? It ought to. The jackass in the cell is none other than Mr. Roberto Russo, also known as Smilin' Bob Russo. Appears he's wanted in Fort Worth for robbery, felony theft, assault, and trafficking of stolen goods. My, my," said Ben.

"Mmm," Nathan hummed. "Ben, I'm going to walk over to the telegraph office. I want to send a couple wires. I want to find out if our guest has robbed any other towns while using his automobile contraption. I won't be long."

Nathan carried his coffee mug while he walked a short distance to the telegraph office. He sent telegrams to the mayors of Bridgeport, Bowie, Nocona, Alvord, and Sunset, asking each of them to respond to his telegram in which he asked if any merchants had been robbed by a man driving an automobile. He also asked for a description of the man driving the auto. After he was finished, he walked back to the office. He had no sooner gotten back to refill his coffee mug when the runner from the telegraph office came through the office door.

"Telegram for you, Marshal," said the young man.

"Thanks," Nathan replied as he took the telegram from the boy's hand.

Nathan tore the envelope open and smiled as he read the note. "Our boy Russo robbed a store in Bridgeport and got away with two rifles and a pistol," said Nathan. "They described him to a T. Thin mustache, scar on his cheek, and a matching coat and pants suit."

Within minutes, the other small towns responded and the young man from the telegraph office came running with the wires. "You're a popular man, Marshal," said the runner. This time, Nathan rewarded him with a coin from his pocket.

With the exception of Sunset, they had all had a felonious visit by Russo and his automobile.

"So now we know that Russo has robbed several stores of firearms, but where in the hell was he taking them?" Nathan mused.

Ben's mind seemed to be elsewhere as he said, "You know, there's a reward on Russo's head. This wanted poster was issued by your Marshal's Service. I think you'd better call your boss in Fort Worth."

"I reckon you're right," Nathan answered. "But this case might also be of interest to your Ranger boys in Austin."

"Mmm," Ben murmured. "I'll call them after you're done with the phone."

After speaking with the telephone operator and waiting a few minutes, Nathan was connected to his boss, Spencer Briggs, the U.S. Marshal Service Area Director in Fort Worth. Nathan had not met Briggs in person, even though Nathan's territory was under his supervision. Nathan had been placed into the Decatur job based on his outstanding record while working in Kansas. Nathan had talked to Briggs on the telephone on several occasions but had never met him face to face.

"Nathan, glad to get your call," said Briggs. "How are you getting along up there in Decatur?"

"Just fine, sir," Nathan answered. "Every day is a new adventure."

Briggs laughed. "Yes, it is. I just heard by the grapevine that you finished your business up at the Red River, and that that Ivan Malone character is no longer among the living. Is that right?"

Heard by the grapevine, thought Nathan. *How in the world did he hear about that? It only happened last week.*

"Yes, sir, that's right," Nathan answered.

"That's good work, Nathan." Briggs paused, then said, "All right, you called me. What's going on?"

"Well, sir, did you ever hear of a character by the name of Roberto Russo?" Nathan asked.

"Hmm, not sure," Briggs answered. "Oh, wait a minute. Is that Smilin' Bob Russo?"

"One in the same," answered Nathan.

"Why do you ask?" Briggs asked.

"Well, sir, I have him sitting in one of my cells," said Nathan.

"What?" asked Briggs. "We've been looking for that character for months. And you say you have him?"

"Yes, sir. Caught him running some stolen guns right down the main street of Decatur," Nathan answered.

Ben started laughing in the background.

Briggs did not seem pleased to hear the laughter on the other end of the phone. "Is that your prisoner laughing?" he asked.

"No, sir. That's my office mate, Texas Ranger Ben Steele laughing," Nathan answered. "You know, I don't have my own office up here. This Ranger sort of came with the office."

"Oh, yeah," said Briggs. "I don't think we can do anything about that for a while. Sorry about that."

Yeah, I'll bet you're real sorry, Nathan thought to himself. The Marshal Service was not known for spending money on office space for their marshals. "We'll probably be able to bring Russo to trial for robbery and larceny. He had a cache of guns in his automobile. Seems he had robbed stores in Bridgeport, Alvord, and here in Decatur."

"No, no. I don't want you to do that," said Briggs. "We need to find out who he was selling the stolen guns to. And then I want to break their chain of distribution and bring the whole mess of them to trial."

"Do you want me to find out who his buyer is?" Nathan asked.

"Well, you can try, but I don't figure he'll talk," said Briggs. "But here is what I want you to do. After you talk to him, oh, let's say Thursday, I want you to bring him to Fort Worth to our county jail. I want you to bring him in after dark, so you are not seen. I don't want his buyer and his cronies to know we have him. Can you do that?"

"Yes, sir. Let me look at the train schedules, and we can call you later to let you know what time we get in on Thursday night."

"All right," said Briggs. "By the way, Nathan, how do you get along with the Ranger, Steele?"

"We get along just fine, sir," Nathan answered. "Why do you ask?"

"I want you to bring him along with you when you bring Russo to me," said Briggs. "Don't ask me why. I'll explain it to you when you get here."

"Mmm," mumbled Nathan. "We'll be there Thursday with the prisoner."

"That's just fine, Nathan," Briggs said. "You let me know about the train schedule for Thursday. We can talk more later." And with that, Briggs hung up the phone on his end.

Nathan pulled the earpiece from his ear and stared at the telephone for few seconds. *Wonder what this is all about,* he thought to himself.

"Is everything all right?" Ben asked.

"Yeah, I think so," Nathan answered. "We need to take the prisoner down to Fort Worth on Thursday."

"Did I hear you say 'we'?" Ben asked.

"You heard me right," Nathan answered. "Briggs wants both of us to deliver Russo."

"Uh, oh," said Ben. "Guess I'd better see what's going on. I'll call Austin."

Minutes later, Ben hung up the phone, and he was shaking his head. "It appears that your boss, Briggs, had already talked to my boss. Looks like I'm going with you on Thursday. He wouldn't tell me what this was all about. He just told me I needed to be on the train with you and Russo Thursday night."

"I think I need a beer," said Nathan.

"You're not alone," Ben responded.

After hiding the keys to the cells and locking the office door on their way out, the two lawmen walked a short distance down the street to the *Second Chance Saloon,* where Ross Simmons soon had two cool beers on the bar in front of Ben and Nathan. For the next half hour, the two men jawed about nothing in particular, but they both remarked that they wished they knew what their bosses had in mind for them. Ross Simmons came and stood behind the bar.

"Hey, Ross. You got anything to make me a sandwich?" Nathan asked.

"Sure Marshal. I've got a couple left over steaks from lunch. I can slice them real thin and make you a real good sandwich," said Ross.

"That's great Ross," said Nathan. "Put some ketchup and mustard and onions on that sandwich and get us two more beers while we're waiting."

"I'll take one of those sandwiches too," said Ben.

When they had finished their sandwiches and beer, both men reached in their respective pockets to get the money to pay Ross for their meal.

"No, no, not for you guys," said Ross. "You two probably saved my life and Jack's life by taking care of Ivan Malone. Your money's no good here."

Nathan put a few coins on the bar anyway. "Consider that your tip for taking care of us."

After waving at Ross on their way out of the *Second Chance,* Nathan and Ben walked back to the office.

"Nathan, I'm going home," said Ben. "I'll see you in the morning."

"Yeah, I'm about to leave, too. But I've got to go over to Pablo's cousin's house. I need to let her know that she needs to feed our prisoner tonight and tell her how to do it, so she doesn't get hurt. See you tomorrow."

One of Pablo's cousins, Rosa, lived in Decatur with her two children. Her husband had been killed in an accident, so Rosa made ends meet by taking on domestic jobs. She welcomed being paid to cook for the jail. She would feed the prisoner that evening and breakfast the following morning. Nathan gave her the key to the office with instructions on how to feed the prisoner so that she would not be endangered.

Nathan left her and headed for Brown's livery to get Wander and hit the road for home.

* * *

Less than a half hour later, in his barn, Nathan removed the saddle and bridle from Wander. After a good brush down and a helping of oats, Nathan turned the horse out into the corral, where he threw a pitchfork of hay. Through with his outdoor chores, he walked to the back porch and began to climb the steps to the porch. Just as he reached the porch floor, the back screen door was opened by Claire May. She was holding Bobby, but then she put him down. Nathan was then shocked to see his son taking tentative steps toward his daddy. The toddler's arms flailed as he stepped toward Nathan.

"He can walk," Nathan laughed. "When did that happen?"

Claire May also laughed. "Just this morning. He had pulled himself up and took his first steps."

They watched as Bobby took three more tiny steps and then promptly plopped down on his bottom. Undeterred, he continued forward on his hands and knees until he reached Nathan, who quickly picked him up and cuddled him.

"Good job, little man," said Nathan. "Won't be long before you're running." He looked over at Claire May and said, "How soon before we put him on a horse?"

"Don't get too antsy, hon. He's still got lots of growing to do before we try that," said Claire May.

Later, after supper and with Bobby put to bed, Nathan, Claire May, and Virginia sat on the back porch enjoying a glass of wine. Nathan had asked Pablo to join them, and he was walking up the path to the house from the barn.

"Pablo, I put your cousin Rosa to work today," said Nathan. "She's cooking for a prisoner we have in jail."

"Oh, that's good," Pablo replied. "She likes to stay busy, and she needs the extra money."

They sat and listened to the usual night sounds. Those sounds were interspersed with the howl of a coyote, followed by a series of yips and yaps of coyote pups as their mother brought them a tasty meal.

"She probably got the pups a rabbit," said Claire May. "Rabbits are really thick around the ranch."

"I saw a red-tailed hawk with a rabbit yesterday. He was taking it back to his nest," said Pablo.

They were quiet for several minutes. Finally, Nathan said, "Claire May, I have to go to Fort Worth on Thursday. I have to take our prisoner to the Tarrant County Jail."

Claire May thought nothing of Nathan's statement. After all, it was a U.S. Marshal's job to escort prisoners from place to place.

"How long will you be gone," she asked.

"I believe I'll be back Friday evening," Nathan replied.

"You're not sure?" Claire May asked.

Nathan then told the others what he had been told by Spencer Briggs, his boss. He was to bring Roberto Russo to Fort Worth after dark and to take the prisoner directly to the county jail.

"Hmm," said Claire May. "It sounds rather mysterious to me."

"Well, that's not everything," said Nathan. "Briggs wants Ben Steele to come with me."

"Now that's odd," Claire May said. "Why would a Ranger be going with you to transport a prisoner?"

"Your guess is as good as mine," Nathan replied. "But I get a feeling that Briggs isn't telling me everything."

* * *

"All right, sweetheart. I should be home tomorrow evening," said Nathan, as he leaned down and kissed Claire May.

It was Thursday morning. Nathan and the family had eaten a quick breakfast, and Nathan was nearly ready to go to the barn to get Wander and hit the trail to town.

Claire May hugged him tightly. "See you tomorrow. Don't hang around with any of those Fort Worth dance hall girls," she teased.

"You can count on it, darlin'," Nathan responded. He leaned down and picked up Bobby and gave him a hug and a kiss. Bobby giggled his approval.

"You be careful, Nathan," said Virginia. She had agreed to stay a bit longer with the Wolfs before returning to Kansas and was sitting in a chair doing the sewing repair to the shirt that Roberto Russo cut with his knife while attacking Nathan. Nathan had told Clair May and Virginia that he had caught the shirt on a nail at the livery barn in town. He did not want to tell them that he had narrowly escaped being stabbed.

"I will, Virginia," Nathan replied. He slung his bedroll over his shoulder and walked to the barn. Ten minutes later, he waved at the women as he rode past the back porch of the house. In another thirty minutes, he had given instructions to Leonard Brown at the Decatur livery that he would come back for Wander Friday afternoon. He and Ben would be taking the train to Fort Worth.

Fidgeting. That would be the appropriate word to describe the two lawmen as they sat at their desks in the Marshal's Office drinking their morning coffee. Rosa had fed Russo his breakfast.

"Whose turn is it?" Ben asked.

"Yours, *amigo*," Nathan replied.

"That's what I was afraid of," said Ben. He rose from his desk and put his pistol on Nathan's desk. He then got the key to the cells and pulled Russo out the back door of the jail so that he could use the outhouse behind the building. He returned in a few minutes and pushed Russo back into his cell. They went to the café for a late dinner. There would be no supper for them other than any items they might be able to purchase on the train ride to Fort Worth.

Darkness fell at last, and Nathan handcuffed Russo's wrists together. As they walked to the depot, Nathan was careful to put Russo on the side away from the back pocket holding his blackjack and away from his holster. Nathan was attempting to take the temptation away from Russo to try to grab Nathan's firearm. Ben was also armed. In the darkness they walked to the train depot. Ben walked behind Nathan and Russo. They stood in the shadows at the depot and did not have to wait for long before the southbound train for Fort Worth arrived. They were the last to board and found a bay of four seats, two seats facing two seats. The lawmen put Russo at the window, and they sat across from each other on the aisle.

Because it was dark outside, and the wheels of the train made a rhythmic, undulating, and monotonous sound, both Nathan and Ben became drowsy, and it was not long before Nathan nodded off. As he slept, Russo got the not-so-bright idea that he could get the key to his handcuffs from the inside pocket of Nathan's vest. As carefully and quietly as he could with his wrists cuffed together, he gently pulled Nathan's vest aside so that it revealed the inside pocket. His fingers moved to the pocket and hovered for a second before getting into the pocket. Suddenly, to Russo's surprise, Nathan threw a right hook that smashed into Russo's face and very nearly broke the prisoner's nose, which almost immediately began to spew blood. Russo's scream of pain could be heard throughout the train car. Fortunately, only a handful of people were riding the night train to Fort Worth, and none of the other passengers seemed alarmed. One man got up from his seat and started to walk to the lawmen's seat, but then turned around and went back to his own seat when Ben opened his vest to reveal his badge.

"I think you broke my nose," Russo wailed.

"You're lucky you still have teeth," Nathan replied.

At that moment, the conductor came into the car while making his rounds, and Nathan asked him to bring a couple napkins. When the conductor saw that Russo was bleeding, he quickly complied. The front of Russo's shirt, vest, and suit coat were already streaked with blood when the conductor returned with the napkins.

"Guess he had a little accident, huh," said the conductor.

"Yeah," Ben replied. "He's what you call a real slow learner."

The remainder of their trip to Fort Worth was completed without further incident. When they disembarked from the train, Spencer Briggs was there to meet them. Neither Nathan nor Ben had ever met Briggs in person, but they were recognized as lawmen by Briggs. The handcuffed Russo was the giveaway for Briggs, and he introduced himself, shaking hands with Nathan, then turning his attention to Ben, "Are you Steele," he asked while extending his hand.

"Ben Steele, Mr. Briggs," said Ben, as he shook hands with the no-nonsense U.S. Marshal Service Area Director.

"Glad you could make it, Steele," said Briggs.

As they walked Russo through the depot, Briggs looked at Russo and could see that the prisoner's clothing was stained with blood. Russo was still holding a bloody towel to his damaged nose.

"Did Russo fall on his face?" Briggs asked, while knowing that was probably not the case.

"Something like that, boss," said Nathan. "Russo tried to get cute and pick my pockets."

"Hmm," Briggs mumbled. "I've got a carriage waiting out in front of the depot. We'll take Russo over to the county jail, and then go get us some breakfast."

Before Nathan got into the carriage, he handcuffed Russo's wrist to his own wrist. He did not want Russo to try to make a run for it. Briggs took the driving seat, with Ben taking a seat next to him. Briggs shook the reins on the two-horse team and clucked to them. He brought the team to a fast walk. It only took a few minutes before the carriage arrived at a rather imposing two-story marble building. Briggs drove the carriage into a porte-cochere where several uniformed officers waited next to an imposing metal door. Briggs climbed down from the driver's seat as Nathan stepped from the carriage.

"These boys will take Russo from you," said Briggs.

The two uniformed officers each took hold of one of Russo's arms while Nathan removed the handcuffs. Briggs signed the paperwork handed to him by one of the guards.

"You might want to get a doctor to look at his nose," said Nathan. There was no response from the guards as they quickly led Russo through the metal door of the Tarrant County Jail. The door closed with a resounding clang.

"Okay," said Briggs. "He's out of our hands for the time being. Let's go over to my office." The lawmen boarded the carriage again, and Briggs drove to a site that was a few streets from the downtown area. He parked the carriage behind a two-story building that had bars on the upper floor windows where the Marshal Service maintained a handful of holding cells for prisoners awaiting transport. He led Nathan and Ben into the building, and they passed two people who were working the night shift at desks in the main office area. They continued on to Briggs's spartanly furnished office.

"I need to get the carriage and the team back to their stalls in our little barn across the street, and then I'll be right back so we can go to breakfast," said Briggs, as he retrieved a set of keys from his desk drawer.

"Keys to the barn," said Briggs. "We have to keep it locked or the thieves around here would make off with our carriage and our horses."

Just as he had said, Briggs soon returned from tending to the horses and carriage and threw the keys to the barn and back door of the building into his desk drawer. "Let's go eat," he said, and the three men walked out the front door of the building. Nathan looked back at the front door to read the sign above the door. In simple letters, the sign read, *U.S. Marshal Service.* "Pretty low-key sign, Spencer," said Nathan.

"That's the way we like it," Briggs replied, as they walked across the street to a small diner that Briggs had said was open nearly twenty-four hours each day except Sunday. The diner was small, with only a few booths and a row of worn counter stools. They found an unoccupied booth near the door to the kitchen. Apparently, a waitress knew Briggs, as she quickly brought a coffee mug and set it in front of him. She turned her attention to Nathan and Ben. "You boys want coffee?"

Ben and Nathan answered her affirmatively.

"I'll be back in a second to get your orders," she said.

After their coffee arrived and they had given their orders to the waitress, the men idly stirred their coffee to cool it a bit, their spoons clanking the edges of their mugs. Their conversation consisted of small talk, mostly talking about their respective jobs, cases, and history.

After they had finished eating and lingered over their third mug of coffee, Briggs broke their silence.

"I reckon you boys want to catch the afternoon train, don't you?" Briggs asked.

"Yes, sir," Nathan answered.

"All right then," Briggs replied. "Let's go on back to my office. I want to talk with you for a bit before you need to leave."

The men stood to leave. Briggs said, "I've got this, boys," and he laid money on the table to cover the three breakfasts. Back at Briggs's office, Briggs sat down behind his desk and motioned with his hand for the other two men to sit in chairs across from him.

Nathan and Ben waited while Briggs seemed to be thinking of how he would start the conversation. Briggs cleared his throat and began.

"I've been wrestling with a problem here in our territory," he said. "That problem involves the jackass you brought in this morning, our friend Smilin' Bob Russo."

"Let me guess," said Nathan. "Smuggling."

"Yeah, you're right, Nathan," Briggs answered. "But not just minor smuggling. The problem is widespread smuggling on a huge scale that reaches all the way up here from the Mexican border. But along with the smuggling comes extortion, robbery, assault and battery, and the list goes on. Here in Tarrant County, I'm figuring that we are up against a syndicate, but I don't know how extensive it is. I don't have the manpower for taking on anything outside of Tarrant County. Therefore, I want to focus only on the bad actors who deal with Fort Worth. There might be a bunch of Tarrant County crooks getting goods from as far away as the Rio Grande, or just a few bad boys running this local operation, but they've got to have a boss somewhere. And we need to cut off the head of the snake."

"Are you making any progress?" Ben asked.

"That's the problem," answered Briggs. "We can't get anyone to talk about it. And that's why I was pleased when you called me and said you captured Russo. If we can get him to talk and tell us who his buyer is, we might be able to make some headway and work our way up the criminal chain. And as strange as it sounds, we are not even sure what contraband goods are coming up here from Mexico. We think that it is liquor, fabrics, and assorted jewelry, but we just don't know for sure. So, this is going to involve the two of you working undercover to follow the trail where it begins in Mexico and ends in Fort Worth."

Briggs continued, "Now, about Russo…"

Ben interrupted him as he looked at Nathan, and then back at Briggs. "Your man Marshal Wolf, here, is pretty good at getting prisoners to talk. Let him have a crack at Russo."

Briggs looked at Nathan. "I've heard," he said. "I'll let you talk to him before you leave town, but right now, I need to tell you what we have planned."

"We?" asked Ben.

Briggs ignored Ben's remark. "Steele, your boys in Austin have been working on a state-wide basis, examining the same problem that we have. We seem to keep stumbling into each other as we try to get to the bottom of these smuggling operations," said Briggs. "For that reason, I asked you to come with Wolf. Your boss and I have worked this out that the two of you will work the problem together. I assume the two of you can get along all right to work together." Briggs watched as the two lawmen nodded their heads.

Briggs went on. "All right then. I'm going to outline your assignment. But I want to emphasize that this might be the most dangerous assignment that I have ever passed along to any of my men. And you two are going to carry it out. Do I make myself clear?" Briggs watched as the two men nodded and mumbled their assent.

For the next hour, Briggs outlined the assignment he was giving Nathan and Ben. He detailed everything that law enforcement agencies knew about the criminal operators and where they worked, which did not take a great deal of time. The criminal element associated with the smugglers refused to divulge any details of their operation. Briggs considered Russo to be a 'small fish' in the bigger pond of criminals. But he could not overlook the fact that even small fish have information that would be valuable in netting larger players. He emphasized again that he was only interested in the Tarrant County smuggling operation and told them that other law enforcement offices would be responsible for their own geographic areas of expertise.

At the end of Briggs's talk, Nathan and Ben looked at each other. They each knew what the other man was thinking. The assignment, while pared down to Tarrant County and the smuggling trail down to and up from Mexico, was daunting for only two men. To them, the assignment seemed almost foolhardy and impossible, but neither man was in a position to tell Briggs that they thought he must be mad, nor could they very easily turn down the assignment. Saying no to an assignment was the same as resigning from your job, and neither man would do that.

Briggs stood up at his desk, signaling that the meeting was over for the time being. "Hansom cabs usually pass by here every few minutes. Hail one of them down and tell the driver to take you to the Tarrant County Jail," said Briggs. "I'll call them and tell them to expect you and to let you talk with Russo."

Briggs walked Nathan and Ben to the front door and watched as the two men hailed a cab. A few minutes later, the two lawmen walked through the same steel door they had seen Russo enter earlier that morning. They checked their guns at the door, giving them to one of the guards for safekeeping. The jail guards then led them to an interview room where Russo was seated at a metal table. His wrists were shackled and fastened to the table. Russo's face was partially covered by tape and gauze. Black and blue shiners surrounded his bloodshot eyes that peered above the dressings.

Russo groaned as he said, "Not you two jerks. What do you want?" Russo was no fool. He knew exactly what the two lawmen wanted. He had been in jail before, and he knew that it was best to just keep his mouth shut.

"Well, good morning to you, too, Smilin' Bob," said Nathan. "Only you don't seem to be doing a lot of smiling."

"Thanks to you, stinkin' lawman," Russo replied.

"I see they got you a new wardrobe, Smilin' Bob," Ben taunted. "It looks good on you." Russo was wearing the jail-issued prisoner's striped clothing.

Russo did not respond.

"Okay, Russo, we can do this the easy way or the hard way," said Nathan. As he said those words, Nathan drew his blackjack from his rear pocket and clunked it down on the metal table.

Again, Russo did not respond, but he now knew that he was in for a bad time against the two lawmen.

Nathan gave Russo a small jab to the side of his head with the blackjack. "That was to get your attention, smart boy," said Nathan. "So now I'm going to ask you a few questions, and I expect you to answer, and tell me the truth. If you refuse, we will make things a bit more painful for you." Nathan then reached over and grabbed Russo's heavily bandaged nose and gave it a small tweak.

Russo howled in pain. "You need to stop, lawman. You got no right to treat me this way."

"Russo, I want to know who you were going to sell those guns to," said Nathan.

"Lawman, first of all I would never tell you, and second, if I told you, I would be a walking dead man," said Russo.

"You're breaking my heart," said Nathan. He slammed the blackjack down on the tabletop, which made a near deafening bang in the small room. "One more time, Russo. Who is your buyer?"

Russo made no comment. His bloodshot eyes continued to peer over the bandages, hate showing in those eyes.

Nathan's blackjack crashed again toward the tabletop, but this time it was stopped from reaching the table by one of Russo's fingers. The knuckle of the finger was smashed and broken. Russo screamed in pain. His breath came in short gasps of pain.

"Russo, I'm going to go on and break every finger on both hands until you tell me who your buyer is," said Nathan.

Russo slumped in his chair, leaned over his shackled hands and began to moan. His moan turned into sobbing. "I'll tell you, but I'm a dead man." He brought his head over his hands as if to protect them from further injury.

"Look at it this way," Ben said. "You'll hang for your crimes, or we put you out on the street. Either way, you're going to be killed."

So quietly that it was indiscernible, Russo whispered. Neither Nathan nor Ben could understand what he had whispered.

Nathan's blackjack thumped loudly on the tabletop. "Do I need to turn up your volume for you?" Nathan threatened.

"Elbert Cantoni," Russo said quietly.

"And this Cantoni character is who you've been selling your guns to?" Nathan asked.

"Yeah, and he'll kill both of you, along with me," Russo said. And then he began to laugh. "You're dead men too." He continued laughing.

"Russo, what does this Cantoni fella do with the guns you sell him," Ben asked.

Russo replied, "I don't know for sure, but I think that he sells them down in Mexico. Russo looked up at the lawmen. "I gave you what you wanted, now let me go back to my cell."

Nathan banged on the interview room door to summon a guard. When the guard opened the door, Nathan said, "He's all yours. We're leaving. You might want to get the doctor back to look at his hand. I think he bumped it on the table."

"Go to hell, lawman. Go to hell," Russo screamed.

* * *

After retrieving their firearms, they stood on the street in front of the Tarrant County Jail. As they watched the traffic going by, Ben spoke. "That seemed a bit too easy."

"I agree," said Nathan. "I have no idea whether Russo was telling the truth or just trying to get rid of us. Maybe Briggs will recognize the name."

"Let's walk back to Brigg's office," said Ben. "I need to stretch my legs."

As they drew near to the Marshal Service office, they did not enter. Instead, at Nathan's suggestion, they went across the street to the diner where they had eaten breakfast. They wanted to talk with one another away from Briggs's office. After ordering, the waitress brought two coffees and two wedges of coffee cake, then left the table.

They sat silently for a minute or two, but then Ben broke the silence. "I gotta tell you, partner, I don't like the sound of Briggs's assignment."

Nathan was not sure how to answer. In truth, he felt the same way, but did not want to sound disloyal to his boss. So, he was silent for a few seconds.

"Well, what do you think?" Ben asked.

"All right, all right," Nathan responded as he clanked his fork down on the coffee cake plate. It was clear that Ben's question was unsettling to him. He responded, "I'm not sure I like the assignment either, but I'm sure as hell not going to tell Briggs that."

"I think we are being used," said Ben. "Our odds of getting through that assignment alive are none too good."

"I can't disagree," said Nathan. "Let's get out of here. The sooner we give Briggs the buyer's name, the sooner we can head for home."

The men left a few coins on the table and walked across the street to Briggs's office.

Briggs laughed when he heard the name. "Cantoni, eh. We have watched that character for months, but we could never see him doing anything that would warrant us busting into his warehouse. His small warehouse is at the edge of the city."

"Based on Russo's statement, can't you just go over and bust into the warehouse," asked Nathan.

"Well, that wouldn't do us much good. Counting Russo, then we would have two small fish," said Briggs. "We want to go after the boys at the top of the operation." Briggs then pulled his pocket watch from his pocket and looked at it. He wound it again before placing it back in his pocket.

Referring to Nathan and Ben, Briggs said, "You boys know the schedule. I'll expect you back here in a week. I figure you're going to the southern border, and you might be there for a month or longer, depending on the outcome of your work. Your assignment is to track down the source of contraband coming to Cantoni in Fort Worth and find out as much as you can about the type of contraband goods that are making their way up here." Briggs then seemed to fumble with his next words. "You might want to get your affairs in order before we meet again." He then rose, walked around his desk, shook hands with

Nathan and Ben, and opened the door to his office. To Nathan and Ben, it was readily apparent that their meeting with Briggs was over.

Back on the street, Nathan hailed a hansom cab that began making its way to Union Depot near the east side of Fort Worth. As the driver wended his way through traffic openings and other vehicles, Ben spoke up. "Not a very personable boss you've got there, my friend."

"Yeah. I never met him in person until today. I was simply appointed to my territory without meeting Briggs. Can't say that I'm impressed either."

Unbeknownst to Spencer Briggs, Elbert Cantoni was the top hoodlum in the Fort Worth smuggling arm, and at this point, he had no viable competition in the racket. By the use of paid thugs and hitmen, he intended to stay at the apex. He would deal with any snoopy lawmen in the same manner that he dealt with criminal competition. They would either be bought out somewhat peacefully, or they would meet their demise.

Chapter Nineteen

Union Station
Fort Worth, Texas

After arriving at the depot, they had only a short wait before they boarded the northbound passenger train that would take them to Decatur. As the sun began its descent in the west, the train pulled out and soon reached its maximum speed. Nathan thought that his brain was distractingly keeping time to the clacking of the train's wheels on the steel rails. He was still upset about the nonchalant attitude of Spencer Briggs. The dangerous assignment that had been given to him and Ben was weighing on his mind, while Briggs sat in his office hatching schemes that might or might not be successful. Tracking down a Fort Worth conduit in the smuggling scheme, in their opinion, was absolutely impossible and insane.

"Let's go to the club car, Ben," said Nathan. "I need a whisky."

Ben immediately rose from his seat and said, "Let's go."

Entering the club car, they sat on a soft, upholstered bench that ran the length of the train car. An identical bench ran the length of the opposite side of the car. A small bar where they had ordered their drinks was at one end of the car. Four game tables sat side by side in the middle of the car, but only one of the tables was occupied. Six men sat at the table playing five card stud. Only mildly interested while he sipped his drink, Nathan scanned the faces of the card players. Most of the faces were nondescript, seemingly ordinary men trying their luck at cards. Their clothing reflected that one or two were working men. Stained work clothes and slouch hats probably meant that they earned their living with their hands. One or two of the others were probably drummers, moving on to the next town to sell their wares. Another man had the look of a rancher. A weathered face, a rough mustache, and a rancher's hat may have indicated that he had spent a day at the Fort Worth stock yards, either buying or selling beef cattle. He wore a lightweight jacket on top of his off-white, snap-pocketed shirt.

Yet another man stood out by the clothes he wore. Light gray pants, a charcoal jacket, a white shirt, a colorful satin vest that sported a watch chain that drooped from one of the vest pockets, and a flat-topped, dark gray, medium-brimmed hat adorned the man's head. His long gray hair was tucked back at the sides and tied at the back. It was the persona and the type of clothing worn by a gambler, a man who made his living at the card table, his seemingly calm eyes never moving from the action on the table.

A haze of smoke from their roll-your-owns hung over the table. Varying amounts of cash sat on the table in front of the individual players. The bench, on which Nathan and Ben sat, happened to be behind two of the players, and one of those players was the gambler, the maven of card games. The deal moved around the table with none of the players benefitting by large bets that would result in a large center pot. It seemed to be a friendly game among amicable strangers.

Nathan finished his whisky and leaned back on the plush bench. He closed his eyes and thought he might fall asleep to the rhythm of the train car wheels. He had very nearly nodded off when he felt his foot being kicked. He cracked his eyes open to see Ben looking at him and then shifting his eyes to the card table. Nathan shifted his attention to the table. The deal had moved to the gambler who was sitting directly in front of the two lawmen. Each player had his hole card in his hands, and each had three cards face up in front of him. As each face-up card was dealt, another bet was placed, starting with the player having the highest hand showing. As a result, the center pot was now substantial. As the fourth card was dealt face up, it was time for each player to make another bet if he wished. As the bet went around the table, four of the players, who had weak hands showing, dropped out. Only the gambler and the rancher remained. Neither player had a pair showing in their face up cards, but each player had an ace face up in front of him. The gambler had an ace and a ten as the two highest cards showing face up. His opponent had an ace and a jack as his two highest cards showing, but neither player knew what was being held as a hole card by their opponent.

With the highest hand showing, it was the rancher's bet. "Ten dollars to you, mister," said the rancher.

The gambler appeared to think for a few seconds before he replied, "Your ten dollars, and I'll raise you twenty," as he put three ten-dollar bills in the pile of bills in the center of the table. The center pile of bills had grown substantially as the previous bets had added to the prize.

The rancher seemed to be deflated. He raised his hand and removed his hat, then used his sleeve to wipe the sweat from his brow, then replaced his hat. But as he brought his arm down, for a split second, he had both of his hands beneath the table, and just as quickly, he brought his hand holding the hole card back onto the table. He continued to hesitate, but then replied to the gambler. "I'll see your twenty and raise you thirty." He drew fifty dollars from the stack of bills in front of him and threw them into the pot.

Now it was the gambler's turn to hesitate. His hole card was a ten. Therefore, he had a pair of tens with an ace kicker. But he thought that *if his opponent had a second ace or jack as his hole card, he was beaten; or was his opponent bluffing?* A gambler is a natural gambler, and it was his nature to play to win. "I'll see your thirty," said the gambler. "Let's see your hole card."

But as soon as the gambler called the rancher's bet, both Nathan and Ben rose from their bench and moved behind the rancher's chair.

The rancher paid them no heed as he placed his hole card ace next to the ace that was already showing on the table. "Pair of aces," he said.

The gambler laid his hole card on the table. His pair of tens did not beat the aces. The rancher reacted by saying, "Well, thank you gentlemen," as he stretched his arms to rake in the sizable pot. But he was stopped. Nathan had pinned the man's right hand to the table, while Ben had his left arm pinned.

"Let's stand up real slow like, mister," said Nathan.

The rancher rose from his chair. But as he did so, a derringer pistol suddenly appeared in his hand, and he tried to get free from the lawmen. He twisted in their grasp and managed to lower his arm holding the derringer. But Nathan pushed the man's hand upward as the derringer fired, sending a bullet through the brim of Nathan's hat and harmlessly into the ceiling of the rail car. But the derringer held two cartridges, and the man tried desperately to bring the gun down to shoot one of his antagonists. In that regard, Nathan helped him and brought the man's arm down with a slam against the edge of the card table. The man yowled in pain and the derringer fired its second bullet. The bullet whizzed by the ear of one of the men still sitting at the table and smashed through a train car window on its path away from the train.

Nathan's blackjack found its target on the side of the man's head. The man slumped but did not fall to the floor. "Take off your jacket, mister," Nathan growled. The man complied.

"Now take off your shirt," Nathan said.

"Hell no," the man said. "And just who the hell are you two yahoos?"

"U.S. Marshal Nathan Wolf, mister. Now take off the shirt or I will cut it off with my knife," said Nathan.

The man glared at Nathan, but slowly unbuttoned his cuffs and then the buttons on the front of the shirt. Then he stopped.

"Take it off," Nathan said, as he thumped the man on the head again.

The man complied, and soon had the shirt off. Instead of naked arms, a pair of odd contraptions were strapped to them.

"Hang on to him, Ben," said Nathan. Ben tightened his choke hold on the man's neck.

"As you can see, gentlemen, this here gizmo held this hombre's little derringer." Nathan placed the gun into the apparatus and pushed it upward where it stayed. But then Nathan pushed a control spring on the apparatus and the gun sprang toward the man's hand where it could be quickly grabbed for use.

"And on this arm, this little gizmo is called a hold-back device." Taking a card from the table, Nathan placed it between the arms of a small clip. Then he pushed the card and device upward on the man's arm. "And now, if I just pull this string that had been wrapped around his upper arm, watch the card."

The card players watched as Nathan pulled on the string and the clip holding the card moved toward the man's hand. "This is where this cheat got his extra ace; not from the deal, but from his hold-back gadget," said Nathan. "Now, one of you fellas at the table, go pull the emergency stop cord," he said as he stripped both devices from the arms of the cheater and threw them on the card table.

A man jumped up from the table, reached up, and quickly pulled the emergency cord. In a few seconds, the men could feel the train begin to slow. At nearly the same time, the train's conductor came bustling into the club car. "Here, now. What's going on in here. Did I hear gunfire?" His face held a feigned, confused look. His eyes roamed about, trying to figure out what was taking place, but his eyes only briefly stopped at the sight of the partially disrobed card cheat.

"Well, you see, Mr. Conductor," said Ben. "This here varmint decided that he wanted to cheat the rest of these gents out of their poker money. And we don't much abide by card cheatin'. So, we need to just let this fella off the train right about now."

"What? You can't do that," said the conductor. "It's against our railroad rules."

Nathan and Ben were silent for a moment. But then, Ben turned to the card cheat. "Do you know this conductor, mister."

The card cheat wagged his head. "No, I don't."

Ben immediately tightened his arm around the man's neck to the point that the man's face was turning a bright red. "Talk to me mister. The conductor is a friend of yours, isn't he?"

The man gagged but managed to gasp out a "yes" answer.

"And you give the conductor a cut of your winnings to keep his mouth shut, don't you?"

The card cheat gasped another, "Yes."

"Well, well," said Nathan. "Mr. Conductor, strip off your uniform coat."

The conductor blustered. "Now see here. You can't do this."

"Oh, I can't?" answered Nathan. "Take the damn coat off before I have to do it myself. And you would find that painful. So, take it off."

The conductor complied.

"Throw your coat and hat on that bench over there," said Nathan. "You just lost your job with the railroad, so you won't be needing your coat and hat anymore."

The conductor did as he was told.

"I will be sure to tell the railroad about your little scheme here, and there is no use in showing up for work again. Now seeing how this is the last car of the train, you two cheaters are going to get on out the back door there and stand on the track. My friend, the Texas Ranger, is going to stand on the rear platform with his gun aimed at the both of you. And then the train is going to start up again and leave you standing on the track."

"What? You can't do that," said the conductor. "We're twenty-five miles from either Decatur or Fort Worth."

"Your problem is not my problem," said Nathan. "You brought this on yourself. You're damn lucky one of the other men at the table didn't shoot your friend, and then maybe you. Now git." Nathan pushed the conductor ahead of him while Ben brought the card cheat. Both men were forced to climb down to the track bed where Ben kept them standing.

Nathan told Ben, "I'm going up to the engine to tell the engineer to get 'er going again. If either one of those weasels give you any trouble just shoot 'em." He said it loud enough for the two con men to hear him before he left to go up forward on the train. As he passed through the club car, he told the card players, "I suggest you divide the pot among all of you. Your friend is not coming back to join you." He then continued through the other cars until he reached the coal car where he yelled at the engineer. In only a couple more minutes, the train lurched forward to continue its journey to Decatur, and Nathan returned to the club car.

As the train gathered speed, Nathan and Ben each got another whisky, but their drinks were already paid for by the poker players, who had broken up the game and were sitting at the table, each enjoying the beverage of his choice. Nathan and Ben sat down on the bench near them. A couple of the men verbally expressed their gratitude for rousting the card cheat and his accomplice.

The professional gambler admitted that he had not seen his opponent's deception. He stuck out his hand to shake with Nathan and Ben.

"My name's Stefano Fox. I've seen a whole lot of cheats in my time, but I can usually spot an opportunist," said the gambler. "That fella was pretty good with his moves. So good that I missed it." The gambler finally released Nathan's hand.

Nathan turned to Ben and asked, "How did you know?"

"Did you look at his hands?" Ben asked. "He may have wanted to look like the innocent rancher, but his hands didn't have any ground-in dirt or callouses on them. Smooth as a baby's butt. Sure not the hands of a rancher."

"I guess I didn't notice his hands," Nathan admitted.

"By the way," said Ben, "you know your hat got ventilated, don't you? Kinda close to your noggin."

Nathan removed his hat and looked at the hole in the hat's brim. "Not again," he said. "This happened once before, and I had holy hell trying to explain it to Claire May. She doesn't like it when I get shot at."

Ben and the circle of card players laughed. "Well, you get to do some splainin' again," said Ben. He took another sip of his drink and continued to chuckle.

A half hour later, the train arrived in Decatur. The lawmen walked past the engine as it released a cloud of steam, and they made their way to Brown's Livery Stable. After retrieving their horses, the two men parted company to go their separate ways, but not before Ben said, "I'll see you at the office, tomorrow or the next day." They waved at each other as Nathan pointed Wander to the trail for home.

As he rode the trail, Nathan's brain was locked onto one primary subject, the assignment that he and Ben had been given by Spencer Briggs. And as was his habit, Nathan mumbled to himself, trying to rehearse in his mind what he might say to Claire May about the work. How could he explain to her that he might be away from home for a month or more? Oh sure, he thought, travelling was a Marshal's job, and days on the trail were common. But that did not make it easier for his wife. In his thoughts, he was seriously thinking that he might have to place a call to Spencer Briggs and resign from the U.S. Marshal Service. How was he going to explain all of his thoughts and reservations to Claire May? He was not looking forward to the conversation. Nearly home, he turned Wander into the tree-shaded lane leading to the house.

Author's Note

To My Readers

Bones Don't Lie is the fourth novel in the Nathan Wolf series. Readers will know that Nathan and Claire May have moved to Texas to take ownership of the beautiful Wise County ranch left to Claire May by her deceased uncle. A reader recently told me in jest that Nathan and Claire May have become almost like family, so he is adding them to his Christmas card list. It is satisfying to know that readers enjoy my books, and it spurs me to keep on writing. Readers can expect another Nathan Wolf book in the series in the future.

Wishing you all pleasant days and happy reading.

James Duermeyer

About the Author

James Duermeyer is a versatile writer and has written non-fiction, historical fiction, and the Western genre. He is a member of the Western Writers of America, and his Western novels include the Nathan Wolf series comprised of award winning *Trail of the Outlaw* and award winning *Singing Creek*. His other novels are *Heroes in Obscurity*, award-winning *Flint Bluff*, *Market Time Conspiracy*, *The Capture of the USS Pueblo: The Incident, the Aftermath, and the Motives of North Korea*.

Now Available!

AWARD–WINNING AUTHOR
JAMES DUERMEYER

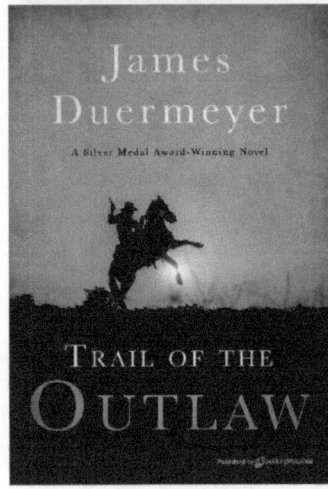

**For more information
visit:** www.SpeakingVolumes.us

Now Available!

R.G. YOHO'S

ACTION/ADVENTURE WESTERNS

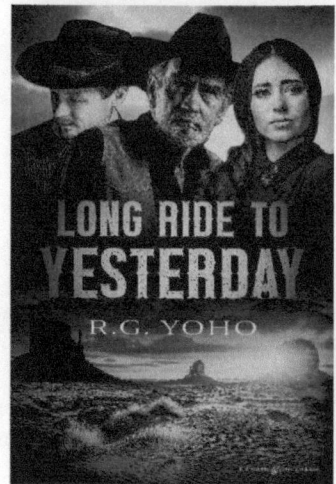
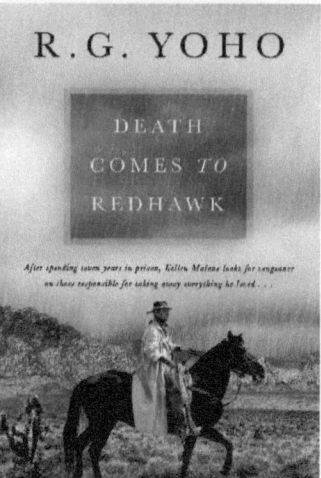

**For more information
visit:** www.SpeakingVolumes.us

Now Available!

ROD MILLER'S

ACTION/ADVENTURE WESTERNS

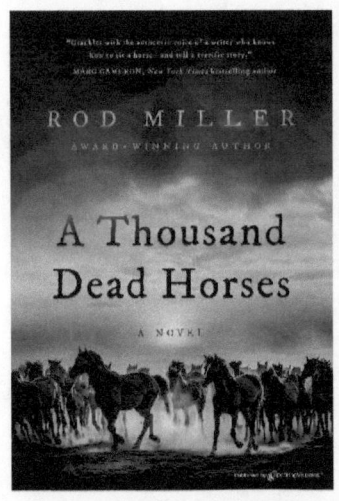

**For more information
visit:** www.SpeakingVolumes.us

www.ingramcontent.com/pod-product-compliance
Lightning Source LLC
LaVergne TN
LVHW041656060526
838201LV00043B/456